Mike Huss

THE MAN WHO CLOSED THE BORDER

Limited Special Edition. No. 7 of 25 Paperbacks

I wrote a dedication to two men for book two which should really be the dedication for this book. I did it because the Grim Reaper had called on one of them and I wanted the second, Peter, to be aware of my thanks before he, too, was called. I am glad to say that he hasn't been so, so far, so good. But the one person who has helped and inspired me more than any other has been my wife Janet who I met in Aden 58 years ago and who has inspired me ever since – thank you.

Mike Huss

THE MAN WHO CLOSED THE BORDER

AUSTIN MACAULEY PUBLISHERS™

LONDON * CAMBRIDGE * NEW YORK * SHARJAH

A CIP catalogue record for this title is available from the British Library.

ISBN 9781035824175 (Paperback)
ISBN 9781035824182 (ePub e-book)

www.austinmacauley.com

First Published 2024
Austin Macauley Publishers Ltd®
1 Canada Square
Canary Wharf
London
E14 5AA

All those folks at Austin Macauley without whom this, and the previous two, books could not have been produced.

Chapter 1

It was Monday morning and he was unemployed. It wasn't going to be for long—he had a new job starting in about three weeks' time—but until then he was entirely his own boss. He had two things he had to do, he couldn't call them jobs because he wouldn't be paid for them but they were, nevertheless, tasks he had to carry out. Janet was still working, and had gone to work on the bus as usual, but she too, would be ceasing work at the end of the week because of the tasks they both had to complete before moving to Belfast; so, they would both be unemployed, something that had never happened to either of them before let alone together.

His first task was to get himself down to the Job Centre and get signed on for the dole; it wouldn't be very much, about £13pw and it would only be for about three weeks but better in his pocket than the government's. The second task was to buy a new car. His HA Viva had been a good little car but it had done approaching 56,000 miles and at about 60,000 it would need a decoke and a thorough sorting out. Although he could do most of the fettling himself, some of it needed special tools which he did not have, nor did he have a garage in which to do the work, and although the car would have been refreshed it would still have been a car with too many miles on the clock and as he was going to be doing a lot of travelling in his new job, it would be better to get something with a lot fewer miles on it. There were a couple of garages on the way into Andover where the Job Centre was located so he would try and kill two birds with one stone.

As he could not be sure how long it would take to view the motors on offer and perhaps test drive one, he decided he would sign on first and then take his time looking for a car. He had never been in a Job Centre although he knew a lot about them from the press and people talking about them. His father told a tale of a man turning up at the company where he worked for an interview and asking to use the toilet before the interview—a not uncommon request. What was definitely uncommon was the guy went into the lavatory smartly dressed and came out having removed his collar and tie, undone the collar stud, presenting an appearance of a right scruff. On entering his dad's office, he sat down, put his feet up on the desk and said, "Look Guv'nor, I don't want this job and you certainly don't want to employ me so tick the box as 'unsuitable' and I'll be on my way."

The potential employer could only tick one of two boxes, 'suitable' or 'unsuitable'. His dad ticked the 'unsuitable' box with alacrity and the guy left; but before he left the building he re-entered the lavatory, replaced his collar and tie and left the picture of smartness and elegance; the picture he presented when he handed in the form at the Job Centre a short while later. It became clear later that the guy did not want to work but to refuse a job offer would result in his dole being stopped, so he had evolved this little procedure to ensure he would never be offered one. Jack's dad discovered this when he rang the Job Centre having discovered from the receptionist what the guy had done.

The Job Centre employee, a Civil Servant of course, was not at all bothered by this deception when it was described to him. Jack over the coming years was to have a lot of contact with Job Centres and very, very few of them were to impress him favourably; most impressed him strongly what an idle, useless lot they were.

He arrived at the Job Centre at ten past nine. The notice on the door which gave their opening hours showed nine o'clock as being their opening time. He was not too surprised that there was a queue of about a dozen people waiting for the doors to open. Only two were women, the rest were men all of whom looked worn down and hard done by. Jack, in his suit, stood out like a thoroughbred amongst Shetland ponies. He felt very uncomfortable under their stares and wished devoutly that he had not worn the suit. Still too late now!

The doors opened just before 9.15am. The people in front of him all made their ways to windows variously headed A to C; D to F and so on so that it was obvious that this related to their names but it took a longer look to find the one for him as a new signer-on. There was no one at that window, nor was there a bell push or other means of attracting attention. Jack stood there for the best part of 10mins and had started to debate as to whether it was worth being treated like shit by the troglodytes who inhabited this dark place when the nearest window to him cleared its last signer-on. Jack nipped smartly over to it and spoke to the woman behind the window, "I have recently become unemployed and would like to sign on please.

"You're at the wrong window."

"But there is no-one at the window I was standing at, can you not sign me on?" The woman looked dreadful, as though he had run into the synagogue and shouted 'pork pie' or something even worse! Rapidly closing her window, she said, "You'll have to wait," and ran away. *That's the first time she's ever moved that first in her life,* thought Jack.

Jack knew about job demarcation from his time with the MOD Civil Servants so he wasn't too surprised at her reaction, nor was he too surprise about there being no one at the window he needed to use, punctuality being another of the qualities that had passed them by. He looked at his watch and thought, *I'll give it till 09.30 and if I haven't been dealt with by then I'll go outside and come back in through the door marked for staff only; find the Manager of this temple to sloth and incompetence and provide him with a bigger fundamental orifice.*

Fortunately, probably for both parties, at 0925hrs a male appeared at the window and said, "Yes?"

"I became unemployed last Friday and I need to sign on please."

The man looked him up and down. Jack had no idea what was going through his mind or indeed if he even had one. The next word from him was, 'Wait.' At which he walked away. To be fair he returned quite quickly with a number of blank forms in his hand. Jack wondered why, since this window was for new people that a supply could not be placed on a shelf under the window but perhaps that would have needed an SEO (Senior Executive Officer) to authorise the expenditure on a shelf and a tray to sit on it and they didn't have one on site.

"Complete these," said the man and he shut the window. There were a couple of tables against the wall which Jack walked over to. There were, of course, no pens or pencils with which to complete the forms. Fortunately, Jack always carried a fountain pen, biro and propelling pencil with him. There were three forms, all asking almost the same questions. They all referred to a P45 asking various questions about the detail on it. Jack didn't have one or even any knowledge as to what it was. He completed the rest of the forms and walked back to the window. After a couple of minutes, no-one appeared. *'Sod this for a game of soldiers,',* thought Jack, so he banged on the window and loudly shouted, "Shop."

The Trog re-appeared, obviously upset, and said, "This is not a shop and such shouting will only get you thrown out."

Jack looked at him for a long, 1000-mile stare and then said, "I would like to speak to the Manager about the abysmal performance of this branch; opening late, no-one working and a speed in performance that would make a slow worm look fast. If, by any chance, he isn't here perhaps you could give me the phone number of the District Manager so that I may speak to him." It was clear from his reaction that the Trog taught turkeys how to gobble. He fell all over his words for a good few seconds and then reached through the hatch and took the forms from Jack. Reading them he asked, politely, for Jack's P45. Jack told him that he had not been given any such document by the Army and, indeed, did not even know what it was. He pointed out that as this Job Centre was in a heavy concentration of Army units that this must be a common problem. The Trog did not respond to that but, looking at a diary, wrote out a slip of paper with Thursday 9.15am and the date.

"That is for an interview for you regarding your unemployed position. Do not miss it or your dole may be delayed or even reduced." At that, he handed the slip to Jack and called out 'next' even though there was no-one else behind him.

Jack left. He walked into WH Smiths and bought the Daily Telegraph partly for its news and partly for the job adverts and then went into a small café for a coffee and a read. Even though he had a job offer which he had accepted he was continuing to look in case something better came along. There was nothing in the paper, the best day was a Thursday but some did appear on other days. He finished his coffee and drove back home stopping at the two car sales garages on the way. He walked around the forecourt of one of them looking at the cars, one a Ford Anglia looked interesting and in his price range but he couldn't find a salesman to help him so he walked out and across the road to the other one.

Almost immediately, a salesman latched onto him but too soon, he wanted time to peruse what was on offer so he sent him away. There were two cars that possibly fitted the bill, another Anglia and an HB Viva, the one that followed the HA he currently owned. Looking around them from the outside there was nothing to choose between them but he couldn't sit in either of them because they were locked. The salesman was still hovering so it was only necessary to gesture for him to come running. From what he had seen of the outsides and his, limited, knowledge of cars he probably preferred the Viva but he didn't want to let the salesman know that so he asked to sit in the Anglia first.

It had done 15,000 miles which was quite a lot for a car that was only two years old. It was in good condition inside although the driver's seat seemed a bit saggy and worn. He said thank you to the salesman and started to walk away past the Viva and he deliberately stopped and looked inside before walking on. The salesman pounced on this and offered to open it up. Acting not too interested he agreed. The first thing that struck him was that the interior was in much better condition than the Ford. The second thing that registered was that it had only done just over 6,000 miles and the third thing, which really did surprise him was that it was an automatic.

Automatics were normally found only in larger limousines. Jack liked the idea of being fully in control of a car especially selecting which gear he wanted. The automatic did not seek to offer that choice until the salesman getting in on the passenger side started moving the gear lever around pointing out that you could select 1st, 2nd or 3rd as you wanted. The car was much more substantial than Jack's HA. The door had a heavier feel to it and a more satisfactory clunk when it was shut. The car was low mileage, in good condition and a good price but why was it such a good price?

The salesman answered the question for Jack without realising it. He said, "Small automatics are becoming the thing but people think the automatic gearbox saps too much power and that puts them off and makes the car slow but these are geared in such a way that this doesn't happen."

Ah, thought Jack, *it's proving difficult to sell, that's why it's cheap.* Indicating disinterest Jack started to get out of the car, paused and then said, "Any chance of a test drive?"

"Yes of course," said the salesman and off they went. It was quieter than his HA both in engine noise and road noise. The gearbox was much smoother than Jack expected and he enjoyed playing with the box changing up and down although he didn't have quite as much control as the salesman had indicated. The upshot was he drove home in his new—to him—HB Viva with £100, not an inconsiderable sum, knocked off the price.

Jack attended the interview at the Job Centre but this time he wore a jacket and slacks. He did not want to give away that he already had a job offer in case they docked his dole—he didn't know how they could or whether even they would attempt to do so but he just wanted to be careful. He was asked questions about his efforts so far to find a job and it was easy to describe buying the papers, registering at the Job Centre and writing off for a job on spec. It became clear that he was expected to make the utmost effort to find a job and if he wasn't

11

thought to be trying hard enough his dole would be stopped. They set up a further appointment for him in two weeks' time but he would be in Belfast by then.

He didn't say anything but wrote a letter to them when he got home to be posted the day before he left England 'signing off' with the explanation he had got a job. He did receive a money order for just short of £40 in due course, worth the being messed around but not worth much more than that. Jack wasn't to know that he would have many further dealings with Job Centres as, mainly, an employer looking for staff, but he would have to sign on again as unemployed in the future, and the more contact he had the lower they sank in his esteem.

Chapter 2

The remainder of his time in England flew by, the biggest problem fitting all their possessions into the car. They managed it but with Janet's feet resting on a box of kitchen gear in the foot well. Jack finished checking over the car on Friday morning, the battery was fine, tyres pumped up with 2lbs per square inch more than recommended to allow for the weight in the car, the oil level fine but the radiator needed a small top up. While he was doing this last, Janet brought out the last travel bag with their nightwear and stuff for that night and Jack squeezed it into the space left for it in the boot.

What he didn't remember was picking up the electric kettle he had used to top up the radiator which he had deposited by the back of the car with the result that there was a peculiar crunching sound, a lurch and a much-flattened kettle on the drive as he reversed back. 'Better than a Mini,' he thought, looking at the remains. Janet jumped out and deposited it in the full dustbin. Jack expected to find a reduction in his security deposit when it was posted to him but the full amount came through so no harm done to his pocket although the kettle was beyond help.

They had a leisurely drive to the ferry at Heysham. They had booked a cabin as the timing was from about 10pm—BR ferries were run for the benefit of the staff not the customers, as with most nationalised industries—and they were due into Belfast just after 7am. The crossing was in fact very rough and they were glad of being able to lie down even if they could only nap rather than sleep. Entering Belfast Lough, the water calmed considerably and they were fascinated by the scenery as the ferry made its way slowly to its berth. Driving through Belfast revealed a grey, wet city with an imposing city centre. Driving out on the Antrim Road was equally impressive. The substantial Victorian house had had its front garden paved over easily creating space for four cars to park. The house was a bit like a child's drawing of one, two windows downstairs with the front door between them and two upstairs. Jack and Janet had the downstairs 'left' flat comprising of a large, high ceilinged lounge a kitchen to the side and a bathroom to the back left and a bedroom to the right behind the lounge.

The landlady opened the door to the flat and welcomed them in. She even helped to unload the car which turned out to be very useful—she deposited their overnight bag on the bed and it promptly collapsed. 'If he thinks he's getting his security deposit back, he's got another think coming,' she said. Jack was just delighted that it had collapsed when the landlady put the bag on it and not him as he was certain that in that case its collapse would have been blamed on him.

She was clearly upset at such a start but Jack reassured her that they would be able to manage with the bed resting on the floor for a few days until she could get it replaced. The replacement arrived on the Tuesday. Brand new it had a clear, see through plastic cover over the headboard which was padded white and when Janet told the landlady that she would like the plastic cover left on to protect it the landlady positively beamed with pleasure. Little did Janet know the problem this slightly loose cover would cause.

On the Saturday night, there was a series showing on the TV starring John Laurie. Each episode opened with Laurie addressing the camera in a totally blacked out scene apart from a light shining up by his chin and illuminating his face in a shadowy, frightening manner, entirely suitable for the horror story to come. They had seen the first two in the series which they had enjoyed although they had not been particularly frightening.

This one, based on the 'Jewel of the Seven Stars' by Bram Stoker involved the curse of the mummy forbidding entry to her tomb. A good story but pretty standard stuff except the female pharaoh had seven fingers on each hand and all the animals in the tomb with her all had seven claws or talons. All the people who entered the tomb were found dead in mysterious circumstances with seven slashes having terminated their lives. It was well presented and did have a scary effect which they both enjoyed. Once Jack and Janet got into bed and settled down Janet kept disturbing Jack, saying, "I heard a noise, something's there."

Jack said, "There's nothing. Go to sleep. That's the last time I let you watch one of those horror things."

They settled back down and then two or three minutes later Jack heard something run across the plastic on the headboard. He leapt out of bed and turned the light on but he couldn't see anything and it was Janet's turn to shush him. Turning the light off he got back into bed and tried to settle down.

Again, he heard a noise and this time he was fast enough turning the light on to see a mouse disappearing down behind the headboard. He couldn't catch the bloody thing, it was simply too quick for him, ducking under the bed, behind the wardrobe and hiding anywhere there was cover. After a futile few minutes Jack opened the wardrobe and took a locked, small suitcase from the top shelf. Opening it he took out his old.177 Webley Junior air pistol, loaded it and waited until the mouse stopped running and shot it.

So much for John Laurie and his bloody scary, horror, stories. Jack was to wish he could shoot bigger targets in a year or so's time. They were to be bothered by two more mice in the time they lived there and although the trap they set out didn't catch them—they were to find out years later that mice didn't like or respond to cheese—but Janet was able to catch them in a corner and release them in the garden out the back.

They were also to be bothered by the neighbour in the flat above theirs. He was a man in his late 50s-early 60s and in the week, they never heard him but on a Saturday night, they would hear him going out about 11pm and returning and hour or so later with at least one other person, sometimes two. Then the music would start, rock and roll, played extremely loud. Knocking on the door and asking him to turn it down was simply ignored.

Banging on the ceiling probably couldn't even be heard, but going out into the hall where all the fuse boxes were and switching his box off did work for a while but he started coming down and switching it back on so as a final resort, as the landlady had indicated no interest in solving the problem at all, Jack switched the electric off and removed the fuse, refusing to return it until 8am Sunday morning that stopped it. He moved out two weeks later, maybe the landlady knew he was going after all because he must have given notice under his agreement, and the replacement was a nice, quiet nursing sister who worked varying shifts and did not party wildly on Saturday nights.

On a Sunday morning Jack got into the habit of nipping across the road to the paper shop while Janet was getting breakfast. Even three months later, he was still looking around to make sure the Colonel didn't see him out with no hat and proper civie uniform of suit or blazer and slacks with a tie of course, such was the imprinting of Army rules. He even decided to grow a beard to show his independence but it was so tatty and miserable he shaved it off but he did keep the moustache.

Chapter 3

The Training Board was situated in a large modern block. It shared the building with all the other boards and the Northern Ireland Training Executive which in fact was the administrative body for all the boards. It wasn't technically an 'executive' but as was the way with government bodies, the tail always wagged the dog. Training Boards were in the process of being set up by the socialist government to improve training in all industries as it was felt that the UK was falling behind France, Italy and especially Germany, in the race to modernise and dominate. A levy was imposed on every separate industry, in reality a tax but the word levy was used to try and disguise what it was, but employers were not fools and when a government makes you pay money it's a tax call it whatever weasel word you like.

Firms were to be bribed with their own money. The levy, imposed differently by different boards, was taken from the company and then, if they trained a little bit, they got a little bit back; if they trained a lot then they got a lot back and if they trained really well, they could get back more than they paid into the levy. At first it worked quite well but, as Jack was to discover, over the next eight years it gradually fell apart, due it must be said largely to the employers.

Each Board was made up of three parties, employer representatives, employee representatives (unions of course, it being a socialist government) and academics. The Board set the policy to be followed. The unions and the academics could out vote the employers and did so, so gradually the employer reps stopped attending the Board meetings so that more and more outrageous policies were passed by idiot academics with no understanding of running a business and unions who couldn't care less at how much damage they did.

By the time Jack was working in a Group Training Association in Nottingham seven years later, the Clothing and Allied Products Industry Training Board was insisting that employers, if they wanted any levy back, allowed girls who were employed as machinists to have time off so they could attend college to obtain a qualification (training you see!) in hairdressing all paid for by the employer who would then lose the machinist they had spent money training to be a machinist. But that was for the future.

For now, Jack was employed by The Clothing and Footwear Training Board of Northern Ireland. There were five Training Development Officers (TDOs), including Jack, and one Senior Training and Development Officer, Sam O'Ryan, who was to resign and leave very shortly after Jack arrived. The vacancy was advertised internally and Jack applied but having only been there for a few weeks his application did not proceed very far! The other four TDOs also put their hands up for the job and Maurice Baldwin got it. For some reason Jack never discovered they never replaced Maurice as a TDO so they proceeded gaily onwards with a team of five.

Jack was scheduled to spend months in the office coupled with occasional visits out with other TDOs learning the levy/grant system and the policies operated by the boards. From January to about Easter all the TDOs spent their time assessing and approving, or not, the claims for levy rebate claims by the companies within scope of the Board. It was a rare situation where a semi-civil servant actually took decisions. The sums of money could be considerable for the larger companies and they were all ready to bung in an appeal if they didn't get what they wanted or expected. Whether they had or had not a qualified Training Instructor was relatively easy to police; policing whether the trainees were trained in a training room/area was more difficult.

A room with a few sewing machines in and a poster on the wall saying, 'Training Room' did not mean, necessarily, that trainees had been anywhere near it—the questioning of recent trainees would often reveal that they had been trained in the traditional manner, i.e., 'sitting by Nellie' where the new girl simply sat by and watched an experienced machinist, Nellie, until they felt they could do it. Such training was common within the industry and turned-out newbies who after six months could produce about 50% of the performance of an experienced machinist.

The TDOs had developed a course for instructors which had been proven to show that with the correct training newcomers could be trained to 100% performance after one week. A fantastic improvement, so fantastic that most companies in the industry did not believe it was possible. It was to take more than a year for the word to spread through the industry that it really was possible if the training was carried out correctly. They had carried out an analysis to find out what were the precise skill needed of a machinist.

Besides some of the basics such as being able to thread the machine correctly, speed was integral to all the training so trainees were taught how to thread the machine and then repeated the exercise over and over until they could do it under the time target—that would differ from company to company, dependent on the different machines in use. When they had looked at the sewing skills, they identified that machinist sewed in a straight line, or in a curved line or a line to a particular point and then changed direction.

The distance sewed varied depending on the garment but rarely did a machinist sew a line much longer than 8" or so before having to re-grip the material. Consequently, shapes for training were cut out of the cloth laid up for cutting in the spaces between the actual garment parts. The trainee would then be faced with a pile of ten pieces of cloth, about 8" long and 4" wide on top of one another. The task, against the clock would be to pick up two pieces of cloth and sew them together from top to bottom in a straight line, put the completed piece down and then pick up another two pieces and sew them together until all ten pieces had been sewn into five joined pieces within the time limit.

Traditionally trainees would only sew a short distance, an inch or two, move their hands, then sew another inch or two and continue on that way until the distance required on the garment had been sewn. The only way, with that bad method, that they could speed up was to try and go faster but there was a distinct limit as to just how fast the piece could be handled five or six times in an eight-inch run. Of course, the new way involved wobbly lines to start with but they picked up sewing a straight line of eight inches in one go remarkably quickly. Since they were using what would otherwise be waste cloth cut between the proper shapes the training was virtually cost free for materials whereas in the traditional sitting by Nellie, they learned on real garments which were often completely spoiled in the early stages of learning as well as the fact that trainees were very slow.

For Jack, the principles were obvious, identify the skill required, break it down into manageable bites and teach each bite until confident before moving on until all the bites were put together resulting in a fully trained recruit or trainee in his new industry. Unfortunately, the Instructor Training Courses being run by all sorts of people did not go into this industry relevant detail; so the Board, who could not run courses on a subject if it were commercially available, having identified that it was not commercially available, had designed its own course which was to be offered to the industry.

The first courses, four of them at the same time, were due to start three weeks after Jack joined the Board and his first priority was to look at the course content and apply his knowledge to it—no pressure there then! The fundamentals already developed were very sound and Jack could only contribute minor changes to the programme. As he was to become familiar with the industry, he was able to introduce some improvements—what he didn't expect was that he would be running one of the four courses three weeks after his start with the Board as Maurice Kennet was to be struck by the flu and rendered *hors de combat* by it. Maurice's course was being run at a further education college and the first he knew about it was a knock at the door on Sunday night.

Standing at the door was his boss. Inviting him in and introducing him to Janet was only the work of moments. Sam was terribly apologetic when he explained that the Board had wanted to score points against the other boards, and the announcement that the Clothing and Footwear Industry Training Board was going to be running four instructor courses at the same time so soon after their creation did cause a bit of a stir. Clearly, he didn't want the other boards to be able to laugh at them so he wanted Jack to run the course for the following week or, possibly two, if Maurice did not make a rapid recovery.

He had with him the course notes and, upon Jack saying, 'Of course I'll do it.' He took Jack through the lessons and the points they needed to make. The course was being run in Ballymena, at one of the colleges there, and the other three were in Londonderry, Enniskillen and Armagh, all four corners of Ulster. He even had a prospectus of the college in Ballymena which contained a good map giving directions how to find it. Unfortunately, it meant Jack would have to travel right across Belfast and back each day. Looked at on the map the distance was about 30 miles but it would easily take, to get there for 9am, about an hour and a half.

For the first morning, he would allow another half hour to allow for finding his way, parking and setting up the kit such as the overhead projector etc. The weather forecast for that night visualised -5C with a heavy frost and icy roads. It turned out to be one of those occasions, very rare occasions, when the forecasters got it right! There was a heavy frost which took some scraping off the windscreen. Getting through Belfast proved not to be too difficult; there was little rush hour traffic at 7am and by the time the traffic was starting to build up Jack was heading north out of the city while the weight of the traffic was heading in. Belfast sits at the head of a lough surrounded by mountains—these acted to trap fumes and emissions to make life quite unpleasant with smog everywhere unless the wind was in the right direction to blow the pollution down the lough and out to sea.

As he climbed up the mountain range, so the number of buildings thinned and by the time he had crossed them he was into quite depopulated countryside. The traffic heading into Belfast thinned and by the time he was about 15 miles north there was surprisingly little so much so that as he ran down a steepish slope to a T-junction where he was due to turn right, he could see just one set of tyre tracks in the frost on the road. He had felt the car tyres squirm a bit a few times so he was suspicious that there was ice on the road, but when he had tried the brakes cautiously miles before it had seemed that there was no ice.

Remembering the time when he had done the same on his motorbike with Paul Air on the back there had been no ice on his side of the road but there was on the other side and he had dropped it with both of them on it when he applied brakes, so he applied the brakes quite hard. Indeed, there was ice the brakes had no effect whatsoever; he released them and applied them again harder and harder until the wheels locked when he immediately released them again.

Called cadence braking a dour old Sergeant from the Hampshire Police had taught them the technique at the tank depot but as it was the middle of the summer, they hadn't any ice to practice on! Years later they had developed slippery water surfaces and kits to lift some of the car weight to reduce grip and imitate icy conditions but that had not been available on Jack's course. Meanwhile Jack was heading for a crash.

Jack had organised the refresher driver training course for all the drivers at the depot on the instructions of the Major commanding. It was late May and they had had a major accident with a tank transporter carrying a Conqueror tank. The all up weight was just over 100 tons. Fortunately, it was travelling at about 10mph through Salisbury when a woman driver burst out of a side turning and smashed into the front off-side wheel which immediately snapped the tie rods controlling the steering.

The driver of the Antar slammed on the brakes but well over 100 tons travelling at 10mph doesn't stop immediately, and with no steering, the vehicle careered across the road and flattened a number of parked vehicles and eventually came to a stop lodged in a baker's shop. The woman driver promptly did a runner and was never seen again. Even though she was clearly to blame the anti-army, ban the bomb, surrender at all costs brigade crawled out of their sewers with demands that all army vehicles should be banned from Salisbury; this despite the fact that detours would add hundreds of miles per year and the consequent costs at two miles per gallon.

The Army PR people immediately went into high gear releasing stories to the press blaming the woman driver, detailing how few accidents per year occurred involving army vehicles and inviting selected pressmen to visit the depot and see just how much training of drivers was carried out. This led to the instruction to Jack to put on a refresher driving course.

The Major, although approving the programme threw a wobbler, when in response to the question, 'who's running this?' received the answer, 'I am,' from Jack.

"Oh no you're not, I've seen you're driving, get in touch with the Hampshire Police and ask them to do it." Before Jack could respond he was gone leaving a very pissed off Lieutenant behind him. Jack was to learn that you could criticise someone for their appearance, their ability to hold their beer, or not, and get away with it but criticise their driving and you faced a wall of shit. All the drivers regarded themselves as professionals, they had completed additional training and were regularly assessed and tested; to be criticised was not on and this included Jack who had slipped onto the courses and had been marked highly for his driving.

But there was nothing he could do about it so on the appointed date this dour, old Sergeant appeared. A quick tour of the depot and an explanation of the vehicles raised a gleam in his eye which developed almost searchlight intensity when Jack said, "We can organise for you to have a drive of a few of these at the end of the course if you like."

The Sergeant spent about half an hour setting up a piece of furniture which comprised a seat a 'dash board,' a steering wheel which didn't work and set into the dashboard was a screen upon which appeared a film shot through the windscreen of a car. It was travelling through a town so there were numerous potentially dangerous areas. The Sergeant started by asking what was plainly a stupid question. The question was, 'who here has or would drive on the motorway at 60mph for a hundred yards with their eyes shut?' The class of 20 drivers all laughed and denied that they would do such a stupid thing.

"By the time this course is over I will ask you that question again and we'll see what your answers are then."

The course started with them all driving police cars, three to a car, with a Trainer Driver marking them. They were not told their scores and they were then subjected to a test on the fake car that had been set up. Each soldier sat on the seat and pressed a button to start the film. They were instructed that when a red light showed around the screen, they were to take their finger off the button and push the button alongside it. The pushing of the second button stopped a stop watch which had started when the Sergeant pushed his button to switch on the red light. The red light sprang on at traffic lights, Zebra crossings, bus stops or where ever took the Sergeant's fancy. The timer was stopping on average at the two thirds of a second mark.

The Sergeant explained that hands responded at the same speed as feet so using fingers on the buttons was a fair test. As he was explaining this he suddenly stopped and said, "Sir, you haven't had a go; let's see how fast your reaction time is."

Jack knew that at some time he would be tested in some way, hopefully one that would not show him to be inferior to the soldiers. Jack duly took his place and pushed the button to start the film. He was poised ready to slam his finger onto the stop button as soon as the red light showed but at the Zebra crossing it did not show; nor did it at the bus stop, the traffic lights or any of the previous places where the red had come on. The Sergeant said to him, when he crossed the Zebra crossing for the second time, "You were expecting me to show the red light then weren't you?"

Jack turned and looked at him and said, "Yes, I was," and as soon as Jack looked at the Sergeant the Sergeant operated the red light. It was out of Jack's line of vision and it wasn't until he turned and consciously looked at the screen that he saw the red light. He reacted immediately but the timer showed that it had taken him three and a half seconds to react—by far the slowest of the class. The class was delighted and Jack was seriously pissed off; he had been well and truly caught. The Sergeant, well aware that Jack was angry, said, "Let's try that again, Sir." This time the red light came on at the zebra crossing and Jack hit the button in.56 of a second, the second fastest of the group.

And the T-junction was approaching and Jack couldn't stop.

The Sergeant then explained that all they had been doing was measuring reaction time with all of them fully expecting the red light to show. "If someone wasn't driving waiting for the red or had, for example, turned to look at their passenger as Lt Hughes had been induced to do, the reaction time could be much, much longer. Now that was just the reaction time to hitting the brakes, the braking distance would add considerable distance to the stopping distance depending on a number of factors, how good were the brakes, what was the road surface like, was it wet or dry, how fast was the vehicle going etc. Sixty miles per hour is 88 feet per second.

"For the purposes of this exercise, let's call that 90 feet per second. It means that when you are alert, ready and expecting it your reaction time distance is 90 feet X 2/3rds of a second i.e., *60 feet before you do anything*. That means if you are driving along the high street at 30mph you will have travelled 30 feet before you start braking. If a small child runs out 20 feet in front of you, you will have run him over and driven another 10 feet before you apply your brakes. That thought should give you the heebie-jeebies! It certainly does me! That is why all police drivers are taught the importance of their reaction time and to be analysing the road conditions in front of them in such a way that they can beat the reaction time delay should something happen.

"I'm not going to talk about braking distances because there are simply too many variables to consider. The figures given in the Highway Code are averages for a car in good condition with good tyres and on a dry road. Your tank transporters, fully loaded are going to take much further to stop than a small car and in the wet the distance doesn't bear thinking about. And that's what all good driving is about, thinking about what's happening ahead of you and being prepared for something to go wrong. Now back to my question.

"Imagine Lt Hughes driving on the motorway, he's driving at 60 mph, well under the limit, and his passenger says something that he responds to by looking at her for 3.5 seconds. Three point five seconds at 90 feet per second is 315 feet when he has not been looking at the road. That is more than 100 yards, at 60 mph, when he has not looked at the road. The legal limit is now 70mph (it had been introduced only a few weeks before across the whole nation). At that speed he would travel more than 360 feet, 120 yards, without once looking at the road, put another way *with his eyes shut*. Now, gentlemen, think about it, be honest with yourselves have you driven at 60mph with your eyes shut for a hundred yards or more?" The response was very different to the first time the question was asked.

And the T-junction was approaching and Jack couldn't stop.

The course then proceeded with a mix of lectures, driving examples and driving with a police driver training, criticising and guiding them. Jack found the most difficult part of the course was to carry out a running commentary of what he was seeing happening in the road in front of him. The course culminated in a 20-minute test drive where the police driver sat there marking their driving, commentary and all. They were then given their marks for the two drives and the course work. The drivers all scored highly representing the professionals they were but Jack came top with 94% for his final drive against 73% for his first one; no-one else had exceeded 65% for their first drive but all had exceeded the second one by, most of them, into the 70s and 80s.

Besides having learned the lessons of how to drive better Jack took from it that if you could test the trainees at the start of a course and then again at the end you could measure the quality and effectiveness of a course. When someone was coming in as a complete learner, it was almost impossible to do but where people were supposedly knowledgeable in a subject it could be possible to test them at the beginning and the end to measure exactly how much people had learned and whether the course had been any good or crap. He resolved to do this wherever possible in the future, on any training course he ran.

And the T-junction was approaching and Jack couldn't stop.

Jack arranged, as promised, for the Sergeant and two of the driver/instructors to drive three Centurions out of the depot and over Salisbury Plain. They returned after half an hour absolutely shattered; all three of them had shaking left legs from the sheer effort of using the clutch pedal. *Perhaps*, thought Jack, *the Sergeant won't be quite so quick to show up and piss off an officer in the future who, after all, had been there, done it and got the T-shirt!*

And the T-junction was fast approaching and Jack was looking at deep shit very soon.

Jack had clearly cleared the thinking time, he had been looking at the tail lights of a van sticking out of the hedge across the T-junction. From the look of it there was a ditch somewhere there because the back of the van was clearly cocked up in the air. Cadence braking was not working worth a dam, there was too much ice and it was too slippery. As he approached the T-junction he could see that the grass verge to the side of the road he was on gradually widened out so that was his option, he released the brakes one last time, obtained what little steering there was and steered up onto the verge applying the brakes on and off in the process and low and behold he pulled to a stop; only just with the front wheels on the road on which he wanted to turn right and his rear wheels on the grass.

The verge was quite rough and it was probably his tyres digging in to the rough that stopped him but whatever it was he was grateful. He gingerly turned the steering wheel to the right and gently pulled onto the road and drove a little past the crashed vehicle and stopped where he would not be in the way of anyone else sliding into the junction.

He walked back to the guy standing by the van. They had a brief conversation that revealed the actual driver had thumbed a lift on a passing lorry and had gone off to find a recovery vehicle. The passenger in the crashed van had revealed within quite a short time that he had been at the end of the queue when brain cells were handed out. It took three goes for Jack's suggestion that it might be a good idea to walk back to the top of the hill and attempt to flag down any vehicle so they wouldn't crash to be understood, and even then then, Jack wasn't sure it had gone in, especially when he said three times, 'It's no my van.'

Jack needed to be at the college to start the class so he could not wait to see if the guy did walk back up the hill but the whole thing did clearly reveal that awareness of the road surface was always an absolute requirement. Jack drove very, very carefully into Ballymena. The closer he got, the wetter the roads became and less slippery and he took the opportunity to speed up when he could. He arrived at the college and parked in the visitors' car park. He couldn't however enter the building. A notice on the door described opening times as 0845hrs. That was no good for Jack as he had equipment to set up ready for a 09.00hrs start. This was to be his first introduction to the approach to punctuality in Ulster. He wandered around the main building to see if he could find any way in. There wasn't a soul!

Chapter 4

Remembering odd items from when he was on guard in Yeovil and Aldershot, he tried to find the boiler room. And sure, enough at the back of the building he found an open door leading into a boiler room. It was all very well to list opening hours but, in the winter, especially the boiler man would have to be in long before that time to get the boilers lit and heating up the water; hot water was needed not just for the domestic kitchens and toilets, but also for the heating for the classrooms and admin facilities.

In more modern facilities, the heating could be timed to switch on at a time early enough for the building to be nice and warm as the people who were to use it arrived. In an old building like this one the boilers had to be lit, stoked up and brought to life by the boiler man—often someone who had been there for years and was the only one who knew just where to hit the right bit of the boiler with the big hammer to get it going! Jack found him.

He was in a little cubbyhole sitting on an often-repaired armchair with his radio on, listening to the music while at the same time studying the racing pages of the Daily Mirror. Jack took all of this in in a swift glance but the thing that caught his eye to linger was a wooden plaque of an Army regiment. The boiler man exploded with a "Who the bloody hell are you?" Jack replied, "Someone looking for an ex Green Trousers." Jack's accent was clearly English and it was clearly Officer Class—his appearance, short hair, business suit and a regimental tie, RASC which no longer existed. The boiler man paused, thought about it and said, "I'm ex Green Trousers." A regimental name from years before when two cavalry regiments the 5th and the 6th were formed into the 5th Inniskilling Royal Dragoon Guards—one of many names over the years the regiment had existed but Jack knew them as the 5th Skins from Aden and as the Green Trousers from the tales the two lads he had spent the night with in jail in Mombasa. "What do you want?

"Well, I spent a night in jail in Mombasa with a couple of Green Trousers in 1966 and I wondered if I could possibly find either or both of them seeing your Regimental Crest. It was now 1969, so not too long for the story to be forgotten and indeed it had not. The boiler man introduced himself as Jim Fogarty, known as Sooty. He had left the Regiment only three months before and had got himself this little number at the college—certain organisations had preferments for ex-servicemen and his knowledge as an ex-driver of armoured vehicles easily fitted him into these boilers that only needed a few shovelfuls of coal and a careful watch of the gauges and pipes for leaks." Looking at Jack, he said, "So how do you know about that then?"

"Because I was the third one, two were Skins and the third was me."

"Cup of tea?"

"Too bloody right, it's bloody freezing out there; I've had a narrow miss on an icy junction and I've got a load of stuff to set up for 09.00hrs start."

"Well, you can forget the 09.00hrs, 09.15 is far more likely but have a swig of this," he had been making a mug of tea as they spoke, "and we'll get your stuff in." They talked as they worked and Jack told Sooty a short version of his career since Mombasa. Sooty started calling Jack 'Sir' but Jack insisted he call him, Jack; he was no longer an officer and he felt he'd get more out of Sooty if he used Jack and he did. Sooty helped him bring the overhead projector and screen into the training room and helped him set it up. "You know," he said, "You are going to be here for the best part of three weeks why don't you just leave this stuff in here and I'll lock it up at night. It will be perfectly safe and save us a lot of humping."

Jack immediately noted the 'us' in the sentence and that's what they did. The kit the Training Board had was all new, latest do-dads and technology. You could, for instance, mount a role of acetate so that you could simply role the written on off screen and carry on. The ones in the college had no such feature so that the lecturer had to write on a square sheet and put it carefully to the side when full where it would promptly cause all the other sheets to fall on the floor and become out of order. Several people, probably lecturers, walked into the room, by mistake of course, and enviously eyed the kit.

As Sooty had told him the course members didn't arrive until 09.15ish and with all the greetings etc. it was 10.00hrs before the class was ready to start. At 10.30hrs two of the class got up and walked out. Jack thought what the hell have

I said to set them off, but Paddy, one of the two men on the course picked up Jack's face and called out, "They've gone to make the tea."

Jack thanked him but the class in turn looked puzzled as Sooty walked in, having tapped on the door, and placed a full mug of tea in front of Jack and walked out. Jack later learned that previously Maurice Kennet did not make any tea or coffee because he was lecturing but this was taken as an affront by the class, they obviously wanted a further 15 minutes each morning and afternoon while waited on by the 'teacher'.

The appearance of a mug of military tea did shake them up a bit. But Jack could not take what was turning out to be a part-time course. So, he spoke to them clearly and in a manner to make it clear that punctuality was next to godliness and lateness akin to failing the course—they started arriving ready for a 9am start and a timely return from lunch at 2pm.

One thing that did surprise Jack was that out of the 10 on the course, eight had never been to Belfast. It was only 30 miles or so and packed with shops, cinemas, pubs, museums etc. which Ballymena could never match. But it was 'too far' for them—incredible to Jack who was driving there and back every day.

When he arrived the second morning, at just after 8.15am, the doors were of course locked so Jack made his way to the boiler room to find two mugs, two tea bags and the other paraphernalia necessary to make two mugs of tea, set out on the little table. There was, however, no sign of Sooty. Knowing that he could not be far away Jack switched the kettle on and had just poured the water into the mugs as Sooty appeared. Greetings over Sooty said he had put the word out to try and find out where the two Green legs who had been imprisoned with Jack in Kenya, were. He expected to hear something within a couple of days.

Meanwhile the course progressed with Jack learning the papers for the following day the night before he did the presentation! There are probably millions of ways to instruct but Jack's was first to find out what the student knew and then lead them onwards by primarily asking questions to guide their thinking to the right answer. One of the subjects covered early on in the programme was 'Why people work?'

The content of the lesson clearly aimed to get instructors to understand why people worked to understand their motivation so that they could be managed to work smarter/better. Listed were eight reasons why people worked starting with money, the most obvious one, and ending with status. In thinking about how he would approach this subject, Jack felt that the detail, while correct in the eight headings, it did not connect all the dots to be of full use. So many of the papers Jack was to read during his six-month induction were research papers presented in the same way.

It was not enough to know that money motivated some people, the supervisor, manager, or in this case, the Instructor needed to know why the individual sitting in front of them was motivated to work there. From conversations Jack had had with his Training Board colleagues and with the managers he had talked to in the visits to factories that he had made he discovered that there was a theory common to them all about why their—mainly female— work force worked and that was for money.

Consequently, most of the payment systems were based on payment by result systems. The sewing machinist would receive a bundle of work, some of the factories had split the tasks up so that a machinist only did one simple job. She would therefore be easy to train quickly and would become good and fast at doing that job. If she wanted more money, then all she had to do was complete more bundles and she would then receive more pay. Simple! The trouble was it did not work for everyone.

Jack began to feel that, using the 'Why People Work' theory there were demonstrably three types of female operative. There were those school leavers up to about 18-20, those about 45 plus, and the third group were those in between. There were, of course individual exceptions as ever, to make life more difficult. He was to come across problems where the girl took her pay packet home unopened, gave it to her mother who removed a pound or two and gave it to the girl and kept the rest.

There was no incentive for these girls to work harder and earn more money because Mum kept the extra! He, with the Factory Manager in one instance, was able to solve some of these by inviting the mother in and persuading her to take a fixed sum from the pay packet and let the daughter keep the rest. Those who were unwilling found a threat of a P45 for their daughter to be a convincing persuader.

The final group, the over 45s did not respond to payments by results schemes very well. Yes of course they weren't going to work for nothing but their motivation for coming out to work was not primarily money. By that age their children were probably grown up and had flown the nest so that they found time in the day on their hands. They were also quite lonely at home—especially the older ones so companionship was a major factor to decide what job they chose.

The greatest example of this came about at a factory near Enniskillen. The factory was a knitwear factory making mainly jumpers, sweaters and cardigans. Virtually the last job was hand sewing of the seams at the cuffs and necks to make sure the seams did not unravel. In the finishing room were a number of largish tables around which sat groups of older women—most over pension age. They would select an item from the box, select the correct colour thread, thread the needle and then sew up the points needing reinforcement. Having done so, they would put the finished garment in a 'finished' box and start all over again. While the sewing was going on the chat was also going on, the owner of the business had a heart attack and died leaving the business to his 18-year-old son.

The son had grown up in and around the business and was well known and loved by most of the staff and especially the women in the finishing section. Knowing he did not have enough knowledge to run the business he hired a Manager to run it for him. The new guy took stock of the business. The knitting machines ran at a set speed and, apart from ensuring they were properly maintained there was little prospect there to increase production but when he came to the finishing room, his eyes lit up. He saw a room full of old biddies talking more than working and saw immediately how production could be improved.

Over the weekend, he had the old tables removed to be replaced by small, individual tables. They were set up in lines and each line was fed just one colour garment; thus, alleviating the need to change the colour in the needle. Each colour would go into one box so that by the time they arrived at the pressing section a box would only contain one colour of garment, simplifying sorting for packing. He also had run in speakers for the radio so that these older ladies could be spurred along by Radio One blasting at them all day, so loud as to make speech almost impossible.

By the end of the week the whole team had resigned. The owner went round to one of their houses and, leaning on their long acquaintanceship, asked her why she had resigned. In essence the answer was that she had come to work to see her friends and chat to them. She had her pension so she didn't really need the money, it was nice but she didn't need it, and not being able to talk, being blasted by that awful bloody music had destroyed her reason for working there.

The company recruited young girls to do the work but it was so boring a job that the labour turnover was horrendous and they ended up re-arranging the section to what it had been, removing the radio and taking all the old workers into coming back. If their performance was too low, then little threats about stopping them talking, bringing in the radio etc. was enough to produce a higher performance.

Initially Jack just had the handout to teach from but as time went on and he picked up stories like this one he added them to the lesson. Other reasons such as contribution to society for those people who worked for nothing for charities, those attracted to profession because of their status and those taking lower paid jobs than their qualifications deserved, such as nurses also came into the discussions.

It was all right to know the reasons why people worked but the important point was to know why that particular individual was wanting to work there in that job. Years later Jack was to work for a man who was convinced that money motivated everyone and could not accept that almost all of the consultants when given the opportunity to earn commission and even foreign holidays by asking a customer for a referral to another company who might then sign up with them, would not do so. As far as the consultants were concerned, they were consultants and asking for a referral was a sales person's job. When the 'bribe' of commission and holidays didn't work and threats of dismissal started if they didn't ask for referrals, resignations shot up.

Of course, some of them were motivated by the offer of extra 'money' but this only proved Jack's point with all generalisations and averages that there was always an odd one out. Some research was published that showed on average that men were more intelligent than women—by 2 or 3 points—welcomed by men and disowned by women, loudly and forcibly; it ignored the fact that when there was a male or female sitting in front of you, you could not assume the man was more intelligent because he might be a lower-than-average male and the female a higher than average female in which case she would be far more intelligent. Jack was always at great pains to stress that one had to see one's subordinates (and bosses!) as individuals and manage them that way—he was to say, not always jokingly, that half his success in life was not managing his subordinates but his bosses!

Lots of the reasons why people work became intermixed as soon as Jack started looking at them, for instance people would apply to become doctors because they wanted to help people, they wanted the status that went with the post and the money. Jack used all these factors to try to get course members thinking more deeply about why the trainee was sitting in front of them and the best way to manage and motivate them. He was concerned that there seemed to be very little thinking going on, we did it that way because it had always been done that way!

Chapter 5

The course covered other subjects starting with the initial interview and some practical tests that the Training Board recommended should be used. One of them was a book to test colour blindness. Devised by a Dr Shinobu Ishihara it contained pages covered in coloured dots. Sometimes there were clearly recognised numbers created by contrast-coloured dots, sometimes there was a line which had to be followed by a finger and sometimes nothing could be seen by the individual taking the test. It was very weird, surreal even, when sometimes someone traced lines and called out numbers that were simply not there to a non-colour-blind person; this last was mixed in with that person not being able to see the numbers that were as clear as day to someone who was not colour-blind.

When a factory made nothing but white shirts, it wasn't a problem but when multi-colours were laid up on the cutting tables once the pieces had been cut up and sorted into single colour bundles or placed in bundles where the machinist had to sort them out, before sewing them together, colour-blindness could be a real problem—someone sewing red sleeves into a green body (red/green colour blindness was the most common colour problem but shade blindness was also a problem; when two or three roles of blue cloth had been laid out and cut up there was often a slightly different shade between the three rolls and machinists had to ensure that sleeves of two different hues did not end up in the one shirt!). About one in ten men had a colour-blindness problem and about one in two hundred women—not exactly equality and nothing could be done about it. For the employer it was important to identify that someone had a colour-blindness problem so a way could be found around it.

Two of the other tests the Board were recommending were downright weird. The first involved dropping a large marble down a vertical tube and catching it when it dropped out the bottom with the hand that had dropped it. The tube was quite short and many of the course participants could not move their hand quickly enough to catch it. The second one involved picking up exactly three pins in one go from a pile on a tray and placing the three pins into a hole in a brass plate. The brass plate had rows and rows of holes and to pass the individual had to pick up three pin amounts and fill a number of holes with them within the 90 second time limit. Again, a large proportion of the course could not pass the test.

Jack spent some considerable time considering this. The tests were supplied by a reputable—allegedly—consultancy. The tests bore no relationship to anything a machinist did so what was their relevance? The women taking the tests were all experienced, high-quality machinists but if they had applied to join a company using these tests they would have been rejected. That was crazy so Jack decided to bin them. The colour-blindness test he kept and a vision test he kept—if someone could not see well enough to thread a needle, they needed to see an optician and get glasses so that they could, an almost blind machinist working on an industrial speed machine would be in danger! Perhaps other work could be found but it was important to find out at the interview stage if someone had a vision problem of some kind.

At the end of the course, each participant had to give a short speech/talk of about 10 minutes on any subject they liked; it did not need to be work related it just had to show that they had taken in the principles they had been taught and they could give a formal presentation. They also had to teach a short, simple practical task for the same reason. On examining Maurice Kennet's notes, he noticed an annotation that he loved immediately. In the formal world talks, presentations, whatever were supposed to be delivered in three parts, an Introduction, a Development and a Summary. Alongside these words Maurice had written:

Tell 'em what you're gonna tell 'em
Tell 'em
Tell 'em what you've told them!

Jack loved it. It fitted so well with Maurice's strong Ballymena accent and it was so much clearer as a guidance than the formal 'Introduction etc.' so he used it when teaching the session and the candidates were marked on had they followed that structure when delivering their presentations.

Seven of the presentations had passed with Jack delighted at the quality in the shape of the presentation and the interest that had been developed. Then it was Paddy's turn.

34

When Jack said, "OK Paddy you're next," Paddy lit a cigarette and puffed on it so hard that he did actually disappear behind a screen of smoke. It was unbelievable. Paddy wouldn't or couldn't get out of his seat and sit at the head of the table. Jack had never come across this problem before. He started asking questions of Paddy like, "What is the title of your talk?" but all he got in reply was a mumble from the other side of the smoke screen.

After several attempts, he gave up and moved on to the next pupil who, fortunately, was not bothered by the experience and gave an excellent presentation. When they finished for the day, Jack asked Paddy to stay behind. The fact that Paddy was terrified was obvious, but having faced real peril in Aden Jack could not understand fear about such a relatively simple task. He asked to see Paddy's notes and they were excellent; he had the *'tell 'em what you're gonna tell 'em'* intro set out, as was the *'tell 'em'* and the *'tell 'em what you've told them'*. Jack decided to withhold judgement on whether Paddy was to pass or not until he had seen the practical demonstrations which were to come a few days later.

Jack spoke to Paddy as they were finishing the day before they were due to start their practical demonstrations and asked him what he was planning on teaching. Paddy said he was intending to teach how to properly sharpen a table knife. At that stage Jack had no idea what a table knife was but he did elicit that it was quite a heavy item which would require someone strong as the trainee.

"In that case," said Jack, "I had better be the trainee." He had intended being the trainee in any case and he said to Paddy, "In view of that and the problem you had with the talk I want you to come in at 8.30am and teach me then before any of the rest of the course arrive." Paddy's face lit up at that and, as instructed, he was there, prompt at 8.30. The task was a relatively simple one but it required that the steps be done in a set order; within 15 minutes Jack knew how to sharpen a table knife—a straight bladed, vertical knife which vibrated up and down to cut through thick layers of cloth.

Where the quality of the cutting was not too critical, the cloth could be cut out with a table knife; where real accuracy was required, with shirt collars or men's jackets for example the item would just be cut out leaving a large margin around it and then cut more accurately by a band knife. As someone new to the industry Jack was to be the trainee quite often and his proudest boast was that he knew how to sew gussets into knickers and was probably the only man who could do so! Paddy's presentation had been structured correctly with a proper introduction, the training had been broken down into logical steps and Jack had had to be proficient at one before moving onto the next and by the end he was competent at sharpening a table knife. Jack considered that in the factory Paddy would only be facing a single trainee and would not be nervous as he had been for the talk element of the course. He therefore gave him a pass.

The remaining practical training sessions went quite well showing that they had taken in what Jack had been trying to impart. The course finished on the Friday and when Jack returned to the office on Monday morning, he found only Tom Magee there. On asking where everyone else was it was to discover that they were all on holiday until the 6th January.

All the factories were closed for this period, it not being economic to open for short weeks with the resulting heating costs, so holiday it was. Jack had not booked any holiday over the Christmas period, Tom was in because he had used all his during the summer when he had taken an extended holiday in America. In fact, that was just about all they talked about all morning there being no real work for them to do. Unusually there was a factory in Portadown that was working the Monday and the Tuesday to meet a valuable and urgent order to produce white shirts for the New Year sales. Apparently, they had a problem with grading the patterns and had asked for Tom, a qualified tailor, to visit to see if he could identify the problem. He was due to visit them the following day, Christmas Eve.

Tom said he did not expect there to be much work done on that day—they would be finishing at lunch time anyway and offered to take Jack with him. Jack jumped at the chance to go with Tom as he had not yet been into a factory, all his time having been taken up with the Instructor Course.

Chapter 6

The factory was an old cinema which had been converted. What had been the ticket office had been turned into a Reception and the interior had been converted into a series of plateaus descending to the ground floor. The flat area had been divided up into a number of departments all of which became apparent once Jack was shown around. They were on time for their appointment but had to wait a good 20 minutes before the boss arrived. As they were sitting in Reception Tom pointed out and said, "Here he comes" and galloping towards them over the field next to the factory was a bloke on a horse. He cleared the dividing fence with ease and dismounted handing the reigns to an old chap who seemed to appear from nowhere but in reality, from a horse box at the side, obviously designed to hold the horse.

With no apology for being late—punctuality, Jack was to discover was a rare event in N Ireland. Introductions over, Tom disappeared off with the boss while Jack was to tour the factory to see the whole process of manufacturing a shirt starting in the Cutting Room. His guide was the Production Manager, a guy by the name of Chris MacAfee, who Jack was to get to know quite well.

The only problem was, was that he was very short and walking alongside Jack he did not reach Jack's shoulder. On their way to the Cutting Room, they had to pass through most of the Sewing room and Jack, as a visitor and a particularly tall, manly and good looking one—at least in Jack's view, attracted a lot of interest and comment. Comments like, "Who's yon big fellah, Chris?"— "Send him over here Chris, we'll show him a good Christmas,"—and others rather more rude and blunt indicated, as Chris whispered in an aside, "They've all had a few and it will get worse or better, depending on your viewpoint, as the day goes on."

Jack had heard one or two tales of the goings on once drink was taken, and indeed had experienced a little of what under the influence women could do at the tank depot, his last posting in the Army, so that he was not too keen to return to the sewing room but return he did after seeing the cutting in operation. The cloth, white cotton, had been laid out on an immensely long table, five feet wide and with an automatic cutter at the end. The pattern paper, was laid on top with the various shapes drawn on it. The pieces were cut out with table knives, exactly as Paddy had explained on the Instructor Course, and then accurately cut out with a band knife.

The band knife struck Jack as being arse backwards. It was an extremely sharp circle of steel which was powered by, in this factory, an electric motor—in others they were still driven by leather belts. It had a sharp edge and a dull edge. The sharp edge obviously cut the cloth but it was on the far side of the blade (so cutting was done by pulling the cloth towards one) so that should the operator nick himself in any way the automatic reaction would be to pull the hand(s) back which would immediately pull them into danger thus, obviously causing more damage to the individual.

If the sharp edge had been on the side facing the operator, then anything happening and the hands would be pulled away from danger with nothing to obstruct them. Although Jack brought this up on a number of occasions over the next three years it was just shrugged off as 'we have always done it that way.' Still seeing it in action added immeasurably to his knowledge. The finishing section took little time and Jack was able to escape through what had been the old fire door for the cinema without having to go back through the sewing room and its possible dangers! Altogether it had been an enlightening visit and Jack much appreciated it.

Chapter 7

The Christmas break passed quietly for Jack but in the Province, trouble was brewing. A 'one man one vote' civil rights movement had been growing since the summer. Sponsored, primarily, by the Catholic Church, there had been 'peaceful' marches, rapidly developing into violence throughout the summer. The Protestant celebrations of especially the Battle of the Boyne on the 12th July had been particularly forceful to counter the propaganda of the Roman Church. Presented to the media as discrimination against the Catholics by the Protestants the situation was becoming increasingly unpleasant and worrying.

Following rioting and fighting over three days and nights in the Bogside area of Londonderry, British troops had been sent in to protect the Catholic population from the Protestants who had become very angry about the way Catholics were trying to seize power. The 'one man one vote' movement was felt to be particularly dishonest by the Protestants. All adults in N Ireland did have a vote in parliamentary type elections—mainly to their own Parliament in Stormont. But unlike the rest of the UK, you did not have a vote in council elections unless you were a rate payer. As many of the Catholics were unemployed—they would argue because they were discriminated against by the Protestants—they lived on benefits and therefore did not pay rates thus being unable to vote.

Jack knew little of the arguments between the two sides but he did feel that the idea of if you did not pay rates, you could not vote in local elections, was a good one and should have been introduced across the UK as a whole—why should people who contributed nothing to the local economy say how it should be run? He felt the principal was fine but in the situation in N Ireland where gerrymandering had been developed into a fine art it probably wasn't going to work. As in Aden the first casualty in war is truth and never once when the Catholics were shouting off about being discriminated against, did they mention the docks in Londonderry, for example, where the workforce was 100% Catholic and where it was impossible for Protestants to get a job.

Jack quite quickly realised that using Catholic and Protestant to describe the two sides was inaccurate. A better terminology in his view was Unionist and Republican. The Republicans wanted unification with the Republic of Ireland and the Unionist wished to remain joined to the UK. As with every packaging there were those who did not fit; there were some Catholics who were not Republicans and there were some Protestants who wanted to join the Republic. Since the summer marches the two sides had become polarised and the Army had had to be called in to defend the Catholics/Republicans.

Seeing an opportunity, the old IRA split and a new branch, the Provisionals announced they were taking over the defence of the Catholic/Republicans because the Army was biased in favour of the Protestants/Unionists. No-go areas had started appearing in the autumn and Protestant families were forced out of Catholic areas with tit-for-tat following with Catholics being forced out of Protestant areas. It is undoubtedly true that the Catholic side was far superior to the Protestants in Public Relations and one of the targets was the RUC (Royal Ulster Constabulary) reserve force colloquially referred to as the B Specials.

Called on in time of need, they were very effective with intelligence because they lived among the general population any way and the country, being so small, everyone knew everyone else. Jack was astounded at how one group would know who the members of the other group were. The Catholics had been brought up in Catholic Schools and the Protestants in Protestant ones. In an attempt to prevent discrimination employers were forbidden to ask what school you went to thus identifying a Catholic or a Protestant Applicant. But this was largely ineffective as either your name (Catholics were always named after Catholic saints and Protestants were often named with names where there were no Catholic saints of that name, for example, in the Training Board where Jack worked there were two Maurices in five staff. As with so many stories in Ireland there actually had been a St Maurice but worship of him had died out in about the 17th century so in the belief there wasn't one many Protestant boys were named Maurice!).

Jack had endeavoured to keep out of the troubles and if someone asked him what church he worshipped in he said he was a Jew. Jack had to travel into the Bogside, a Catholic area, where he was often stopped at a checkpoint manned by uniformed and armed men. Demanding to know what his business was to be entering the area Jack would show his Training Board identity card and tell them he was visiting Tootal Shirts or whatever factory it was. He would be entering this area on a daily basis for frequent periods of time and he began to be recognised by the regular gunmen manning the road blocks.

One of them took a dislike to Jack—Jack disliked him in equal part—and insisted on searching Jack and his car every time he came through. On one occasion he asked Jack, when Jack had answered 'Jew' to the question what religion are you, "But are you a Protestant Jew or a Catholic Jew?"

Jack looked him straight in the eye and said, "I'm a Buddhist Jew." The gunman looked at him for a few moments and then passed him through. Jack was just able to keep a straight face but he felt that he would be facing problems in the not-too-distant future. There were other religious jokes flying around the place, another one being the Protestant Leader, Ian Paisley was out for a walk on Lough Ney and was run down by a speedboat! Vicious yes. Anti the other religion yes, but most of them were very funny.

Jack, on his way home, was stopped three nights running by a temporary road block operated by the Ulster Defence Regiment which had been formed mainly from the old B Specials. The attempt by the IRA, spurred on and supported by the Roman Catholic Church, to discredit and get rid of the B Specials had succeeded and failed in that, yes, they had certainly got the B Specials disbanded by lies and false evidence to the British Government but the men and women of the B Specials had mainly joined the new Ulster Defence Regiment and thus the source of intelligence and manpower was still available to the forces of law and order, and once they had been trained to the British Army standards, they were a much more effective force than the B Specials had ever been.

The training was contributed to by Jack. The road block on his way home was hopelessly operated. Jack came round a bend to see a long straight in front of him. It was, in fact, the only straight on the entire journey home. The problem was just a few yards into the straight was a cross roads. It was notorious for accidents because, coming around the bend at any speed meant that you were into a car coming out of the cross roads before you knew it. It was also dangerous for vehicles slowing down to turn either left or right at the cross roads who regularly were hit from behind by fast moving traffic.

The first soldier of the road block was positioned perhaps 20 yards beyond the cross roads, the two Landrovers forming the block were staggered across the road about 10 yards beyond the first soldier and the final soldier was about 10 yards beyond the last vehicle. Nice and balanced that it looked it was in fact hopeless. Anyone intent on evil coming around the bend could avoid the block altogether by turning left or right at the cross roads. Someone wishing to avoid the road block from the other direction had about half a mile of straight road to turn around in and vanish into the distance.

On this last occasion Jack could see an open top car, with four scantily clad young females in. The car behind them, with just one male driver, and then Jack, both of them were was waved straight through whilst the soldiers chatted up the girls. As he drove away Jack thought what a good way to get safely through a road block, follow a car full of semi naked females. He reached over to his glove box and somewhat precariously wrote down the number of the car with just the one male driver. He drove into Ebrington Barracks on the way home; it was the base for, amongst other Army units, the 5th Bn Ulster Defence Regiment and Jack soon found himself sitting in front of the Adjutant.

Jack started with, "I think I have just seen an IRA smuggling operation in progress and I think it was aided and abetted by your road block out on the Limavady road." It took a moment or two for Jack's statement to sink in.

"What the hell are you talking about and who are you?"

Jack paused and said, "Until a few months ago I was an officer in the Army; my name is Jack Hughes and I saw a temporary road block, which I must say was in completely the wrong place, was laid out badly, operated badly and they stopped a car, a Triumph Herald Convertible with the top down on a February day, containing four scantily dressed young ladies, or perhaps females might be a better description, who drew to them virtually the entire crew of the road block like flies to shit. The following two cars—there weren't any others—were waved through without any inspection whatsoever. What a wonderful way to ensure your terrorist cars are never searched or even stopped; all it costs you is four freezing cold little temptresses."

The Adjutant looked at him. "Do you know that the car with one driver, I think you said the one in front of you, was actually carrying a terrorist?"

"No, of course not but what a great way to operate. It might have been the first time they had tried it out without anything or anyone wanted in the following car or it might be the umpteenth time they have done it. But I am sure the soldiers I saw would have fallen for it every time."

"Would you mind waiting for a moment," at that the Adjutant stood up, tapped on the door to the side of the room and disappeared through it. Jack sat there studying the paperwork on the wall and was just about to start looking at the paperwork on the desk when the Adjutant reappeared at the door and asked him to come in. Sitting at a desk was a half colonel with the badges of the Rifles on his uniform.

"What was wrong with the layout of the roadblock; you did tell my Adjutant that it was all wrong didn't you?" Jack paused to get his thoughts in order before he spoke because he didn't think he would get a second chance and said, "May I have a piece of paper; a picture saves a thousand words," and being handed a pad by the Colonel he drew a straight line from top to bottom which curved off to the left at the bottom. An inch up he drew a horizontal line across the page. He then drew a dot to represent the first soldier two inches above the cross roads, two lines across the road an inch above the soldier and then another dot an inch above that.

He said, "anyone for any reason whatsoever can come around that bend, see the roadblock and then turn left or right down the cross roads thus avoiding the mobile roadblock. The soldiers in the roadblock have no way of knowing if the car or cars that have turned off have done so legitimately or not. Although not necessarily legitimately someone coming along from the top of the page has the best part of a quarter of a mile or more in which to see the road block and turnaround to avoid it." Jack stopped and looked at the Colonel.

The Colonel said, "How would you organise that roadblock then?"

Jack looked at him, deliberately paused and then said, "I wouldn't. Whoever is in command of that patrol can set it up anywhere he likes but not there. He clearly needs some training about the positioning and the operation of an effective roadblock. It is too dangerous for all and sundry there. Your warning man would have to be around the corner and out of sight to slow traffic down enough; a wrong 'un could accelerate around the bend and drive through before anyone in it could react. Your cut-off man might have a chance to shoot but he would be shooting straight down the straight with a good chance of hitting an innocent instead. Wrong place; to try and improve it would be like trying to re-arrange the seats on the Titanic," Jack stopped and looked at the Colonel.

The Colonel said, "When can you join us?"

"Next week," said Jack.

"Wait till you hear from me; for all I know you may have been thrown out for telling Colonels how to run their commands." He said this with a smile on his face. Jack wondered if any check would throw up that he had done exactly that with the Lt Colonel commanding the Junior Leaders' Regiment a couple of years ago!

"One thing," the Colonel said, "You'll need to get rid of the fuzz on your face." Jack had had a moustache when he was in the regular Army and had joined a beard to it once he had served his Short-Term Commission.

"No problem, Sir, I didn't much like the thing anyway." Jack gave the numbers of the girls' car and that of the one behind it to the Adjutant and left. He wondered how Janet would take it because they had not discussed the matter but, in the event, whilst not exactly happy about it she could see the need for expertise to be introduced to the UDR as what she had seen of it, she had been mightily unimpressed too. She also was happier that Jack would be armed going around and at home since the IRA had started murdering people, they were suspicious of in their homes.

Jack was to fit two chains; a mortice lock and the Yale lock was already there to the front door as well as slide bolts. Similar locks were fitted to the back door and locks to all the downstairs windows so that any attempt to break in would be noisy and slow, hopefully slow enough for Jack to seize his pistol and defend the house. A bit dramatic sounding but there were already a number of dead soldiers and policemen who had taken no precautions at all—the worst one Jack knew of was where a knock at the front door at 10 o'clock at night was answered by a five year old who opened the door and let the two murderers in to shoot his daddy dead in the living room. That could not have happened if the basic rules had been followed. Jack was determined that the murdering bastards would not succeed like that with him. And they didn't but Jack was to experience a number of nasty turns.

Chapter 8

Jack heard nothing about the car numbers ever again. He was invited to see the Colonel about three weeks later. Shown into the Col's office by the Adjutant Jack was left alone with the Colonel. "I took a ride out to the place you described and you were absolutely right. My soldiers do need training. The Regular Officers are myself, the Training Major, who has not yet been appointed, and a Royal Signals Staff Sergeant to look after the communications. All the other officers, Company Commanders, the 2i/c, the Adjutant, Uncle Tom Cobbly and all are ex-B Specials. They are brave men, they are able men but, for the most part they have not been army trained. So, everything they do is as they did it in the police, in many ways very similar to the Army but quite dangerously different as you have already seen in some respects.

"You are too junior, experienced though you are, to take the Training Major's role. I am talking to you like this because your record indicates that you can be trusted. You and I are the only people in the battalion cleared to Top Secret-UK Eyes Only, so I propose to use you in a soft, led by example way. I do not want you, in any meetings of officers, to speak up showing off your superior knowledge; that would not work. I want you to speak only if asked a direct question and answer it in a subordinate way.

"I propose to give you, eventually, 2 Platoon, A Company, they cover the road we both know and the areas around it. Your normal duties will be to take out two Landrovers, eight or nine soldiers and patrol your area. You will check on a number of sites, set up roadblocks as you deem fit. However, before that I want you to do something a bit different. As I've said, you will eventually take over 2 Platoon but before that I want to use you in a way that will spread your knowledge and skill across all the other Platoons. Patrols are normally eight or a maximum of 9. More than that is too much for the Landrovers and all the kit they carry but we also normally have more men reporting for duty than we need for the patrols.

"So, I propose to bunch the leftovers together, they will all be from different Platoons and you will form a two, or even three, Landrover patrol if the numbers allow it. Then, when you start setting up proper roadblocks, border checks etc. the men from all those different Sections or Platoons will learn how it should be done properly and spread the skill back into their own patrols the next time they go out. I think that after about three months you will have trained enough soldiers that the knowledge will be well spread throughout the Battalion. From time to time, you will take part in larger exercises as ordered. Are you willing to take that on, as a Lieutenant and paid accordingly?"

Jack did not have to pause, he said, "Yes, Sir."

"Good," said the Colonel. We have a small exercise this weekend, advances to contact, setting up defensive bases, patrolling and breaking contact all of which you will be familiar with, out at the training area near Magillagan Sands. Do you know it?"

"Yes, Sir, I visit a company there which makes ladies costumes from Irish tweed which the Priest, who runs the place, smuggles across the border in the boot of his car. He also runs a mushroom farm there to create employment for males as they won't work on sewing machines; that's still women's work here."

"How on earth do you know that?"

"Because he told me when I bought a skirt and top for my wife from him. He seemed quite proud of the fact; he compared it to the Prime Minister transferring his live stock from the Ulster side of his fields to the Republic side of the fields which straddle the border whenever authorities from either country appear."

"I do not want this conversation repeating to anyone. Your military knowledge is superior to any of the officers starting with the Company Commanders and working down. The Adjutant is the Adjutant because of his knowledge of all of the ex-B Specials; ideally, I would like you in the role but you do not have the people knowledge that he has. However, I will move you into the Operations Room in an Operations role, if you want, in about three or four months when your knowledge has been dissipated throughout the Battalion. What do you think to that?"

"I think it would suit me fine, Sir."

"Good. The Adjutant will take you over to the QM and get you kitted out. You can draw a.38 Smith and Wesson straight away; you'll have to fill in all the forms and that but we will be getting Browning HI Powers in a few weeks so I shouldn't go buying a shoulder or belt holster for the.38 because you'll only need to change it again. I'm sure the Adjutant will be able to answer any questions or sort things out but if you feel you need to speak to me that can be arranged any time you want. See you at Magillagan."

The Stores were so close to the Colonel's office that he hardly had chance to speak to the Adjutant before they were there. There was time for him to explain that as the Battalion had only just been formed, they were being supplied from a regular army stores whilst theirs was being built and kitted out. A Lieutenant was just coming out as they entered. Jack immediately recognised him and was just as quickly so in return. It was Lieutenant Mike Huss who Jack had last seen in the Officers' Mess in Tidworth when he had sold most of his kit to him.

"What are you doing here?" Jack asked.

"I have just been posted in to join the Ordnance Field Park squadron and have just been making my number here. I wondered if I would ever come across you as I knew you were moving to Northern Ireland from our conversation at Tidworth but I didn't really think I would. I must rush as I have an appointment but I'll catch up with you some time."

In fact, he did catch up with Jack and they became quite friendly in the two years or so that Jack was to remain in Londonderry.

Chapter 9

It felt strange to put on the combat kit then cover it with a large top coat as travelling as an individual in combat kit posed considerable danger. The IRA were approaching their apogee of murder and bombings. They had commenced peace talks with the British Government, largely because it was self-evident that, they were losing the 'war'. The Government had flatly refused some of their extreme and somewhat stupid demands with the result that on what was to be called 'Bloody Friday' they detonated 19 bombs and killed nine people and injured 130 'just to force the government to concede to their demands'.

In fact, it hardened the Government's determination to destroy them and there followed a series of ambushes and captures of active IRA men. Some were killed outright and others were captured. With steadily improving techniques, riddling the IRA with informers, and public horror and revulsion at the IRA behaviour the numbers of active members had been steadily declining. They had knocked on the door of a policeman and when it was opened by his three year old son, they had pushed their way into the front room and shot him to death in front of his horrified family.

They had done this before and Jack puzzled at the stupidity of a policeman having such lax security—it had undoubtedly led directly to his murder. They had stopped a mini-bus containing 13 men on their way to work, had sent away the one Roman Catholic amongst them and had then shot the remaining 12, Protestants, to death. That was perfectly alright for them to do but if an armed, in uniform IRA man had been shot that was murder. The hypocrisy of them was overwhelming. While there were what might be described as dedicated patriots to the cause, the majority were just murdering scum. At the start of the conflict, they claimed to have an army of 1500+ soldiers. By this time the active numbers had been reduced to not more than 150 and the end, although still far distant, was definitely in sight.

Jack arrived at Magillagan, took off his civvies and reported in full uniform. The day was taken up mainly in basic infantry training, something which Jack had not wanted to do in the Army having done so much of it in the Army Cadet Force and during basic training at Buller Barracks and Mons Officer Cadet School as well as at the Junior Leaders' Regiment. Here however it was different; this was for real and the volunteer soldiers had to be trained to a very high standard, especially in anti-insurgency training, as soon as possible.

Part of the day was spent in setting up and operating road blocks and the skill associated with it and when it became known that Jack had operated such road blocks in Aden (*see 'It must have been the compo'*) in a real insurgency situation much more attention was paid to what he said.

The last hour of the day was spent zeroing weapons. Jack chose an SLR (Self Loading Rifle) and a Stirling SMG for his personal weapons, the.38 pistol he didn't fire; unless you could actually stick it in someone's belly and pull the trigger it was of no use whatsoever although he did intend to zero his Browning when he got it—it wasn't much more accurate than the.38 but at least you had 13 rounds to fire around the place and some of them might just hit what you were aiming at! He grouped both the SLR and the Stirling within two inches at 50yds and as most engagements were likely to take place at that range or less that was good enough for him. It did draw some attention to him as well.

A Colour Sergeant he did not know introduced himself as having been nominated to form a battalion shooting team—hear we go again thought Jack—and would Jack be willing to try out for it. Jack agreed that he would but as things turned out he never did.

Jack attended his first duty on the following Tuesday evening. He arrived just before 18.00hrs to find a Corporal and seven soldiers waiting for him. Having signed in and introduced himself the first job was to draw weapons. The Corporal drew a Stirling Sub Machine Gun (SMG) and the soldiers SLRs. They and the Armourer Sergeant were surprised when Jack asked for his SLR which he had zeroed only the Saturday before. Each soldier was issued with an extra magazine into which they were to place the 10 rounds they were also issued with.

The Corporal explained that the pink card (changed since Aden, thought Jack, where it was yellow) ordered that empty magazines were to be kept on a weapon at all times and the loaded magazine was to be kept in an ammunition pouch on their belt. Jack asked the Sergeant for a second loaded magazine for each soldier and was refused the request; at which Jack then wrote on a piece of paper, '*I order you to provide an extra magazine for each of these soldiers, including me as we will be firing on the range and need the extra ammunition,*' and signed it.

The Sergeant smiled and issued the magazines and rounds. Jack, as a Marksman, could easily fire seven, aimed, rounds in 10 seconds and having only 10 rounds per man if they were ambushed or got into a fire fight was patently absurd. As was having to keep an empty magazine on the weapon and the loaded one in a pouch. The pink card, with which they were all issued, blandly stated that this procedure prevented the accidental discharge of a weapon possibly with deadly consequences and anyway anyone looking, intent on mischief, would not be able to tell just by looking that the weapon was unloaded. Jack instantly knew that that had been written by some bloody Civil Servant miles from any danger just intent on some extra security for which they could claim credit.

As with all versions of the card, they were to change colour and instructions several times over the next few years, the ultimate responsibility rested with the minister, at this time, Margret Thatcher's Willie. Jack was to have passing contact with Willie in the near future and in circumstances which Jack heartily approved.

Jack told the Corporal that he wished to act as an observer, at least at first, and he was to take out the patrol, stopping to set up road blocks or not as usual, to follow the route(s) he would normally take and stop for a break as normal. The Corporal looked at him for a moment and then, thinking better of it, said, "Yes, Sir." He turned to the soldiers who, having heard Jack, were already starting to get into the Landrovers and ordered them to mount.

Jack took the front passenger seat in the second Landrover and they drove around to the exit of the camp, Ebrington Barracks. At the gate the first Landrover stopped and the soldiers dismounted. Funny, thought Jack, that isn't necessary and he then noticed that there were boxes, about 18" deep, 3' long and 2' deep full of sand. The four from the first Landrover lined up facing the boxes and pointed their weapons into the sand. On the order of the Corporal, they removed the empty magazines from their weapons and clicked one of the loaded ones onto them.

The empty magazines they then placed in the other pouch than the one with the second loaded magazine. Jack's Landrover had by that time drawn up behind them and with nothing being said the three Privates dismounted. It was obvious all eyes were on Jack who got out and joined the line. The second group followed the same procedure as the first, Jack included, and then got back into their vehicles. They drove off.

The drive was a mixture of showing their presence and then stopping on a section of road and setting up a temporary road block. The placing of the vehicles wasn't quite right and the positions of the soldiers could have been a bit better— some were too far out and apart and some were too close but the overall operation was much better than the ones Jack had been used to seeing. He put it down to the training on the previous Saturday but he noticed that cars with pretty girls were always stopped! That bit had not been absorbed yet.

Although they were driving around their general direction was towards the power station where Jack was expected to inspect the guard. Some of the roads were quite narrow and twisting but the two drivers sailed along them and it was obvious that they were very familiar with the roads. Jack made a bet with himself that they always drove this route at this time and when they arrived at the power station the guard was ready for them and they were ushered straight into the canteen where, speaking for the first time, the Corporal pointed out that the canteen was due to close in half an hour and they needed to order their supper straight away. Jack joined in and selected a meal and afterwards took the Corporal, Corporal Fernyhough aside. He started by asking, "What's this about loading charged magazines onto weapons?"

Fernyhough replied, "Sir, you will have noticed that no order was given to load. We simply stopped at the gate, by the defence against an accidental discharge pit, and each individual loaded his weapon if he wanted to. The general consensus is that if we are ambushed, we need to fire back immediately, it's something we covered again as recently as last Saturday, to start shooting back straight away while moving from the ambush site into cover ready to prepare to attack the ambushers. If we have empty magazines on our weapons and have to go through all the rigmarole of taking off the empty magazine, placing it in the pouch, removing the charged magazine, loading it onto the weapon, cocking it and then firing back we will be firing back from heaven or hell because we would be well dead.

"We have all agreed that we would rather disobey the order and live to face a court martial rather than have some pious fucking hypocrite, who never ever faces danger, saying unmeant words over our coffins. When we do get back, assuming we do, we will dismount at the gate and unload without a word being said. I hope you will not upset this arrangement, Sir and understand that the sandpits are there with the compliance of those more senior than you or I and who understand the dangers we face start with the fucking idiot high ups."

The look on the Corporal's face was more than expecting an answer. Jack read an unspoken warning into it that, if he rocked the boat, he might not live to regret it. While that might seem extreme the fragging of unpopular officers in Vietnam was becoming a bit of a scandal. Officers who unnecessarily endangered the lives of their troops were rapidly disposed of. Clearly risks to life had to be taken—that's what soldiers were for—but not needlessly and Jack understood instantly that empty magazines on weapons was a needless danger.

"I understand," said Jack. "Would I be correct in thinking that the route we followed tonight is the same as always?"

"Yes, Sir."

"And we always have supper here at this time?"

"Yes, Sir."

"Can you see the obvious danger in that?"

"You mean using the same road every time to the power station?"

"Yes."

"There is only the one road, Sir."

"And what about the time?"

"Well, that does vary a bit depending on how long we spend on road blocks but we must be there by 21.30 or we won't get supper."

"OK, let's get back on the road," and with that they carried on the patrol. On arrival back at the barracks the two Landrovers stopped just inside the gates and the soldiers disembarked and unloaded their weapons, again with no orders given as the Corporal had forecast. Unlike the regular Army, the soldiers became civilians almost immediately and split up going their individual ways. It was too early in the morning for the QM's Stores to be open so Jack planned to return at lunch time.

When he returned to the barracks at lunch time, he found Lt Huss in the QM's Stores.

"Hello, what are you doing here?" Huss asked.

"I could ask the same thing of you," Jack asked and they both laughed.

"I'm about to ask for 2 and a half inches to the mile maps of this area, the one inch to the mile is quite good but they don't show enough detail especially across moorland and similar."

The Sergeant who had been ear wigging the conversation as hard as he could disappeared as soon as Jack looked at him and then returned with two maps, necessary to cover the quite large area Jack wanted to examine. Mike said to him, "I'm just about to have lunch in the Mess and lift a glass to the patrol that caught that bastard Priest last night care to join me?"

Jack hadn't a clue what he was talking about but lunch and a beverage sounded just right so he said, "Sure."

Mike ordered a gin and tonic and Jack joined him.

"What's this about a Priest then?"

"Well, last night a patrol of two 3rd Anglian Landrovers patrolling the Albert Clock area in Belfast saw a motor with Republic number plates parked in a side road. They could vaguely see people inside it which made them instantly suspicious. That area is notorious for ladies of easy, if expensive, virtue and it could simply have been a couple at it or it, given the Free State number plate, could have been innocent or somewhere it shouldn't be. So, the patrol stopped, one in front and one behind, and they dismounted and approached the car. Shining in a torch caught an almost naked pair frantically getting dressed. Ordering them out of the car revealed a young woman and an older man.

"They could still have been terrorists but it appeared unlikely, when the prostitute started giving them some gob. Not prepared to take that the Corporal decides to make like difficult and demands identity cards or other proof of who they were. The woman simply tells him to 'fuck off' at which he says, 'We can do this the hard way or the easy way. You prove who you are and we let you go on your way to earn more tricks; if you don't, we'll radio for the police and tell them there's no hurry so you could be waiting for two or three hours before they arrive—that'll knock a hole in your earnings for tonight'."

Meanwhile the man had been frantically trying to silence her to no avail. His actions seemed to be a little over the top and he refused identification three times after which the Corporal says, "As you are driving a foreign car you might be anybody so I think we had better get the police here to sort you out."

At which the guy reaches into his hip pocket, at the same time saying over and over, "There's no need for that," and produces a Republic of Ireland driving licence. That was fine but the thing that really exploded them was the photo clearly showed him wearing a dog collar and describing him as 'Father' rather than 'Mr'!

The Priest kept asking them not to report him; he hadn't actually done anything wrong (they weren't sure about that, certainly they, as the Army, couldn't do anything but the police could surely think up something about 'lewd and lascivious behaviour in a public place') but his entreaties worked in the end and they let him go. The following morning it was all over the front pages of the protestant leaning newspapers. It was pretty certain that it didn't leak from the soldiers—they had no opportunity to get to a telephone for a start—but the one they hadn't considered was the whore who was described in the most derogatory ways by the priesthood and the opportunity to get back at one of them was too good to miss.

"I have bought half a dozen copies of the story and will be displaying them where they will do the most good or harm depending on your point of view," said Mike.

Jack laughed and then said, "If you don't mind me saying so that seem a little bit hard on a bloke who was just trying to have his end away?"

Huss paused for a moment and then said, "You obviously aren't up to your history. In 1415, a bloke by the name of Jan Hus, John Huss, my great, great keep going with lots of greats, predecessor, was given a 'safe conduct' pass to the Council of Constance, to explain his teachings. He had built up a huge following, so large that his chapel, called Bethlehem, could not hold the more than 5,000 worshippers who regularly turned up to hear him preach and some estimates, at the outside meeting, said the number was closer to 10,000. His teaching of Christianity was quite different to that of the Roman Catholic Church, a more spiritual version which, quite honestly, I don't understand.

"It was a lot more like that of the Gnostic Christians who had been hated, feared and attacked for centuries. But he did preach certain policies or creeds which were an anathema to the Roman Church; firstly, he wanted the officers of the Church to conduct the services in the language of the people, he lived in Prague and spoke in Bohemian when conducting his services which the people loved. When the services were preached in Latin, very often in bastard Latin by barely literate priests, the people could not understand what was being said which gave an undeserved and abused power to the priesthood over the people which the priests had been quick to benefit by.

"The previous Pope had excommunicated him for preaching against the sale of indulgences whereby people could spend a shorter time in Purgatory before progressing to heaven if they paid Priests to say lots of Masses for their soles and purchased the indulgence. Rich people could, of course, afford to pay but the poor could not and they were condemned to eternity in Purgatory. The excommunication wasn't enforced fully and Huss continued to preach supported by the King of Bohemia and a growing number of followers. He also taught that during the taking of Communion the wine did not actually turn to blood, as the Roman Church taught, nor did the bread actually turn into flesh, it was symbolic.

"Imagine what the Roman Church was teaching then, and even today, in the countries where the population is less well educated was that to commune one had to eat flesh and drink blood, a bloody nonsense if you'll excuse the pun."

Jack laughed, "He also decorated his Chapel with paintings, the majority of the population being illiterate, the first painting that one saw on entering the Bethlehem Chapel was of the Pope sitting on his throne with his feet being washed by a number of Bishops. The one next to it was of Jesus washing the feet of his disciples. A very visual and deadly portrayal of the level to which the Roman Church had sunk. Incidentally, when the Communist leaders under the Russians were looking for a Czech hero, not a king or saint or any of that sort of rubbish, in their eyes, they discovered Huss who was enticed to the Council of Constance, by being given a safe conduct by King Wenceslas, to explain his teaching and defend himself.

"There had been a new Pope who was concerned by the growth of Huss' teachings, in fact the real forerunner of Protestantism a hundred years before Luther, and who as soon as Huss arrived, declared the safe conduct null and void. He was tried immediately, condemned and burnt to death within an hour and a half of arriving. Unfortunately, for the Church that was not the end of Huss and his teachings. His followers rose in armed revolt and there followed the Hussite wars. Two Papal armies were destroyed by the Hussites; they mounted cannons in heavy wagons, a form of primitive tank if you like, and moved them around the battlefield as needed.

"Unfortunately, the Papists, unlike the Native Americans, worked out that if you shot the horses the wagons weren't going anywhere—something the American Indians never did in the westerns and the coaches continued to escape; not the Hussites I'm afraid to say. The main part of the family fled to Sweden where in the 1600s, Dr Magnus Huss became the Padre for the first Swedish Foot Guards. Initially he did well and received a gift of engraved, stirrup cup, glasses from the King which we still have.

"Unfortunately, he started teaching using John Huss' philosophy as well of that of Luther and other prominent Protestants which got him sacked. Part of the family fled to England initially settling in the North East in South Shields. They set up a ships' chandlery business and opened branches in Cardiff and London as the firm prospered and grew. They even outfitted Scott's expedition to the Pole and from which he didn't return. Nothing to do with the provisions but it was about time for a Huss to cause trouble in history—I think by the way things are going I should be the next one and you can be sure that forgiveness and loving the bloody Roman Catholic Church will not be part of it. What sort of organisation is it which burns people alive to save their immortal souls while at the same time eats flesh, drinks blood and buggers little choir boys? So, a long answer to your question but I hate them and everything they stand for."

Jack said, "Well, I did ask and what I've seen of their antics here hiding terrorists, weapons and explosives in churches doesn't exactly endear me to them either."

They went their separate ways having arranged to meet again quite soon. Although Jack found many of the people, he worked with were very friendly he and Janet were not welcomed into any particular circle of friends which already existed. Consequently, they built up a small circle of friends amongst the English population working and living around them.

Chapter 10

Life suddenly became very busy for Jack. His commitment to the UDR took off; his involvement with the church in Belfast took off with Jack teaching an open circle every Friday evening and Janet announced she was pregnant and did not think she should travel so far, each week. It was almost exactly 75 miles from their home in Strathfoyle to the church in Belfast. Although 'A' roads for most of the journey apart from the last few miles into Belfast they were narrow and rough.

Mileage had been building up on his HB Viva and Jack was starting to worry about it; he was travelling long distances visiting factories and although the expenses he was paid were supposed to contribute to wear and tear, the wear and tear was way ahead of the wear and tear expenses money. But help was at hand; the Training Board was a semi-civil service organisation, the terms and conditions exactly matched that of the civil servants to whom they answered although in theory they were an independent agency the reality was that they were a government department in all but name. This had created a particular problem.

Civil servants did not have government cars provided, they either claimed expenses for using their own cars or, if they were lucky, could book a pool car. Neither was working out for the Training Development Officers of the 10 training boards and agitating for the provision of cars with the job had been increasing. The resistance came from the civil servants who were jealous of the idea of these quasi-civil servants getting cars when they could not.

However, Jack was heading for 35,000 miles in his first year and when you consider that a car in those days was heading for a major decoke and service, possibly including engine rebuilds at 50-55000 miles Jack's Viva wasn't going to last very long at his current rate and the wear and tear allowance looked fairly pitiful. He was therefore more than pleased and delighted to receive a memo that the provision of cars to TDOs had been approved in principle and that a committee (of bloody civil servants from the controlling Government Department, of course!) had been set-up to investigate the best vehicle for the role. The memo asked for any recommendation from the TDOs as to what they thought was the best vehicle for the role they carried out—Jack for example often carried an overhead projector and six-foot screen which was a bugger to fit in the Viva and it had, indeed, cut some of the upholstery when being put into the car.

On the basis that he didn't think they would provide an estate version of a Rolls Royce Jack replied that for the high mileage, load carrying capability the Cortina Estate would be the best car in his opinion, The committee to examine the problem was set up of all civil servants, not one of the Training Bboards was represented nor, other than the initial request for recommendations, were anybody from the Training Bboards asked to comment on the vehicle they proposed as being the best one for the job. They came out with the Morris 1100 4 door or 1300 two door (they were the same price).

Given that this car had the worst boot space of any car on the market at the time it became immediately obviously that the civil servants had stuffed the TDOs of whom they were inordinately jealous. Although there was uproar at this stupid and vexatious decision there was nowhere to go to appeal as the more senior ranks in the civil service, SEOs of not exactly fond memory of Jack's recent experience, did not receive cars and would therefore automatically support their juniors against any appeals by the TDOs. Time was to prove the arbiter, repairs to the interiors, any large items of equipment and the costs of hiring vans frequently soon proved the decision wrong but the civil service never admitted to errors—they couldn't because they never made any! And blame was placed utterly on the TDOs although there was never an attempt to fine any of the TDOs for damage as was permissible under their terms and conditions.

As for Jack he chose a 2 door 1300 on the basis that he had sadly missed the power of his 2,600cc Morris Isis, exactly twice the power, but utterly superior in comfort and performance. Janet on seeing it when he first brought it home was to say, "Why have they given you a Post Office van?"

It was to be many years before Postman Pat was invented but it was nevertheless an accurate comment!

Chapter 11

Jack visited a lingerie manufacturer in Maydown, only a short spit from where he lived at Strathfoyle. It was to visit a modern factory, English owned, which had claimed pretty much the maximum of Training Levy back of which Jack was a little suspicious as they had not, to his knowledge, sent anyone on the Instructors' Courses Jack had been running since his appointment to look after the North West Region. He met the Production Director, Jim Keegan, the Operations Manager, David Sharpe, and the Personnel Officer, Julie Collier, the last two being English. They did meet the requirements for the claim they had submitted.

The Instructor was a girl who had attended the course whilst employed by another company so she was no problem. Jack left having agreed to return to look at the Supervisor Training about which the management had some concerns.

When he returned a week later, he started off with a meeting with the Director. Besides his concerns about his Supervisors, he detailed other, more general problems which they were experiencing. One was a security problem which wasn't a security problem. For two Fridays in the last month, they had received telephone warnings that there was a bomb in the factory due to detonate in 15 minutes. They had had no option other than to sound the Fire Alarm and have every one evacuate the factory and to call the police.

The police and Bomb Squad duly attended and found nothing. The police did however tell the Production Director that false warnings had been made to two other companies on the Industrial Estate. Those two companies, as his, did not finish until 5pm on the Friday. Situated in the middle of the Estate was a Training Centre which taught unemployed people, mainly men, new skills, plumbing, plastering, painting etc. so that they could gain employment.

That Centre finished at 3pm on a Friday and quite a few of the trainees were married to women working in the companies that had had the warnings. Because of the time taken for the police and Bomb Squad to arrive and inspect the premises took longer than the time left to work all the employees in the three companies had toddled off home with their partners.

The problem for the three companies was that they could not ignore the warnings people could be killed so they were at a loss what to do. Jack thought about it for a moment and then said, "Why don't you put a notice up on the noticeboard saying that the roughly two hours lost would have to be worked after the factory had been declared safe by the security people. That would obviously mean working two hours later and really buggering up the finishing time. I would also put in that the authorities had told us of this little ploy and would be carefully checking the phones in the Training Centre to try to catch the perpetrators of the hoax. Obviously, you take the employees safety and security very seriously and would never ignore a warning in case it was real but if you ever did find out who the hoaxer was you would report them to the police, or something like that." They did it and the hoaxes stopped. Jack's standing rose enormously.

Jim Keegan brought up a number of problems they faced one in particular not involving training but more in the way of discipline. The company manufactured all sorts of ladies delicates, knickers, bra-slips, slips, nighties and anything for which they could get an order. The problem was attachments such as bows. A strip anywhere between an inch and two inches wide was cut from a roll; it was then fed into a lockstitch machine by hand which had a special foot which folded it in such a way that it came out the other side as a tube.

That tube had then to be measured and cut so that the resulting short piece could be tied into a bow to be then sown onto the garment. Apparently, it was normal for machinists waiting for work or for their machine to be repaired to be asked to produce some bows. Most of them hated doing it especially as they were just paid a flat rate for this work which for most of them meant lower money. They discussed the possibilities re: disciplinary action, paying a higher flat rate, concentrating the work on the few machinists who didn't mind doing it but none of these seemed to be a satisfactory answer.

They had been discussing Supervisor training for a few minutes when the receptionist stuck her head around the door and said that there was a woman from the Job Centre there who was demanding to speak to the boss because they didn't employ enough disabled people and she was going to issue proceedings against the company unless the director spoke to her.

Jim apologised to Jack and said I'll just have a quick word with her if you don't mind and get rid of her—they are always trying to place people with us but we only have skilled jobs and really don't have anything for disabled people. Jack said he certainly didn't mind waiting and moved to a seat at the side of the room. The woman who was ushered in looked as though she ate nails for breakfast, hammers for lunch and bashed them in for dinner. She lost no time in pleasantries but started right in, "You are a major employer, you employ more than 200 people but you have no Registered Disabled People in your employment. I am seeking to place two young women who are only mildly educationally subnormal and I refuse to accept that you have no jobs for them. They might take a bit more training than a normal person, I can help with a grant for the additional costs of that, but I do not accept that you cannot employ them. By law you are required to employ 3% disabled people in your work force which means you should have at least six people here. You have none and unless you employ these two, I intend to refuse you permission to recruit anyone at all until you have at least six disabled people in your employment."

Jim interrupted her, "You know very well that the 3% figure was introduced into the disability legislation just after the end of the Second World War when about 3% of the potential work force, ex-servicemen and women, as well as civilians injured in the bombing etc. were in need of work. That was more than 20 years ago and the number of disabled people has been steadily decreasing, so much so that there aren't enough to go round. That sounds a bit flippant but it's not meant to be, it is just a statement of fact. When you take out of the number of the terribly injured or disabled people who are incapable of doing any work at all, the number of disabled people who could work is very small.

"We have complied with all your requirements advertising for disabled people to apply in every vacancy we advertise but we never get any applicants. Now you force your way in here threatening to effectively close me down…"

Jack, who could see the back of the woman's neck going red and her body tensioning up ready to attack, thought he had better interrupt here or he would be in a third war and two was already enough.

"Can I ask just what these girls can do in your estimation and what could they not?" Jim introduced Jack and sat back. The woman composed herself, looked at some notes in a file and explained that the girls, twins, scored between 5 and 7 percent below the normal percentile so they should be able to carry out any normal skill level jobs but they would not be able to carry out any really skilled machining.

61

Jack asked, "Would they be capable of being taught to thread a sewing machine?"

"Oh yes they have done some simple sewing at school in Domestic Science."

"What about measuring a length of cloth tube and cutting off designated lengths, say three inches?"

"Oh yes they could do that." Jim had sat up and was looking intensely at Jack, you could see he knew where Jack was going.

"Could they then take that three-inch length and tie it into a neat bow?"

"I'm pretty sure they could do that." Jack explained the job of tying bows, the importance of it being done properly and to a high quality. He explained that the machinists did not like doing it because they saw it as being a lower status and were unwilling to do it. Bringing Jim into the conversation Jack suggested that based on what they had been told about the girls they would probably need 26 weeks training and would there be a training grant available for that length of time? The woman asked if she could see the job in action so they all headed out to the lockstitch machine with the special foot and Jim measured, cut up and tied a few bows.

"Right," she said, "I'd like to bring them in sometime next week and have them try the job. If they can do it to your satisfaction then I am sure we could find a training grant for each of them for 13 weeks each."

Jack left the two of them to arrange the timing for the visit and went for a pee. When he returned to Jim's office, it was to be met by a much warmer attitude than had previously been the case. Jack explained that in the sessions he taught about job satisfaction, from the text book, he had always been a bit bothered because it didn't seem to take into account different levels of intelligence and ability. He explained to Jim that as the woman had been talking, he had "seen" the bow tying job as too simple and beneath them for the machinists but that it might be hard to do for the twins and therefore satisfactory completion of the task would be rewarding for them rather than something demeaning and below their perceived status for the machinists.

In the event the twins tried out for the job and were up and running long before the 13-week training grant ran out putting money in the kitty for the company, a great job for the twins (their attendance was to prove excellent) and happier machinists who no longer had to produce bows. Jack modified his ideas about job satisfaction. The text books compared high skill to low skill jobs and implied that more satisfaction was achieved the higher the skill level needed.

Jack had just learned that the satisfaction was related directly to the individual. It was how demanding the job was to the individual. The twins found the relatively simple job of making bows demanding for them and they achieved considerable comfort from achieving it well; the fact that someone else found the job too simple and non-satisfying was irrelevant, the individual had to be fitted to the job if possible.

There was a lot of press information about Volvo trying an experiment in the assembly of their cars. They had moved from a production line where the individual did the same task time after time. To reduce training time the tasks had been so deskilled that people could be taught to do them in just a few minutes. They would therefore carry out that function hundreds of times a day. Going home they would record no job satisfaction whatsoever so, instead of there being a line down which the vehicle progressed gradually taking on the appearance of a car, the line turned into a team area where the group of individuals organised between them who did what job and for how long.

It was assumed, and hoped, that the people would work as a team, rotate the jobs, be responsible for self-inspection and produce fault free vehicles. There was an enormous amount of publicity with the hope this would lead to the end of boring jobs and frivolous walk outs. Jack was unable to find out very much about how successful the scheme had been, but his dad, following a visit to Ford's huge place at Dagenham said that there had been some conversation there, which he had not taken much notice of because it didn't concern him, but which seemed to be that it had not worked, the stronger members of the team bagged all the good or easy jobs and bullied the weaker members into doing the worst jobs—human nature in full flow thought Jack! It also made him consider the differences between intelligence, education and common sense—they were three quite different things.

Chapter 12

Jack and Janet had slowly built up a small number of friends, all of them English. Two of them worked at the twin's factory. In fact, Jack sold his Viva to David Sharpe who had been looking for a car for his wife. Julie Collier was the Personnel Officer and during one evening when they were out at a local restaurant Janet said she had been driven out of the job she had only started that morning because she was English and the women in the office where she had started a clerical job, were all Catholic and had demanded she be fired.

Julie immediately offered her a job with them, suggesting that as she obviously was not a machinist, she might find being an Examiner suitable. It, she said, was not one where she would be very popular because any faults found meant that the garment went back to the machinist who would have to repair the fault thus losing manufacturing time and earnings.

Janet had been working there for about two weeks when Jack received a phone call in the office from Julie. Normally Jack spent most of his time out visiting companies so Julie was fortunate to catch him. Without any pleasantries she said, "Jack, I think you had better get over here as quickly as you can. Janet is unwell and I think it might be German measles so, as she is in the early stages of pregnancy, (10 weeks) you need to get her to a doctor as quickly as you can."

"I'll be there in 15 minutes," said Jack and put the phone down. Outside of speed limits in towns there was no maximum speed limit in N Ireland and even if there had been Jack drove as fast as he could. Janet was in Julie's office and in a very tearful state. Giving Janet a quick hug, Jack said, "Come on were going to the Doctor's straight away."

On the way, they discussed what little they knew of Rubella, the medical name for German measles but that was pretty well nothing. Arriving at Reception Jack explained the situation and they were asked to wait until the next Doctor was free (there were three in the practice). They only had a wait of 10 minutes before they were seen by Dr Stanley. He examined Janet behind a screen and then arranged for them both to sit in front of him. He confirmed that the diagnosis was Rubella and offered an injection but said it was probably too late to prevent some damage to the foetus.

Jack asked, "What damage could be done?"

The Doctor replied, "Well, we have been reading recently quite a lot of research which reveals that Rubella is a lot more serious than had traditionally been suspected. We suspect, now, that it could cause blindness, deafness and spasticity or worst of all, all three. It is so bad that I can offer you an abortion if you want one. I can see that shocks you both so I have something to do in the office and I will come back in a few minutes to see you, but if you want to take a day or two to think about it fine, but if you do want an abortion then I must say, unpleasant as it is, it should be done sooner not later."

At that he got up and walked out closing the door behind him. Nothing was said for a few minutes and then Jack turned to Janet and said, "What do you think?"

Janet looked at him and said, "What do you think?"

Jack took a moment to gather his thoughts and said, "Whenever the subject of abortion has come up in the press, TV or radio we have always been against it except if the mother's life is in danger. I don't think anything he said could cause something as serious as that but we can ask him that when he comes back. He also didn't say what the chance of the baby being affected was; is it 10%, 50% or 100%, so we need to ask that as well. We have always said that life is created at the moment of conception, not birth, and therefore an abortion will kill a living being albeit a very tiny one in the early stages of pregnancy. This might seem to be a test of our beliefs. To agree to an abortion, I believe I would be a party to murder. You have always agreed to that so what do you think now?

"I haven't changed my mind but I would like to hear what the Doctor has to say in answer to those two questions." Jack put his arm round her in a clumsy hug and then said, "I'll go and get him." Jack found him in reception and they both returned to his room and Jack asked him the two questions. He gathered his thoughts together for a moment and then said, "As regards the chances of the foetus being affected at this stage, I can only estimate it at about 50%. During the first twelve weeks of pregnancy, roughly, the foetus is forming into a baby. After 12 weeks it is fully formed and is only growing. That is why taking care, no alcohol, diet etc. are so important in the first 12 weeks particularly. Now Janet is at 10 weeks and it could be possible that the virus will have no effect if the foetus is a fast grower so to speak.

"However, if Janet is a slow developer so to speak, the foetus might need another 3 or 4 weeks to fully form, so that's how I arrive at 50%. I think the chance of the Rubella being life threatening in respect of Janet is nil." There was a small café next to the surgery. Jack asked the Doctor if it would be ok if they went and had a cup of tea and then came back? He said it would be fine.

The tea was a bit unwanted but they talked through what the doctor had told them. Jack said that as there was no life threatening issue, he was therefore still of the mind that abortion was murder and if it was intended, they have a handicapped child then so be it. Janet took some time in replying when she did, she said, "Like you I believe abortion is murder. I am at the stage where I have felt very faint stirrings of movement and I can't bear the thought of killing my baby. So, I think we should go ahead even if there is a risk of some problem or other."

Jack leaned over and kissed her gently and they made their way back to the surgery and declined the offer. From then on Janet was placed on an 'at risk' list at the hospital. Every time she went to the hospital, she saw a different doctor otherwise the treatment was fine. When she saw one in late September, the Doctor said, "Not long now Mrs Hughes, only three months," she replied, "Three weeks!"

The Doctor looked at her and said again three months. Janet retorted, "three weeks doctor."

He gave her a long look and then studied her notes again. He then asked her, "Is your husband a small man?"

She replied, "Only if you call six feet one inch and 200 lbs small." The conversation ended at that point! Three weeks later there was no sign of even the first hint of birth. On the Saturday morning, which was nine days after the due date, at 3am, Janet woke Jack and told him he had better run her to the hospital. Jack was proud of himself in that he didn't try to put two legs into one trouser leg, or panic or anything he simply drove her to the hospital but quite quickly— at 3am there wasn't a lot of traffic.

After waiting for an hour or so a nurse came out and told him that he might as well go home because it was a false alarm, but as she was nine days overdue, they were going to keep her in to induce the baby the next day i.e., at 10 days which was the normal practice. Jack drove home and went to bed. At 3pm the next day, the normal visiting hours' time, he arrived promptly at the hospital. He stayed until just 4pm, throwing out time, when Janet said, "You'd better call a nurse I think I'm just starting."

Jack had to wait out in the stairwell where there were a couple of chairs. Janet was pushed past in her bed to the lift which ran up the centre of the stairwell on her way to the delivery ward. A nurse told Jack to wait there in the stairwell. At one o'clock in the morning he was still there having watched a succession of women being wheeled past and then back holding a baby a while later. At one o'clock, a nurse passing by asked him if he had had a cup of tea or anything. When he replied no, she said, Oh, you poor thing you'd better come along with me and took him to the nurses' room and made him a mug of tea which couldn't have been more welcome. Having finished it he returned to the stairwell thanking the nurse profusely.

As he did so another nurse who was wheeling a bed with a soon to be mother in it into the lift called out, "Congratulations Mr Hughes," and at that moment the lift door closed leaving Jack in a bit of a state. There wasn't a soul around and he was contemplating catching the lift to he knew not where when a Sister came out of the ward and said, "Oh, there you are. Congratulations Mr Hughes you have a beautiful baby girl." Jack looked at her and then put his foot in it— in fact both feet full force.

"Are you sure it's a girl?" asked Jack. All the time Janet had been carrying they had somehow drifted into the habit of referring to the baby as 'he'. That wasn't based on any knowledge (no scans in those days!) it just happened hence his 'are you sure…'

The Sister looked him up and down and said, "Well, you know Mr Hughes we are all highly trained here and it isn't so difficult to tell the difference."

Jack felt about one foot tall. He was saved from further embarrassment by the Sister directing him to where Janet and the baby were. But the trouble wasn't over for Jack. Janet wanted to know where he had been when she was wheeled back. Had Jack known the trouble he was in he would have said he was in the lavatory but he didn't so he said, "I was having a cup of tea with a nurse." Thereafter that came back to haunt him with, 'and another thing…'

Over the years (at the time of writing the baby is now 51! Whenever the subject of abortion came up Jack and Janet had a strong opinion. The 'baby' is just as beautiful now as she was at birth but she is profoundly deaf. The problems arising out of that have not altered the opinion of both of them, abortion is murder. You dear reader, are entitled to your own opinion even if it is wrong!).

Chapter 13

Jack used the two-and-a-half-inch map to find routes across the heath around the power station. Although a bit rough on the Morris 1300's Hydrolastic suspension, when he tried them out in daylight, they were certainly passable for a Landrover. Jack also checked out the meal times at the canteen at the power station and it was perfectly possible to eat anytime between 18.00hrs and closing at 22.00hrs. So, the second time Jack took a patrol out it was very different. Different routes both on metalled and unmetalled roads; different times and different places for road stops.

The one thing that stood out on the second journey was the walls of Londonderry. From one spot on the wall, high up, he could see down into the Bogside. A misnomer if ever there was one, the area was full of new housing. All rented from the Londonderry Development Commission, the same people from whom Jack rented his house on the other side of the river Foyle, they were modern, clean and bright although that didn't prevent the IRA trying to portray the place as indeed a bog side that poor, hard done by Roman Catholic people were thrown in to rot by those rotten protestants.

For a while segregated estates had been forming. Estates where the Roman Catholics were in the majority started threatening minority protestant families and after numbers of them had been threatened with being burned out or shot by the IRA they had wisely moved out. There being no obvious place to go the protestant communities started forcing out Roman Catholic families where they were in a minority so that there developed 'one side' housing estates; in Londonderry that was the Bogside and 100% Roman Catholic and in Belfast the Falls while the protestants occupied the Shankhill. There were other areas around the country mainly in Roman Catholic Armagh and in Tyrone but in more modern towns, Coleraine for example, a university city, there were no obvious divisions whatsoever.

Looking over the wall Jack could see the entrance to the Bogside. He could see the sort of pill box that the IRA had built and the three men manning it. All three were wearing uniform, the IRA version, looking like what they were, rank amateurs with nothing fitting properly, berets straight out of the box looking more like pancakes on their head with the body sticking out a bit like a wing. One of them was lounging behind what looked like a.30 Browning machine gun precariously balanced on top of the sandbag wall and the other two were armed with rifles, one an Armalite, which the IRA was to make famous, and the other an unidentifiable carbine of some sort.

Taking the microphone from the signaller Jack called his base. For once reception was clear and he was able to report what he was seeing. At the other end a SSGT (Staff Sergeant) acknowledged the report and nothing else. Jack asked if he should take any action and the SSGT simply said you have reported it and that's enough. Jack could not believe what he was hearing. Trying again he said, "There are three armed men, blocking access to a public road. They are clearly in the uniform of the IRA and they are armed. We chase these buggers all over the country trying to catch them and here are three of them in plain view, which I could easily capture or shoot and you are telling me to do nothing. Do I understand that correctly?"

"Yes."

"I need you to put that in writing so I can collect it when I return to camp."

"This is Sunray (the Colonel). You will take no action and report to me on your return. Confirm."

"Wilco, out." Jack was fuming.

The Sergeant with him said, "It's always the same, Sir. These bastards are murdering our boys and we can't do anything about it. It's not right so it isn't." Jack said, "Although I have to report to the CO when I get back that doesn't mean that I have to do nothing if he doesn't give me a clear explanation." The rest of the patrol was carried out without incident and when they got back to barracks Jack went to report to the CO.

"I know, I know, I know," said the Colonel on Jack reporting to him, "don't tell me it's wrong, unfair etc. I agree with you but that's orders and orders are orders."

"You mean like the orders Lt Col Mitch, Mad Mitch disobeyed in Aden when his Highlanders were being shot by those Arab bastards?"

"Oh yes you were there weren't you?"

"Yes, I was and I met him twice when he came in to our office."

"Well, much as I would like to emulate him, I am not going to chuck my career down the pan here in this political cess pit. So, to be clear. You will obey the orders on the Opening Fire card at all times. If those men had shot at you, you would have been perfectly entitled to shoot back but the Army is here to assist the civil power and we do not have the power of arrest. The RUC of course do, but don't call them to a situation like that because their hands are tied too; they would not be allowed to arrest them and they would have to wait for those IRA bastards to fire first and what do you think would be left of them or you it that Browning opened up on you?"

Jack didn't answer but saluted and walked out.

The situation of 'no-go' areas was to continue for an unacceptably long period. During it the IRA built up areas where they imposed their bloody will on the people. This build up, of 'no-go' areas, had gone on almost entirely within the rule of Edward Heath. The troubles, with the civil rights marches, had started in summer 1969 and by 1971 were well established. Jack had joined the UDR in late 1970, his daughter was born in October 1971 and it wasn't until late July 1972 that something was to happen about them. On the 21st July 1972 the IRA exploded 20 bombs across the country.

On the 31st July 1972 the Army went after them in their 'no-go' areas. It was one of the biggest operations the Army had taken part in since the 2nd World War. Unfortunately, the operation was given away in Londonderry by Willie Whitelaw. When Jack arrived for duty on the 31st, a Monday, Ebrington Barracks was buzzing. Eventually Jack sorted out most of what had happened. It was all gossip and chatter but it seemed to be true.

The operation had been planned for quite a while—the Army always had ready plans for any eventuality; they even had plans to invade America! The Bloody Friday (the multi-bombing, not the shooting at the parade), as it had become known was the final straw and Edward Heath, the Prime Minister could no longer go off sailing in his 'little dinghy' when the going got tough and had given, if not his blessing, the OK for the operation. Some 5,000 troops had been secretly amassed in Londonderry, many of them being brought in on ships up the river Foyle at the last minute—they had to be careful because the work force in the docks was entirely Roman Catholic and it was dammed certain they would tell the IRA if they had known.

In Ebrington Barracks Whitelaw decided he wanted to address his old regiment so they were drawn up in three sides of a square so he could address them. A battalion of soldiers takes up quite some space so, all neatly lined up, they were quite a way from him when he stood on his little box to address them.

Realising they probably wouldn't hear him he told them to break ranks and come closer which they did. But what they also did, once they were close, was to about turn and turn their backs to him. Even a fool can recognise that action so he stormed off. Had that been all then probably all would have been well, but it wasn't; he had himself driven round to the BBC offices in Londonderry, one floor below Jack's office, and went on air. He broadcast that there was to be a major exercise, that evening starting at 21.00hrs, and that people should keep off the streets.

Jack, on reporting for duty, was sent to the Operations Room. He had been doing this for several months. Starting at 18.00hrs he would read Orders to see what, if anything was scheduled for that night. Most evenings, about two per week it was just routine. This night the Col was there. He was holding an envelope labelled 'Operation Motorman' and it became clear that it had been opened several days before because the whole battalion had been called out.

They were briefed in their sub-units and left the barracks shortly before 21.00hrs. They spread out along the border with the Republic and at 21.00 promptly they closed it. They closed it because Jack gave the order over the radio to initiate Operation Motorman effective immediately—he thus became the man who closed the border—in that part of the world anyway! No traffic, vehicles or on foot was allowed to cross in either direction. It wasn't long before the locals started to use the small, unapproved roads which crossed the border in their hundreds only to discover they were closed as well!

Meanwhile other regiments had surrounded the Bogside and promptly at 21.00hrs receiving the order to execute Operation Motorman they headed for the 'no-go' areas. The IRA had been bragging that no British troops would ever be allowed to enter, they were prepared to fight to the death and the last man and bullet to prevent it. The troops, heavily armed and supported by armoured vehicles, bracing themselves for heavy casualties had a bit of a surprise. There wasn't a soul there!

The pill box point Jack had seen was empty but the Browning had been left there so quickly had they run. There were also tales of rifles lying in the streets where they had been abandoned in the rush to run. Gradually a picture emerged that following Whitelaw's broadcast they had all run for the border, it being only about three miles away on average so that they had been clear and away by about 18.30hrs, about half an hour after the broadcast. This time Jack's night on duty was a bit different—in fact it went on for a further 10 days before he was stood down!

The IRA had the ability to listen in on the Army net so messages were either sent in code or not sent. With Exercise Motorman Jack was able to sleep for a few hours in the middle of the night on a camp bed in the office but he was frequently interrupted. To collect reports that were really too long for coding— the troops weren't exactly qualified signallers—Jack flew in a Scout helicopter every day to each of the main road blocks. He delivered messages and orders and collected anything they were reporting.

It wasn't the first time he had flown in helicopters but it was his first time in a Scout the front of which wasn't much more than a plastic bubble. He could see down through the floor and watch the ground passing by. However, it was a bit disconcerting when they flew over the Bogside to see a bloke in an alleyway firing up at them. As it happened, he was using a shotgun and they were flying too high for the shot to reach them but it was a bit pissing-off to find that his report of the incident was simply ignored. He never knew why.

At the end of 10 days, they were stood down and returned to being a civilian, part-time soldier. His boss was full of questions but when Jack didn't answer them, he assumed that it was secret. In fact, there was very little to report! Back in January he had had to report everything and anything when he commanded a roadblock on the Border the Sunday after Bloody Sunday.

A 'peaceful march' had been planned, starting in the Bogside and ending up somewhere or other, Jack never knew where, in protest and anger at the shooting of 13 civilians by the Parachute Regiment in Londonderry—another supposedly peaceful march—where in McGuiness, one of the IRA leaders carried out a lead position allegedly in the political wing of the IRA called Sinn Fein. In reality they were all the same organisation, and even more than 40 years later the Paras were being blamed for the 'massacre' even though clear film existed of McGuiness firing a pistol at the Paras from the shelter of the marching crowd.

He had no concerns that the Paras were returning his fire and his 'people' were being killed. Truth is always the first casualty of war! On the following Sunday Jack stopped a coach full of more than 30 men- no women- crossing from the Republic into N Ireland. When asked where they were going, Jack received a mouthful of abuse so he disembarked from the coach and called for a police patrol to attend as he was very suspicious about them.

The police took their time in responding and took a good two hours to interview each member of the coach party. At the end of the time, they ordered the coach to turn round and recross the Border. They didn't like the look of them either. Talking to some of the road block commanders, during Motorman, they had received plenty of abuse too, but that hadn't got the abusers through the Border either!

Chapter 14

There were only six boot and shoe manufacturers in N Ireland and as the majority were in the North West, Jack's area, he had been given responsibility for all of them to ensure uniformity of approach. On his first visit to one of them in Coleraine he arrived just as an ambulance was pulling away with its lights flashing and siren going. Arriving at Reception Jack was asked to wait. After about 15 minutes the Personnel Officer arrived full of apologies. She explained that a new member of staff, a Skiver, had just had a nasty accident on the skiving machine.

Jack had no idea what that was so he just expressed sorrow at the situation and good wishes for a speedy recovery. Starting the formal part of his visit the Personnel Officer offered him a tour of the factory which he leapt at. She explained to him that there were great changes going on in the industry because of foreign, much cheaper, competition. Traditionally shoes and boots had been made of leather. This was changing with the introduction of manmade materials replacing leather.

At the start of the manufacturing process, design and approval for that particular design, costings etc. occurred first and there was a small unit which concentrated on making the new designs and discovering the best way to make that particular shoe or boot. If leather was to be used then the first stage was to select an appropriate hide. The hide was then marked up for where the pieces were to be removed. Some areas of the hide could only be used for certain areas of the shoe.

To cut them out, a Clicker placed the knives on the leather and then operated the press which forced the knife through the leather. The cutter was driven by a leather belt system at the side of the room which drove a number of machines attached to the shaft. As the shaft spun a protrusion on it swiped across the knife with a clicking sound, hence the name of the job operator. The knife(s) were the shape of the piece of leather to be cut out, for example if it was to be the sole then a knife, sole shaped sharp on one side and blunt on the other, would be placed on the hide in the area for soles.

There might be several knives of the same shape but different sizes to be placed on the leather and cut out in one go. The uppers of the shoe were cut out in a different area of the leather and eventually all the pieces needed would be cut out. Quite often there would be a lot of the hide left which was unusable for shoes/boots but could be used for other products. Getting the maximum out of a hide was a very skilled job. But as things were changing for manmade materials where a sheet would be identical all across it the knives could simply be placed tightly, side by side, so that virtually none was left over.

The sewing room was similar to that of a shirt manufacturer but the machines were much more substantial with more powerful motors, much thicker needles and bigger areas under the foot to allow for the leather thickness as opposed to the thickness of a shirt. The biggest problem with sewing two pieces of leather together as a ridge formed if one piece was sewn on top of the other. The industry got round this problem ingeniously with a miniature 'bacon slicer'

The machine was called a Skiver and there was a narrow slot, just thick enough for the edge of the thickest leather to be inserted. Inside was a round, spinning blade, just like the Grocers for bacon, which when the leather was passed through the slot trimmed the edge at a 45-degree angle which meant that two pieces of leather, butted up to one another could be sewn through in the angle so that there was no ridge once they were sewn together.

Explaining and demonstrating this to Jack the Personnel Officer explained that a Supervisor had just been showing a new starter the machine and said, "You can see that the slot is too narrow for your fingers to go in," and before he could say anything she (the learner) said, "Mine will fit," and put them in the slot.

From then on demonstrations were done with the machine switched off because that young lady had 45-degree finger tips to show how Skiving was done! Being the easiest job in the factory the word originally meant the easiest but became the word for someone dodging the job entirely! Such is life.

Jack worked with all six shoe manufactures and was so successful that they invited him to the informal get togethers that they had monthly to discuss problems of common interest, including the Training Board. After seven or eight months of this Jack was asked to attend a meeting in London, on their behalf, to represent them at the City and Guilds meeting to consider the training and examinations following it for the industry. Jack reported this to his boss because he couldn't just disappear off to London for a couple of days and especially because of who would pay the travel expenses.

When he told Maurice Baldwin, his boss, about the request he was astonished at the result. This had never happened in any of the 15 or so training boards, and it put the Clothing and Footwear Industry Training Board well into the lead regarding relationships between the Board and its industry members. His boss was so excited he rang the Chairman of the Board there and then. Jack enjoyed the praise but remembering Mons and the attempts to establish competitions between the Platoons he remembered that his platoon only won when there was a tangible prize, i.e., crates of beer and with nothing forthcoming in the way of a bonus as a result of his success he wasn't too fussed!

Jack enjoyed the visits back to England and on two occasions was able to take Janet and the baby with him. They were left with his parents to make a fuss of and as the two working days were Thursday and Friday, they were able to use the Saturday to visit Janet's parents and then travel back to Strathfoyle on the Sunday.

Alison gave every indication of being a normal, healthy baby but although she could see, and looked at and took an interest in her surroundings, they were unable to determine if her hearing had been affected by the Rubella. The normal test for hearing was for Janet to sit Alison on the floor and attract her attention with a toy while the Health Visitor sat behind Alison and blew a whistle, beat on a drum and made other noises. A 'normal' child would hear and look for the source of the noise.

Alison sometimes responded and sometimes didn't. Jack was concerned because watching closely the Health Visitor was sometime intruding into Alison's sight picture so that her responding and looking was more to do with the fact, she could see what was going on out of the cornier of her eye rather than responding to the sound. Overall, the facilities for deaf children were pretty well nil in Ireland and Jack and Janet started having conversations about returning to England.

Chapter 15

One Monday morning Jack's boss, Maurice rang him to say that they were expecting visitors from England and he wanted Jack to help to entertain them. It turned out that it was the Chief Executive of the English Clothing and Allied Products Industry Training Board and his deputy. By this time there were 15 boards operating in N Ireland all of which, bar one, had been set up after the English equivalent.

The odd one out was theirs. Clothing, and footwear, was a major industry in N Ireland but only a relatively small one in England, consequently the English Board was only now being set up, some three or four years after the Irish one, and the two of them were visiting to make their number so to speak and to see how the Irish Board functioned to see what tips they could pick up.

Some 60% of all shirts sold in England were made in Londonderry and great strides had been made in the training of instructors and supervisors, much of it achieved by Jack, and word of this had spread so that they had specifically asked to meet Jack and accompany him on some visits. Jack drove halfway to Belfast on the appointed day and met up with Maurice and the two visitors.

On the way back to Londonderry Jack was quizzed by the two of them but initially at least, it was nothing to do with the Board and how it operated but about the troubles and the effect it was having. He was a little surprised that, having answered their questions, they indicated that the picture Jack painted was substantially different to that received from the people in Belfast. All Jack could say was that as an Englishman he probably viewed things differently to the 'natives' who had grown up with the divide between Catholics and Protestants.

They were particularly interested in seeing companies where the Instructors trained by the Irish Board operated. Jack knew this from the briefing he had received from Maurice and had made arrangements to visit Tootal shirts. *(This factory was to be sold off in 1987 as part of a restructuring by the Holding Company).* The visitors were extremely impressed when the Factory Director explained that the traditional "sitting by Nellie" which resulted in a trainee taking six months to reach about a 50% performance (quality had to be 100% from the word go) had been reduced to 100% performance in a week with the training carried out by the board-trained instructors. The supervisory training was slightly different.

When Maurice had called all the Training Development Officers to a meeting in Belfast, it was to discuss the creation of a Supervisors' Training Course. Legally the Board was not allowed to offer training that was commercially available elsewhere. There had not been a problem creating and offering the Instructor Training since there were no organisation in N Ireland at that time offering such a course. From the impressive results achieved by the Instructors a demand had arisen for the Board to offer Supervisor training.

The problem was that there were a number of different organisations offering such training thereby barring the Board from offering it. The meeting had arisen because companies were saying that they had sent supervisors on these courses but the company had seen no improvement in their performance as a result. Hence the meeting. A general discussion took place and after a while, feeling that it was going nowhere, Jack said, "We're all sitting here talking away about subjects they should be taught but isn't the starting point, 'what does a Supervisor actually do?' I've met some in various factories and seen them repairing poor stitching, carrying work around and disappearing off to the cutting room to get something re-cut but as to what they actually do all the time I don't know."

Silence reigned. Eventually Maurice said, "Jack's right. Back to basics we need to know what they actually do and whether they should be doing that before we can design a programme. I suspect that the majority of their time is spent on activities that have to be done but which probably should not be done by a Supervisor. That may account for why the courses that they have attended have taught them marvellous things but when they get back to the factory, they have to do all these other jobs which prevent them from doing the proper job.

"I think we should each invite reps from the best companies in each of our areas to a meeting and discuss with them the issue of supervisory training and see if we can get two each to commit to their Supervisors recording how they spend their time. And this is what they did. The recorded results of how supervisors spent their time—they worked out a standard list of actions so that comparisons could be made between different companies—was quite extraordinary. Something like 80% of their time was spent on non-supervisory duties and only 20% on 'managing' tasks."

They all reassembled in Belfast to discuss the data. Although they all more or less knew that supervisors did spend time on non-managing tasks, getting recuts, carrying work from one machinist to another, handing out new colour threads, repairing badly done work to save the garment—it really was astonishing just how much was not proper work; it had to be done of course but why by the Supervisor.

After the initial reactions the conversation died. Just what should be the subjects taught on a supervisor course in such circumstances—it was pretty obvious why attendance at the courses on offer did not result in any improvement; the minute they returned to their factory they had to carry stuff around, there was no time to manage!

The silence became a bit prolonged. Eventually Jack said, "I think we should talk to Mary Peters." (She was the golden girl of N Ireland having just won a gold medal at the Olympics and had announced that she was setting up a health club). The others all looked at him as though he had gone crackers. "No," he said, "seriously. Most of their time is spent in physical activity, carrying work between machinists, popping up to the cutting room to get an item recut, fetching new colour threads, buttons, labels etc.; so, we should be getting them fit so that they can carry a bundle under each arm, run between machines etc."

Everyone laughed. "I'm sort of being serious," said Jack. There is no point in us offering a course which would be fundamentally the same as what is on offer now. We need to select, say a couple of our companies each again and get them to commit to looking at changing the operation, i.e., how should the work move, conveyor belt, reorganise the layout so that the machinist once she has done her bit passes it forward to a bar behind the girl in front who will just reaches behind her for the next piece etc or get someone else to carry it around. The solution is likely to differ from factory to factory dependent on what they are making but if the management won't commit to these changes, then there is no point in us running courses teaching skills, they will never be able to use."

There was another long silence then Maurice said, "Jack's right," and that's what they did. Jack took the visitors to one company where they had installed a conveyor belt system so that when once a girl had finished her bundle, she put it back into the open topped box and it was whizzed along to the next girl in the construction sequence or into temporary holding—no, just in time here yet; the machinist could be sent threads, labels, bows etc. with the box load and pass them on in the box when the work moved. It was particularly effective because, although they just made shirts, they were all of different kinds and the order of make-up varied.

The other factory made just about anything they could get an order for, shirts, blouses, slips and bra-slips even yellow dusters! Here the Supervisor had a work station and a 'gopher' carried the work including delivering and collecting buttons, threads, labels so much so that the Factory Manager told the visitors that the gopher had saved £1,000 in the first week by the proper utilisation of the ancillaries which would either have been taken home by the machinists or thrown into the bin.

The visits to the two companies were very successful and the two from the English Board were very impressed by Jack as well as the results of the Supervisor Training Course. So much so that the Chief Executive took Jack aside and told him that if ever he wanted to move back to England, he would guarantee Jack a job with the English Board. Jack noted his contact details in his little black book!

Chapter 16

The English Board members were not the only visitors Jack was asked to squire around. Visitors arrived from Cambridge University to fact find to form part of a report on Trainability Testing. Traditional interviewing techniques had been brought up to date in recommendations from the Training Board, to some degree, with the introduction of eyesight and colour-blindness testing.

The great weakness in the interviewing by all the companies was an inability to determine at the interview if the individual could in fact be trained to sew at the speed and quality required of a machinist. Some companies had introduced sitting the person (most of the time a girl, but in the men's tailoring companies and shoe manufacturers men were the preferred sex.) at a sewing machine and getting them to sew something but it was unstructured and very hit and miss. The Industrial Training Unit in Cambridge had been looking at this same issue and had developed a trainability assessment (they didn't like 'test') which they wished to try out for machinists.

The method had originally been developed for assessing potential bus drivers and had achieved very impressive results. Now they wanted to try out the principles in other industries. Again, more willing to be progressive companies were selected in each of the regions and invited to a meeting in Belfast. From that three companies were selected to have their normal interviewers trained in the technique before being turned loose to use it.

Basically, the interviewer used a script to instruct the potential employee at every stage. They were given no practical instruction by the interviewer demonstrating what was required, they were simply read a script which they were able to follow or not. Those who could not follow the instructions exactly were rejected. The ones who could were offered a job. The success rate of these people was very good, something in excess of 90% but Jack had a little niggle in his mind that not all those failures would necessarily be failures at the end of the improved training they had introduced. He was never able to satisfy his worries on that score but he did in a later job.

Jack got on very well with the two women from Cambridge and invited them to dinner at his home on their second night. When they entered his house, Jack took their coats and hung them up in the hall. When he took his own jacket off, the look on their faces was a picture. Exposed in full view was his Browning Semi-Automatic pistol in its shoulder holster. He had to explain he was in the UDR and, as such, was potentially a target for the IRA. Jack wanted to keep good relations with the Industrial Training Unit because he had a feeling that he would need them in the future.

Dinner went off fine and Jack ran them back to their hotel afterwards. When he met up with them the following morning, the senior of the two patted him where the Browning was carried and said, "We'll be well protected today then." The rest of the visit went well and Jack obtained contact details from them for the future.

Chapter 17

Although Jack spent most of the time with the UDR running the Ops Room when he was on duty, he did still command patrols on occasions. One was to confirm that he needed to move his family back to England. The troubles were getting worse and the personal danger for him was increasing. It wasn't helped by stupid commands putting him into more danger than was needed. On this particular night Jack had a patrol of three Landrovers carrying 13 soldiers plus himself. They were approaching the border on an unapproved road when they passed an open gate into a field with a car, a Morris Minor 1000 in it.

Jack was sitting in the back of the Landrover facing towards the offside of the road and, as the gate and car were to the nearside, he couldn't see it but the lad sitting opposite him was looking in that direction and saw it. He called out, "There's a car in the middle of that field and it's a bloody Belfast number plate!"

Jack called for the driver to stop. He was pleased to see the professional way they dismounted and took up all round cover. Jack knew from running his first Instructor Course, in Ballymena, when he first arrived in N Ireland that eight of the ten people on the course had never been to Belfast 'because it was too far away!'

So, for there to be a Belfast number plate on a car, about 25 yards from the border, in the far North West was unexpected and needed to be investigated. Jack congratulated the soldier on his perspicacity and quick reaction and a short while later was to wish that the little bastard had had his eyes shut and missed it altogether!

Sorting out his plan Jack confirmed the positioning of the various soldiers and then with the Sergeant standing by him went onto the radio and reported the car and its number plate to Operations. He was told "to wait out" which he knew from working in Operations that they were contacting the police and getting the number plate checked. After about ten minutes they came back on the air with, 'is the car locked?'

Jack replied, "Not known, over."

"Find out, over."

"How, over?"

"Try it, over." The correct response to that should have been 'wilco out' but Jack could not believe what he was hearing. Here was a suspicious car, parked in the middle of a field, within about 25 yards of the border, which ran along the hedgerow at the far side of the field, where they were open to being ambushed and shot to pieces or blown up by a bomb in the car to be detonated either by opening the door or detonated from a distance as soon as someone approached it.

So, Jack went back onto the radio, "Are you serious? It does not create an immediate threat, where it is, so it can easily be left with us guarding the immediate area, until a bomb squad can get here. Why can that not be done instead of risking lives unnecessarily, over?"

"Carry out the last instruction, over."

"Have you listened to anything I have said? It is an obvious ambush site, a trap to take out a number of soldiers, so I want to know who is giving such a stupid order and why, over."

A new voice, "This is Sunray, execute the order you have been given, over."

"Wilco, out" was all Jack could say, Sunray being the call sign for the Col. So how to approach this mess with the minimum risk? Jack called in the boundaries of the soldiers setting a closer perimeter but still sufficiently far away from the car to be safe, and detailed some of them to do as he was to order. First, he had to make sure, as far as possible, that there were no terrorists hiding in the further hedgerow.

He detailed off the Corporal to bring two men with him and Jack explained that the first thing they were going to do was search down the hedgerow to their right and follow it down to the hedge at the far side of the field through which ran the border—this might have been just this side, through the middle of the hedge or run along the far side; Jack didn't know and he was fairly certain no-one else did either—so they would then traverse the border hedge and return, hopefully, down the left had side. Jack then detailed one of the soldiers to come with him to follow the route again but this time the soldier would lead very slowly as Jack followed shining a torch close to the ground to see if he could spot a cable or wire running out from a hedgerow, probably the border one, to the car.

Having done that and finding nothing Jack had to decide what to do next. While he was thinking Sunray came up on the radio for a sitrep. Jack told the radio man to send 'wait out' with some pleasure and then turned to the Sergeant, "Gather together all the rifle slings that we have, and any rope, and combine them together to make as long a cable as possible."

Jack could see the hesitation in the Sergeant and said, "I'm going to attach it to the door handle, if I can, and use it to open the door." The Sergeant looked at him. Of course it was dark and difficult to see all the detail, but it looked like relief on the Sergeant's face. Jack's mind had been working ever since the presence of the car had been spotted. The Army had spent much time and money, well some anyway, on training Jack as an officer so the economic argument went, a soldier should be risked before an NCO, and NCO before a Warrant Officer and all of them before an officer.

There was also the issue that the officer knew more than a more junior rank and to lose that data and the command presence of the officer would be bad policy. Jack had no problem with this when, for example, patrolling where they might be ambushed a Private Soldier led with the officer somewhere in the middle of the patrol; that way if they were ambushed the officer in the middle would survive the initial assault and take command of the following action—if he had been leading and killed with the first shots the patrol would be leaderless.

They had been taught this at MONS OCS and it had been standard Army practice for centuries probably. For Jack, who had displayed on numerous occasions an unwillingness to accept the norm—everyone knew what the training was and the practice which followed it—so that Jack, if he had been planning an ambush would have targeted his initial fire at the men in the middle of the patrol hoping to eliminate the command and control immediately at the commencement of the firefight. Of course, everyone knew that so that the command function would not be placed in the middle. And thinking about that quietly, and sometimes not so quietly, that that was crackers!

Following that logic, Jack should order someone more junior to approach the car and open the door, the expensive command and control function should not be risked. It seemed clear to Jack that the Sergeant initially thought that Jack was going to order him to open the door hence the look of relief when Jack said, 'I...'

Jack had also been brought along on the premise that an officer should lead from the front and not ask/order soldiers to do something he would not do himself. Lead or order? Order or lead? The radio crackled again asking for a sitrep.

"Tell him, wait out." Jack enjoyed making the Col wait. After all he wasn't the one in danger, Jack was! Taking the rope, which wasn't much longer than seven or eight yards, although each rifle sling was quite long, in the order of four feet, the problem was that, because they were made of such stiff canvas, tying them together used up such a long length the final rope was quite short. Taking it Jack approached the car and shone his torch on the handle.

Fortunately, it was of the type that pulled to open, had it been a button to push in he would have had more trouble. He slid the end of the sling under the handle and then gently secured it back on itself making a loop. He then laid down on the ground as far from the car as the rope and his outstretched arm would allow and pulled—if he was going to be blown to bits there was no point hanging around. He had done it this way in the hope that explosives taking the line of least resistance would explode more upwards than outwards.

In the event there was no big bang and Jack's sphincter muscle could relax from its miniscule size it had been when he pulled the handle. He opened the door fully and shone his torch carefully inside. Fortunately, again, it was a basic model with only a parcel shelf, no closed glove compartment to hide something nasty. Returning to the Radio Operator he took from him the handset, sent his call sign and reported, "The door was unlocked and there is nothing in the vehicle, over."

"What about the boot?" came back from Sunray.

"Wait out."

"Fuck, fuck, FUCK," the last said with very considerable feeling!

"Well, Sergeant, how do you feel about opening the boot?" Jack could not resist asking him just to see his reaction. Jack sort of formed the opinion that the Sergeant wasn't too keen. There was no way to attack their crude rope to the boot handle so Jack, taking a deep breath just opened it. Various bits of rubbish, clothing, and pop bottles met his eye but nothing that looked decidedly dangerous nor did it go bang when he opened it—which was quite a relief.

Taking hold of the radio handset Jack just pressed the send key and said, "Nothing found, out." The 'out' ended the conversation and prevented the Col speaking. Walking back to the Landrover Jack got into the front passenger seat of the middle Landrover to be followed by the members of the patrol. The Sergeant opened the door and asked, "Where to now, Sir?"

Jack looked at him and then said, "To the nearest pub and you can buy me a large double brandy—that's for opening the door; then you can buy me another one for opening the boot and then you can buy me another one because last week the terrorists used a radio detonated bomb in Belfast for the first time." Jack gently closed the door and ordered the driver, "Pub."

They saw no-one when they returned to barracks just after 05.30am just as it was getting light. When Jack reported for duty the following week, it was to the Operations Room; in the messages for Duty Officers which said, 'In the event of the discovery of a suspicious vehicle the area immediately around it is to be cleared and its presence reported to the RUC and Bomb Squad.' The Col, Sunray, never said a word to Jack about the incident but the Adj, passing him in the corridor, said, "You can claim for clean underwear on expenses if you wish!"

Funny though it was Jack had finally made his mind up that he was going to see what the CEO of the English Training Board could offer him. He felt he had done his share. Not many of the inhabitants of N Ireland were coming forward to fight for their own safety and coupled with the complete lack of facilities for his daughter it was time to move. However, N Ireland and its troubles had not quite finished with Jack.

Chapter 18

When he rang the English Board, he was put straight through to the CEO. After the normal pleasantries Jack explained that he felt it was the right time to return to England and so he was ringing to take up his offer of a role which he had made to Jack during his visit to Londonderry. The CEO said, "Well, I can offer you two posts immediately. One would be as an Area Adviser a bit like the role you fill but much less detailed and only concerned with visiting companies and trying to persuade them to become involved with the Board or, which I think might be much more to your liking, a Group Training Officer's position in Nottingham.

"Although we have many more companies in England making clothes and allied products than N Ireland, they still represent much less of the manufacturing capacity of this country than does the industry in N Ireland. We have many small companies who we cannot support directly by the Board but what we have done is to try to persuade numbers of them to group together and employ a Group Training Officer of their own. We pay 25% of their salary as a grant and support them in any other way that we can. We have already set up three and the next one is to be in Nottingham.

"The Area Adviser there, a Barry White, has been canvassing companies and 20 of them have expressed interest. The next stage would be to advertise the position but responses have not been too good in the first three areas and filling the posts has taken some time. I am confident that Barry could sell them on interviewing you and short circuit the process especially if you come with a high recommendation from the Board which you would. How quickly could you get over to England for an interview?"

The group idea sounded great to Jack. As it was Friday, he said, "Monday."

"Perhaps not quite that quick," laughed the CEO. "We will need to get them to appoint a management committee and set a date so I will give Barry your contact number if you give it to me now and he will get in touch with the arrangements. How does that suit you?"

"Great," said Jack. The interview went ahead a couple of weeks later in Nottingham in what was to be the Group Training Officer's office. It comprised a small office, a large training room and a small committee room. All had been built in one of the factories in the heart of the Lace Market, an area loaded with clothing manufacturing companies, was freshly decorated and furnished. They had even organised a Secretary, part-time for Jack.

Parking was difficult but as it was envisaged that he would spend most of his time out in the companies within the Group, 20 in all with exactly 2000 employees between them, comprising men's suit manufacturers, lingerie, shirts, blouses, bra-slips, men's fashion jackets and one, major company manufacturing all ladies underwear, pyjamas, slips etc. for a major chain store (*must be careful with names as they are still in existence even if they are a bit of a shower!*) even if the manufacturer was modern with all the latest machinery and manufacturing methods.

But N Ireland wasn't quite finished with frights for Jack. Once he had received the job offer in writing, with an increase in salary of £750pa plus a Cortina! Jack resigned giving a month's notice. One of the companies in Nottingham, manufacturing high end ladies dresses and costumes, trouser suits and a small blouse line owned a Coronation St, end of terrace type house around the corner from the factory. Divided into two flats, Jack was offered the use of the ground floor one, a bedroom, living come dining room with a kitchen and bathroom in an extension at the back, it was ideal for Jack to use while he looked for a house to buy.

Until then he and Janet had lived in rented places and had decided that now was the time to buy. The flat was too small for all three of them so Janet and Alison were to stay with Jack's parents in Crowthorne with Janet visiting by train at the weekend to view properties discovered by Jack. Well that was the intention but it didn't quite work out like that.

The run down to leaving was very busy. Arrangements had to be made for a flight for Janet and Alison to fly from Belfast to Gatwick to be met by Jack's parents on the Tuesday before Jack flew into Leeds/Bradford on the Saturday to collect his car, his brand new Cortina which had made him the envy of the Board colleagues when they discovered what he was going to drive, and which was to be left for him to collect at the airport—he would then drive to Nottingham to meet the removers at the flat to drop off some of his furniture and the rest at one of the factories.

On the Thursday, the removers were to load the majority of his furniture with the bed, a table and a chair being collected on the Friday morning. Jack was to drive to Belfast on the Friday afternoon and stay overnight with Maurice who would drive him to Aldergrove in the morning for the flight to Leeds/Bradford.

Resigning from the UDR was not difficult, just a letter with a date, but the worrying bit was when should he hand in his pistol? He wanted to retain it to the last possible moment, obviously, so that meant handing it in on the Friday morning, they wouldn't let him take it to Belfast and hand it in there. So, Friday morning it was. On the Thursday he had to go to Coleraine for a final meeting of the Boot and Shoe Advisory Committee.

As he drove out of the estate a Cortina was coming along the other way at some speed. "Prat," muttered Jack as they narrowly missed one another on what was quite a narrow road. There were two men in it. It was when he saw their brake lights go on that he became slightly worried. They were hidden by a bend in the road very quickly but Jack kept an eye on his rear-view mirror and very shortly they appeared behind him.

Accelerating to maximum speed, Jack shot along the B road to the A2 where he turned left for Coleraine. It was no good, even flat out his Morris 1300 was slowly but surely being overhauled by the Cortina; there wasn't even enough traffic to slow his pursuer down as there had been in Aden the last time he had been chased. *(See 'It must have been the compo'—book one of the trilogy.)* After about 2 miles, on a long straight stretch with no traffic the Cortina drew up alongside him and the passenger in the front waived him to stop. Slowing to a stop Jack drew his pistol and held it low down pointing through the driver's door at the man who got out of the Cortina, dressed in civilian clothes, and walked over to him.

He was not apparently armed and he said a cheery hello as he approached. Jack waited until he was at his open window and said, "I have no idea who you are. I am an officer in the UDR and am pointing a gun at you at this moment. Who are you and why have you stopped me?" The man froze.

"Easy, easy, I am a police officer." *Bugger,* thought Jack*, he's going to do me for speeding but, hold on, there is no speed limit on any main roads in N Ireland,* "and I am going to reach into my pocket and pull out my Warrant Card."

"Very slowly," said Jack. He did and handed the Warrant Card to Jack. Jack looked at it, examined the photo which was the usual horrible likeness and satisfied that he was indeed a police officer Jack said, "You still haven't said why you have stopped me."

"I'll explain that in a moment, Sir, but first I would like you to stop pointing that pistol at me and produce your authority to carry a concealed weapon." Jack produced his ID card and the authority which the policeman examined in that very slow and annoying way they have and then handed them back. In the meantime, Jack had returned the Browning to his shoulder holster.

"I believe you live at 9 Greenfield Park and will be moving out very soon, is that correct?"

"Yes," said Jack wondering how on earth he knew that and why it was of interest.

"I have been allocated that property, once you have moved out, and because of the problems with squatters I would like to put some furniture into the house, before you leave, so that if anyone should move in it will be breaking and entering and I will be able to throw them out immediately. If the house is empty, then its squatting and I can't get them out except through a long and awkward process through the courts."

Relieved, Jack laughed and said, "You damn nearly got yourself shot for that and if this bloody little Post Office van had been any faster, you'd never have caught me but that's life. I am on my way to Coleraine and expect to be back at Greenfield Park by about 3pm. I shall be moving out tomorrow morning about 11am once the last of my furniture has been removed. You are welcome to move anything in that you want to, all of your furniture if you want, this afternoon or tomorrow morning."

"Right you are," said the copper, "Thanks for that and I'll bring most of my stuff round tonight," which he did.

He said, "Cheerio and thanks," and they parted. Although, in the event, it had not been needed Jack was ever so pleased that he had not already handed the Browning in and once he did so the following morning, he felt very naked and exposed as he drove to Belfast. He left the car at the Head Office and went home with Maurice who had offered to put him up for the night and run him to Aldergrove Airport in the morning. As he sat in the Departure Lounge, he thought back on some of the events but the main point that popped up was his visit to the Spiritualist Church in Colchester where the Medium had said, "I see you in Ireland with two pips on your shoulder," five years later it had come true for the Lieutenancy and the move to Ireland."

That had been exactly right. Proof, if proof were needed, that there was more to life than just life! He caught his flight as scheduled and arrived in Leeds/Bradford at 11.30hrs completing a full and eventful three years.

N Ireland had not quite finished with him. His collection of his Cortina had been very simple and he had revelled in the luxury of it as he drove relatively slowly down the M1 running it in carefully. He had had a narrow escape when a giant wheel from a lorry flew over the central reservation narrowly missing him and all but destroying the little A30 behind him. The removals lorry turned up and he unloaded the furniture for the flat and it then delivered the rest to the factory. It had all been collected in a furniture removals van but it arrived on the back of an open lorry covered by a tarpaulin which had not done a very good job and some of the items were wet.

The carpet from his lounge had gone missing somewhere on route and he had to process an insurance claim for that but, all in all, it had gone reasonably well and he was glad to be back in England. He then drove down to Crowthorne arriving just after 19.00 hrs to meet up with Janet and Alison and the rest of his family. He returned to Nottingham very early on Monday morning in time to start his new job at 09.00hrs. That evening, returning after dark he parked about thirty yards up the road and as he walked to the flat there were a couple of almighty bangs behind him.

Acting on his training he leapt over the low wall beside him landing on a soft flower bed which proceeded to decorate his new suit copiously with mud. When he peered across the wall it was to see two young lads running off up the road laughing their heads off. Jack knew it was the 4th November because that was his job start date but he had forgotten all about Bonfire night, and fireworks, because they had been banned in N Ireland for the three years he lived there. He used all the Anglo Saxon he knew and then some as he climbed over the wall and made his way to the flat. *That's two bloody walls I've jumped over,* thought Jack, *and there won't be a third—and there never was.*

Chapter 19

Jack was to spend the next six years in Nottingham, as the Group Training Officer of the Nottingham and District Clothing Industry Group Training Association. It turned out to be a very happy six years with the only bug bear being how to shorten the name of the Group!

The job, answering to a Management Committee at a meeting once a month initially, involved carrying out a training needs analysis for each member company and from that developing training plans to meet the identified needs. Well, that was the original intention but by the time Jack had carried out a training needs analysis in the first three companies—in itself a problem since nobody wanted to be last on the list and there had even been an argument as to what order should be followed, alphabetical, reverse alphabetical, should the names be put in a hat and drawn out, in the event they went for the hat version but by the time Jack had carried out the three it was clear to him that they all had the same needs with very little difference between them.

The three needed trained Instructors and a training room; this could simply be the last row of machines shut off by free standing screens or a proper room in those big enough to warrant it and space for it. The supervisors were all like those Jack had seen in N Ireland working very hard but doing the wrong things with a consequent need to look at the job and how it could be improved. Management training had been there none! And because of a shortage of recruits into the industry it became clear that Jack would be spending a large portion of his time talking in schools in an attempt to persuade leavers to join the industry.

The Training Board was very keen to develop the Group Training Associations and they appointed an individual, Stan Baker to be the contact man between the Groups (12 in all eventually) and the Board and who, with Barry White was to make a trio with Jack achieving many developments within the Nottingham Group so much so that five years later it was turning away applicants to join because it had grown to 36 companies with more than 6000 employees between them.

He put a proposal to the committee that rather than carrying out a training needs analysis in each member company he should sent to each of them a 'standard model' which they could study before he visited so that at his visit they could point out where their needs differed from the norm—not much as it turned out—and these differences could be incorporated. This was accepted and all of the Group benefitted by a much quicker process.

Jack set up a number of Instructor courses immediately because he knew that that would produce the most immediate and spectacular results. He pruned the instructor's course, that he had run in N Ireland, and reduced it from three weeks to two. The improvement in results in the individual companies started showing almost immediately and, like Ireland, there soon started a demand for a supervisor's course. While he took the same route i.e., chose three of the more eager companies and started them off with the selected supervisors recording how they spent their time he went off to a course that was being constructed by the Clothing and Allied Products Training Board. They had been very impressed by what the Irish Board had done with supervisory training but had decided to start at the top and start with management training.

The Irish Board had considered doing that but felt that it would be better if by carrying out the supervisory training they could persuade the management to come to them asking for training rather than going to them to tell them they needed it. They had looked at the problem that supervisors were doing the wrong work and had carried that forward to the management on the assumption they were probably doing the wrong work, probably the supervisors and no-one was actually doing the management work. They had invited Jack to attend because of his involvement in the supervisory training in Ireland and were interested in his input into the course they had planned in outline. They also hoped that some of Jack's companies would be willing to attend the first course and introduce what was being proposed into their companies.

Starting with the premise what should managers be doing had concluded that the starting point should be an analysis of the business potential and where, if it was, it was falling down. They started with an average company which they defined as being 100 sewing machines/machinists; working 40 hours a week represented a potential of 4,000 production hours out of those 100 machines. When no-one of the course members, two other Group Training Officers and 5

Training Board staff reacted to that figure Jack did. Somehow it leapt of the projector screen that the maximum production hours were not 4,000 but 4,000 x 3 = 12,000 hours if you worked three eight-hour shifts, the machines were quite capable of working 24 hours per day even if the machinists weren't so the maximum potential output was 12,000 hours per week and by operating only one shift the factory had already lost 8,000 hours or two thirds of its potential production.

This suggestion by Jack raised an enormous hullabaloo with the majority of course members disagreeing with Jack but he was adamant, those machines could potentially run 24 hours a day and to run only 8 was creating a potential loss—just to stir the pot a little more he suggested that they could run seven days if they wished making the total potential production hours in excess of 16,000.

The course leader eventually brought the discussion on this point to a close accepting Jack's argument that there was a potential for 24 hours production per day but if a company chose, as a policy, to run only 8 their starting point for loss was 4,000 potential hours and the other areas they were to come on to provided lots more potential argument, for example, should one start with labour turnover as a potential loss before machine breakdowns or should it be the other way round? They determined on a long list of potential losses only some of which would apply to a particular company. Jack felt that the course had enormous potential for all the companies in his group and arranged a date for a course to be run by the Board. It took some talking because Jack wanted the course run over a weekend.

For the Board staff that was almost heresy but for Jack's people many of them were owner managers and they could not get out during normal working hours—many of them had not had a holiday for years because of this problem and even those who closed their factories for 'Wakes Weeks' could only take a few days of the fortnight because of having to catch up with work that they could not do at other times. So, Jack offered the course to his members on the basis of starting the course with dinner on the Friday night and finishing mid-afternoon on the Sunday. They would be run at, variously over the next few years, the Palace Hotel, Buxton, the Peveril of the Peak Hotel, Dovedale and a hotel in Bakewell which claimed to have invented the Bakewell Tart but there were never any tarts there when the courses were run! *(Yes, I know they say 'Pudding' but tart makes the better joke!)*

The courses proved enormously popular and those companies taking advantage of them benefitted to such a degree that Jack started to receive requests for places from non-member firms. Discussions in the Exec Committee resulted in a policy of limiting attendance to member companies but, recognising the opportunity to put a few bob in the kitty, Jack ran instructor and supervisor courses for individual firms that were not members and which were too big to comfortably fit into the group so they were offered associate membership and courses run for them were charged at a modest figure.

Chapter 20

Almost all the Group members had recruitment problems. The industry was poorly served by 'the rag trade' tag. A comedy series on the television of the same name did not help. The image portrayed was enough to put any school leaver, and more importantly their mothers 'no child of mine is going to work in a factory' from joining the industry even though the potential earnings were far greater than that in any office. Jack had a conversation with a neighbour across the road whose son played with Jack's daughter. He was a teacher of mainly woodworking but he also had, as a little earner on the side, the role of Career's Master. Jack attended a careers convention and was dismayed. There were professional recruiters there, the three armed forces had major stands with films showing all the attractive sides of the forces, foreign travel, sport etc., none of the square bashing or being shot at of course.

Banks, the NHS and other big organisations were there and had Jack accepted an invitation to man a stand all he would have had was the table provided by them, the chairs provided by them and a letter headed piece of Group Training Association's paper! Not very impressive! Jack did accept an invitation to speak at the neighbour's school but with no handouts rather than a list of Group members for anyone to contact if they wanted a job in the trade, it was pretty useless.

At the next Executive Committee meeting Jack put forward a proposal. He had talked a video equipment supplier into lending him a video camera, tripod, video display unit and a tape recorder—the minimum he would need. He proposed two main uses for the kit. The first was to make a film of a garment being produced—preferably something simple like a slip or nightdress—starting with a designer doing a sketch, producing the patterns, having the cloth cut into the pattern shapes, being stitched together by a sample machinist, and so on through the processes until the finished garment went out of the factory.

This would obviously be used in school and conferences to promote the industry. The second main use would be for training, especially to tape interviews, for an interviewing course he was about to run, and to tape course members presenting their talks etc. on the Instructor's Course. There might well be a million and one other uses but those two would be a good start. The whole kit would cost almost exactly £1,000 but would be money well spent. The Exec Committee agreed, it went to the next main committee meeting and was approved there and shortly thereafter Jack was trying to make out how the bloody thing worked. There were millions of wires (oh yes there were!) with none for only that one hole only, and it turned out that the kit was so heavy that they had to buy a trolley thing to move it around.

Jack made a video lasting 20 minutes showing a designer sketching out a diagram of a slip and then all the stages that were followed to end up with a packaged garment going out of the factory. It showed sample garments being produced for the sales people, patterns being produced, grading (sizing), cloth being laid up, cut, sorted into colours, sewn together, buttons etc being added, pressing and packaging with examination going on at stages. As word spread around the Careers Advisers and Teachers that Jack had a video film and that it was good, he started to receive invitations to speak in schools, colleges and conferences.

One posh girls' school which had previously showed no interest in having him speak to the leavers suddenly contacted him with an invitation to speak. He did and the video film went down well but it was the questions afterwards that didn't go too well. One of the questions asked was how much machinists were paid. Jack answered with that as it was payments by results system the amount varied from machinist to machinist but during training it was at least £10pw and a really good experienced machinist could earn more than £50pw.

This last did not go down well with the teacher who exclaimed, "But that's more than I get!" Jack's response that he could arrange for her to be interviewed for a job the next day did not go down well revealing the prejudice of academics to factory workers and the implication of their being worth more than any mere factory worker.

Jack even received an invitation to speak at the national conference of Careers Teachers and Advisers at Kent University in Canterbury. The organiser even asked him to be a little controversial! Which he was! At that time there was a considerable movement in academia that spelling wasn't important, work should not be marked with red ink lest it upset the poor child, freedom of expression being more important; teachers were increasingly being called by their first names, uniforms were disappearing and potential employers were generally despairing at this attitude. Jack dropped in his controversy at the end of his delivery. He didn't do so earlier in case they stopped listening to him.

He said, "Now I am aware that there is much national debate about spelling and other changes in the academic world. I would start by asking a rhetorical question, is it the job of schools to educate children in isolation or is it to prepare them for the world of work? My view is the latter in which case spelling not being important means that your salary will be paid each month to someone else because the Wages Clerk cannot spell your name correctly and anyway, they only paid half because although they used the right method to calculate it, they got the answer wrong. Spelling correctly is very important and so is getting the answer right—I do not care what method is used simply that it is right. If, of course, you believe that education exists in a vacuum then you are wrong again. Any questions?"

Surprisingly he didn't get any questions nor was he asked to speak ever again at the conference.

Eventually the careers work was taking up more than half of Jack's time. Although the Group employers were quite pleased with that, the recruiting of school leavers into the Group companies was noticeably better, Jack did not enjoy doing so much of it.

Chapter 21

Although Jack was not to realise it for many years it was the training, he evolved at this time which was to create his future career. Following the Second World War both Tory and Labour governments concentrated on passing legislation to get the country up and running. The quality of training in the UK was being passed by Germany, France and Italy and that had led to the Industrial Training Act 1964 and the creation of the training boards in an attempt to improve the training nationally which hadn't moved on in many years. Train drivers, steam trains, took at least 5 years to train yet during the war this had been reduced to ten weeks.

Jack's dad had been an apprentice toolmaker and he always said that the first year he made the tea, the second year he was allowed to drink some and it was only in his third year and onwards that he started to learn anything! That meant his real training was only three years long. Jack knew that if it was anything like 'sitting by Nellie' in the clothing industry with a proper training needs analysis and training programme derived from it then that three years could have been reduced to one year or less.

Certainly, the unions and the Labour party felt so, so they had introduced the Industrial Training Act in 1964. But more importantly, as it would turn out for Jack, a part of that Act had set-up Industrial Tribunals. Because many employers disagreed with the levy assessments made against them by the Training Board the Government had set up Tribunals to hear appeals against the Levy. The Tribunal consisted of a Chairman, who was always a lawyer—generally a Solicitor but sometimes a Barrister, a rep appointed by an employers' organisation and a rep appointed by a recognised trade union.

It was meant to be a non-legal operation with employers encouraged to represent themselves rather than by a lawyer. In fact, Jack never came across an employer appealing against any levy he made so he had no direct experience of them. However, once the Industrial Relations Act 1971 was to introduce the concept of unfair dismissal. Initially claims were heard in the Industrial Relations Court but this was soon changed to the Industrial Tribunal, (nowadays the Employment Tribunal), about three years later.

(In the future a chap by the name of Tony Blair was to introduce and enormous amount of new legislation appertaining to employment law but it was as nothing compared to the mid-sixties to the mid-seventies all of which was to effect Jack in ways he could not have imagined!) The first of the laws to really effect employment was :*(I have listed all of the significant ones below to illustrate just how much was passed and why it was to have such an effect on Jack in his role of Group Training Officer, but you don't have to learn them!)*

The Industrial Training Act 1964—set up the Board for which Jack worked in N Ireland, an appeals process to a Tribunal and, indirectly, the Group Training Association for which he worked from 1971—1978

The Redundancy Payments Act 1965
The Equal Pay Act 1970
The Industrial Relations Act 1971
The Contracts of Employment Act 1972
The Health and Safety at Work etc. Act 1973
The Trade Union and Labour Relations Act 1974
The Sex Discrimination Act 1975
The Race Discrimination Act 1976

(The Disability Discrimination Act didn't come in until 1995—so much for concern for the disadvantaged in society, like Jack's daughter! Followed by religion and age, the last of which came in and out again in the 21ˢᵗ century!)

Jack's direct involvement started one day when he was visiting one of the smaller members of the Group. They had been talking about equal pay and sex discrimination and the owner had asked Jack just how you would prove that you hadn't discriminated on the grounds of sex when offering someone a job. Jack thought about for the moment and then said, "Well, you'd have to be able to show that the person you offered it to was the best one applying and that would mean being able to show the records of those selected for interview and their interview records to show the best one had been selected."

There was a long silence and the guy then said, "What interview records?"

Jack realised that this wasn't the facetious reply that it sounded, it meant that there were no records because he didn't keep any. Not too difficult to understand why, he only employed five machinists and three of them had been there for years.

"Can I see the Personnel Records that you keep?"

"Sure." At which he reached into a desk drawer and pulled out an old-fashioned school exercise book. Jack caught a glimpse of some other, older and tattier ones underneath. There was a name per page with the very basic details, name, address, NI number, phone number and references to the rate of pay, whether they paid the full stamp or not and other odd bits of info.

Handing it back, Jack said, "Right, we need to set up a system, hopefully only one page per person interviewed/employed which will contain all you need to know plus be a record in case it should hit the fan later." Picking up his pen and pad from his brief case Jack quickly sketched out a document. The first third or so would act as an application form with basic questions, name address, age little bit about previous jobs, titles and wage/salary. Jack asked what else do you ask and the guy quoted a couple of questions which Jack added. Then the second third (running over to the other side of the page) Jack set out a basic interview sheet listing appearance, punctuality, claimed experience and again added a couple more points that the guy made.

Jack also added boxes for the colour-blindness test (Ishihara) and the eyesight test both of which Jack recommended. Later Jack was to add a space for the trainability assessment he had learned from the Industrial Training Research Unit at Cambridge which he had first come across in Londonderry but which he had not yet introduced to the Group. The final third of the page was given over to recording any information not already included above such as pay, sick pay, promotions and any special training or skills learned during employment.

"Now you need to get someone to type that up for you and produce a few copies. Then it is a question of keeping them. Use something like a clip file and file all those you take on in it. For applicants who you don't interview at all just write on the application why not, lives too far away, no previous experience, wants too much money or whatever the reason is; don't, obviously write anything discriminatory down like 'woman wants a man's job' or anything racial because they would be illegal and then put them in a file cover with the date on the outside and perhaps the job title applied for.

"You can also file there the application form/letter and completed interview section with the marks awarded, I would suggest marks out of ten, for the no-argument issues like punctually, appearance etc for those unsuccessful applicants and keep them for at least seven months—applicants to tribunal must normally do so in three months but for discrimination issues they have six months to make a claim. That's the least I think you could do and obviously if rejected people have higher scores than anyone offered a job you will be in trouble. What do you think?"

"Well, it's a right pain in the arse having to do it but I can see that with only one piece of paper bunged in a file, winners or losers, it won't be much of a problem." They carried on discussing matters and Jack eventually left and went home. He did not expect, at the Exec Committee in two weeks' time, that the subject would come up with two of the members asking him to do a similar exercise for them! A quick survey around the committee showed considerable interest and it was only a couple of weeks after that that Jack had put together a one-day course the uptake of which involved every company in the Group apart from the one he had produced the form in the first place. This movement into Personnel, rather than training, was to provide Jack with the experience and knowledge which enabled him to obtain the next job in his career.

Jack had been with the Group for nearly six years and during that time it had grown from the original 20 companies employing 2000 people to 36 employing over 6000. Some of them, the large ones, were associate members paying a relatively small annual fee but also a fee it they wished to send someone on one of the courses. The courses ranged from the very first instructor one to senior management/owner ones—most of those being run at weekends, when the individuals were free to attend, and using input from the Clothing and Allied Industries Training Board where appropriate.

There were now 12 Groups throughout the country and the Group Training Officers had formed an association, electing Jack as their chairman, to liaise with the Board on matters of mutual interest. From the press and the Board, he became aware that the Board was increasingly worried that employers nationally were becoming concerned about the working of the Boards and the Levy/Grant system. At the beginning it had been relatively simple for Jack to reclaim the Levy for the Group members and even to make a slight profit for most of them.

The Boards were funded from their Levy imposition of the companies within scope of that Board and, as more and more employers had reclaimed the Levy for the training, they had carried out so the amount available had decreased. Boards had largely achieved their basic remit and the businesses had improved their training systems enormously. However, the Boards kept looking at new areas and there weren't any that most of their clients wanted them to look at. Boards were made up of one third employers, one third unions and one third academics.

The attendance by the employer reps while good at the start had started tailing off. Consequently, some of the grants were union and academia inspired and loathed by the employers, for example within the clothing industry their Board had introduced a requirement that employers had to release younger employees for further education courses at Colleges of FE, to improve their education and employability. All well and good but in practical terms it meant that a 17-year-old girl had to be released to college to study hairdressing AND TO BE PAID FOR THAT RELEASE by their employer!

Jack's Group were incensed by this, to be released for a designer course, mechanic or something related to their industry was fair enough but this was too far! And Jack was getting it in the ear at every company he visited. It was not surprising therefore that employer groups around the country were forming to agitate to the Conservatives to do away with the Training Boards when they got into power at the next election (they hoped!). Jack thought about it and came to the conclusion that if that happened it would not be too long before Group members started looking at what they were paying to be members and that this would go up by 25% due to the loss of the Training Board contribution to Jack's salary. It was an industry which was starting to struggle in the face of cheap imports from Asian and Far East imports and therefore the future was starting to look a little bleak—time to start looking and move on. And that is just what he did.

Chapter 22

The advert appeared in the Daily Telegraph in the jobs' page on a Thursday. It said they were seeking to recruit a Personnel and Training Manager for a new position. It was a wholesale, retail and cash and carry operation in the grocery trade. Based in Wellingborough in Northamptonshire the company sites were spread over East Anglia and the South East of England. Amongst the qualifications listed was a degree. Jack didn't have one but if British Oxygen regarded his commission as being equivalent to one (he had been approached by them through Officers' Records when due out of the Army) why should he argue so he wrote off. As it was the first application, he had made he did not really expect to be in with a chance but he received an invitation to an interview so he went!

The Army had taught him the value of reconnaissance and although not quite the same thing he thought it might be a good idea if he went to the library and looked at what they might have about the company. It was the first time that Jack had ever done such a thing and was quite amazed at what a very helpful Librarian was able to dig up for him. When he arrived at their offices in Cambridge house, five minutes early as per Army rules, he was after only 10 minutes shown into the MD's office. He introduced himself and the other man present who was introduced as the Financial Director. After the pleasantries the first question asked of Jack was, "What do you know about Terry Linehams?" The name of the company.

"Well, you are structured through three main operating divisions, retail about 40 shops, cash and carry's 14 C&Cs and 4 distribution depots delivering to about a 1000 Spar stores. Head Office here in Wellingborough, 650 staff and £80 million turnover last year. You are growing, have never had a dedicated Personnel and Training function before and you have just lost an Industrial Tribunal." The two of them exchanged glances, only later did Jack discover that no-one else interviewed had been able to describe the company in that detail—the advert had described the three divisions but not the numbers.

He was immediately asked what he knew about the Industrial Tribunal and could only tell them the name of the Applicant and the fact that they had lost on the grounds of unfair dismissal. He was told that it was going to appeal and they had every expectation of winning. (In fact Jack was to attend the Appeal Hearing at the Employment Appeals Tribunal and listen to the case whilst still working his notice with the Training Group. Linehams did win it and it became of immense value to Jack over the succeeding years because it set the rules for Incapability Dismissals rather than Disciplinary ones.) The interview seemed to go well as far as Jack was concerned although the Financial Director seemed a bit off.

About 10 days later he received a letter offering him the job.

He started at the beginning of November 1978. Although he didn't know it, he was going to be there for the next 10 years and achieve quite extraordinary results. The beginning was far more humble. He was given a clapped out old 1100cc Ford Escort until his Cortina 1.6L Estate came through—it was supposed to be a waiting list of only six weeks but in the event, it was more than three months. Originally it was to be a saloon but he had persuaded them that he would be travelling between the more major units to run training courses and would need the extra carrying space of an Estate.

They had agreed but would not upgrade it to a GL 2.0litre to match his car at the Group. He would in the future be given responsibility for introducing a car policy at his next job and the sensitivities he experienced in this one was to stand him in good stead.

In the Training Board he had only advised companies what to do about training, in the Group he had been much closer to implementation but still advising, in this new role he was to be responsible and would be able to actually put into practice ideas he had developed.

Initially he spent time in the Head Office where he was provided with an office, something not too usual as most of the building, a purpose built one, modern, sleek and clean, very much unlike most the clothing industry that he had worked in for most of the last 10 years. He got his own office because he would be interviewing people either for employment, disciplinary or promotion and that needed to be done in private. Secretarial services were provided by the Financial Director's secretary.

Nominal hours were 9 to 5.30 Monday to Friday but when travelling to sites the days could be much longer as Jack had practiced arriving at sites to be visited at opening time and depending just how much he was to do there leaving at finishing time. In the Group, spread generally quite close around Nottingham, this had been no hardship but now with sites the other side of London and with London to cross—the M25 was years away—it made for some very long and hard days.

Initially Jack visited the four main distribution depots and several of the bigger Cash & Carrys. The retail shops, mainly under the Spar logo but including several other names which had been taken over when the previous owner failed (running a successful grocery, tobacconist and confectionery shop was not as easy as it seemed!) but the names had not yet been changed. The common denominator was, of course, people although the rules applying to their employment differed enormously dependent on whether they were covered by the Retail Wages Council or the Wholesale Grocery Joint Industrial Council.

Both bodies set rules for minimum wage, holidays, sick pay, overtime and some other rules. Following the election of a Labour Government after the war, the unions, whose baby the Labour Party was, demanded payment. In many industries the unions had been unable to organise effectively to negotiate on behalf of members within them.

For example, hairdresser shops rarely employed more than two or three hairdressers and the first one to complain about pay and conditions and 'we should join a union' very rapidly found themself out on the street with their belongings in one hand and a P45 in the other. The unions came up with the idea of a wages council which would be made up of employers in that industry, academics and unions. (Yes, the model for what later became the Training Boards!).

The decisions of that council would have the effect of law and would set at least minimum pay, usually as an hourly rate and per age range, when overtime started and the minimum rate for it, in the week, on Saturday and Sunday, sick pay and maybe some other factors peculiar to that particular industry. It was always open to employers to pay more but they could not pay less than the minimum. In Jack's case the retail shops came under the Retail Wages Council. Many if not most employers hated this form of compulsion because the balance of power sat with unions and academics with the employers unable to do anything to prevent stupid decisions. Theoretically there was an appeal to a

Government Minister but it was very unlikely that an appeal by an employer against union and academics would be successful.

Other industries viewed the goings on with considerable suspicion and trepidation starting with sheer incompetence through to communism by another name, so before a Wages Council could be foisted on them, they set up their own organisations to do the same thing but better. These were called Joint Industrial Councils, in Jack's case, for the Wholesale Grocery and Provisions Trade. The Council was made up of employer and union representatives, equal numbers on each side with each side electing its own chairman, secretary and member for an Executive Committee. Companies could join or not as they wished but if they did not, they faced the risk of a Wages Council with the three party control.

As a result, the vast majority of the companies joined voluntarily. It still set minimum pay, sick pay etc but the negotiations each year took place between the employers and unions within that industry and they managed to reach agreement each year, sometimes happily sometimes not so happily until the last year when Jack led as Chairman for the Employers' side and agreement was not reached of which more anon!

The 'contractual' employment paperwork, in his new employer, varied from non-existent to abysmal. Records were nominally kept at each site for that site and it was patently obvious that it needed sorting and quickly. The Contracts of Employment Act 1972 had nothing, actually, to do with contracts of employment save for that an employee should receive a Contract of Employment STATEMENT of Main Terms and Conditions(it wasn't itself a contract!) within a certain period of starting and that there should be certain statutory notice periods.

Jack started in 1978, only 6 years after the Act, and not even a nodding attention had been paid to it. The first stage for him was to get copies of the Retail Wages Council and Wholesale Grocery JIC details and swot up on them. Linehams had made the first steps into using word processors which gave Jack a huge flexibility hitherto unavailable. He was determined to produce the necessary documentation to meet the requirements of the law, the company's needs and what would be the best procedure to implement and issue them using as little paperwork as possible. It was quite clear immediately that he would not be able to produce a one page document to cover all eventualities as he had done in the Group Training Assoc., a few years before.

He arrived at a number of documents as an absolute minimum. He would need:

* A generic handbook covering the company as a whole;
* A Statement of Main Terms and Conditions of Employment for retail staff;
* A Statement of Main Terms and Conditions of Employment for Cash & Carry staff;
* A Statement of Main Terms and Conditions of Employment for Wholesale Distribution staff; and
* A Statement of Main Terms and Conditions of Employment for Salaried staff—he hoped he could get away with just one of them with the addition of standard paragraphs for variances between the different sectors for example an Appendix for those issued with company cars.

He also needed to consider how he would operate the Personnel Records system. From what he had seen in the first few sites he visited the system was a shambles. Most of them had been taken over and no attempt had been made to standardise documentation whatsoever. It took very little thought to decide that the records should be held at Head Office. The issue was how should that be done and again it took little thought to go back to the original document he set up for the Training Group members; he needed a single sheet of paper that acted as the application form for the first third, the interview record for the second third and the employment details for the third—the third could also be used to notify changes to the record e.g., new married name, new address etc.

This form would be used to create a file in Personnel and the Wages Department. Jack intended they should be printed self-carbonating so that the underneath, second copy could be kept on site for their records. In getting to know the new company it became obvious that the one department every single employee notified of changes was the Wages Department—people always made sure of that so that they got paid! Jack used that to keep his Personnel Records up to date when they were computerised years later.

He collected a set of documents into a folder and had a fancy cover put on it with a clear see through cover over that, produced a copy for every director and attended a Board meeting to put his proposals to them. He was greeted with complete silence when he finished his delivery and it went on so long that he was just starting to get worried when the MD said, "Bloody brilliant, get on with it."

A couple of days later Jack was called to the MD's office. The MD said, "What I'm about to tell you is ultra-confidential and is known only to you and me. I am about to be promoted to Group (the holding company) to head up an acquisitions and development team. The announcement won't be made for another 10 days or so. I want you to know that I have been very impressed by the way you have performed since you joined us two months ago. I do not imagine you will have any problems with the new MD, who will be announced in a week or so, but in the very unlikely event that you should do so give me a quiet bell, here's my private line number, and I will sort it out. You are looking puzzled (Jack was!); you weren't everybody's first choice for the job let me say so if there is a problem let me know. Understood?"

"Yes, and thank you very much."

"Now the official reason I asked you here; you know from what you identified as a problem in the handbook that we do not have a standard pension scheme. Almost every company or shop we have taken over have different terms, pay holidays etc as you have sorted in the recommended standard documents you put to the Board the other day. With pensions it's even a bigger bloody mess as you have already identified. We have been working on that but it's highly sensitive so that has been done for us by an outside body. I want you to ring this guy, (he handed over a card) and arrange to go and see him in the next day or so, at his premises, and ask any questions or point out any problems that you can see with the draft scheme."

At that he handed Jack a file with a mound of paper in it along with a booklet headed 'Pension Scheme Draft'. Then prepare a paper for a special Board meeting I am calling for a week from now before I move on. Any questions?"

"No, but I might have once I've read this lot—can I come and speak to you before I see this guy?"

"Only if you absolutely have to. It's all pretty straightforward and I've got an awful lot to do so try and sort it yourself—I'm sure you'll be able to."

"Ok," said Jack and left.

As he walked back to his office, he was thinking only the MD and the FD were involved in interviewing me which means that I was not the FD's first choice and more worryingly, he's going to be the new MD or otherwise why warn me off? Oh, great he thought, two months here, no protection for unfair dismissal for nearly a year yet—absolutely bloody great. Still the MD had made a clear offer to support him so let's hope it's going to be ok he thought.

A week later the MD and FD disappeared off to a Board meeting. Jack knew why and listened amusedly to the speculation as to why both Directors had disappeared to a Group Board meeting. No-one was kept in suspense for long because, on their return, everyone was called together and the MD announced he was moving on and the FD would be the new MD. The place was buzzing for the rest of the afternoon with speculation but by the following morning the new regime was in place and it was as though that had always been the situation.

At ten o'clock, Jack was sent for by the MD. It seemed funny to see him sitting in his new office and it had crossed Jack's mind a few times during the previous few days as to who would be the new FD and if he, Jack, would still continue to report to him or her. He was not left in doubt for long.

Having gone through the social pleasantries, the MD announced, "Jack, you were not my first choice for the job; I favoured another of the short list of three. However, I was wrong; I have been very impressed at the speed at which you have settled in and what you have achieved in that time. I was particularly delighted to report to the Holding Board yesterday that not only had we not paid any Training Levy to the Distributive Industry Training Board but that you had even achieved a small payment back from them.

"In two months, you have achieved more than all the other Personnel people in the Group companies have done, most of them having been in post for years. Well, done. I want you to keep that up and continue to report to me; you will not report to the new FD, whoever that might be, but you will be, with me, setting out a recruitment programme for that post and some others we'll talk about over the coming days. Now, what have you got for me regarding the suggested pension scheme?"

One of the reasons Jack had decided it was time to move on was he was now 34 and there was absolutely no chance that the Training Group would provide a pension and he knew enough about the subject to know that the longer he was in one the better it would be. The proposed scheme he had been asked to look at was a final salary scheme which meant that a scheme member would 'earn' $1/60^{th}$ of their final salary for each year they were in the scheme. In Jack's case that meant 31/60ths, or just over half of his final salary as a company pension. He would also receive a pension from the state which meant a very comfortable retirement. There were all sorts of funnies in the way it was calculated, it wasn't the actual final salary that would be used but an averaging system to give the best figure and even then, it was the 60ths of 2/3rds of the final pensionable salary, but overall, it was a good scheme and he welcomed it. He said so.

He was then asked how he recommended that it should be announced to the staff. The problem was that they had 41 retail shops, most of them with only a tiny staff, 14 C&Cs with as few as 20 and as many as 120 staff and the 4 distribution depots had more than 150 staff each making 650 in total. With some 61 sites in total, including HO and a petrol station in Northampton which had been picked up along the way somehow, it did not seem logical to Jack that he could visit every site and deliver a number of talks in each one—they could not shut down for him to do this in one go—so there had to be a way to deliver it more robustly.

The retails shops could probably be done by getting the Managers together for half a day, training them and then sending them back to their stores to deliver to their staff. The large distribution depots would have to be done as perhaps three or four talks in each in one day making four days and then the smaller C&Cs done the same as the retail shops and a two part delivery in half a day at the larger ones.

For the scheme to be viable a large percentage of the staff had to join—this had been made clear in the paperwork with which Jack had been provided. He suggested the programme he had outlined since he didn't believe there would be much of a take up if the announcement of the scheme was done by some sort of memo or letter. The MD said to leave it with him for a few days and he would get back to Jack.

Jack thought about it a bit and then sat down and planned a programme whereby he would talk at the significant sites about the new Contract of Employment Statements and the pension scheme at the same time. It would be virtually the same delivery to the collections of managers of the smaller units except they would have to return to their units and do the delivery of the talk to their own staff. When he took the plan to the MD it was instantly approved. There were always the few smart arses who refused to sign the 'new contract' even though Jack pointed out that they were not signing that they agreed it, only for receipt.

Jack made it abundantly clear that since the documents only set out on paper the conditions they were already working under, and that, by continuing working they indicated that they had accepted the conditions, there were still a few who would not sign. So, Jack had a form printed which said 'I refuse to sign for receipt' and got most of them to sign that! For those that still wouldn't, and there were a few, Jack signed on the form Mr So and So refused to sign for the Statement that was handed to him and stuck that in their file anyway. He was never to have any sort of comeback. More than 77% of the staff offered the pension scheme accepted it which went down well with the MD since the highest uptake in the other Group companies was 58%!

The pension scheme was to come back again and again over the rest of Jack's working life, partially because every six months or so the company expanded by taking over others and partially by a succession of governments mucking about with pensions, so much so that there were more laws passed relating to just pensions than that list of employment legislation quoted above. In one job Jack was to have to talk to trunker drivers at 2am in the morning as that was the only time, they were in the depot—trying to be enthusiastic at that time was somewhat difficult!

There is almost a standard saying in life that things come in threes but it isn't strictly true, if nothing else because it depends when you start counting and stop, but it was to seem that the rule of threes particularly applied to problems needing sorting at the same time.

Chapter 23

Three problems landed on Jack's desk within the space of three days. The General Manager at the Distribution Warehouse near Orpington rang regarding a problem with a female member of staff, the Manager of the C&C just outside Hastings rang with a problem with a male member of staff who would not wear his uniform coat and the Manager at one of the retail shops, also in Hastings, who had a member of staff who refused to fill shelves because the tins were too heavy.

The female, Orpington, one sounded worse and worse as the manager recounted the tale. She had worked for the company for 14 years. No formal disciplinary action had ever been taken against her but there had been a number of informal warnings for time keeping, absenteeism and quality of her work. Each time she had improved for a short while but the process then started over again. Whether she knew her Supervisor was about to move into the formal system that afternoon was not known. But that morning she had stood up and announced to all and sundry in the office, about 11 of them, that if she should faint her Doctor had said that the length of time she was unconscious should be recorded! She then sat down and carried on with her work as though nothing untoward had happened. "What should he do?" The Manager asked.

Jack hadn't the faintest idea (no pun intended!) *If in doubt, ask questions to give yourself time to think*, thought Jack, so he did. Whilst he gained some background information that didn't help, but the Manager did tell him that she worked in a general office in the warehouse, a very old one, which was up a steep stone staircase about 16 feet up. Fainting at your desk whilst sitting down was unlikely to be too dangerous, even if somewhat unpleasant and worrying, but fainting at the top of those steps and tumbling to the bottom was likely to be very dangerous, potentially even fatal.

Therefore, it could not be ignored. Not knowing the site, not having been there yet, Jack could understand the Manager's concern so he asked, "Do you have any one a bit more than a trained first aider at the site, perhaps a nurse?"

"No, the first aider we do have is on holiday at the moment."

"How many staff work at that site?"

"About half of them." *I am going to like this guy,* thought Jack, *not a lot but I do like him.*

"Okay the old ones are the funniest—how many are employed there?"

"Just over 250."

"Well, as an aside, you should have more than one first aider but that's for another time. Do you have an Auntie Nellie, an older woman that they all go to with problems?"

"Well, there is Doris in Accounts that the women seem to go to, even some of the men sometimes."

"Could you ask her to take this girl aside, what was it, Melanie, and ask her what this is all about? I don't think we should be talking about a man asking her at this stage; what do you think?"

"Why do you think it's something to do with women's problems then?"

"I don't know," said Jack, "but fainting comes about from shock, the sight of blood, loss of blood excitement/stress on meeting the Beetles and what else?"

"No idea, I assume you want me to do that now?"

"The problem's not going to go away, is it?"

"Ok I'll ring you back."

As soon as he put the phone down it rang and it was the manager at the Hastings C&C to say that a member of staff wouldn't wear the new uniform coat that had just been issued to him. Throughout the Company it ranged from no uniforms at all to different ones at different sites depending on what they wore before Linehams had taken them over. A number of designs and colours had been provided to the old MD but he had done nothing about it. The new one dumped the lot on Jack's desk and told him to sort it. Jack just called a number of staff in from the General Office, most of whom had worked in one of the retail or C&C sites and asked them to choose.

It was pretty well unanimous, they went for the plain Burgundy coat for the men and a white background, cross check in black, burgundy and yellow with Burgundy collar, cuffs and pocket tops for the women. Jack felt that if he put it out to full consultation he would get as many choices as the number of people he asked. Whatever he did would have some come back and with so much work to do with the introduction of the Contract Statements and pensions stuff he thought, 'stuff it—send order sheets for sizes and male and females with a few replacements as a reserve and get them issued.' The orders had started arriving in the stores about 10 days before and this was the first problem that had arisen.

"Why won't he wear it?"

"He says he's a pacifist and doesn't believe in wearing uniforms."

"How long has he worked for us?"

"Just under four months."

"What's his work like, is he in a union, is he an ethnic minority, has he had any previous disciplinary warnings and is he pregnant?"

"He's definitely not pregnant, he's barely ok as a worker, not in a union to my knowledge and no previous formal warnings but there have been a few informals for two absences on a Monday, timekeeping, late back from tea break, that sort of thing. And he's white and rather posh."

"One final question, has he worn a uniform before?"

"We never had them before."

"Got a pen and paper to hand?"

"Ready."

Dear Mr Smifff,

Since you have failed to obey a reasonable order from your Manager you are suspended with immediate effect.

You will be notified of the time and date of a disciplinary hearing to examine the matter. At that hearing you have the right to be accompanied or represented by a fellow employee of your choice; you have the right to state your case and you have the right to appeal against the decision I take.

You will be asked if you will obey the order to wear your protective coat and if you say no your employment will be summarily terminated without notice or payment in lien and any accrued holiday pay will be forfeit. If you agree to obey the order it will result in a Final Written Warning being issued to you which will lapse after 12 months providing there has been no further incidence of indiscipline.

Yours sincerely.

"And copy it to me. OK?"

"That seems a bit harsh."

"Not really. He has refused a legitimate order. If he decides to comply then he'll have a final written warning for the refusal which will lapse providing he doesn't do it again which he isn't likely to do but if he does, he's out. It will show the rest of the staff that refusal to obey a reasonable, lawful instruction costs you your job and he's the first one in the company to refuse. Getting the elbow will send a strong message to all the others that wearing it is a jolly good idea. And from what you've said he won't be much of a loss anyway."

Jack was thinking of his policy of getting rid a wrong 'un, a weak link, asap, but he would not say that to the Manager. "Make sure you have a witness with you when you hand him the letter and then get him straight out of the C&C. OK? Let me know when you are going to do the hearing and I will make sure that I am available on the phone if you need to speak to me. Never be afraid to suspend a hearing while you think about it and then reconvene when ready."

No sooner had Jack put the phone down and it rang, this time from the Manager at a Hasting's Spar shop. She introduced herself and then explained that she had a female member of staff who was refusing to fill shelves with stock on the basis that the outers of beans or vegetables or other tins were too heavy for a woman. The Manager did not accept that as the outer boxes were wheeled to the aisle and set down on the floor from goods-in by, as it happens a woman, they were then opened and the tins placed individually in their place on the shelves so the actual weight being lifted was less than a pound.

"Has she done this work before?"

"Yes, a bit, but she was mainly on the main till but the till was often down on cashing up, nothing very much at one time but building to a total of between £8 and £10 per week. As there could have been a number of people on the till during a shift it is impossible to pin down whether it is simple mistakes in giving change or someone helping themself to a bonus each week, I can't prove it but I think it is down to her so I moved her off the till and have had her filling up, facing up etc."

"Well, two things, you need to change your till procedures so that the till is totalled up every time there is a change of operator. The second is have you put all of the till operators to facing up or just her?"

"Just her."

"So, you suspect she is the thief?"

"Well, err, yes."

"Why?"

"Because the other two have been with me a long while and there was never a problem until she started."

"Ok. How long has she worked for us?"

"Nearly three years."

"And have you suspected her for all of this time?"

"Pretty well. The losses started about two weeks after she started. There are always some problems with balancing the till but if it's due to genuine mistakes then the till should be up as much as it should be down. With her it's always down."

"But if there are others on the till, does that include you as well?"

"Yes, sometimes if the operator has popped to the loo or something like that and a customer needs serving but not for any period of time."

"So apart from the fact that the losses started after she started what evidence do you have it's her."

"Just a feeling."

"Ok, that's not enough to justify sacking her; we'd lose hands down at Tribunal. Let me think about it and ring you back in a few minutes."

As soon as he put the phone down it rang. It was the manager from the Hastings C&C to say that he had handed the suspension letter to the lad and he had stormed out in a huff shouting, 'my Mum's a solicitor and you'll be hearing from her.' Jack said, "Let me know if you do—don't say anything to her at all, just refer her to me."

Jack didn't expect to hear anything more but he was wrong in that. In the meantime, he sat and considered what to do about the woman refusing to fill shelves. There wasn't a problem about the refusal; but there was a problem about the security of the tills and for that he needed to speak to the Director of Security. He was an ex-police Detective Inspector, a Scotsman known as Taffy. Jack didn't ask! He made it clear that although the instructions were that all tills should be 'zedded'—terminology for returned to zero at the end of the particular operator's shift—the reality was that in small stores it was impractical although it was enforced strictly in the C&Cs where the sums of money in the till were hugely larger and therefore losses potentially much larger.

Taffy offered to send one of his Security Officers into the store on a 'routine visit' which Jack accepted and they agreed the visit would be on the following day. However, nothing was to come of it. Jack rang the Manager at the store and told her that he had not been able to find anything that said women should not be asked to lift weights just that they should not be excessive; there were rules laid down in the Factory's Act but they clearly did not apply here and even then, they were considerably higher than one pound. He then set out the same procedure as he had for the lad at the C&C refusing a reasonable management instruction and dictated the same letter again. He also asked about what had happened about shortages since she had been taken off the till—a question he should have asked originally. Pretty well nil was the answer he got.

When he put the phone down it rang immediately again, this time the General Manager from the Orpington Depot to tell him of the conversation between the Aunty Nellie and the fainting girl. In apparently some distress the girl had told her that she was experiencing very severe bleeds during her period and had told the Doctor that she felt faint during those times hence the instruction about timing the faint. Jack thought about it for a moment and then said, "Right, we need that confirming by her Doctor. Get a letter typed up to the Doctor explaining that the girl is an employee of ours and a patient of his, explain what we have been told, explain that she works up a steep, stone set of steps and ask about safety, how long the problem is likely to last etc. Type up another letter, again addressed to the Doctor but this time from her authorising him to speak to us. Get her to sign it and you sign the other one and get them off as quick as you can—deliver them by hand if you can. Then produce a third letter to the girl saying that in view of her situation, don't spell it out, which makes it dangerous for her to work at the moment she is being suspended on medical grounds, on normal pay, send her home, someone with her if you think it necessary. Fax me copies of all three please."

"Christ, am I glad you're dealing with this," he said.

"I'm not," said Jack, "you are I'm just dictating letters!" In the event all three of them blew up over the next couple of days; the mother was indeed a solicitor and was on the phone to the C&C Manager, the mother and father of the Shop Assistant were, one a Union Regional Officer with ASTMS and one an Union Area Official with the ASLEF; and the Doctor phoned Jack to say that the fainting girl had been into his surgery and instructed him not to answer the questions in the company's letter. Jack thought, that's nearly as good as being back on the streets in Aden without ammunition but not quite as bad as approaching a Morris 1000 to see if there was a bomb in it though! It was not surprising therefore that Jack found himself on the way to Orpington two days later with meetings set up for the fainting girl in the afternoon and the conscientious objector and the weight lifter refuser the day after that.

It had been quite a good drive down through London, just after the morning rush timed to get him there for noon with the meeting with the girl at 2pm. However, life being what it is as he turned off the main road into the industrial estate a lorry in front of him threw a half brick, which had been lodged between two rear off-side wheels, into his windscreen which immediately smashed, and turned opaque with extremely limited visibility.

Jack had had a similar thing happen to him before when he was driving in the dark down a country lane into Belfast and then his immediate reaction had been to punch a hole through the screen to enable him to see. Big mistake. For the rest of his journey pieces flew from the edge of the hole and he ended up wearing sun glasses in the dark to protect his eyes—bad all-round! Then he had swapped cars with a colleague and driven back to Londonderry in his car while Jack's had been repaired. Besides the inconvenience and visibility problems he learned that a broken screen shed bits into the heater system which threw them out at a rate of knots in small, dangerous pieces for the rest of the time he owned the car.

So, this time, being daylight anyway he was able to see enough to drive slowly the remainder of the way to the depot without knocking a hole in it. While he did his business at the depot a windscreen repair company, with whom they had a contract for all the cars, vans and lorries was prevailed upon to come out immediately and repair it on site.

After that it went from bad to worse! The girl had sent a message in that she could not attend the Depot because she was too unwell but Jack could go to her home if he wanted. Jack did not want to! But having driven the best part of a hundred miles and for three hours he had to see her. It turned out that she only lived a few hundred yards from the Depot, so, taking the female Supervisor of her office with him, Jack found himself knocking on her door at 2pm.

The walk had been interesting as the Supervisor had opened up to him about the girl and her family as being a right weird lot. The two parents, the girl and her brother went to Butlin's every year sharing a one bedroom chalet. Jack didn't think that odd, he had often shared with his parents and sister but it was when the Supervisor said that the four of them shared the one bedroom in their three bedroomed house that it did start to sound a little weird. She was apparently a very talented trombone player and had won a few competitions at Butlin's and her brother played a triangle to accompany her.

They arrived before any more could be revealed only to discover that the girl would not let the Supervisor in but would allow Jack, insisting even, that he come in. Jack did not want to. He would have no witness and he wasn't sure if the girl was alone. *Rules are for the guidance of wise men and the observance of idiots*, thought Jack, as he sent the Supervisor back to the Depot, and the idiot is me! He wasn't even sure he should ask how she was given the nature of the alleged problem so he started with, "I understand that you told your Doctor that you were withdrawing his permission to answer my questions. Is that correct?"

"Yes," she said.

"Why is that?" asked Jack?

"Because it is too embarrassing."

"Okay," said Jack, "but if your Doctor doesn't speak to me I have almost nothing to go on. All I know is that you warned people that there was a risk of you fainting and I am told that if that happened at the top of the stairs up to your office there is a risk of you falling and not just injuring yourself but even of you being killed. How can I allow that situation to continue? I can't so unless I know how real that risk is I cannot allow you to work…" At that the girl burst into tears and sobbed, "You're going to sack me after all these years."

"I didn't say that. I said I cannot allow the risk to go unassessed." At that moment the front door opened and a woman appeared at the door to the lounge where they were sitting. The girl immediately leapt up and rushed over to her sobbing, He's going to sack me, Mum."

The girl was about 5ft 10inches tall and her mother just about 5ft so that the girl putting her head on her Mum's shoulder was bent almost in two, very bizarre and the looks the mother was giving him would easily have peeled paint off the Mona Lisa. Jack said, "That's not correct, I have just said that I cannot allow her to return to work until the risk she presents is quantified. I cannot do that without a Doctor's opinion and since she has refused to allow her Doctor to talk to me I will have to take a decision based on what I know and that is very little. What I do know says she cannot return until I know more."

"What will you do if you do know more?"

"That depends on what it is. If she is likely to get better quite soon then she will be suspended for medical reasons until she is better, if she is not going to get better or it will be a very long time then she may be paid off." At the word 'paid' the woman's face lit up.

"Go and make us all a nice cup of tea," said the woman. "How much would she be paid?"

"Well, I can't tell you exactly but she is entitled to 12 weeks' notice and since she clearly cannot work it that would be paid in lieu. She has…" At that the girl came in with a tray on which was a tea pot, two cup, a small pot of milk and a bottle of pills.

Putting it down the girl said, "I haven't brought a cup for myself because I am going to kill myself." At which she picked up the bottle of pills, took off the lid and poured the lot into her hand.

"Don't be silly dear," said the mother, "give them to me," and took them from her. "Now you were saying how much she would get," she said to Jack.

"Well, as I said, 12 weeks' pay in lieu of notice, she has 4 week's accrued holiday…" the girl got up and walked, almost ran out of the room, "pay and she may have some accrued from this year." At that the girl rushed back into the room with a huge carving knife in her hand and screamed, "I am going to kill myself," and at that slashed the back of her left wrist. Jack and her mother both grabbed her and for a few minutes all hell was let loose with the three of them flailing about and sending the tea and the furniture flying. Jack had managed to grab the knife hand in his right hand but the corner of the blade was digging into his little finger, cutting into the scar from when he had jumped into the barbed wire during training in the Army.

The mother grabbed the girl by her head and was shouting, "Stop it, stop it." Gradually the struggling stopped and the girl released the knife into Jack's hand which by now was quite covered in blood. The girl rushed out of the room. Jack didn't care where she'd gone and if she had gone to get a gun to shoot herself, he would quite happily have loaded it for her. He took a handkerchief out of his pocket and wrapped it round his finger at the same time saying to the mother, "Your daughter is clearly very sick. You need to get her to a Doctor as soon as possible. I will write to her, copy to you, terminating her employment for medical grounds."

"Will you let her come back when she's better?" Jack was pretty astounded at that and had to think for a minute.

"If she gets better and provides a medical report to that end then I will consider it but I make no promises. For now, I need to get this hand attended to at the Depot. Goodbye." At the Depot the General Manager sent for the First Aider who applied antiseptic to the quite deep cut and a couple of butterfly pressure plasters to hold the cut together and seal it up. When he finished telling the tale the GM said to him, "And what if she does apply to come back?"

Jack said, "I told the mother I would consider any application and I have; she's not coming back and make sure you never have a vacancy if she applies!"

Jack finished his other business at the Depot and as soon as his car was repaired, he drove to his hotel for the night. Quite a day he thought broken windscreen and a cut finger. He'd been closer to bare steel that afternoon than he ever had in eight years of Army service!

The following morning, he arrived at the C&C at 8am as it opened. He had arranged for the disciplinary hearing to be heard at 8.30am and, while he had most of the information, he needed, he needed to prepare the Manager for his role, which he did.

At 8.30am, Mr Smifff arrived but he was not alone. He was accompanied by his mother. After the introductions in the Manager's office Jack explained to her that she had no right to attend or represent her son but he was confident in their company procedures and he was prepared to allow her to sit in and listen, providing she did not interrupt, and he would give her the opportunity to say anything she wanted to say before he adjourned to take his decision. He also explained that normally the C&C Manager would conduct the hearing but as it was him her son had refused the order from Jack was going to conduct it on the grounds of fairness. At that he asked the Manager to describe what had happened when the lad refused which he did. Jack then asked the lad if that was an accurate description of the event. The lad replied, "More or less."

"Which bit was less?"

"Well, yes, it is correct." Jack turned to the Manager and said, "Tell me about Mr Smifff's work record."

"He joined us exactly four months ago, since then he has been late five times, not too seriously—about five or six minutes each time; he has been spoken to informally several times about being late back from tea breaks or lunch and he has been absent 3 times, twice on a Monday and once a Friday." Jack knew this because he had been through it with the Manager earlier but his mother obviously didn't because she was looking daggers at her son.

"Leaving aside the issue of the uniform for a moment, is that record correct?" asked Jack. The lad didn't answer. "I'll take that as a yes," said Jack. "I'm not at all impressed with that record and I have to say if you worked for me, you would have been long gone. Now you did refuse to wear the coat, didn't you?"

"Yes."

"Why?"

"I am a pacifist and will not wear a uniform of any kind."

"Are uniforms, in the sense of war or fighting, not restricted to armed forces? Surely a company garment in whatever style or colour as an identity all staff share, that you see in shops, airlines etc are different, they are not war like in any way, are they?" The lad said nothing.

So, Jack asked the $64,000 question, "If I order you to wear the coat, will you?" Again, the lad refused to answer. "Would you like to say anything Mrs Smifff before I ask your son to take you to the canteen for a coffee while I consider my decision?"

"Well, I know that record isn't very good but he is very young and if you give him a second chance, I will make sure he works to the highest standards and wears his coat."

"Thank you," said Jack, "I will send someone to fetch you as soon as I am ready."

The two of them got up and left the office. Turning to the Manager, he said, "What do you think?"

"Well, I sort of thought, before you came that giving him a second chance with a Final Written Warning would be the right thing to do but as I had to look at his record which I sort of knew wasn't good but until I wrote it out for you, I didn't realise quite how bad it was. If he's that bad now, what will he be like when he's been here long enough to be protected by an Industrial Tribunal?"

"I agree," said Jack, "can I have a coffee whilst I consider the decision I have already made?"

The Manager laughed and picked up the phone and ordered two coffees. Then he sent for the Smifffs. "I have carefully considered the details I have heard. Normally, in a situation like this as your suspension letter says, you would be given the opportunity to obey the order and compliance would result in a Final Written Warning, refusal would result in summary dismissal. In this instance I am looking at an individual who not only refused a reasonable order but who has the most appalling record as well. In addition, you refused to say if, if given a second chance you would wear the company coat. It is my view that you should already have been on a Final Written Warning for that appalling record in which case another Final Written Warning could not happen anyway.

"There is no point therefore in me asking you yet again if you would obey the coat wearing order and if you said 'yes' that would mean a second Final Written Warning being issued which is a nonsense. As it is, as a Final Written Warning had not been issued but should have been I am terminating your employment with one week's pay in lieu of notice with immediate effect for misconduct. I will confirm this in writing within a few days as well as your right to appeal against my decision should you wish to do so." The two of them got up and left without saying a word. The Manager said, "Thank you. Do you think he will appeal?"

"I have no idea but any such appeal from a decision I take has to be heard by the MD and I cannot imagine him making a trip all the way down here for that toe rag. If he does, I'll write the rejection of the appeal letter by the MD and he will sign it. Appeals do not always have to be heard; maybe if the employee is long serving and the original decision could have gone either way it would, but with one like this no chance. I have another one at the retail shop in Hastings so I'll be on my way. Just be a little bit quicker getting into the formal procedure with new starts because as you said if they are that bad when they are not protected how bad will they be when they are?" And he left. What he didn't know was how quickly word of his action got round the company; it was certainly in Wellingborough by the middle of the afternoon.

At the shop he went through with the Manageress the girl's record and discussed how it would go. The girl turned up on time and this time not only did she have her mother with her, but her father too! They confirmed that they were union officials and insisted on representing their daughter. Jack insisted they didn't! He explained that the company did not recognise either union and would not, under any circumstances, recognise them by the back door de-facto by allowing them to do so. He said he would let them attend because he knew it would be a fair procedure but only as witnesses for their daughter. They agreed to that.

The Manageress's office was tiny and the five of them filled it to overflowing, so the Manageress and the father had to stand. Jack remembered the story he had been told about Elizabeth 1st getting so fed up with the time Privy Council Meetings went on for that she hit on the idea of having the chairs for the Council, *probably benches* thought Jack, removed for everyone except herself. She thus did two things, shortened the meetings by a huge amount and created the role of Chairman, ironic that that should be thought of as a male role because the first chairman was a woman! Jack told her this was a disciplinary hearing, exactly as he had at the meeting a couple of hours earlier at the C&C.

And then asked the Manageress to describe what happened. He then asked if that was an accurate description and the girl agreed it was. So, he asked her why she refused. She said, "Well, really I am a Till Operator and I shouldn't be filling shelves."

Jack said, "You are not a Till Operator according to your contract (he had long given up on referring it to its proper name of a Contract of Employment Statement or Main Particulars of Employment!) you are a Shop Assistant and Assistants can and do, do all tasks asked of them."

As he spoke, he removed from his brief case a copy of her contract and a copy of the relevant section of the Retail Wages Council's documentation describing Shop Assistants duties and handed them to the mother who was nearest to him. He then carried on by saying, "also at the end of the Job Description it says, as the final point, 'and such other duties as may be reasonably asked or ordered' so I ask you again, why did you refuse because I understand you have carried out general duties around the shop since you started?"

The girl paused for so long that Jack thought she was not going to answer but just before he demanded an answer the girl said, "What if I'm pregnant?"

Before Jack could react, the mother interrupted and said, "You're not, are you?" Before the girl could answer Jack interrupted, in turn, and said, "I did, before the meeting tell you that you were here on sufferance and were not to interrupt because if you did, I would ask you to leave, but I can quite understand why you did and I shall overlook it in the circumstances 'cause I would probably have done the same in your circumstances, so, are you pregnant?"

"Well, no but if I was, I wouldn't have to, would I?"

"Well, since you are not it doesn't apply but I will give you a short answer. Leaving aside women who have very severe medical problems during pregnancy who would probably be medically suspended in very severe cases of not being able to work at all, they would not be dismissed, for 'normal' pregnancies, which are mainly the norm; there would be no change to the duties to start with at all except for those carrying out duties involving X-Rays, dangerous chemicals, those prescribed by law, where the law forbids a pregnant woman from working there, they would be found other, safe work or they, too, would be medically suspended.

"Many women do not even know they are pregnant until two or three months gone and the first impact, once they do know, is to be checked out by a Doctor and then notify the employer. I don't propose to go through all of that procedure just to say that depending on the job the individual's duties would be changed to keep her and her baby safe. As a Shop Assistant neither filling shelves with weights as small as this, (he held up a 15ounze tin of beans) or working on the till, would be regarded as being too onerous.

"However, by the later stages of pregnancy working at the till might become too dangerous. As you know, it involves lifting, sometimes, not heavy so much as awkward, items where you have to pick it up and then swivel to move it from one side of the till to the other and a lot of that could be laborious, no pun intended, repeated many times during the day so you would have to be taken off and given much lighter work filling shelves etc."

The girl's face was a picture. Jack turned to the parents and said, "Right, as I said before the meeting, I am now giving you the opportunity to say anything you wish to say before I adjourn to consider my decision?" They looked at one another and then shook their heads. Jack adjourned by asking them to go round to the café a few shops along and come back in half an hour. They left. "What do you want to do with her?"

"Well, she's quite a good worker, no timekeeping or absenteeism and the quality of her work is OK, I wouldn't put it any higher than that but there is the issue of the shortages and as they have stopped whilst she is not on the till I am not sure if I want to keep her."

"OK. I don't think she will refuse when they come back to do the duties, I think her parents will make sure of that because they know firstly, that she doesn't have a leg to stand on by refusing and they will know that she'll have trouble getting another job having been fired from this one; so if I issue her with a Final Written Warning but keep it tight to the refusal so that if she should be late by 5 mins once it won't cost her, her job and if she goes on the till you will need to ensure proper zedding is done to pin it down to her—how do you feel about that?" She nodded.

And that's what he did as she agreed she would obey the order. It wasn't entirely the end of the matter though because a couple of months later the Manageress rang Jack to tell him she had resigned and left—she was pregnant which she probably suspected at the hearing and her parents, discovering the fact, had thrown her out and she had gone to live with her boyfriend and his parents in Dungeness, which as neither of them had transport meant that she had to leave. *There's nowt so queer as folk,'* thought Jack, *'it's a funny thing, life.'*

Chapter 24

Life became hectic, fascinating and very demanding very quickly for Jack. An unfair dismissal claim arrived from the Industrial Tribunal; the holding company took over another Group which was a mirror image to Jack's except instead of it operating with Spar Wholesale Delivered Depots it covered the VG Group. Now comprising some 10 companies almost all of them multi-function in that they all had wholesale depots delivering to retail shops, they all had cash and carrys open to traders and they all had retail grocery shops, under Spar, VG and other names plus a few odds and sods such as a chemists and a petrol station owned by Jack's own company, but besides the attraction for expansion and consolidation savings offered by the purchase there was a Computer Centre in the other group and that was a major attraction, Jack was told, for the purchase.

As Jack was to find out the Computer Centre was to get him into some trouble quite quickly. It didn't take a genius to work out that there would have to be rationalisation and that a leaner, single function company with responsibility for just one of the functions i.e., just one cash and carry company would control all 80 plus cash and carrys. It would have been nice to deal with just one problem at a time but, of course, life is not like that, and he was to have another problem involving sales at one of the Distribution Depots and with such big changes likely to the structures of the company ahead it would be necessary to shine in the meantime in every respect to be sure of staying and not going!

His immediate problem was the Industrial Tribunal, especially as Jack had been involved in the dismissal. Linehams had been handed, a few months ago, a single cash and carry that had gone bust (a technical term you understand!) and which had been purchased by the Holding Company. The Operations Director on the first visit to the C&C took less than two minutes to realise why it had gone bust! It was a tip. The Manager had been there for 12 years. It was filthy; the layout made no sense at all, products were just shoved on the shelves any-which-way; there were no promotions on the ends of the aisles, or indeed anywhere at all; there were no uniforms and the staff did not respond quickly to calls to attend the checkouts with customers waiting.

Having walked the C&C the Operations Director summoned the Manager to a disciplinary hearing the outcome of which was a Final Written Warning listing 41 items which were to be improved within a month or he would be dismissed. That had taken place before Jack started but the OD consulted him a day or two before the Disciplinary Hearing was to be heard. In the month he had been given not one of the 41 items had been complied with—not one!

Because he had been the Manager of that C&C for 12 years dismissal might be hard to justify so Jack offered to attend the Hearing with the OD and he was only too happy to accept. Jack had drafted the letter summoning him to the hearing and it contained the three rights plus details of the issues causing dissatisfaction as for previous disciplinary hearings he had been involved in before.

At the start of the Hearing Jack explained his rights again and what would happen. The Manager asked for the Assistant Manager to accompany him. Jack was not happy about that and explained that although, if he insisted that would be allowed, for a subordinate to know what had happened to his superior in the event that the superior was not to be dismissed was unwise but the Manager insisted and so the AM attended. Jack even offered to suspend the hearing to allow another Manager to attend if he wanted but he insisted on his AM being with him. The OD started by asking him if he had received the Final Warning Letter containing the 41 items. The Manager agreed he had.

"So, what have you got to say for yourself?" asked the OD.

"Look, if you're going to sack me, just sack me I'm not going through all this rigmarole," said the Manager. The OD and Jack just sat there somewhat stunned. The OD was obviously about to speak and it seemed to Jack that he was about to say, 'OK you're sacked' not being known for a man with a lot of patience, so Jack jumped in and said, "Hang on, this is your chance to speak up for yourself. Are you really saying you have nothing to say? Take item 1 in the letter, the spilt ketchup. Did it really sit there for the 3 days as the OD says? Why didn't you get it cleared up?"

"I did ask Bill but he didn't do it."

"Why not?"

"He didn't want to."

"Did you tell him or ask him?"

"Asked him."

"When he didn't do it why didn't you tell him?"

"That's not my management style to tell people—I always ask."

"And have they discovered that if they don't do as you ask you don't then tell them to do it, in other words, they can just ignore anything they don't like?" The Manager did not reply. Jack continued through the remaining 40 items with unsatisfactory answers to all of them. Although the Manager was sent out at the end of the Hearing for half an hour the decision to sack him took a lot less than that. He was told he was sacked, that it would be with pay in lieu of notice, any accrued holiday pay due would be paid and he was told of his right to appeal if he disagreed with the decision. Jack wrote the dismissal letter for the OD's signature and that was that. Except it wasn't because the unfair dismissal application was submitted to the Industrial Tribunal one day before the three month three-month time limit was reached.

Passing the application to Jack the MD asked him whether he felt we should resist it or pay him off. The appeal case that Jack had watched at the Employment Appeal Tribunal had cost the best part of £5,000 and if they could settle for less than that would it not be worth it? Jack replied that if he did it, and it was supposed to be set up so simply that both Applicants and Respondents, i.e., companies, could represent themselves without involving the costs of lawyers.

Jack said he would like to go and see an ordinary Tribunal in action and then decide if he felt he could do it. If he did do it and lost then that would be time to think about involving lawyers and fees but not until then. The MD agreed and a few days later Jack found himself watching a Tribunal in Cambridge. It was very informal with the ex-employer going first and explaining why he had fired the Applicant. The Chairman wrote down all that was said so it was quite slow going and he interrupted all the witnesses from time to time to understand the evidence being presented.

Once both sides had presented their cases and the employer had had a second go recalling a witness to rebut something the Applicant had said that hadn't been asked of the witness in cross examination, the Tribunal withdrew to consider their decision. They took less than half an hour and the application was thrown out giving a fair dismissal decision. It had all been, as described on the tin, very informal, lots of cross talking and no legalese whatsoever. Jack was confident that he could run a case and told the MD so.

What had become clear in the Tribunal he watched was how much attention was paid to the details provided on the IT1, the Application to an Industrial Tribunal, and especially on the IT3, the Respondent's Response. So, he took a lot of time and care with the reply including attaching a copy of the Final Warning Letter, the letter summoning the Manager to the Disciplinary Hearing, the notes of the Hearing and the Dismissal Letter following it. He also made reference to the fact that the Manager did not appeal against his dismissal.

Tribunals would develop a jaundiced view of Applicants who did not exhaust their company's procedures before going to Tribunal. Jack also asked for a Pre-Hearing Assessment based on the company regarding the application as being frivolous, unreasonable or otherwise vexatious. This PHA process had been introduced because employers foresaw that dismissed employees would make a claim to the Tribunal out of revenge to mess them about and incur thousands of pounds in costs for applications that had no value whatsoever. In the event the system did not work because Tribunals almost never issued warnings although Jack was to succeed in getting a couple of warnings issued in the future, but not on this occasion!

Jack kept in touch with the AM, explaining he would need to know if the Manager wanted the AM to attend the Tribunal as a witness so that arrangements could be made to cover for his absence, he running the C&C on a temporary basis. By so doing he was able to find out that the AM did not want to go, if asked, and he asked Jack if he had to go. Jack explained that if he refused the Manager could obtain a Witness Order from the Tribunal requiring him to attend and if he failed to do so he could be fined up to £1000!

"Why don't you want to go?" asked Jack.

"Because he was an idle bastard and deserved everything he got. He deliberately ignored the OD's and Area Manager's instructions as being bollocks. By rights he should have been sacked years ago and it was largely down to him that we went bust, so I don't want to give evidence to help him win his case."

"Well, thank you for telling me about that. If he doesn't call you and we did, would you be willing to say, on oath, just what you've just said to me now?"

"Bloody true!" The Manager did not ask the AM to be a witness so Jack took him himself! Came the day, attempts by ACAS to conciliate a settlement being refused by Jack, the three of them arrived, Jack, the AM and the OD, in Cambridge.

When they booked in Jack asked the clerk if the Applicant had any witnesses and was told no. So it came as a bit of a surprise to find the ex-Manager sitting with three men. Two of them were sitting at the Applicant's table with the Applicant and the third one sitting behind them. Jack sat on his own at the Respondent's table, the one to the left as you look towards the three Tribunal Members. In those days a Tribunal was made up of one member nominated by trade unions, one nominated by employers and a legally qualified Chairman, usually a Solicitor but sometimes a Barrister, who sat in the middle.

Although the Lay Members, as they were referred to were never introduced it normally did not take very long to determine which side of the fence they sat. Later on, Members were to be appointed from ethnic or other interested sides, if a case involved sex harassment of any kind, then at least one woman would be on the Tribunal, or a race case an ethnic minority Lay Member would sit—Jack was never to discover if a Gay Member was ever to be appointed in cases involving gay persecution or harassment.

Piled up in front of the two to Jack's right were a number of books which were thicker than any book Jack had ever seen. It became clear from the Chairman's opening remarks that one of the two was a Senior Barrister and the other a Junior Barrister. The third man turned out to be the Instructing Solicitor employed by the ex-Manager! Jack was starting to experience that going down for the third time experience by the time this had become clear!

However, he relaxed a bit when the Chairman said that as the Applicant had legal representation, he was going to ask the Applicant to go first. Jack had been expecting to go first as that was the convention except for cases of alleged discrimination when the Applicant always went first. When he asked Jack if he objected, he said he had none as quickly as he could. The lead Barrister looked as though he wanted to object and took a while before saying that he had no objection.

"Right, it's for you to start," said the Chairman and we don't require an opening statement from you; the paperwork is particularly clear on what happened and the fact that your client is asking us to declare that he was unfairly dismissed is abundantly clear."

"I would wish to point out," said the Barrister, "that it is not my intention to call evidence to rebut all 41 items for which the Applicant was dismissed. I shall show that one of them was patently unfair and unjust as an instruction and that therefore all the other 40 would fall by the same reasoning." The Chairman, who had been looking down writing, looked up with a look on his face that Jack could not interpret but which was clearly not in agreement. He said, "What would you say to that Mr Hughes?"

Jack knew he was being asked to object but it took him a moment or two to think about it and on the basis that attack is better than defence he said, "That's absolute rubbish. Even, (he didn't know at that stage of his career that Barristers were referred to as 'my honourable friend' and all other representatives, solicitors, trade unionists, legal execs etc were to be referred to as 'my friend'! To Jack they were the enemy and were to be treated as such, so he simply referred to the Barrister as 'he' or 'him' as the case went along!), if he could demonstrate that one of them was unfair there is no way that can mean that all 40 others were also unfair. Quite the opposite in fact all 40 could just as easily be fair; it is up to them to prove their point and that they will not be able to do."

"I am with Mr Hughes on that, but it is your case and you are entitled to run it anyway that you wish within the normal rules. No doubt if you decide to proceed on that basis, you will address some argument to us to support your case. Proceed." At that the Barrister called the Manager who was sworn in by the Tribunal Clerk and the case started. Jack expected a long build up and lots of questions as to why the dismissal was unfair but he simply asked the Manager if the 41 items listed were a fair comment of the state of the C&C and the Manager simply said, "No."

He then asked him what do you say about point seven. This point related to the pricing and ticketing of crisps. The OD had done a deal with the crisp manufacturer starting with that if he placed their crisps in all 15 C&Cs what price would he charge? The price was extremely good and the deal was done. The Printing Department produced special posters to promote the deal which were stuck to boards which could be stood on, by and near the stacks of crisps on promotion. The problem was that, in this case, the setting of the promotion material was so sloppy that there was only one board on the pallet load and as customers removed the boxes so the board fell over and the 'look at me, see what a good deal I am' became lost.

No boards had been attached to the ends over the pallet, or to the aisles, or at the entrance to tell customers of the promotion. In fact, just one board had been slung on the pallet and had rapidly started to deteriorate at its mishandling and all the other boards had been left slung in a pile in Goods-in. As the OD had done the deal personally, he had made sure, in speaking to, and confirming in writing to the Manager, that he took a very dim view of this and it was to improve immediately.

He had made it clear to the Manager that the other boards should be displayed around, and where that should be, and he had directly ordered that the individual boxes of crisps should be ticketed to show the code and price—exactly as was done with all other products. The Applicant in response to his Barrister said that he had not had the time to do it but he would have done so but the AM (Area Manager) arrived back in the afternoon before he had had chance to do so. The Barrister then asked him if the same answer would have been given to all the other 40 points and he said, "Yes."

At that the Barrister then said, "No other questions, Sir."

Jack was as surprised as the three Tribunal Members. The Barrister had obviously not heeded the Chairman's comments at the commencement. Jack was not going to complain! Jack started off by asking him if the notes of the final disciplinary hearing were accurate and he agreed they were. Then Jack asked him, since he had started off by refusing to take part in the hearing but just said words to the effect that just get on and sack me, I'm not going to go through this process did that not imply that he was guilty as charged, had no real answer to any of the charges and was admitting so straight away? It was clear to all that he didn't want to answer the question, if only because of the time it took him but he eventually said, "No."

It was very simple for Jack to say, "Why then did you not start answering the 41, 41, points?" Jack repeated the 41 twice for effect.

"It would have been a waste of time because he had already decided to sack me."

"But you did not know that, did you?"

"I was sure he would."

"Based on what?" No answer was the stern reply, so Jack pushed further and asked, "Wasn't it really because you knew you had no defence and were conceding from the very start?"

"No."

"Oh, I think it was," said Jack, "but let's move on. You have just said, to your lawyer, that the reason that you had not had time to get the crisps priced because there wasn't time before the AM came back, do you still maintain that?"

"Yes."

"So what time was it the AM came back?"

136

"I've just said."

"No, you haven't. All you said was that there had not been time before the AM came back in the afternoon…" The Barrister interrupted and said, "Sir, he's bullying the witness. The witness has already answered that question." The Chairman looked back through his record, he had been writing down everything said, and said, "No, he hasn't. Mr Hughes is quite right, he only said in the afternoon and that is not a time so answer the question," to the ex-Manager.

"Just before closing."

"What time was that?" asked Jack.

"We closed at 5.30pm."

"And you didn't have time between noon and 5.30pm, five and a half hours to do that job?"

"No."

"That's ridiculous, isn't it? It can only take, what, five minutes to ticket the boxes?"

"Oh, much longer than that, at least an hour."

"Rubbish," said Jack, and he then interrogated the Manager as to how many boxes were left on the pallet, many of them having been removed and knocking the sign about whilst that was happening. Eventually he agreed that there were only 15 to 20 boxes to be done but he argued that the ticketing of them would take quite a time because the ticketing machine had to be set up and then they would have to remove the top layer or two to get access to the lower ones. At that Jack reached down and picked up his briefcase from which he removed a ticket gun. "This is the gun we're talking about, isn't it?"

The Manager agreed. "Do you remember the code and the price?"

"No."

"Does Code 127 and £13.50 sound right?"

"Yes, about that." So, Jack set 127 and 1350 into the gun by turning the two little knobs. He did it quite quickly because he had pre-set those numbers into the gun anticipating events and knowing he would appear much quicker if he had pre-set them than if he had to do it for real because he was not practiced in this skill but the real people would have been able to do it quicker than he had pretended to anyway. He then squeezed the trigger handle quickly 20 times sticking a ticket each time onto the back of his hand.

"That didn't take long did it and before you say the layers had to be removed, I agree with you but the ticketing, setting the gun and sticking on the ticket takes no time at all does it?" The Applicant did not reply but this time Jack did not press him because it was obvious that he had made his point. "So, if I am exceedingly generous that it would have taken 10 minutes you still maintain that you did not have time, just ten minutes between noon and 5.30pm?"

"No."

"What day was it this happened on?"

"A Tuesday." As he said it Jack could see in his face that he realised just what he had said.

"Yes, it was a Tuesday—do you want to check your diary that the 15th was indeed a Tuesday?"

"No."

"What time was closing time on a Tuesday?"

"Eight pm."

"Eight pm. Eight whole hours after noon and the time the OD left. Why did you answer five thirty before then?" The Tribunal Members all fidgeted which said to Jack that he had scored but he had not finished. "Do you still maintain that you did not have 10 minutes in eight whole hours to do something that the OD had told you to do immediately?"

"Yes."

"Well, what else were you doing? You didn't get the smashed Tomato Ketchup mess cleaned up which I would have thought would have been your very first priority given the danger and mess it presented because it was still there three days later so what were you doing?"

"I was just busy."

"Would it surprise you if I said your Assistant Manager will say in his evidence later that you did nothing at all, all the rest of the day?" The ex-Manager just glowered at him. Again, Jack let it go feeling he had made his point. Jack started to say, I have no further questions, Sir and then stopped. "Sorry, Sir, I do have just one more question," and turning to the Applicant said, "You would not have ticketed those boxes yourself would you, you'd have told the Assistant Manager," and at that point he took a stop watch out of his brief case and said, 'John, get those bloody crisps ticketed. The OD is on my back. Get them done ASAP' and he stopped the watch. "That took exactly eight seconds. Do you want to insult this Tribunal's intelligence and insist that you did not have eight seconds, just eight seconds, in eight hours to get the crisps ticketed? Jack did not expect a reply nor did he get one."

Jack called the OD who gave his evidence, mainly affirming the accuracy of the warning letter, the notes of the final hearing and the accuracy of the dismissal letter which set-out all the dissatisfactions of the 41 points and he explained that so bad had been the response to the letter setting out the targets he was expected to achieve he did not believe that giving him some sort of extended Final Written Warning would have resulted in a better performance. The Barrister had seen his case go down the toilet with Jack's cross examination of the Applicant and did a very perfunctory job of his cross examination of the OD who was easily able to destroy the points the Barrister was attempting to make.

Jack did not call the Area Manager as he could not really add anything other than to say the same thing that all the documents were accurate. Jack debated whether he should call the Assistant Manager for him to confirm that the Applicant had done nothing to try and get any of the problems sorted out but as he didn't know what the Barrister might know about the Assistant Manager, he decided it was a risk he would not take.

With both sides having summed up the Tribunal withdrew to consider their decision. They were only gone 45 minutes. Everyone having resumed their seats the Chairman announced, "This application fails." Jack didn't know at that stage in his tribunal career that most Chairmen would announce their findings of facts, briefly, regarding what the claim was by the Applicant, what the Respondent said in defence and would then go through all the points, especially of disagreement between the parties, and made findings of fact supporting one side's arguments with the expression, 'we prefer the evidence of…' rather than coming out with it's a pack of lies by that lot.

It would therefore take a while seeing whose evidence they preferred before it became clear whether you were heading for a win or a loss and even then, it wasn't until the very end that the Chairman would say, 'this application therefore fails/succeeds'. The suspense throughout what could be a long list was murderous but just occasionally the Chairman would start with, 'this application fails/succeeds' so that one could sit with misery or delight whilst the details were read out.

So, Jack was able to immediately relax but he was also pleased when, as part of the facts, the Chairman stated that 'Mr Hughes had gone further than a Tribunal could ask of a reasonable employer when he had interrupted when the Applicant was apparently prepared to give up his right to defend himself when he specifically made the Applicant answer each of the 41 points contained in the

Final Warning Letter. The Applicant tried to tell us that the decision to dismiss him was already taken, and we could understand that he might feel it would be inevitable that he was to be sacked but he cannot have felt that by any actions taken by the Respondents who went out of their way to ensure that he defended himself although it is easy for us to understand that, knowing as he did, that he had made no attempts whatsoever to comply with any of the instructions in the FWW he would be justified in anticipating the termination of his employment.

'His defence here, today, that he did not have eight seconds in the whole period of eight hours in which to instruct the AM to get the crisps priced is simply not credible. His representative argued that they would show that the item relating to the crisps was unfair and that unfairness applied to the remaining 40 other items; since they have singularly failed to show that there was any unfairness in that instruction whatsoever and if we accept their argument that the other 40 follow the same pattern of treatment then it inevitably follows that their allegations against the 40 fail also...'

Jack thought, *hoist by their own petard might be appropriate at that point!*

Jack arrived at work the following morning to discover that the OD had already spoken to the MD regarding Jack's performance. He was glad it had not gone the other way in which case he would probably have never conducted another case and his life would have followed a very different course.

Chapter 25

The next project Jack became involved in was to look at the sales performance at one of the East Anglian wholesale delivering depots. With about 275 Spar and a few company-owned shops the Board decided that there was a need to quickly look at the operating model so that decisions could be taken regarding the restructuring of the wholesale delivered side of the company. Delivering goods obviously cost money. In theory the bulk buying into the depot, all four of them in fact, should mean that the savings could cover the costs of delivery so that the prices delivered would be competitive. However, it was becoming obvious that many of the shops they supplied could buy the goods cheaper from Tesco's or Sainsbury's than the depot could deliver them at; hence the business was in a slow and inevitable decline if something was not done to improve the situation.

Having received his instructions Jack went over to Boston and spent three days going through the operation. The director was certain that with a bit of training the sales force could sell more thus enabling them to buy more from the supplier at a cheaper price and thus remain competitive. He spent the first day with the director and then the second day out on the road with two of the sales team. On the third day, a Saturday, he arranged for all the sales force, nine of them, very unwillingly, to attend a meeting. He started the meeting by saying he expected that they were pretty pissed off by having to work on a Saturday and so was he, but if they didn't, they would be looking for a new job in the near future and that would piss them off even more.

He supported his assertion by showing them a set of statistics which showed decreasing sales, increasing costs and figures to show the growth of the major supermarkets who should not have been their competition at all but they were for the simple fact that they could sell cheaper, at a profit, than they, the depot could buy at! From his day out he had formed the opinion that they didn't actually have a real sales force, they had a bunch of order takers and very expensive ones at that. He didn't think it would be very wise to say that to them especially as he didn't really have any figures to support his view.

So, he explained that for the next fortnight they would be expected to record how they spent their time. He was thinking back to the work he had done in the clothing industry and how the supervisors spent, or rather wasted their managerial time carrying out the wrong tasks and that training them to do the wrong thing was a waste of time and money so he explained a little about the exercise he had carried out in that industry and the benefits that had accrued from it.

From the time he had spent on the road with the two reps he had formed an outline aide memoire but he involved the team in adding to it and improving it so that they recorded the same activity the same way across their diaries. He also arranged to come back the following two weeks, two days each time to go out with four different reps to get a good feel for the job.

Although the jobs of a supervisor in clothing manufacture and a salesman in grocery selling would appear to be very different the same type of information came back. For example, they actually only spent 8% of their time selling or attempting to sell. They spent 23% of their time driving. Most of Friday was spent driving to all their customers collecting their order books for the next week's delivery.

From what he observed and the figures he analysed from their diaries, sales figures from the depot and costs involved in salaries, cars, petrol etc he came to the conclusion that the whole process was fundamentally flawed. The turnover every week of the small village stores varied very little. Promotions made very little difference and passing on price cuts to customers did not produce any great increase in sales so the shopkeepers simply kept their normal prices the same and pocketed the difference between the sale price and the lower cost as profit for themselves.

Some of the stores were so small that when Jack looked at the total purchases by the shopkeeper for the week the profit did not cover the cost of sending in the Salesman. In other words, they were losing money every time a Salesman called. In fact, when he looked at the figures in total nearly 70% of visits cost money. When he delivered his presentation to the Board, starting with the suggestion of the replacement of the majority of the sales force with telesales based in the distribution depot offices who would simple telephone the shop for their order he was not entirely surprised that they didn't like the idea! However, when he started to argue his case, the MD cut him off, in fact he hardly presented his case at all when they moved on to other matters. He was asked to stay back when the meeting broke up.

The MD announced, once the Board had gone, that he had not wanted Jack to go into his report in detail because it would no longer concern him as in two days' time there was to be an announcement of the restructuring of the company and the wholesale side of the business would no longer concern Jack as he was to be part of one of the three interim Cash and Carry companies which in a few months' time would become one national cash and carry company. He was asked to keep all this to himself for the next two days and even longer for the creation of the national company as there would be a huge amount of work to be done regarding the restructuring with, unfortunately, the likelihood that quite a number of people would be losing their jobs.

At present there were 10 MDs that would be reduced to one for the distribution company, one for the retail company and one for the national cash and carry company albeit that initially there would be three MDs for the three C&C companies but that would be reduced to one in a few months. As Jack took in the numbers, he also took in that there would not be the same number of Heads of the Personnel Departments as there were now and that meant that his head might be one of the ones to roll. The MD had been watching Jack closely as he gave out the information. He clearly saw Jack's dawning of the danger and quickly interrupted to say that he was to be the MD of the C&C Group and he wanted Jack to be the Head of Personnel and Training in the new Midlands Company.

That was to be strictly between the two of them and whilst Jack would officially have to apply for the role when it was advertised within the whole group he was not to worry because he would be successful! For the record he said he had believed that Jack's report on the future structuring for the wholesale distribution depots was the way to go but he had cut the discussion short because it was no longer their concern. He said he would forward it to the new MD of the distribution company but, knowing him as he did, it would be ignored. And it was!

Chapter 26

And it came to pass that the cash and carrys were split into, initially three companies, North, Midlands and South with Jack as the Head of Personnel and Training for the Midlands company still called Linehams at that stage; and then, as he knew it would be, it was announced that the three would become one company, based in Northamptonshire, and, again the post was advertised with all three Personnel people from the three C&C companies applying but also five from the other parts of the Group. Jack was the man as far as personnel and training was concerned as far as he was concerned but he wasn't so sure that he was the man for the new Board. Initially there were 87 units, some in competition with one another, indeed on the same industrial estates and streamlining them would clearly be a first priority.

The major job losses would be in the two Head Offices which would be closed. A few of the key people would be moved to Wellingborough, if they were willing, but most would lose their jobs. Starting with MDs there was only a need for one so two would go—but probably into the Group. Jack was duly interviewed by a group of three Directors and had to wait several days while the other applicants were interviewed to know the result. He was driving along the M62 heading for the M1 and home when his car phone rang.

It was the MD asking him to cancel his appointments for the following day and come to a meeting with him to start at 9.30am and last for most of the day. Jack obviously said he would and then, having thought about why and concluding it wouldn't take a day to tell him he hadn't got the job so he must have got it, he asked, "As it wouldn't take that length of time to give me my P45, can I assume that I've got the job?"

"Clever bugger," said the MD and rang off! Jack laughed and let out a huge breath—it had been very stressful waiting for the decision because he knew the Personnel Heads of the other two C&C companies well enough to know he couldn't work for either of them so that if one of them had got it he would have been looking for another job; they were both prone to self-abuse and weren't worth the space they occupied on this earth. He was so delighted and relieved he'd got the job and thinking about what he might have to deal with the following day that he completely drove past the exit to the M1 and had to drive on to the M18 to be able to turn south!

Jack was not involved in the MD moves, that was handled by the Holding Company, but almost all the others were and it was a quite unpleasant time for Jack. He didn't feel too much concern for the most senior people losing their jobs, they had after all been the ones to run the companies taken over quite badly. The people he felt most sorry for were the middle and junior levels who through no fault of their own who would find themselves at the Job Centre signing on as unemployed.

The exercise to sort out the C&Cs would turn out to be a major task and would take the best part of 18 months. The performance of the company as a whole was poor. The original Linehams units were profitable but nearly all the others, some 73 units, had been taken over because they were failing. Linehams was the only company of the 10 forming the Group initially which had a Methods and Systems Department, commonly referred to as Work Study. To sort out what needed to be done in each C&C the Work Study Practitioners would go first to a C&C to measure the amount of work in it, measured by how many attended hours were needed to operate it and once they had done this, they then looked at how many attended hours were actually being worked.

By the end of the exercise, it turned out that 86 had too many attended hours and only one had too few. Jack's job was to then reduce the attended hours. Right from the start Jack took the view that although it would inevitably attract attention as 'carrying out loads of redundancies' the reality was that the number of hours worked in total were to be reduced and that did not necessarily mean, if possible, that anyone should lose their job.

Redundancy is an emotive term, perhaps the most emotive in the employment jargon. Someone caught stealing and is therefore sacked had only themself to blame. In a potential redundancy situation, it was the job, not the individual carrying it out, which was to go. The individual may be entirely blameless but the employer is saying go forth I have no need of you anymore. The legislation around redundancy is complicated and was evolving rapidly at the time Jack became involved. The definition, in law, is, of course, lengthy and mouthy. Jack chose to define it more simply, but nevertheless accurately, as 'the need for work of a particular kind has ceased or will cease, has diminished or will diminish, at that site'.

There was a requirement in law to consult, initially that was limited to trade unions only even if the staff likely to be made redundant were not in the union and did not want the union to represent them! Eventually both by changes to the law and by case law it became mandatory to consult meaningfully (some employers consulted and then totally ignored what the employees had said so that Tribunals introduced the word 'meaningfully' thus moving 'consult' much more towards 'negotiate'—a different meaning entirely!).

There were also rules requiring specific periods of consultation depending on the potential number of redundancies contemplated. This last proved to be a real headache for Jack because, when he invited the National Officers of the three main unions with which they had agreements, he had no idea how many they might be. He stressed, restressed and re-restressed that he hoped that there would be none at all and since the approach looked at attended hours and he had no idea how many people might want to volunteer for redundancy or want to reduce their hours he could not give any figures.

He was able to argue that as the rules related *to numbers at that site* it would be and the numbers would always be less than 30 (some of the branches did not employ that number in total!) the requirement to consult for 30 days would never be triggered. He only got this one through when he printed off the legislation to show '*at that site*' since they tried to total the number for 87 C&Cs which likely meant 99 days of consultation!

The first hurdle was to reach agreement on the procedure to be followed. Some of the branches were covered by LIFO (last in—first out) agreements, some had appraisal agreements and the majority had none at all. Normally the process would be to go with the agreement in place and only change it afterwards.

Jack could not countenance that. The company was in serious trouble. In the North West Region, comprising 23 C&Cs, 21 were losing money, some quite a lot, one was breaking even and one a satisfactory profit. That one was the only ex-Linehams branch, all the others had been taken over recently. Jack presented to the three main unions that if the branches were to be saved then they needed to keep the very best people and the not so best would be selected for redundancy if it became necessary to carry out compulsory ones. When two of the three argued for the LIFO to be the system, not surprising since they had been the ones to negotiate that system into those branches in the first place, Jack countered with, how can it be justified that someone who had a string of current warnings, live, keep their job when someone with an exemplary record but one day's service less should lose theirs? It could not be justified and when it became clear that Jack was not to be moved on this, they agreed.

They agreed a process where a full time official from the union would attend the C&C and be present while Jack spoke to the staff in two halves. Jack would then, having explained what the company proposed, leave the union official to speak to the staff and after that Jack would speak to any members of staff individually who might want to reduce their hours or volunteer for redundancy and tell them what money they could expect and date of leaving etc.

In the event in 87 branches, there was not one single suggestion in addition to those proposed by Jack, produced by the staff or unions; so much for consultation. In addition, Jack had had delivered to the site the day before he arrived, the new uniforms which formed part of his presentation along with large photos and posters of the way the depot was to be modernised, cleaned and presented—more like a modern supermarket than a traditional warehouse—to make them more attractive to work and shop in. It was a huge expenditure and development of the company, not just firing a few cleaners to improve the bottom line. In the event the process was to take almost 18 months in total interrupted time and again by the acquisition of new companies and sites.

The exercise was draining trying to balance the wishes of the C&C Manager's and apparent fairness in that they all saw it as an opportunity to get rid of certain members of staff who had annoyed them in some way or other. There was also the problem, in those depots that had union agreements for LIFO to save a later starter and get rid of a longer serving one who was top of the unwanted list. Jack was to achieve all of them but it took utmost ingenuity to do so and cost Jack no end of sleepless nights.

Although he generally worked through one Region before moving on to another, they did spend a lot of time in identifying depots which might cause trouble and left them to the last. In the North East there were eight depots covered by one particularly militant union which had a policy of no compulsory redundancies. The National Officer had made it clear that that policy was for public consumption and that, if there were a need for compulsories, there would not be a problem.

However, the Regional Officer, a particularly militant individual, intent on going somewhere in the union and politics, made it clear to Jack at their first meeting that there would be no compulsories under any circumstances—even if it meant that the whole place would close in that case, and she confirmed that she would agree to closure but not some redundancies to save the place! Jack found that an almost impossible position to understand and didn't accept it. He knew that if any of her three depots were to need compulsories he would speak to the staff and he didn't believe that they would all volunteer to lose their jobs for the sake of two or three compulsories.

In the event after the first visit with her she was so disgusted that she walked out and refused to attend the other two which suited Jack just fine. It was caused by what happened at the first one. After he had spoken to the first half of the staff, he left her with them to say whatever she wanted to them. 'This was then repeated with the second half.

He only received three questions from the staff when he invited them to ask having delivered the 'this place is losing money and this is what we propose to do about it' speech. The first question he got, more of a statement from a young man who announced he could not afford to buy a tie the wearing of which was to be a requirement of the dress code being introduced with the new uniforms. Jack challenged him by questioning whether there was a charity shop near him where ties sold for 50p or less and he couldn't afford that? Jack was too long in the tooth to offer to buy one for him—he'd end up buying one for every male in the company as the word spread round but when the lad said he couldn't Jack said to talk to his Manager who would give him a sub out of his wages to be repaid at 10p per week which attracted laughter, and in the event, the lad turned up wearing a tie without a sub.

The second comment came from a young woman who announced in a broad Geordie accent that there was *'nae way she was climbing nae ladders in a skirt as she wore nae knickers and no-one was getting a free look at her ha'ppenny for free!'* After the laughter died down Jack, ignoring the double negative, said that he had said nothing about wearing skirts only that staff were to be clean and smart, wear proper shoes, not trainers which were no protection if they dropped tins on their toes when filling up so she could continue to wear trousers, if that was what she wore now. The third point was about ties again but this time if they could take them off if it was a hot day to which Jack answered that the Manager would give permission if it was that hot but not today, which elicited laughter as it was snowing outside.

Unknown to Jack the union she-devil had tried to stir up trouble by referring to Jack's statement that one way of saving money would be that there would be no overtime at overtime rates unless in an emergency. He had said that they would be recruiting weekend and evening staff who would work at time rate and therefore no overtime would be available except for cover for someone who had not turned up or for stocktaking which would continue to attract overtime.

The she-devil also tried to stir it up with the second group of staff and when that, too, failed she stormed out of the depot saying to Jack as she passed that this lot did not deserve to be in the union and he could do with them as he wished. She did not attend at the other two depots and everything went smoothly including one compulsory which was manufactured to get rid of one the Manager particularly wanted gone. There were no repercussions.

The Swansea C&C was one Jack wasn't especially looking forward to visiting. It had a fearsome reputation for militancy, as did three others from the old South Wales company, mainly it was felt due to bad management, senior management failing to back up local management when faced with union intransigence about something or other and in the case of Swansea particularly there were poor relationships between the male and female staff where each group had its own Shop Steward, a male for the males of course and a female for the females—both of which Shop Stewards were constantly trying to achieve a better term or condition than the other.

As part of his delivery to the two halves, about 70 staff in each, he also delivered the news that there would not be two recognised Shop Stewards in future, only one, to be elected by the membership, and a deputy who would only be consulted in the absence of the main Steward. One of the questions he got in response to this was what would happen if they did not agree to this. Jack made it absolutely clear that unless all the proposed changes were agreed to, including, of course, any other changes the staff might suggest that management agreed to, he would close the C&C since it was losing so much money the losses could no longer be tolerated.

That was greeted with complete silence which in the event was a good sign— they had never been resisted before, the previous senior management always having conceded when faced with union opposition; and they had no strategy agreed beforehand for resistance, especially as Jack had agreed the process with

National Officers of the union. Because trouble had been expected at Swansea the Regional Director had been in attendance, albeit that he had half hidden himself at the back of the canteen when Jack had been speaking!

Jack delivered the standard speech and then started seeing the staff who had expressed an interest in reducing their hours or volunteering for redundancy. He had with him the male shop steward who, after the first person had been shown the amount of money he would receive and who had volunteered immediately for redundancy, asked Jack what he would receive if he volunteered. Jack told him, it represented, most of it paid tax free almost a year's net pay. Having seen that he then asked that, if he did volunteer, how quickly he would be allowed to leave.

Jack did not take long to say, "You can go now, this minute, if you want."

The Shop Steward looked at him for a moment, reached out his hand to Jack and shook it saying, "Thanks very much. Can I say goodbye to a few people before I go?"

"If you really want to you can but I would think it better if you perhaps came back on Friday with any other volunteers to collect your P45 and monies due and you could perhaps go for a drink with them after closing."

"That's a good idea. See ya," and off he went. In moments the RD came in to tell Jack that the female Shop Steward wanted to volunteer for redundancy what should they do?

"Accept, tell her, her money amount and let her go immediately, just like I've done with the male one!" The RD just looked at him until he had absorbed what Jack had said and then laughed as he rushed out of the room. Everything else went smoothly and the C&C became profitable almost immediately.

One event to get Jack into trouble was the development of computers and their introduction to the company. One of the main reasons for the purchase of the VG Group was to get their hands on their Computer Centre which was based in Coventry. Not long after the takeover Jack, along with the other nine Heads of Personnel was invited by the Holding Company Personnel Director to a meeting in Coventry to be briefed on what the Centre could provide for Personnel.

Jack was a bit peeved as he had already spent some time and effort looking into this issue. It had been clear for some time that the manual systems he had inherited as they had taken over company after company were inadequate, slow and inaccurate. Some of them amounted to little more than the proverbial back of a fag packet whilst even the best were little more than piles of paper with no real structure. The one area which did seem to be accurate most of the time was the Wages Department. Employees always ensured that they told Wages of any changes to their circumstances so that they would always be paid. Jack had concluded that somehow, he had to ally Personnel Records with Wages but how?

Then luck intervened. He read a story in the press that the National Coal Board Computer Department was looking to sell its services to companies or organisations to mop up the spare capacity it was developing by default as the mines, who were its primary user, closed down. Jack knew that the Wages Department at Linehams had sent off a computer tape every week which contained the wages information. The NCB processed the tape into wage packet print outs and despatched them to the Lineham's sites to be made up into wage packets. So, Jack contacted them and invited them to come and see him.

They brought with them a 'kit' which they called Wizard and demonstrated it to him. It comprised a keyboard, VDU and modem which operated through a phone line. In essence it was a search engine which would investigate any data to which it was connected and print out the information it had been instructed to seek.

As Jack watched, the more excited he became. It meant that if he had this kit on his desk and it was connected to the Wages Department data, he could call up all the Managers' salaries searching by branch turnover, and list them in any order he told it to do so. This could be linked to the gross profit performance in the Accounts Department so that performance against turnover could be listed— an important figure when salary increases were being considered annually. The best thing of all was that with the exception of the individual's job title all the information Jack was likely to need to issue Contract of Employment Statements, Handbooks etc or carry out the likely data searches Jack needed to, was put into the computer at the commencement of employment by the Wages Department.

Jack had produced a form very early on when he started that Managers used when something happened to an individual, in three parts it gave starter information, when promotions or wages changed part two was used and part three was used when they left. All Jack had to do was ensure the Managers completed the job title properly and that was entered into the computer in Wages and the Wizard search engine could then find anything required. The demonstration by the NCB had happened the week before the Computer Centre invite arrived, so Jack had already had a meeting with the MD about his intention to use the Wizard system which, as it happened, was very fortuitous.

When he arrived at the Computer Centre, they wouldn't let him in! What was now the Cash and Carry Company had not got around to issuing company photo ID cards and in fact didn't do so for the next 10 years! Because he didn't have such a thing the Receptionist in Coventry wouldn't let him in, even though his name was on the list and the idea someone knew Jack Hughes from Lintwoods Cash and Carry Ltd was to visit that day and an imposter had rushed in ahead of him seemed more than a little fanciful. He was forced to stand in Reception, no chairs, for some 10 minutes whilst the Personnel Director, Jim Tunn, was sent for to vouch for him. He then had to wait another 20 minutes whilst they produced a photo ID to hang around his neck.

Jack had always had a thing and was to continue to do so for the rest of his life about wearing a name badge so once they handed this thing to him, he stuck it in his brief case ostentatiously. The Receptionist cleared her throat and started to speak but before she could really get going Jack said, "You now know who I am and I know who I am. I don't care whether I go that way," pointing to the inner corridor or, "that way," pointing to the exit.

"If you say I can't go that way," pointing to the corridor, "unless I put that thing around my neck then I'm going that way," pointing to the exit. "Which is it to be?"

With a look that could kill a lesser man she buzzed the corridor door open. "Thank you," said Jack and walked through. The Receptionist had told him to turn left at the end of the corridor but out of bloody-mindedness he turned right and had a wander around the building. He was never once stopped and asked who he was or what he was doing even though he wasn't wearing a label and certainly could not have been recognised by anyone because no-one knew him. He walked past two or three offices with their doors open and no-one in them so he concluded that, in fact, their security was a joke.

Eventually having walked around the whole building he arrived at a door which opened to reveal Jim Tunn who said, "Ah there you are I was just coming to look for you, come on in." So, Jack did to be greeted by people sitting around a large table with name boards with Jack's name in front of an empty chair. Sitting down he had trouble seeing over a huge stack of green and white striped computer paper. Jim introduced himself and then the Manager of the Computer Centre. In turn he introduced what turned out to be the proverbial computer geek.

He launched straight in with, "On the top of the paper in front of you there is a print out of all your employees in alphabetical order which is the first data we can provide."

Jack leaned forward. Picked it up and dropped it on the desk on the far side of the stack of paper. "The second pile is a list of all your employee…"

Jack interrupted, "I have always been taught that the customer tells the supplier what they need not the supplier telling the customer what they are going to get. I have never, ever, been asked for an alphabetical list of my employees and I cannot foresee any time when I would want such a thing. What I do need is a computer system that will enable me to enter all the data regarding my employees and ask it to tell me which of them have First Aider qualifications, or list who have TU dues deducted every month and to which union are they paid. Can your system do that?"

"Well, we would probably need to tweak the programme but yes it could."

"And how long would it take from when I asked you to print out all the £75,000 to £100,000 turnover Depot Managers' names would it take to provide the information?"

"Well, once we had got the programme right, and depending on the priority we gave to the request and the time of the month, for example we would be running the accounts at the end of the month then it might be possible to get you a reply at a quiet time, in, say, two weeks."

"Two weeks! And how long would it be before the programme is ready?"

"That I could not say. It would depend on a budget being authorised and then finding a programme with the ability to write the programme; say six to nine months."

Jack looked at him. He wanted to use Anglo Saxon but decided the prat wouldn't understand it so he simply said, "Nothing you have said or shown me is the least bit of interest to me. I have had an offer from the NCB to provide their Wizard system which would answer my questions as fast as I can type in the question. Six to nine months and then maybe weeks before I can get an answer to a question; I need an immediate answer, for example, when in a disciplinary hearing; is of no use whatsoever to get an answer weeks later. Thank you for the demonstration it was most illuminating," and at that he got up and left leaving the pile of print-outs on the table.

The Receptionist at Head Office greeted him with a blunt the MD wants to see you as soon as you come in. He thought, the magic of modern communications, the Holding Company Personnel Director had obviously telephoned and complained.

He had and the bollocking came to a quick halt when Jack said, "It doesn't do anything I want. It does lots of things that I don't want. It is three times as expensive, for Personnel for this Company, as the NCB Wizard system I have already seen and told you about. If I can't have Wizard then fine, but I won't use the services of the Computer Centre because it doesn't do anything I want and it will be at least two weeks every time before I would get what I wouldn't ask for; that's not the speed of light, a snail could do better."

A few days later he received a memo from the MD reminding him that he was authorised to spend up to £10,000pa on his own authority under the company policy. Henceforth Wizard worked for him.

Chapter 27

Jack was at a meeting in Durham one Monday with the NE Regional Director, David Isling, when he received a phone call from his Secretary to say that he had to be at a meeting in Leeds the following morning at 9.30am. It was to be in a building he would recognise when he got there and it was only a few along the road from Leeds football ground. While he was on the phone David's phone had also rung and he had received the same message. Jack didn't recognise the address as such and David confirmed that it was not the address of the Leeds C&C which they had acquired quite recently when it had gone bust.

Jack had been intending to return home to Newport Pagnell that night but David suggested he stay with him that night and they could travel down together the following morning; he, David would catch the train back whilst Jack went home after the meeting. Jack spent a very pleasant evening with David and his wife, Sue. Jack and David had worked closely together when David was in charge of the introduction of the new electronic till system and Jack had stayed with him and his wife before so it was very pleasant to catch up. However, it was to be the last relaxed pleasant evening Jack was to have for a very long time.

When they drove down the road the following morning looking for a building, they would allegedly recognise it was to be amazed at the sight of a huge new building, still with builders on site, with a huge Lintwoods sign on it! Parked around were a number of cars including the MD's. There were no office facilities so the Board of Directors ended up sitting on planks placed over carpenters' saw horses amidst the workers.

The luxury was extended further when they were served builders' tea—no la-di-da coffee here—and they had even made an attempt to get most of the stains off the mugs! The MD gave a little speech in which he explained the development of a number of new cash and carrys had been on going but due to their takeover bid for another company it had had to be kept secret. The building they were in was scheduled to open on the 1st November and they were here to start the planning process for it.

Running parallel they were also to plan for a new cash and carry to open in Glasgow on the same date and four further cash and carries in Edinburgh, Stirling, Perth and Inverness shortly after. A stunned silence followed and then a subdued clapping and cheering. Once it stopped the business started by the MD going around the table to each of the Directors in turn setting out what he expected from them and answering their questions in turn. Jack, having spent so long going around reducing staffing in all the C&Cs was delighted at the idea he would now be recruiting, not dismissing people, but as the others were speaking, he started jotting some notes which gradually had him thinking, *'Oh shit!'*

When it was his turn, the MD confirmed what Jack expected that his role was to be responsible for the recruitment of the staff. He responded by dropping a metaphorical fart of deadly carpet creeper performance, "I assume that the staff over in the old C&C in Leeds will be transferred here, so assuming most of them do, it may be that some live so far, the other side of the old one that it would be too expensive or impractical for them to get here but the bulk should do so. However, topping them up will be a problem and Glasgow is going to be a nightmare. How many staff are we going to need?"

The MD looked at the Ops Director who said, "Well, as this is all news to me as well, I don't know. How big is the building?" The MD told him. A quick calculation came up with about 138. Jack then asked, "Fruit and veg. Butchery? Wines and spirits…"

The MD interrupted at that point and said that information would be provided very soon to which Jack said, "Well, can we look at dates for a moment. How long will it take to fill up the place with stock?"

A month was the reply from the Ops Director. "So that brings us back to the 1st October. It will take a month to train all the staff before that so that brings us back to the 1st September for them to start. For salaried staff to give notice to their current employer, I assume we will want to pinch as many qualified staff as we can from competitors, which means that they will have to give notice on or before the1st August. We will have to interview them before that so allow another month to interview several hundred staff from whom we will need to select those to start, which brings us back to 1st July.

At that faces started to look concerned as it was already the 2nd. "We will have had to advertise about a month before that and we will have had to know what we are looking for before that to be able to design and place the adverts in the best media which I would guess is a local paper and the Job Centre at least. We will also need premises to do all that which means we should have started more than 2 months ago! And you won't give me the staffing requirements for a few days when we are already too late! I need to fly to Glasgow tomorrow and start the ball rolling, I need to hire a car and find the best Job Centre to use as not all of them will have the facilities we need. Oh, and you needn't look so worried I'll get you your people but it would have been better if I could have known about this something like three months ago. As it is it is going to need a miracle but I am used to that!"

There was a bit of a stunned silence when they realised that the work needed to be done and the time scales involved could not be rubbished the thought of failure showed especially on the MD's face.

Not surprisingly he was the first to respond and gave immediate permission for Jack to fly and hire a car—something which had been tightly controlled before because of costs—and in fact he said, "Whatever you need Jack. Just keep me informed if you need anything else. Keith make sure Jack gets at least an outline staffing plan this afternoon." The meeting broke up shortly after that. Jack had a quick word with Keith and David during which they agreed that the plan to be provided would be used for both Leeds and Glasgow. Jack ran David to the station and then headed back to Wellingborough. He had no idea as to how he was going to get the staff required only that he was committed to doing it on pain of death or worse! He stopped at the first services he came to on the M1 for a pee, cup of tea and a burger and to ring his Secretary, but not necessarily in that order.

He asked his Secretary to book him on the first flight to Glasgow in the morning, to arrange for a hire car to be picked up at the airport, a small Escort or similar would do—that ought to please the MD that he had not hired a Grenada which was his company car—and to find out the address of a Job Centre in the middle of Glasgow nearest to, and he gave her the address the MD had given him for the new branch, and to make an appointment with the Manager at the Job Centre an hour or so after the plane due time at Glasgow.

As a sweetener to the Manager, she was to say that he wished to discuss recruitment for 140 jobs to be created by their new enterprise. He also asked her to get a box of application forms from stationary for him to take with him. And finally, he asked her to remain in the office until he returned, as well as the two

Personnel Officers, as he would need to discuss with them his future movements along with those of his two Personnel Officers and some of the admin staff. He then went and grabbed his burger. And yes, it's obvious he'd had his pee first!

When he got back to Wellingborough just after 6.30pm it was to find the place a buzz. The excitement about expansion auguring as it did good for the future after what had been a difficult couple of years was palpable. Not five minutes after he had arrived the Ops Director's secretary tapped and came in. She handed him the proposed staffing plan the MD had ordered prepared and wished him luck in filling it.

To Jack that said his pointing out the problems of getting the new staff in time had spread throughout the company. And Jack still didn't know how he was going to achieve it. He left the office eventually just after 9pm knowing he would have to be up at 4.30am in order to get to Birmingham airport for the 6.30am flight.

With a wheeled travel bag full of stationary his arrival at Birmingham, flight and collection of hire car—an Escort—all went smoothly. Driving into Glasgow at the start of the rush hour was not so smooth but he did make slow progress but could not find the Job Centre. Having driven the length of the road three times he was certain that it wasn't on that road and so therefore the address he had been given was wrong. Spotting a small Newsagents, he risked parking on the double yellow lines and sped in to ask if they knew where it was, delivering papers etc almost certainly meant they knew the area.

Behind the counter was an Asian appearing man who once Jack asked if he could tell him where the Job Centre was, replied with a strong Scott's accent, "It's away doon the reet, Jimmy. First turning on the reet is the Crescent and if you turn doon there you'll find it on the reet." Laughing, Jack thanked him and rushed out. Talk about preconceived notions, seeing an Asian Jack had expected a Peter Sellers goodness gracious me accent but the chap was obviously a second generation Scott and had grown up there with a broad Scott's accent. *Well, you learn something new every day,* he thought.

Sure enough, the Job Centre was where he said it was and Jack parked up and walked inside. Over the next two years or so Jack was to have a lot to do with Job Centres in Scotland and England and what a lot of Jobsworths they were. The manager was, at first, very helpful but when Jack asked which would be the best paper to place a recruitment advert in, he went bananas. It became abundantly clear that he did not want a big advert in the paper telling applicants to collect an Application Form from the Job Centre. He even telephoned his boss who then spoke to Jack and he tried to persuade Jack not to place it. Jack however was determined.

He made it clear that he needed to attract people who were already working in the cash and carry industry, or similar, and he didn't feel that many of them would be regularly attending a Job Centre looking for another job. The job night was Thursday so he entered into the advert that completed application forms had to be returned on the following week Friday. As he worked out the dates the way in which he could organise so many interviews gradually formed in his mind.

He came up with a plan that involved turning up at the Job Centre on the Monday morning following the Friday closing date with a team, himself, a clerk and his two Personnel Officers. They would take with them a load of pre-printed letters which invited the addressee to an interview at a time and place. The individual's name and the time would have to be written in by hand. A group of 15 would be invited in at the same time. They would be introduced to the company, its terms and conditions and expected manner of working in an address that was to last no longer than 30 minutes and then they would be interviewed individually during 15-minute interviews.

Apologies would be given to the ones who would have to wait the longest to be interviewed; the interviews would be carried out by three interviewers, two from Personnel and one an Operations Area Manager who would have the new building in his area. Jack felt it important to involve Operations in the process partly because he could not have his own entire department of experts tied up in the process and partly to involve Operations so that they couldn't then place any blame purely on Personnel as they had been involved in the decision taking.

Each expert would have a list of five applicants each of whom would be interviewed for a maximum of 15 minutes. As he was thinking about it his first thoughts were that 15 minutes wasn't very long, but his/her application form would have already been studied for them to have made the interview list and they would have been spoken to for 30 minutes so any questions they might have asked, and taken up time with, would already have been dealt with in the 'common' to all of them delivery. Any way they didn't have any more time if they were to get through the numbers they needed to. He devised a simple grading system to select those for interview from their application forms.

Ideally, they were looking for C&C Assistants, someone of several years' experience in working in a C&C preferably food, alcohol, cigarettes, meat and white goods; lived not too far away (the wages were too low for someone to afford heavy travel costs!), they must have a good work history, not too many jobs in too short a time, show good reasons for having left them, average education qualifications and present a well written application form. Any one meeting those criteria would be graded 'A' and included on the 'for interview' list; anyone with no C&C but retail shop experience would be 'B' and only included on the list if there were insufficient 'A's and one missing criteria, whether C&C or retail would be a 'C'.

Jack hoped they wouldn't need to include any Cs. A similar grading system was shot together for the other categories of jobs but with the appropriate adjustments. In the event the system was to work extremely well and was used throughout the recruiting for all five openings in Scotland. In the event the interviews had all to be held in hotels as all the Job Centres could not provide the space needed.

Jack received an anguished cry from the Job Centre on the night the advert appeared in the paper that they had run out of the 350 application forms with which they had been provided for applicants within hours of the advert hitting the streets! Easily solved of course he had another 500 delivered overnight and even then, they ran out and needed more.

Jack, Gloria, one of his Personnel Officers and Nicki, one of the clerks, met at Head Office in Wellingborough at 7am on the Monday and made it up to Glasgow by midday. The Job Centre staff were surprised at their arrival, knowing they were driving up they didn't expect them until near the end of the day and they were astounded when Jack indicated that they wished to be shown the office that had been allocated to them for the sifting of the application forms.

In fact, in Glasgow and the other Centres that they worked they were to discover that a work ethic was noticeable only by its absence—for example, the Manager came in about 4.45pm to indicate that they were just about to close and looked positively shocked when Jack indicated that they anticipated working until at least 5.30 to 6ish. He disappeared and reappeared 5 minutes later with a set of keys and asked Jack to lock up when they left! Jack did. When they reappeared the following morning at 8.30am there was no sign of any staff so Jack let themselves in.

It was interesting to note that the staff arrived at 9am and later, none before so that they certainly were not open and ready for business at 9am, their official opening hour, and indeed by the time they'd all made themselves a drink, had a

160

chat about the telly the night before etc it was not much before 9.30am before they were really ready for business—about as bad as the one when Jack signed on when he left the Army. This pattern was to repeat itself throughout their working in Scotland.

The process of selection worked well and towards the end of each day they stopped assessing the applications individually but combined their experience of those graded to that time to be able to decide who should be offered an interview. Once decided the forms were handed to the clerk, Nicki, and she produced the letters inviting the selected ones to interview two weeks later. They finished the applications by 11.30am on the Friday and were on their way home by noon.

Returning two weeks later, this time without a clerk, they carried out the interviews with two groups of 15, one after the other in the morning and the same again in the afternoon thus interviewing 60 people a day for the first four days and only 30 on the Friday. They were very impressed by the general appearance and standards of the applicants—it was clear that there was high unemployment in Scotland unlike in London where they struggled enormously to recruit enough staff for the new C&C in Barking in all Jack was having to find staff for seven C&Cs in total! In fact, the process and the quality of the staff recruited for the five new C&Ss in Scotland worked very well. Only in Glasgow was there a problem one.

Jack used the Depot as a base, borrowing the Manager's car, when he made the initial approaches to the other four Job Centres across the country, except for Inverness where he had to base himself in a hotel to start with, it being too far from Glasgow to travel daily. Using the canteen on a couple of occasions he became aware that every time he did so there would be a strong Scot's accent voice going on about the bluidy English and when were they going to bugger off back to England and leave them alone.

When this happened a third time Jack became pissed off, looked about and identified the voice and then left the room. He found the Security Officer who was visiting that day, described the gob to him and instructed him to invite the individual to leave the premises and never return. He heard no more about the bluidy English but he was sure the sentiment didn't disappear!

Chapter 28

All in all, Jack was to spend 10 years at Linehams/Lintwoods. By the end of that time, it had grown from the original, multi-function company of 14 cash and carries, 41 retail stores, 4 distribution depots and a few bits and bobs employing some 600 people and £80 million of turnover to a single function company of 104 sites including 1 bonded warehouse, 1 huge Head Office, a petrol station and 101 cash and carries. It employed 5,500 people and turned over just over a billion pounds. Jack had thus overseen and led the acquisition of at least 10 companies and the work necessary to combine them into a single functioning entity. Along the way he had, at first attended the Joint Industrial Council (JIC) for the Wholesale Grocery and Provisions Trade, covering some 90,000 people, as a representative of his company and, in quite short progression, been elected to Chair the Employers' side.

Following the Second World War and the election of the first Labour Government they had started, in repayment of their debt to the unions, to impose legislation to improve the lot of the working man—they weren't too concerned about the working woman—and particularly in those industries or professions where the unions had not been able to organise. They had done this by the setting up of Wages Councils comprising equal numbers of employer, union and academic representatives. They set the minimum wages, hours, overtime, holidays and sick pay for their industry. Early ones were for the hairdressers and retail food shops. Jack had some initial experience of that with all the retail shops that Linehams had owned.

When he attended his first meeting at the JIC he was quite frightened. He was now operating at national level amongst national figures and he was only too sure that he would be out of his depth. However, by the end of the meeting he had become mightily unimpressed with some of these national figures, on both sides of the industry, who clearly knew little but spoke a lot! Having resolved for the Employers' side meeting, before he went, that he would say nowt and listen a lot he found it almost impossible as they were talking such ill-informed rubbish and they had to be corrected before meeting with the union side.

They listened and they accepted what Jack said, to his surprise, and it was perhaps not too surprising therefore that a year later he was elected to Chair the employer side. There followed several years during which he established a sound reputation as a safe pair of hands. During that time, he came to know and not trust the representative of their major competitor. He was to meet him in less pleasant circumstances in the future.

During the 10 years Jack was to handle some 200+ tribunal cases. That would seem to be an enormous number for just one company to undergo but divided out it meant about 20 a year across more than 100 sites and 5,500 employees or ex-employees in most cases! It almost became a joke that the rule of three applied. They always seemed to have three on the go at any one time but no sooner would they finish one than another one would start! It was at a time when unions were encouraging any member who had been dismissed to make a claim, no matter how trivial or unwarranted it was, in the hope that the employer would offer a small sum to settle as a 'nuisance settlement'.

Jack became very angry at this. One union in particular would immediately register an application no matter how unjustified. Jack began to use more and more a process, in the legislation, designed to eliminate frivolous, vexatious or otherwise unwarranted applications. The wording was to change over the years as a variety of governments tried to refine the working of the system. Initially a Pre-Hearing Assessment (PHA), then a Pre-Hearing Review (PHR), it was a Tribunal hearing which would take a look at an application to see if it was such a waste of time that the Applicant should be warned off. If they were warned off but continued with their application and lost then they risked having costs awarded against them.

Lacking such a warning the Applicant could not be pursued for costs, a founding principal of the process that an employee (nearly always ex-employees!) could make an application without fear of costs. It was open to the Respondent to ask for a PHA and Jack started doing this with every unjustified claim. Partly because the Tribunal system did not understand the law and partly because so many Tribunal Chairman were biased and or ignorant of the law, many of them were part-time Chairman operating solicitor's practices of their own and just turned up to a Hearing for the not inconsiderable sum they were paid for so doing; they were very reluctant to hold a PHA, which if it issued a warning would mean no nice Tribunal to preside over and thus no fee.

But the biggest problem was that there was no evidence taken at a PHA. Evidence is when a fact is stated on oath or affirmation and the Tribunal reaches its decision based on that evidence. At a PHA each side stated its case as to why there should or should not be a PHA, and, of course, they tended to contradict one another. Applicants, or more correctly their representatives were not slow to catch onto that where the parties did contradict one another the Chairman would always let it go without a warning as there was no evidence on which to base one! Thus, most of the time a PHA was a waste of time. Over 29 years Jack was to handle more than 650 Tribunals and ask for somewhere in the region of 150 PHA/PHRs but was only to obtain five and in only two of those was he able to get the Applicant warned off. The first one he ever did he won.

The Manager of one of the C&Cs in Oldham telephoned Jack one Monday morning asking for advice. The story he told amused Jack no end even though it was serious in nature. The Butcher, a young man of 25 or so and who had been there for some four years had been having an affair with a female customer. The lad heard, via the grapevine, that the woman's husband had found out and blacked her eye for her.

Hearing this the young man had, on a wet, cold, Sunday night, gone looking for the husband. Not finding him at home he had started a search of the local pubs and, going into the Dead Duck, had spotted him across the bar. Shouting out, as he advanced, 'Oy I want a word with you,' he headed for the husband. Being, shall we say, a not too salubrious pub, the staff were well versed in handling trouble and interspersed themselves between the two protagonists before blows were struck.

A member of staff had immediately telephoned the police who arrived in the shape of a wet, bedraggled and pissed off with life Constable. He quickly resolved the situation warning both males to be gone or else. The husband and wife went home but the Butcher went to another pub and had a drink or two. His resentment continued to build with each pint and by the time he had reached six it had reached boiling point, mainly because he was explaining to himself, he hadn't even hit the bastard just once. So, he resolved to do something about it and took himself off to their house. The husband answered the door to a loud knock and as soon as he did so the lad punched him straight in the face.

It was a good punch, a punch which gave much satisfaction but which did not put him down or end the matter; in fact, it stirred up the husband and he responded in kind. The resulting noise, shouting and the two of them rolling around the front garden attracted very quickly an appreciative audience, pouring out into the rain, regardless of it, and some from their windows where they proceeded to cheer on the entertainment. Unfortunately, around the corner was a, by this time very wet, cold and even more pissed off Constable. Hearing the noise, he investigated. Separating the combatants to loud boos from the crowd he was not best pleased to discover the two from the pub he had warned off earlier!

Having been nice once he was not inclined to give second chances so, calling for backup, he arrested the two of them and had them carted off to the nick. But for the incident he would have been off shift in 15 minutes now he had to process the two arrests so he threw the book at the pair of them. The Butcher did not enjoy his night in the cells. Having relayed all this the Manager added that the husband had been in to complain to the Manager and had informed him that his wife would not be trading with us in the future amounting to a loss of about £500 per week.

Jack, as was his want, asked him what he would like to do about it and he said he wanted to sack the bastard! Jack then set out what he had to do. His guilt or innocence would be judged by the Magistrates' Court. The relevant company rule indicated that a criminal offence, committed outside of employment but clearly connected to it, fell into the bounds of a potentially gross misconduct offence but it meant that his guilt or innocence would be judged by the criminal court and not the company.

Obviously, there was the issue of the loss of the sales each week, a not inconsiderable sum in any event so the Manager would have to get the lad to a formal meeting any way to set the route ahead. Jack dictated the letter over the phone, at which he would be asked to set out his version of events. If he refused to attend, or wouldn't speak, because his Solicitor advised that he shouldn't he should simply be told that the matter was being considered as potentially gross misconduct and that if he was convicted by the court, he would have to attend a disciplinary hearing at which his future would be decided.

A few days later, he pleaded guilty in Court, was fined £120 and was bound over to keep the peace for 12 months. As it was clearly a criminal offence connected to his employment and also because the Company had lost sales of

£500pw because of his actions it was a foregone conclusion that his employment was terminated for gross misconduct. What wasn't foreseen was that he would make an application to the Industrial Tribunal for unfair dismissal!

Jack thought about it for all of a nanosecond and then fired off a request for a PHA on the grounds that the application was clearly vexatious, clearly unreasonable and had no prospect of success. He, given the reluctance of Tribunals to grant PHAs didn't really expect to get one but he did. He prepared thoroughly. He had developed in his head a three point plan for Tribunals. They were Preparation, Preparation and Preparation!

First, he prepared by considering what the Applicant's case was, then he prepared the Tribunal's case and then finally his own case based on considering all three! The Applicant's case was set out in the IT1 (Industrial Tribunal form 1). This was supposed to set out the full details of the Application but they varied considerably in quality. It gave the Company the basis of what they would have to defeat. He was also very interested in who, if anyone, was representing the Applicant.

A jobbing high street solicitor was nothing to worry about and a Barrister not much more so, but a Trade Union full time official specialising in representing members was probably the most to be feared because he would be well prepared, knowledgeable and unlikely to be frightened by threats of costs. He obviously knew what the Company's case would be but he found it useful to speak to relevant managers who had been involved especially for details of what was being said after the dismissal, especially by the ex-employee to his/her mates still employed. Finally, he had to research the law, the case law and anything else he could find out about that particular Tribunal Office before sending off his IT3 Response. Liverpool, for example was notoriously left wing and very anti employer whilst Shrewsbury was exactly the opposite.

It appeared that the Butcher was not represented since the communications between him and the Tribunal were all by him but that did not stop Jack asking the Clerk when he checked in if there was a representative. The answer was 'no' so Jack relaxed just a little bit. The hearing was listed for 10am but they weren't called in until 10.45am and it was quite obvious that the Chairman was not a happy bunny about something or other—the two Lay Members, one from a union and one from an employer looked decidedly uncomfortable. Jack was to attend others of a similar atmosphere!

166

His opening remarks addressed to Jack were quite abrupt, "Well, Mr Hughes, you have asked for this PHA why do you say this application has no prospect of success?"

As Jack started to say his piece the Butcher, Mr Smifff, started interrupting. The Chairman was not happy at this and his first words were to tell Mr Smifff to be quiet; as he didn't so the Chairman's language got stronger until his last words, "Mr Smifff, shut up, if you say another word or interrupt again in any way, I will throw you and your case out. Now Mr Hughes what do you want to say?"

As this was one of the first cases Jack had handled, he had not yet formed the opinion that whoever upsets the Chairman first, loses, but this one started him well on the way to that opinion!

Jack drew the Chairman's attention to the small bundle he had prepared. He started with the Contract of Employment Statement and Mr Smifff's signature for receipt of it. He next pointed out the page extracted from the Company Handbook pointing out that committing a criminal offence out of employment but clearly related to it would be regarded as gross misconduct and liable to summary termination of employment. He had included a clipping from the local paper reporting the case and that Mr Smifff had pleaded guilty.

He pointed out that as a result, not only had they suffered the bad publicity as the paper had clearly named the employer but also that they had lost, on average, some £500 in sales every week. He finished by drawing attention to the letter summoning Mr Smifff to the disciplinary hearing, the notes of the hearing and the dismissal letter which contained the right to appeal which Mr Smifff had not done.

He finished by saying, "The procedures followed were fair by any measure, the offence was admitted and the damage to the company was considerable. For the Applicant to bring this case was clearly vexatious and without any prospect of success and I ask you to issue a warning that if he proceeds with it and loses you will order costs against him."

"Right Mr Smifff, you have heard what your employer has to say, what do you want to say?"

"What I do outside of work is nothing to do with them. I'm still giving her one like..." At this the two Lay Members and Jack burst out laughing but the Chairman, keeping a completely straight face, said, "Be that as it may, that is of no interest to us whatsoever. Look at the bundle your employer has produced, page 5, is that your contract?"

"Yes."

"Yes, Sir."

"Yes, Sir."

"Is that your signature?"

"Yes, Sir."

"Did you read it?"

"No, Sir."

"Why not?"

"Too much bloody paper."

"Your employer says that they have lost £500 per week as a result of the lady concerned no longer shopping there, is that true?"

"No. It was nothing like that amount." *Oh god thought Jack, I hope I didn't misread 500 pounds for 500 pence, but before he could think any further* the Chairman asked, "How much do you say it was?"

"More like £800 to £850 per week." Jack relaxed!

"Mr Hughes, what do you say to that?"

"As I said before, Sir, I believe the £500 to be an average but if the Applicant wishes to argue that it was £850, I won't argue with him." The Chairman with the slightest smile on his face said, "No, I don't suppose you would. Wait there," and at that the three of them stood up, as did Jack, and off they went. Normally Applicants and Respondents were kept apart in separate waiting rooms etc so that they couldn't start fighting if nothing else, so Jack was a little surprised at this. Wondering whether he should speak to Mr Smifff he was surprised before he could do so by the return of the Tribunal. They hadn't been gone two minutes! Sitting down the Chairman immediately said that they could see no prospect of success with this case whatsoever and they were therefore issuing the warning requested by Mr Hughes.

At that the Clerk, who had followed them into the room, took the envelope the Chairman was holding and gave it to Mr Smifff. What was immediately clear to Jack was that the warning had been produced before the hearing, there certainly hadn't been time in the two minutes or so that they had withdrawn for the letter to have been produced. Still, Jack enjoyed that one and retold the tale many times over the years that *he's still giving her one like!* He was also glad that no-one at any stage asked the question if the Manager of the C&C knew that the affair was going on! The answer to that one might have been somewhat embarrassing.

In the 200 or so that Jack was to handle during the 10 years he was there, there were many that were memorable but not really of significance. They all taught that the most important step in winning at Tribunal was the procedure followed in the disciplinary or capability hearing. Jack would come to believe that that amounted to 95% of the success in winning. It was not until he joined what would turn out to be his last employer that he became familiar with the 'any difference test' which was an argument available to an employer (actually in all cases ex-employer but the Tribunals never referred to 'ex' only the employer). There was also the issue of contribution, just how much had the employee ('ex' again!) contributed to their own dismissal. More of those two later.

Shortly before Jack's time at Lintwoods came to an end he conducted his first ever case at the Employment Appeal Tribunal. A full blown Appeal Court, but just for Industrial Tribunal appeals, later to become The Employment Tribunals, it functioned through a Judge as the Chairman and two Lay Members who were senior members of their respective sides, union and employer. As the Company had grown Jack had appointed an Industrial Relations Manager, to augment his two Personnel Officers as the business had grown and demand increased.

She turned out to be probably the worst recruitment mistake he ever made. Initially things had gone well then in just one week disaster struck. At their biggest C&C in Manchester a Security Officer caught the Senior Shop Steward in the car park with a packet of bacon he had not paid for. When he was stopped, he immediately offered the explanation that there were long queues at the Checkout and he was intending to return and pay for the bacon once he had put it in his car and the queue had died down a bit. When this was reported to Jack, he thought all his Christmases had come at once.

The guy had been a troublemaker for years. He had been suspected of theft for years but had been too clever to be caught. He also had ambitions of becoming a full time official of the union and used the most trivial of reasons, even creating some of them himself for publicity in his cause. Two weeks before the General Manager had rung Jack because he had been caught, past the checkouts but not yet outside the building, again by a Security Officer, who really should have let him leave the building but he moved too soon and his excuse that he had been taken short and needed to go to the lavatory before the checkout was difficult to disprove.

On Jack's advice the GM conducted a formal disciplinary hearing, with the full time official from the union present (as was required by the company procedures and the law) and Jack. Suspending the hearing to allow him to consider his decision he said to Jack, "I would desperately love to sack the bastard but I think it's a bit too thin. What do you think?"

"The man is a thief. He will do it again it's just a matter of catching him— easier said than done I know. However, what we can do is issue him with a letter that is effectively a Final Written Warning. It will say something like *I am giving you the benefit of the doubt on this occasion but should your honesty ever come into doubt again you will be fired. Anything at all, break the rules at all no matter how minor especially if it potentially involves theft and you are out and you are reminded that it is always the company policy to prosecute under such circumstance...*" And that was what they did.

Now that the same thing had happened again Jack contacted the full time official to tell him what had happened and the time and date of the hearing. When offered the opportunity of being present he said, "No bloody chance. Sack the bastard he was lucky not to be sacked last time, I thought you were more than fair and it's none of my remit, or the union's, to defend a thief. Sack him."

Unfortunately, as it turned out Jack could not make the hearing at the last minute and had to send the new Industrial Relations Manager in his stead. He instructed her that whatever the Shop Steward said, even if he called Jesus Christ as a witness who supported him, she was to authorise the General Manager to sack him. It did not matter if there was a bright star in the sky and three Kings on camels he was to be sacked. In fact, if he was not sacked, she would be! He explained in great detail why and therefore expected it to happen.

The hearing was scheduled for the Friday at 10.30am. Jack had had to go to the Holding Company Head Office in Milton Keynes and was there until late not getting back to Wellingborough until after 6pm. When he did arrive it was to find a note on his desk telling him to go immediately to the MD's office which he did. Consequently, he didn't leave the office until gone 9.00pm, a not very happy bunny.

Jack operated a roster for Saturday and Sunday mornings and had not been due to go in the following morning but as a result of the meeting the evening before he had to go back in on Saturday morning. As a result of that meeting, he had to go to the Rushden Cash and Carry at 8.30am first and then on to Head Office, arriving just after 10.30am. When he arrived, it was to find another note on his desk instructing him to go straight to the MD's office. He was more than a little annoyed because the Rushden problem could easily have been dealt with by telephone but the annoyance, he felt was just about to get worse.

The MD opened with, "I have had Reg, the GM at Manchester on the phone, livid, that he had caught the Shop Steward stealing and that, on your orders, he had been told that he could not sack him. Did you tell him that?" Jack looked at him dumbfounded.

"No, I did not. I sent Christine, the Industrial Relations Manager, to sit in with him whilst he conducted the disciplinary hearing, take the notes etc and…"

He stopped and then gestured to the MD's phone, "May I?" Following a nod, he picked up the phone and dialled his Supervisor's extension—he knew she was in because he had seen her car in the car park—in fact she had parked in his space not expecting him to be in. When she answered he instructed her to come up to the MD's office as quick as she could. It was an uncomfortable silence as Jack knew if the MD believed Reg then he was in trouble. The Supervisor tapped on the door and entered.

Jack said, "You were present on Thursday when I spoke to Christine about going to Manchester weren't you?

"Yes."

"What did I tell her?"

"You told her he was to be sacked. That if she didn't ensure he was sacked you would sack her."

"Any questions?" The MD shook his head and thanked her. He then said, "I didn't think it was true. I think you should also know that during the last two Saturdays she, unsolicited, brought me in a coffee and ran you down quite badly. She also intimated that she was sexually available if you were no longer the Personnel Director and she was." That stunned Jack, so much so that he literally did not know what to say. The MD let the silence last for a short while and then said, "I will leave you to deal with her."

"Oh, I will," said Jack and left the room. On his way to his office, he stuck his head into the Personnel Department Office and catching the eye of the Supervisor indicated his office, now. Passing the Industrial Relations Manager's office, he stuck his head in there too and said, "My office now." Once both women were present, he said to the IRM, "Why did you not fire the Shop Steward yesterday?"

"Well, when he said there was a queue at the checkout the General Manager confirmed it, so I thought it unsafe to sack him, especially as he was the Shop Steward."

"When I briefed you, I told you he was likely to say that and that it was not acceptable as an excuse since he had been specifically warned about such action didn't I? Also why do you think that your opinion as to his guilt or innocence amounts to anything? When you first started and again when I was briefing you, I repeated that if Reg believed he was guilty then he was—there was no need to prove beyond all reasonable doubt; it would simply be enough to have a reasonable belief. I went through that didn't I?"

"I don't remember you saying that."

"Oh yes he did," piped up the Supervisor.

"Why did you tell Reg that I had directly forbidden you to allow his sacking?"

"I did no such thing."

"Reg told the MD that you did." She remained silent.

"Why have you been running me down to the MD?"

"I've never done that!"

"The MD says you have, on the last two Saturdays you were in." At that the Supervisor interrupted and said, "Oh yes, she has. She's been running you down to me, almost every time we speak."

"Well, here's what's going to happen," said Jack, "I'm going to the lavatory and when I come back, I expect one of two things to have happened. Either I find your instant resignation letter on my desk and you gone, or if you are still here, I will sack you. I will sack you for disobeying a direct order, for running me down to the MD and anyone else and for the mistake you made."

"Mistake?"

"Yes, offering your pussy to the MD; if it had been your arse, you might have succeeded but the mistake you made was, he fancies fellas not sheilas." At that Jack walked out with the laughter of the Supervisor ringing in his ears and a stunned look on the face of his ex-IRM. When he returned the Supervisor was still there holding two letters and no sign of the IRM.

The Supervisor said, "This one's from her, she's gone but I don't think you've heard the last of her and this one is from me." Taking it Jack opened it thinking as he did so that it was her resignation as well but it wasn't. Consisting of three pages of A4 closely typed, she had set out all the details of the things the IRM had said about him and, interestingly, the MD. Clearly the Supervisor had not had time to produce this in the time it had taken him go to the lav which she confirmed by saying that she had been so concerned about the lies she believed she was being told that she had set it all out and had intended to give it to him on the Monday but as he had come today she had given it to him now.

Jack thanked her profusely for the letter and the trust she had shown in him and she walked out of his office laughing and muttering *offered him your arse!* Jack just prayed that the MD never found out that he had uttered such a calumny about him!

Chapter 29

The IRM left him one last present. A few days after she had gone, he received a Tribunal decision through the post for a case she had conducted. They had been suffering quite severe stock losses in a large C&C in the North East. One day the Assistant Manager walking out the back door noticed a pile of rubbish by the back door, presumably put there ready to be thrown out. Something about it did not look quite right so he stopped and had a closer look. Under some layers of cardboard, he found six bottles of whisky and several packs (outers of 200) cigarettes. Looking around he could not see any staff members watching him so he replaced the cardboard and walked away.

Reporting to the Manager straight away, they both then kept a careful eye on it. They gave up after a couple of days in the belief that someone must have seen the AM finding the goods so they had been warned not to go near the stuff. Then the Manager received a tip off that a number of staff were involved in persistent stealing. Six staff were named and the Manager, realising this was way beyond his ability to deal with reported it up the line. Investigations were carried out by the Security Department part of which involved talking to the local police.

They asked for a staff list which revealed that six staff, all male, had criminal records and these were the same six the informant named. Two of them had served time for Grievous Bodily Harm and were regarded as quite dangerous by the police. The six were immediately suspended and an investigation started. Fingerprint examination of the goods proved useless as a number of staff were identified as having handled the bottles, including two of the suspects but they could have done that legitimately putting them on display. It took six weeks for the investigations to be completed.

During that time a second informant came forward naming the same six but she only did so on the assurance that her name would be kept secret—the same basis as the first one. Given the very real fears that both informants and the management had, it was decided never to reveal that there were two informants since it was felt that to do so would have enabled the thieves to identify them. It also meant that they could never be named or used if the case(s) went to Tribunal. During the six weeks the losses stopped which meant the company had not lost about £6,000 based on the previous loss rate.

Four of the six had been with the company long enough to bring claims to Tribunal and two had not. Jack estimated that, if they lost, they would have to pay out about £4,000 to the four of them so they took the decision to conduct disciplinary hearings and sack them. Not surprisingly they all submitted claims but two were immediately struck out as they had insufficient service to make applications. It took 15 weeks for the cases to come to hearing, all four of them together, and because Jack had been involved in conducting a Tribunal elsewhere his new Industrial Relations Manager had conducted the case. When the decision arrived, just after her jump-before-she-was-pushed leaving, Jack was a bit surprised that they lost.

He read the decision through a couple of times that day and then thought about it overnight. The following morning, he went to see the MD and told him the result.

"Did we lose because of her presenting a bad case?" He asked.

"No, I don't think so, much as it pains me to say so," said Jack. "I think the Tribunal went bonkers. There is two pages of speculation that the informant might have been the thief and had given a false tip off to direct suspicion elsewhere; that the informant believed what he said but was wrong, when he believed they were guilty but they weren't, and they go on speculating on what might have been the truth for two pages of A4 but the one thing they don't do is consider what if the tip off was true? I think that just might be grounds for an appeal—they didn't consider the employer's defence!" And that's what he did.

Jack was notified that there was to be a Review Hearing on date, place etc—normal procedure to sift out those with no legal grounds for an appeal, just a 'I don't agree with the decision and want another bite at the cherry' claim.

The Employment Appeal Tribunal was based in St James's Square, in London, at that time and only later moving to the Embankment. There were two waiting rooms, not this time for applicants (Appellants) and Respondents, but for smokers and non-smokers! Generally, appeals were conducted by lawyers for both sides, not the employer and ex-employee so they didn't need to be separated in case they got a good old punch up going as happened sometimes at Tribunal hearings. The surroundings were much grander, the property originally being owned by Lady Astor and in Jack's case the hearing was conducted in the Gold Room. It was, literally, all gold, wallpaper, woodwork, ceiling and doors, if somewhat faded and tatty, all very, very, grand. In fact, so grand was it that Jack started to wonder whether he should be there! He did not have long to wait before he was shown in by a clerk.

The Chairman was a Judge, sitting in the middle, and on either side of him were the two Lay Members, this time Jack recognised one of them as a well-known trade union leader but the other one was unknown to him. He quickly laid out his papers on the Lectern, as opposed to Tribunals where everything was done with everyone sitting, at the Employment Appeal Tribunal the person addressing the EAT did so standing. Having everything sorted Jack looked at the Chairman who asked if he was ready and when Jack said he was he invited Jack to start. Jack had decided to keep it as simple as he could.

He had been unable to find any case law that might help but more importantly had been unable to find any that might count against him. The ex-employees had not attended to represent their arguments nor had they sent any legal representation. So, Jack simply laid out the case as he had done to the MD shortly before, summarised that as they failed to consider if the tip-off was accurate was the dismissal fair? He was asked a couple of questions by the TU leader, quite hostile at first but once Jack said the union had refused to represent them at the disciplinary hearings his attitude changed recognising, as did Jack, that such a refusal normally only happened when the union believed overwhelmingly that they were guilty.

Jack waited in the Waiting Room for about 20minutes and was then called back in. He stood when the EAT entered and remained standing when they sat down expecting to be addressed re the decision but he was told to sit down by the Chairman. The Chairman said, "I am pleased to tell you that we have reached a unanimous decision but before I tell you what it is I would just like to say on behalf of myself and my Lay Members what a good job you have done in presenting your case and how nice it is to see an employer with the guts to speak for himself rather than all these dam lawyers."

Jack smiled. "Now stand up please."

Jack stood. "We think there is much in what you say Mr Hughes. We have very carefully read the Tribunal's decision and there is indeed no word whatsoever that they considered that the tip off might be true and it is our opinion that they should have done, even if they then went on to discount it, they should have considered it and they did not. We are therefore allowing this case to go to full hearing and you will be notified of the date in due course. Good day to you." And with that they got up and left. Jack was delighted both at the decision and at the comments made about his performance.

(It did not come to hearing for nearly 18 months and by that time Jack no longer worked for Lintwoods and it was to be three years after that before discovering the outcome.)

Chapter 30

Jack was making his way back home down the M18 from the Retreat Monastery he used for running his middle and senior management training courses—weird to be served a pint in the evening by a Monk in a habit—one Friday afternoon when his phone in the car rang. It had only been fitted a couple of weeks before and while it had proved very useful on a couple of occasions it had also proven to be a nuisance and this was one of those times. It was the MD asking where he was. He told him halfway along the M18 which was followed by, "Were you planning on driving straight home?"

"Yes, I was. I should get there about 7.30pm if there aren't any holdups it being Friday night and all."

"I need you to come into the office. What's the earliest you could get here?"

"About the same time, subject to the traffic as I have just said."

"Ok, see you then. Ring me if you are going to be much later than that," and he rang off. Jack wasn't a happy bunny but it was obvious something was up and he would just have to wait until he got to the office before, he found out what it was.

Walking into the MD's office just after 7pm he discovered that the Marketing Director was with the MD. The MD immediately said, "We have a major problem that is costing us a lot of money and you are just about the only man in the Company that I know is not the guilty one." *That's a weird way to start a conversation,* thought Jack.

The MD continued, "a competitor is coming out with promotions identical to ours, and I mean identical, three or four days before our promotion starts so that ours is blunted and we're losing money. Some of the suppliers are complaining because we aren't achieving the sales we and they hoped for and they are talking about stopping discounts for promotions with us. That would be disastrous. This competitor can only be doing this if someone in Lintwoods is leaking confidential information about the forthcoming promotions to them. Now I know it cannot be you because you don't see marketing information…"

"Oh, thank you," said Jack to laughs from both of them.

"Do you remember a manager from Oldham little—they had three C&Cs in Oldham, known as little, big and the other one—called David Thomas?"

"No, I think he left shortly after we took Wright and Brown over, I certainly never met him."

"Well, we have been using Private Detectives and they have traced the information as far as him, he works for some new start business we don't know in Oldham, you don't remember if he was friendly with any of the other Wright and Brown Managers?"

"No sorry, as I said I've never met him and, although I went to Oldham little shortly after he left, I never met him and the Assistant Manager, if I remember aright went with him."

"Well, that was our last hope. I don't know where we go from here," said the MD and put his head in his hands. Jack sat in the silence for a minute or two and then said, "Why don't I go and ask him?" Both of them looked at him in astonishment. The Marketing Director looked at him and speaking for the first time said, "What do you mean?"

"Exactly what I said. Drive up there, walk in and ask him. I might just have to introduce myself first, probably as someone retained by Lintwoods to identify the guilty leaker and sue them for damages if they won't tell me. I'll probably need to work on what I'm going to say but something like we've traced the chain to you, we're not really interested in you but the next person in the chain but if you won't tell me who that is I'll sue you for every penny you've got and then some to ensure we break the chain; we will, of course, involve the police—you've got five seconds or else—along those lines sort of thing."

They looked at him for some time until the Marketing Director said, "You'd do that?"

To which Jack replied, "Not as frightening as opening the door of a Belfast number plated Morris Minor."

"Do it," said the MD. So, Jack did. Having got the name of the competitor Jack went into his own office and looked up the address on one of his A to Zs—he kept a set which virtually covered the whole country in his office. He knew it took about three hours from his home in Newport Pagnell to Oldham but the C&C he was heading for was on the far side so he estimated his time to be three and a half hours. He rang them and ascertained that they opened at 8.30 on Saturday mornings which probably meant that the staff would start arriving about half an hour before that. So, he needed to be there about 8am and that meant leaving home at 4.30am. *That'll teach me to volunteer—I should have known that from my Army days,* he thought! Being a Saturday meant lighter than normal traffic so he had time for a quick pit stop before arriving just before 8am. He parked in their car park with a clear view of the door of the building. Building! It was half a dozen old asbestos sheet garages standing side by side with some sort of prefabricated shed at one end. None of the garage doors opened and, as Jack discovered when he walked in to the shed, holes had been crudely knocked through the side walls of the garages to allow access through the six. The floor was hardened earth with goods just standing on the earth. Some of the piles, particularly sugar he noticed had split packages with sugar and other contents spilt out. It was disgusting, unhygienic and unsafe.

He wondered how on earth (no pun intended!) they had got away with it from Trading Standards and the Health and Safety lot. It was easy to spot the guy he thought was the manager because he was the one in the suit and seeing him arrive Jack had followed him in. Jack was dressed as his best 'legal'; double breasted navy blue pinstripe three piece suit, brilliant white shirt and his old RASC regimental tie. Walking straight into the Manager's office he introduced himself as he said he would to the two MDs the night before and watched the blood drain out of David Thomas's face. Jack started to count down from five and had got to three when the door behind him was thrown open and an Asian looking man walked in. Cheerily he greeted them and asked who Jack was.

Jack did not want to say to a stranger and simply said, "Someone who is just leaving, but I will be in touch," and at that he walked out swearing under his breath. He drove out of sight of the building and then stopped. He rang the C&C and asked to speak to David Thomas. Once he heard Thomas say hello, he started, 'five, four, three...' when Thomas interrupted him and asked, "Why are you going after me, I'm not the one betraying my employer?"

To which Jack replied, "My employer has lost a huge sum of money as a result of your impacting the promotions and if they can't get at traitor, they'll get at you to break the chain, starting with suing you for at least a million pounds or alternatively you can just whisper the name to me and walk away free, so which is it to be?" Jack let the silence run and then started, "Five, four, three..."

"Kieran Hill, the Manager at the other Oldham."

"A very wise decision if I might say so. Goodbye Mr Thomas, this is the last you will hear from me, unless, of course, you are lying in which case we will come after you for two million." Jack rang off and then rang the MD. He rapidly described the events and was gratified to receive a fulsome thank you and congratulations. When he went in on the Monday morning and asked the MD what he was going to do about it, it was to discover that he had made a statement to the Fraud Squad on the Saturday and they had raided his house on the Sunday! All that was left for Jack to do was to write to the prison where Hill was being held dismissing him for gross misconduct.

Chapter 31

In early 1982 the Holding Company got rid of the Chairman who had created the whole group and replaced him with a bit of a City Whiz kid. Initially the holding company had been based in Northampton but as the group grew a number of the HQs of the C&C company, the Holding Company and the Pharmacy group were based in a building on the other side of Wellingborough and Jack had been moved there when he was promoted to the Personnel role for the whole C&C company.

The three companies' senior executives, all fourteen of them, shared a dining room. It could only seat 10 but as people were often away it was nearly always possible to get lunch if you wanted it. One benefit meant that you could easily talk to someone from Holdings if you wanted to. Unfortunately, Jack didn't get off too well with the new Chairman. Jack had been going out one lunchtime, the cook being on holiday, with the MD and the Ops Director when they bumped into the Chairman. He needed to borrow a car so Jack gave him his keys. He wasn't too impressed when he got it back as the guy had obviously eaten a sausage roll or pork pie whilst driving and had left the detritus all over in the front. Jack debated as to whether to say anything but came to the conclusion since he was new to Jack that discretion should be the better part of valour.

However, a few weeks later the issue was to reappear. Jack was in his office when Reception rang to say there was a policeman in Reception asking for him. As this happened from time to time anyway Jack wasn't particularly surprised or worried and asked for him to be shown up. He was expecting to be addressed about some personal problem or other regarding an employee so he was somewhat taken aback to be told that he was to be reported for driving without lights in fog a short while before.

As the copper was talking Jack suddenly realised that he was talking about the lunchtime when Jack had loaned the Chairman his car. It had indeed been foggy in the morning but by the time the three Directors had gone out a lunchtime

182

in the MD's car it had largely cleared up. Jack could particularly remember the day because they had driven past a number of cars, parked at the side of the road, which had obviously been in shunts because they all exhibited damage one, a police car, had been especially banged about. As Jack explained about the Chairman using his car and leaving it in such a mess, he must have struck a chord with the copper because he opened up in return and told Jack that the Inspector involved was also regarded as a bit of a bastard by the rank and file.

Apparently, he had driven out to the first accident, which involved the first police car, a necessity that a senior officer attend any accident involving a police vehicle, and having parked his police car, walked along to the other one and just as he got there when he heard an almighty bang, turned round, only to see his car with another one, an old Volvo, halfway up the boot of his! He had turned to the said Constable, sworn, and then ordered him to take the number of any car passing by without their headlights on. The Constable was still taking numbers at lunch time when the Chairman drove past even though the fog had long cleared. Jack was delighted to take the copper to the Chairman's office and leave him to it.

Unfortunately, that was not the end of the matter. After the copper had left the Chairman appeared at Jack's door and it was clear that he was not a happy bunny. At one stage Jack thought that the Chairman was suggesting that Jack should take the hit but he wasn't having any of that but he did tell him about the conversation he had had with the copper. Several weeks later the Chairman appeared at his door again and told him that he was due in court the following day and he expected Jack to be there as his witness to the fact that the fog had cleared by lunchtime.

Jack did not really want to get involved and suggested he would be better getting a report from the Met Office but the Chairman was adamant, so Jack went. Whilst nothing was said directly it was made clear that if he still wanted to be in employment when the share option scheme matured in three months' time then his evidence should be forceful and favourable to the Chairman.

The share option scheme had been introduced almost three years before and, unlike most schemes where the executive was simply given the shares as a reward, in this scheme the participants, the 60 or so senior executives in the whole group, had to double the share price, by their successful running of the group businesses, or they would not receive the options. In fact, as they neared the three year anniversary date it looked like they would have increased the share value by more than six times generating quite large sums of money for the participants and shareholders.

Jack had been following medical advances in the treatment of deafness, particularly caused by Rubella, and had been in correspondence with the House Ear Institute in Los Angeles about cochlea implants for his daughter. That would cost an enormous sum of money which in normal circumstances Jack could never have afforded but with the share option scheme money, what was left after the Taxman had stolen his 60%, plus a loan he could just about afford it. The only condition he still had to meet was that he had to be in employment of the group at the anniversary date which of course the Chairman knew.

In the event the court case progressed with the Chairman giving his evidence supported by Jack's evidence that the fog had gone by lunchtime. The prosecution tried to put Jack under pressure but he countered with the Constable's story about still logging cars at lunchtime on the orders of the Inspector and that seemed to satisfy the Magistrates. The one thing that always puzzled Jack was that the Chairman didn't use a solicitor.

Jack did manage a little satisfaction a week or two after receiving the share option money, when over lunch, one day, the conversation turned to recruitment and the Chairman demanded to know what Jack was doing in the way of recruiting Graduates implying, although not actually stated, that he was remiss in some way.

"Well," said Jack, "seeing as you had me go yesterday and sack the Midlands Regional Director for incompetence, and he was indeed incompetent, and seeing as how he was the only Director in the company who had a degree, I think that speaks for itself." Jack enjoyed that. Shortly after that the Holding Company moved to Milton Keynes to very luxurious offices and out of Jack's proximity.

Chapter 32

The last major incident which Jack got involved in, although he didn't know it was to be the last at the time. Happened on Christmas Eve. Jack had called into the Rushden C&C on his way to Wellingborough to interview a member of staff and sign some legal documents for her. When he arrived at his office it was to be greeted by a message to ring the Chairman urgently. A few weeks before the MD had been promoted to be Chairman of the Retail Company and the Cash and Carry Company, with the Marketing Director being promoted to Managing Director.

On the basis that reconnaissance is always a good thing Jack stuck his head around the MD's door and said that he had an urgent message to ring the Chairman did he have any idea what that was about. The answer was 'no' so he rang the Chairman. The Chairman simply said to get over to Milton Keynes, the Retail Chain HQ ASAP. So, Jack did. He was shown straight in to the Chairman's office who proceeded to tell Jack a tale.

He suspected, no knew, that the Marketing Director there was taking bribes from suppliers to place orders with them and he was going to interview him and wanted Jack with him when he did so, so that he could then sack him. He said that he believed that he was involved with at least five suppliers and had a diary that showed payments to him from one of them.

He proposed getting him and accusing him of taking money from the five of them but wasn't too sure how to progress after that hence he was asking Jack's advice as to how to proceed from there. Jack was more than stunned if only because the retail company had its own staff including a Security Director and a Personnel Director (well Human Resources Director a title Jack hated—he felt people were not resources they were much more important than paper clips, blotting pads or desks but, along with so many other Americanisms, the term was taking over) but Jack was unsure why he was there so asked.

"Because you're sharp, can smell bullshit from 10 miles and have bigger balls than a bull and will need them with this bastard. You also have immense experience of conducting these sort of hearings which I don't have."

That's true, thought Jack, *when he had been promoted to MD of Lintwoods and had set-up the firing of one of the Regional Directors, the day after he was appointed, but had left it to Jack to deal with, so true to form it was happening again.* He also took the opportunity to think what he should say. He started with, "That doesn't sound right to me…"

"What do you mean?"

"You have the diary for one which is obviously pretty hard proof but how much absolute proof do you have about the other four?"

"Well, two of them have only started trading with us since he was appointed and the other two are not companies we would normally trade with."

"The problem we have is that he knows absolutely certainly and without any doubts, who he is on the take from and so if even one of them you name is wrong, he will know that your information is faulty in that respect at least and will be likely to clam up. He'll know that the suppliers will not be too willing to admit their guilt in bribing him so silence will be his best policy."

"So, what do I say then?" Jack thought about it for a moment and then said, "I think you should start by introducing me as a Senior Executive of the Holding Company and are there at your request as a witness. That should start to put him on edge. Then you simply say 'I have been handed evidence that you have been taking bribes from suppliers and you are prepared to give him this opportunity to tell you about it in an informal meeting.'

"Should he remain silent or deny it, you will turn it into the formal system and suspend him, 'Then stop and let silence do the job.' Obviously, I have no idea what he will say but you must simply reply to anything he says by saying, 'tell me about it' unless of course he tells you then listen and ask questions as appropriate. If it gets a bit too silly, 'oh yes you did—on no I didn't', then I will step in and I will anyway if you look at me or I feel it would be appropriate for me to do so. I'll sit to the side of him but slightly back so that I am not in his immediate eye line."

The Chairman nodded and at that Jack stood up and arranged two chairs facing the Chairman's desk with the one on the left about a foot further back than the one on the right. The door to the office was to the right so that with Jack sitting on the left chair the empty one would be nearest to the door and inviting to the Marketing Director when he came in. Jack nodded again and the Chairman picked up the phone and asked his Secretary to ask the Marketing Director to come to his office immediately.

It was only moments before there was a knock at the door which was immediately opened by the secretary allowing the Marketing Director to come in. He said good morning to the Chairman and then looked enquiringly at Jack. Jack stayed sitting and the guy sat down. The Chairman said, "This is a Senior Executive of the Holding Company and I have asked him here today to be my witness as I have been handed some very serious evidence that you have been taking bribes from suppliers. That is, of course, a very serious matter and I wanted to give you the opportunity to explain it. So why have you been doing it?" *Not quite right,* thought Jack*, but close enough.*

The guy shrank a bit in his seat and said, "I haven't."

"You have."

"I haven't."

"You have and I have the evidence to prove it."

"I haven't and I think I want my solicitor present before this goes any further." The Chairman immediately looked at Jack. *Surprise, surprise* thought Jack*, thought Jack, now I need to say something but what—quick, think!*

By this time the guy had shrunken down on the chair and was hugging his knees in a very closed, defensive posture. Jack said, "That would be a pity and, anyway, you do not have the right under the Company Disciplinary Procedures to be accompanied by anyone other than a fellow employee or your union rep. However, this is so serious that I am prepared to allow you to have your solicitor present if you continue to insist on it but in such circumstances, I would feel the need to call the police in. They, of course, have much greater powers than do we, for example they would have access to your bank accounts which will clearly show evidence of such transactions…"

At that the guy sat up straight and smiled saying, "You can check my bank accounts all you like you will not find a single entry which is not legitimate and which I can account for." *Shit, shit, shit,* thought Jack*. By his words and body language he knows that he hasn't paid any of the bribe money into the bank. Think, think, think! The Chairman was looking decidedly unhappy at this point.*

Jack deliberately delayed responding for a good ten to fifteen seconds and then said, "You are quite right, people on the take like you are usually clever enough not to pay the evidence into their accounts but they are almost never clever enough to hide the negative evidence which a good Forensic Accountant, and we have some very good ones at Holdings, find in no time at all."

At that, the guy started to shrink down again so Jack, believing he was on the right route said, "The money is normally spent and sometimes saved. If spent it is usually on luxuries so for example, there should be a record of how you paid for your wife's new BMW 7 Series. (The Chairman had told Jack that that was what had first made him suspicious because the guy wasn't paid enough to afford one of them).

"There should be invoices, paperwork for the car traded in, a HP agreement or similar; there should be records of rates, gas, electricity, that holiday to the Seychelles, all sorts of things should show as coming out of your bank account but they did not come out of your bank account because you paid for them with the cash bribes. If you have saved some then there will be bank/building society savings books with a lovely trail of entries in; even if you have popped over to Switzerland of other nice safe banking areas you must have account details and the police will find them because we will call them now and you won't be able to get home quick enough to hide them."

By that time the guy was an absolute picture of dejection so Jack paused and nodded at the Chairman while mouthing 'again'.

"You have been taking bribes, haven't you?" The guy looked up and almost whispered 'yes'. "From Wellbeings?" The one he had the diary for. "Yes," and the Chairman named the next three to which he said 'yes' to each but when he got to the fourth the guy said 'no'.

Jack had a little smug feeling at that. After a bit more conversation about amounts the Chairman stood up and said, "Wait there," and walked out. By this time the guy was quietly sobbing. *Tough,* thought Jack. The one thing he wasn't going to do was talk to him so he busied himself writing notes of the meeting so far especially the detail about the bribes. It must have been a good 30 mins before the Chairman returned and when he did it was with two policemen, one in uniform, who promptly arrested the Marketing Director and took him away.

What Jack didn't discover until later was that the Chairman had arranged with the police that instead of going down from the top floor in a lift or walking down the stairs, they had walked to the far end of the top floor, most of which was open plan office space, and down one floor and back along the whole length of that floor and the same with every floor in the building so that virtually every employee in it saw him being taken away by the police.

"And just think," said the Chairman, "that bastard was on a salary three times greater than yours."

Jack looked at him and said, "What happens now?"

"Well, first, thank you for your help. Your approach was absolutely right if I'd gone my way, I'd have blown it, so well done. I expect the police will want to take a statement from you. Once he's seen a solicitor it's possible, he might try and deny his actions and say that we bullied him into a confession but that'll not stand up for five minutes with your notes?"

"Yes Sir, I have been writing them out whilst we were waiting and you had better have a look at what I've written so far, I haven't quite finished, in case I've got something wrong."

The Chairman quickly scanned the notes and agreed that they were fine. At that the Chairman asked, "You going back to Wellingborough now?" The time was pretty well mid-day and the office would be closing for Christmas at 1pm and he would be pushed to get there for that time but there were some last-minute presents in the office he needed to collect so he said, "Yes." At which the Chairman handed him a package for the MD and asked him to deliver it! *A bit different to last Christmas,* he thought.

Then they had had the Christmas party on the Thursday night which had become a bit out of hand because, against Jack's advice, staff were provided with unlimited free drinks. One of them, a new employee in the Computer Department, had become very drunk and was trying to drag a number of the young females onto the dance floor to dance with him. No one would because of his evident drunkenness but, just as the MD and Chairman walked into the room, he dragged a girl onto the floor and promptly fell over. She escaped leaving him on the floor gazing up at a somewhat annoyed MD that this should happen just as the Chairman came into the room. "What on earth are you doing; get up from there at once."

"Fuck off," came the reply.

"How dare you speak to me like that."

"Fuck off."

"Do you know who I am?"

"No, but you can still fuck off."

"I'm the Managing Director and this is the Chairman." This last bit said in slightly awed and honoured tone.

"Well, he can fuck off too." At that the MD started calling for Jack who was eating in the room next door. When they met, almost apoplectic by now, all the MD could say was I want him sacked immediately.

Jack simply said, "Leave it to me," and went and arranged for a couple of his mates to take him home. The following morning Jack sent for him and said, we can do this the easy way or the hard way. The easy way you accept a Final Written Warning without us going through all that disciplinary palaver or you can go down the official route which will mean being suspended until after Christmas, then a disciplinary hearing and you will be sacked for gross misconduct. Which is it to be?"

The guy took the FWW. Later the MD sent for Jack and asked if the guy had been sacked. Jack said, "No. I told you before the party that we needed to put out a notice reminding people that it was a formal company function and that normal disciplinary rules etc applied but you accused me of being a party pooper and refused. A Tribunal knowing that we provided free alcohol with no controls over the amount any one consumed will say it was, in part, our fault and would not find a summary dismissal to be fair. Plus, he's black and will play the race card that previous party staff misbehaviours, and there have been some, were not fired, because they were white. So, I've given him a Final Written Warning and if he does anything, anything at all in the future he's out."

Reluctantly the MD agreed. As it happened, they were the last two in the building and, as they walked out into the car park, who should be standing by the MD's car but the lad; he had broken open the petrol flap and was busy peeing into the tank. The MD looked at Jack, Jack looked at the MD and nodded and the MD said to the lad, 'you're fucking fired, my lad, and the bill for that is coming out of any pay due'. One for the book, fired in a car park with his willy out!

Jack wasn't to know that this would be his last but one Christmas working for Lintwoods.

Chapter 33

The Holding Company made a bid to take over their biggest competitor. It was so big that the Monopolies Commission stepped in and for months the takeover was delayed whilst the Commission heard evidence. Jack was even called. The trade unions jumped in by objecting to the takeover arguing that there would be blood everywhere with people losing their jobs by the thousand. Jack was called, along with the letter jointly written by the same trade unions thanking him for the manner in which the original restructuring of the company had been done resulting in only four compulsory redundancies out of 85 branches and some 4000 plus employees. So much for blood down the walls!

In the event the Commission allowed the takeover to go ahead but by this time the City had been buying up shares in the competitor like mad in anticipation of huge profits to be made when the offer was eventually made. The Chairman had warned financial journalists to warn the buyers that he would not pay an inflated price for the competitor but they ignored him and bought and bought. When the offer came it was at the original value calculated when the offer was first made and the speculators were being offered sums considerably below what they had paid; so, perhaps not surprisingly, the offer was refused and the bid failed.

As far as Jack was concerned that was that and life progressed as normal until a few months later when he was driving in to work one Monday morning to hear on Radio 4 that Lintwoods had been sold to the competitor. That news really was a bombshell. In that instant Jack knew his job had gone. The taking over company, and he had been in that position at least a dozen times, always kept their own staff and fired the staff of the taken over company.

There were the odd exceptions but as Jack knew the competitor well, sitting on the Wholesale Grocery Joint Industrial Council with their MD, who he did not rate at all, knowing them as he did, he knew he would be for the chop. When he got to Head Office, the place was buzzing with speculation cut short at 9.30am when the Holding Company Chairman, with the C&C and Retail Company Chairman arrived. The Chairman of the Holding Company read a short statement, which made politicians statements seem like the acme of truth, and then invited questions.

No one spoke so Jack thought, what have I got to lose, my jobs gone anyway so he asked why was it that we had to hear that we had been sold on Radio 4 and not from you. The answer appeared to be something like City rules which was bullshit so Jack asked another question which elicited another bullshit answer but did reveal that the terms of the takeover forbad the Holding Company, or any of the other companies in the Group, from approaching and poaching any of the C&C staff, but with a smile and a wink the Chairman said, "But there is nothing in the agreement which stops you approaching us and I can indicate any such approach will be favourably looked upon."

Jack looked at him, then stood up and walked over to the window and in an exaggerated manner looked out. He said, "Nope, no pigs flying by so I guess no approach," and he walked out of the room.

The MD disappeared that day only a few minutes after the new MD appeared. The Operations Director went the next day and the Finance Director the day after. Day by day the Board disappeared. Jack was expecting the call to go at any time but nothing happened. The new MD had sat on the Joint Industrial Council with Jack as Chairman, a peculiar juxtaposition, and the annual negotiations for pay and conditions was on going at that time. For the first time ever, the unions had refused the employers' final offer and were in the process of collecting votes for industrial action. *Jack always thought the correct term should be industrial inaction! So*, he wasn't too surprised to find the MD coming into his office and asking what action he, Jack, would have taken if the company had not been taken over.

"Well," said Jack, "I would have recommended to the Board that we pay the Final Offer increase from the beginning of April as usual, announce that that was what we were going to do to all staff and see what happens. It's my belief that the gap between the amount the unions want and the employers' offer is so small, about seven pence an hour, that as some 75% of our staff are female they will, being much more sensible than the males and far less macho, will work out that going on strike, the unions' suggested action, would lose them, for a full-timer, £90 per week. It will take a long time, at an extra seven pence an hour, should they be successful with the strike, to get back that £90 let alone the same for each other week lost, that they will just accept it and get on with it. So, I would just go ahead and do it."

"Paddy (the Personnel Director of the taking over company) thinks we should pay the extra."

"I don't," said Jack. At that the MD got up and left. Eight weeks after the takeover, when the union action had collapsed with the other employers going down the route Jack had recommended, Jack was fired. Lintwoods had paid the additional seven pence and with the taking over company doing the same they were the only two in the industry to do so, thus putting their costs up compared to every one of their competitors. Jack smiled as he was fired and, had the MD had good hearing, he would have heard Jack saying some rude words about that fucking idiot Paddy and the MD.

Jack had formed a bad opinion of Paddy from his first dealings with him. Almost immediately after the take over a problem arose in Middlesbrough. There were two C&Cs there, literally across the two sides of the road on a T-junction. Lintwoods one was very successful and Paddy's one wasn't and it was the manager and Assistant Manager of the opposition who had resigned and left without working their notice leaving a situation that had to be dealt with. It would have been dealt with in due course by either Paddy or Jack but now it had to be sorted immediately.

It was decided that Paddy and he would go because the intention was to close one of them anyway and the resignations had at least solved the problem of which manager and Assistant to retain. Paddy drove a 405 Peugeot diesel, diesels being their company policy, so Jack, who drove a petrol 2.8GL Granada, wanted to see what a diesel was like; he might not want the job, even in the very unlikely event they offered him the post, if the diesel was as bad as it was said they were. In making the arrangement Jack had suggested they meet outside the Wellingborough HO at 6am so that they would arrive in Middlesbrough, with a stop for breakfast, easily before opening time.

Paddy had reacted to this time with horror. He wanted to meet at 9am i.e., the start of work and then arrive just before noon in time for lunch! Eventually they compromised on 7.30am but even then, Paddy was half an hour late. When Jack went to get into the car, already feeling angry at the delay which he saw as deliberate, he was greeted by a tip which would have made the local Council quite proud. There was a half-eaten sandwich, two or three empty cans of pop, sweet wrappers, crumbs and debris all over the seat and on the floor. Jack took one look at it and said, "If you worked for me and I saw your company car in that state I'd fire you. If you think I'm travelling in that shit heap you've got another think coming. I'll go in my car, you can come with me or drive yourself," and at that walked over to his own car.

By the time he had got seated, Paddy was showing no sign of getting out of his car so Jack drove off. He stopped at Preston Services for breakfast but Paddy did not appear, nor indeed did he appear in Middlesbrough until half an hour after Jack. Jack spoke to his staff to explain that the new lot were going to close their branch across the road and the staff would be transferred into this one as they anticipated that enough of the customers would also transfer to enable them all to be retained in employment. After that Jack went home.

When he had been called into the MD's office who was sitting behind his desk with Paddy sitting beside him. There was just the one chair and Jack was invited to sit down. He asked, "I'm going, aren't I so is there any point in me sitting down?"

The MD had a dopey look on his face which in reality said it all but he did say, "Well, I'm very sorry to have reached this decision but…"

Jack interrupted and said, "Look I know the score. Is that for me?" Gesturing to a white envelope on the desk. The MD nodded so Jack picked it up and started to walk out.

As he went, he said, "I packed my personal stuff weeks ago. I'll be gone in five minutes." The MD said, "If you have any queries about the package or the car, please feel free to contact Paddy at any time."

"If I have any, I'll contact the organ grinder not the monkey, thank you," and walked out. Being sacked, especially when you knew that you could do the job miles better than the bloke who'd got it, hurt a lot but Jack knew after eight weeks that he could not work for that lot and the way in which they worked, or didn't, most of the time. The one thing he was pleased about was the decision he had made a few days after the takeover to cancel the purchase of a new house in Kettering. He had seen it but when he went to talk to the Agent it was to discover that there was already an offer on it so he had left his details in case it fell through.

It did and he received a telephone call telling him it was now his if he wanted it. As it was the Wednesday following the takeover and he knew his job was in very considerable danger he told them he would ring them back in a few minutes and went to see the MD. He had sat with him on the negotiating committee for the Wholesale Grocery JIC and knew him quite well.

He told him about the house and asked the $64,000 dollar question, "I know it may difficult for you to answer this but, should I withdraw from the purchase as I may not have a job in a short time?"

Without a pause, he replied, "Yes, go ahead with the sale."

"Thank you." And Jack walked out. He telephoned the estate agent and cancelled his interest. Jack had never trusted him during the meetings and knew that the guy was lying the moment he said to go ahead with the purchase.

Jack was able to go back to his office without meeting anyone and he only had his brief case to pick up as he had, as he had said to the MD, taken his personal stuff home weeks before. To the few people he saw it just looked like he was going out as he had done numerous times before and it was just the odd cheerio or goodbye which suited him, he really did not want the fuss attached to permanent goodbyes.

Of course, it did not take long for word to get around and he was contacted by lots of people and even attended a farewell party one evening but as far as he was concerned it was tomorrow, he was worried about not the past. As it was one of his Personnel Officers contacted him a few years later having been unable to tolerate the standards introduced and he was able to secure her a post as an Area Personnel Consultant with Delta.

Chapter 34

Jack was fired at the end of September. He had been paid everything he should have and had also been offered the services of a consultancy specialising in helping senior personnel acquire new positions. Jack had refused to use such agents in the past when taking over companies and releasing their senior executives since he didn't believe they were any good. His experience with this one proved him largely to be right and the only thing that made Jack take up the offer and contact them at all was the claim they made that they always had jobs to offer because companies approached them rather than advertising in the press with all the work and cost that involved. Jack was interested in their jobs not really in how to apply! It turned out, of course, that they actually had no jobs on their books at all which Jack took to be vindication of his attitude to them in the past as being right. In fact, in the three months Jack was on their books they made no introductions for him at all.

One evening Jack received a telephone call from the ex-Marketing Director of Lintwoods who said he had been to a Recruitment Consultancy that day in London and walking down the corridor had seen the name of the ex-Personnel Director of Lintwood's Holding Company on one of the doors but hadn't actually seen the guy himself and was telling Jack that fact and offered their number if he wanted it. Jack thought about it. He hadn't really rated the guy when he had had to carry out some of the policies dictated by the holding company and had been in his bad books for the computer centre incident, but, hey, what if he could point Jack at a job or two.

Jack consulted his little black book of phone numbers and addresses because he could vaguely remember recording the guy's home phone number which he thought might be better to use than the office one. He did have the number and it was still the right one. After the normal convivials Jack explained that he had been told of his working for the Recruitment Consultancy and since Jack was looking for a job, could he help?

"No, that's not me as hard as it is to believe there could be two of us with the same name!" Jack was disappointed that that possible route to a job was slammed shut in his face but when the guy said, "Why don't you give me your details in case I hear of something," the door slipped slightly open again. *Nice guy*, thought Jack, after he did so and ended the conversation.

He didn't really expect anything to come of it so he was quite surprised to receive a call from him the following day! In it he explained that as a holding company and semi-venture capitalist they had been looking at taking over a company which would need a Personnel Head as it had never had one, and had grown to the size where one was really needed. He said he had not said anything the night before because they had not had confirmation that their bid had been accepted and he had also wished to speak to the Chairman/MD about Jack before doing so.

They had heard that morning that the bid was successful and the boss man would be quite happy for Jack to be considered for the vacancy without going through the normal recruitment rigmarole. He explained that as he obviously knew Jack, he would not interview him but he would invite him to Dorking, where they were based, to meet his Deputy who would interview Jack but only from the point of updating his folder.

He would then send Jack's details to the new MD they had just appointed for him to directly interview Jack as Jack would be working for him. Jack was quite happy with that and the quasi-interview in Dorking went well. He was a bit put out to discover that the company for which he would be working, if successful with the MD, was in Stoke on Trent thus necessitating a move.

Jack had attended the interview in Dorking and subsequently on the Monday of the week before Christmas attended one with the MD in Stoke, it took place in a Tudor style house in one of the five towns and it was explained that it was being closed down with everyone moving to the Hub on the outskirts in a months' time. The hub was a purpose built unit broadly square, where lorries bringing in parcels from their individual depots reversed up to the goods-in side and unloaded onto conveyors and then drove around and backed up to its depot bay on one of the other three sides.

Parcels flowing from the in-bays flowed automatically around the warehouse to the bay of the truck destined to take those parcels to that particular location. In all there were 75 locations so it was quite a size. The cost had, of course, exceeded budget, one of the reasons they had gone bust and been bought out.

One other problem, not to become obvious until the summer, was that it was built with air conditioning in mind but as they had run out of money, they could not afford the equipment so the building had been finished without it. However, the design meant that no opening windows had been fitted, it was all glass and steel and once the temperature rose in the summer it became an impossible hothouse in which to work and the hastily bought in air conditioning machines were simply not able to cope, but that was a problem for the future!

Jack's interview with the MD went well and Jack left feeling good about it. However, the last comment, that I have someone else to see and will be in touch with you soon, was not so good. When it reached Friday lunchtime, and Jack had heard nothing, he thought *that's it, the 'someone else to see' has got it*, they will have finished at midday for the holiday. However, he was in the study at 3.15pm when the phone rang. He was just reaching out to a pad by the phone at that moment so the phone only gave half a strangulated ring when he picked it up.

It was the MD and he offered Jack the job, which Jack immediately accepted and after a short discussion it was agreed that the MD would collect Jack on the 2nd January and drive them both up to Stoke. When Jack came out of the study his wife was in the kitchen and the two children in the lounge. It was clear that none of them had heard the phone and so knew nothing of the conversation. So, Jack decided to surprise them. He said nothing, but went out on the Saturday morning, Christmas Eve, and did some extra shopping. He bought a radio controlled, build it yourself, model car for his son, a colour TV for his daughter and a high-fi music centre for him and Janet.

Both children had been asking for these as presents for months before Christmas but with Jack having lost his job had modified their 'demands' accordingly. When he got home, he banned all three of them to the kitchen so they could not see him bringing the presents into the study. He then banned them from the study on pain of no presents or worse. Wrapping them was a problem because they were quite large and almost all the wrapping paper had already been used. He further could only find one tag!

Unknown to him Janet had started to worry that he had flipped and gone out and spent all their money! This became a certainty the following morning when having opened all the presents, bar the special ones which were still in the study, Jack banned them all to the kitchen again while he moved the presents from the study to the lounge; it took a while, especially to display them advantageously, so Janet was becoming dead certain he had flipped. When they were called in their eyes lit up on stalks as they opened the presents. The label, which had been carefully displayed on the top, was dropped to the ground and was only read by Janet when, in response to her question, "What have you gone and done?"

Jack handed it to her. It read:

From the Personnel Manager, Personnel Director Designate of APD to the Hughes family wishing them a very Happy Christmas.

Janet looked puzzled and said, "Why have we got these from him, whoever he is?" Jack kept smiling and gradually she realised as it took a moment to recall the name of the company he had visited on the Monday. It was one of those moments fondly recalled during the rest of their time together. Not very many, in fact none, fondly recalled moments, were to occur during the year Jack was to work for APD.

It was only on Jack laughing that she put two and two together and realised. It was one of the best Christmas's they ever had and she always said she was sure that he had flipped and spent all their money.

Although he didn't realise it at the time when he started Jack was only to stay for a year at APD. Initially his main task was to grab all the paperwork relating to personnel and produce a proper Statement of Main Terms and Conditions of Employment and a Company Handbook. The introduction of the new paperwork went smoothly with only a few minor objections to deal with. The one major issue was the Shop Steward of the drivers. APD employed just over a hundred of them split between the trunker drivers who delivered parcels to and from the Hub to their depots around the country and around 25 drivers who delivered and collected parcels to customers in the Stoke area.

There were an additional 180 local delivery collection drivers employed at the 18 depots APD owned scattered geographically around the country. In addition to the 18 they owned the other 55 depots were run by franchisees and they used the APD documents for their employees. Many of the local drivers were in fact subcontractors and Jack learned a lot about the law and such individuals during his time there.

The Shop Steward was a trunker driver based at their Carlisle depot and, it was rumoured, had ambitions for a full-time employee career with the union, thus he was a pain in the arse manufacturing frivolous excuse after frivolous excuse to cause trouble. Given sorting him out as a priority by the MD Jack thought about how he could neutralise him for a few days. What he did was to create a Works Committee.

There had never been such a thing and initially the MD was against it. However, Jack pointed out that it was the intention of the Government to force workers onto the Board of Directors of companies and to improve representation and communication between employers and employees, especially designed to give unions more power, so they needed to get ahead of the game and reluctantly he agreed. To get matters started Jack chose representatives from each of the main departments and appointed them to the Committee—there were to be elections of members in the future but Jack didn't quite manage to get around to organising them before he left! In structural terms there were two groups of employees at the Hub, those who worked during the day and those who worked at night processing the arriving and departing parcels.

Since the largest number of staff worked during the day Jack chose the daytime for the Committee meetings. To represent the drivers, he chose one of the van drivers based at Stoke who was the unofficial deputy Shop Steward anyway and who stood in for the Shop Steward during his absences as necessary. He was a far more reasonable individual, an ex-driver from the Royal Army Service Corps and who stood a little bit in awe of Jack when he discovered his Army record. At the first meeting the Committee raised a number of issues, most of which had been long running, and a continuing sore.

One of them was the provision of toilet paper! The Company bought the cheapest, poorest quality, hard, shiny stuff that failed to wipe cleanly! They wanted the relatively new, soft stuff which did a much better job. So, Jack agreed that one and most of the others which cost very little to remedy. Some, like locks not working on the toilet doors, cheapest available again, took a little longer, but it was resolved. When the Shop Steward asked for meetings with management, as he had always done, it was rejected as all requests were to be submitted to the Works Committee.

Although he complained to the full time official of the union, whose job he wanted (and who knew that!) he got short thrift as his deputy attended and a complaint that the Company's behaviour was anti-union was rejected. Jack continued to ensure that requests from the Committee or complaints were quickly resolved smoothed the previous unsettled relationships enormously and none from the Shop Steward ever succeeded—the staff were not daft and his power gradually withered away.

One day the Hub Manager and the Security Manager appeared at Jack's door. *Not good he thought.* It turned out that looking, by chance, down a long aisle that led to the clocking in/off point, the Hub Manager saw an employee clock out two cards—commonly a fiddle and normally a gross misconduct dismissal offence, which Jack thought would be the issue, but no, they didn't want to sack the bloke and they wanted Jack to find a way not to sack him since every time it had happened before the individuals concerned, the clocker and the benefiter off the clocking had been sacked! It turned out that the reason they did not want to sack the 'benefiter' was he was the only person who worked in International Parcels and was the only guy in the Company who knew the law and processes involved.

(At that time International meant the Isle of Man but they did intend to expand on to the Continent!). The additional problem was if they did not sack the 'benefiter' how could they justify the sack, or not, of the 'clocker'? *Gee, thanks very much thought Jack. What to do? Need time to think—ask questions.*

"Is this the first time you think it has happened?" asked Jack, thinking as he said it from his experience it was highly unlikely that a crook was caught the first time, they cheated the rules?

"Oh yes," said the Security Manager. Jack knew from his personnel file that he was an ex-Detective Inspector of the local police, with a good record of convictions at a time when confessions were routinely obtained by a good kicking out in the Yard! And boy did he have big feet! That answer, and Jack's subsequent questions and investigations, were to reveal that the guy was as thick as two short planks and not capable of being a night watchman let alone a Head of Security. Jack's response to that answer was, "I bet it wasn't. Do we know where the International guy was at knocking off time when the offence occurred?"

"I think he had gone home much earlier as he was on 'job and knock' (being allowed to finish once all the work was finished—short for job done and knock off work) and there wasn't much international work that night so almost certainly he went home early," said the Hub Manager. Not really knowing where to go next Jack asked, "Where does he live and how does he travel to work?"

"He lives out just by the motorway. I think he scrounged a lift with one of the Trunkers that night." Jack looked at the Security Manager who simply stared back—he had learned as a young copper how to go dumb when faced with authority just as Jack had in the Army.

"Didn't you tell me, during my induction, that a log was kept of each vehicle when it left the Hub, number, driver name and the name of any passenger?" asked of the Security manager.

"That's right."

"Well, in that case would it not be a good idea to check the logs and find out if he did ride a trunker and which one it was?" Before the guy could answer Jack carried on, "And since I bet it wasn't the first time this happened, wouldn't it be a good idea to check the previous four weeks or so to see if he had travelled with the same trunker, or another one or two, before?"

They both nodded and got up and left. It took them an hour to come back and the hangdog look they both carried as they came back in indicated that Jack was right. They had, having found so many repeats gone back six weeks and discovered that he had travelled with the same trunker every night for six weeks; they had then stopped feeling they had done enough. Jack, having had time to think about it whilst they were gone then said, "And what about the clock cards, have you checked them?"

"What for?" asked the Security Manager.

"You told me that you saw a man clock a card and then another card. Those two cards will show exactly the same time, won't they and if the same guy has clocked both cards every time, they will show exactly the same time every time, won't they?" Jack could tell by their looks that that had not occurred to them so they went away again.

This time they were back much quicker. For the six weeks the two cards were identical. "Do you still want me to find a reason not to sack him?" Jack asked with a smile.

They didn't have to answer for Jack to know their decision. "The problem is," he said, "as he's on job and knock if he had finished all his work, he would have been able to go home early and be paid for the full shift, so, if that is so, what offence has he committed that would make it gross misconduct and thus justify summary dismissal?" Now they really were flummoxed especially the Security Manager he looked exactly like a bulldog chewing a wasp.

Jack let them suffer a little and then said, "Since he's gone on that same trunker there is a reason for it, isn't there? I don't really know what it is but it's likely to be because they are mates and/or he's the only trunker that goes past his house. Since we know he's always been on the same one it means he always goes at the time of that trunker which might mean he has had to leave work undone to catch it. Is there any way to check if he's gone home leaving work undone?" They looked at one another.

"The best thing to do would be to check his work station tonight and the next few nights, if necessary, to see if he leaves parcels unprocessed," said the Hub Manager and that's what they did. Those conversations took place on Tuesday and the pair of them re-appeared in Jack's office on the Friday with big smiles on their faces. Tuesday and Thursday nights he had gone home leaving about half a dozen parcels each night unprocessed, the Wednesday night had been a light night and everything had been processed.

In the meantime, Jack had sat down with one of the IT people and by examining the records for the previous three weeks for the parcel acceptance into the system at source date and the date which it had left the Hub he had been able to determine there were eight nights, out of the 15, when parcels had not gone out the same day they had arrived, which they should have done. This evidence, added to what had been discovered on the Tuesday and Thursday was more than enough to support gross misconduct dismissals for both miscreants. Thereafter Jack was looked upon with some sort of awe.

However, he was held in no sort of awe by the Group Chairman who attended all Board meetings. Jack as a Director Designate did not attend all the meeting but was called in as necessary and needed. Immediately Jack met him it put his hackles up. He couldn't say why, it was just that all the hairs stood up on the back of his neck and his system seemed to be shouting, WARNING, WARNING, THIS GUY'S A WRONG 'UN. It had only happened a couple of times before in his life and on both occasions, it had been right so he decided to take special care with this one. At the very first meeting Jack found himself under attack for not having stopped the recruitment of two extra staff shown in the staff numbers statistics. Jack made the point that he had not recruited the people, did not know who they were or that there was supposed to be a moratorium on recruitment.

The response was that they had bought the company to turn it round from loss to profit and one of the biggest costs were staff so they were to be reduced not increased. Jack then asked if the Department Heads could be told no recruitment except with his approval but this was refused. He asked if he was to carry out a redundancy exercise and was told no; so, he asked if he couldn't stop people being recruited or make people redundant how was he to control numbers? The Chairman simply moved on to the next item on the agenda.

Afterwards Jack asked the MD what the hell was going on and what he was expected to do? The reply, to ignore him and just get on with his other duties was not helpful. So, he did his old soldier, *'fuck him'* and carried on.

In one of the meetings the subject of bonuses came up. Jack was more than put out when it became clear that the Group Chairman was proposing a system based on the performance of the Company as a whole. He believed that this would incentivise every employee to work harder. Jack was unhappy as he had experienced such schemes in the past and they did not work; certainly, some people were incentivised but many were not and they just sat back and let the others work harder. And in any event Jack felt that it was better to incentivise people to work smarter not harder but when he discovered that the Chairman was proposing a variable rate bonus, that is only a 5% bonus for the lowest paid, 10% for middle management, 25% for senior management and 50% for Directors he was angered, especially as he was damn sure that the Chairman would probably get a larger bonus still.

"As the higher your rank the more you get paid you will automatically receive a higher figure, based on everyone receiving the same percentage, why should someone senior therefore also be on a higher percentage and doubly benefit?" He asked.

The Chairman simply moved on to the next subject with no discussion or decision having been taken. Jack didn't think he was going to enjoy life the next time the subject came up.

One thing he did enjoy was working out a new car policy. The existing one didn't exist! There were hire cars, rentals, drive your own and get an allowance and every version you could imagine including people not having a company vehicle who should, and those having one that shouldn't. Each person's nominal salary was secret, unless they chose to share it about, so that their value to the Company was not always obvious. The problem with a company car was that it stood there for all to see, so the bigger and more expensive the higher the standing.

One way to avoid that was to pay a grant and let someone buy and run their own so that a young, single person living at home with mum and dad could top-up the grant and buy a more expensive car than their boss who, having a family and lots of bills might buy a much cheaper car and spend the difference on life. Both their individual choices, but when the subordinate parks an expensive limo against the second-hand wreck driven by his boss problems arise—Jack knew because he had had to deal with them in the past.

Analysis of staff salaries seemed to indicate that they were in five levels so it would appear sensible if he had five levels of car but no manufacturer produced five separate models which could be matched so it meant that he would have to choose a bottom of the range and a top of the range i.e., a base level Cortina and a Ghia Cortina for two of the salary levels, if he went down that route. What he enjoyed was going to all the major car makers and talking to them about adopting their range for his company. He was able to test drive a huge range of vehicles some of which were rubbish and some of which were brilliant. A case in point was Alfa Romeo. The top of the range 164 was brilliant and the noise of the 3 litres just heavenly.

The noise was even better in the 75 but he gave it back early after only two days as being unsafe—unsafe that is for his licence as he found himself driving like a lunatic just to hear that 3 litre at full chat. The small range, the 33, would have had to be split between the 1.5 and 1.3 litres but the 1.5 was so powerful it was almost impossible to exit from a side turning on a wet road without enormous wheel spin. In the end he had settled in his mind on the Vauxhall range, the alternative one being Ford although there was little difference between the two ranges Vauxhall were prepared to offer a better deal but he didn't quite get to recommending it to the Board before events prevented it.

He returned from the old offices one day and as he drove up to the gates of the Hub the alarms started sounding. He had to wait while one of the Guards was on the phone until he finished the call then called out to Jack that one of the parcels had split and bullets and explosives had fallen out onto a belt. He motioned to the guard to let him in, drove to his parking space and hurried in against a flood of staff making their way out. He was able to see where the Security Manager and Hub Manager were standing by a belt about 50 yards down the building and made his way there.

Immediately, the Security Manager started gesturing for him to leave but Jack called out that he had some experience with explosives and ammunition and might be able to identify what they were looking at. The parcel had somehow caught a corner at a T-junction and had been ripped open. Bullets were scattered over the belt and on the floor. Jack could tell at a glance that they were rifle bullets, probably.303inches or 7.62mm in diameter. Just one close glance told him what they were. The vast majority of live rounds, or bullets, were brass cased with a pointed, copper jacketed bullet sticking out at the pointy end. The other end contained a recessed percussion cap. Sometimes, with smaller rounds, there would be a rounded lead bullet sticking out.

Blank rounds would have the brass case and percussion cap but the pointy end would be crimped together with no obvious bullet present. The ones he could see had a copper jacketed bullet but the casing was a steel colour and it was ribbed with shallow grooves running from end to end all around the casing. He could see the base of one and there was no percussion cap present. As Jack was taking this in the Security Manager was flapping like a good 'un and going on about ensuring the area should be cleared, the firefighting hoses run out but not too close in case the explosives blew up etc, etc.

As he got closer Jack could see a hand grenade lying on the ground and a couple lying on the belt. A Mills 36 Grenade, used for primarily trench and bunker clearing was about the size of a cricket ball but had a segmented body, roundish, but the surface looked like a chocolate bar with all the separate segments. Normally it would be the ubiquitous khaki colour but these had red paint running in all the channels between the segments—definitely non-standard, but it did have a leaver lying against the side of the grenade with a split-pin through the top holding it in. Picking up one of the grenades, Jack started to unscrew the cap in the base of the grenade. The Security Manager, face a lovely shade of white, was backing away as far as he dared, spluttering away as he did so. As the base cap came off Jack could see that it was not fused. To be fused it would have had to have had a .22inch. cartridge case with a fuse cord coming out of the pointy end and ending in a detonator.

Screwing the base cap back on Jack threw the grenade to the Security Manager, shouting 'catch' as he did so. He didn't catch it because the moment Jack shouted, the Security Manager fainted! Jack had recognised straight away that the rounds were display rounds with no cordite, flash-less powder, gun powder or other explosive ever having been anywhere near them.

The silver colour of the casing was designed to catch the eye for a display or bandoleer of some kind; they could even be used for dry practice at loading magazines and for bolt action rifles for practice of weapon handling but you could drop them, put them in a fire and nothing would happen—except they might just melt! Having seen them and the red paint on the grenades Jack knew that they would not be real, in the sense that they would not have any explosive inside them, indeed they would have been removed from the production line before the filling room and would never have had any explosive in them to start with let alone removed later. And, as with the rounds, the grenades could have been put in a fire and they would not have exploded.

The thing that did surprise Jack was the Security Manager's actions. Having read his Personnel File Jack had read that he had been called up for National Service, he was about 10 years older than Jack and the last National Serviceman had been released about two years before Jack joined as a Regular; his file said he had served his two years in the Royal Military Police which had led to the Police Force when he was demobbed and it seemed inconceivable to Jack that he had not recognised dummy rounds and grenades. He made a mental note to do a little checking when he had the time but in the event, he never had the chance to do it. Needless to say, Jack was immediately struck off his Christmas card list!

He continued to come under pressure from the Chairman regarding staffing until about the third time it happened Jack insisted that it be minuted that he did not have the authority to control staffing levels in any manner whatsoever at which time that pressure stopped. It stopped only to be replaced with pressure regarding the Distributive Industry Training Board Levy.

When the boards were first set up it was possible to, by carrying out lots of approved training, to get back from the Board covering your industry, more Levy than you in fact paid out—Jack had in fact achieved this for the six years he had worked for the Group Training Association in Nottingham. However, as the years had gone on, the Boards had increased in size thus their costs had increased and since these costs had had to be deducted from the Levy on that industry there had been less and less Levy to be repaid to companies demanding more and more money back.

Indeed, for this and other reasons, the Tory Government under pressure from industry had started to do away with the Boards. Unfortunately, APD came under the Distributive one which still existed. Jack had tried to argue that they came under Road Transport, not Distribution, but had been unsuccessful—it would still have been under a Board but Road Transport was a much more sensible and reasonable one to deal with than was Distribution which, to be polite, was so far up its own backside as to be coming out of its own ears!

The problem Jack faced was that to achieve a full rebate of the Levy he would have had to send about 6,000 staff on training courses every year when they only employed 1750 in total! Each Board meeting the subject of the Levy rebate was raised and each time Jack got a load of grief because he was failing abysmally in the Chairman's eyes. Previously, the Company had simply sent off a cheque for the amount and ignored the Board—it had saved a lot of administrative work and had been regarded as good value for the time saved! Jack had set about claiming and the balance debit for that year would have been less than £300.

It did not seem a sum that should be worried about to Jack but the Chairman obviously did and when he started to hint that Jack should submit extra claims anyway Jack became worried. Eventually he asked for a comment to be minuted that said, in effect, Jack had worked for a Training Board and as part of that work had had the job of checking claims, he thus knew the processes extremely well and knew that any sort of audit would rapidly throw up that false claims had been submitted. He was not prepared to risk his personal reputation, or even prosecution, with such a fiddle and that was that.

He was utterly dismayed to discover a few weeks later that the Minutes of the Board Meeting had been 'adjusted' to omit that comment. He discovered it because the Holding Board's Personnel Director's Assistant, who had updated his CV when he first visited Dorking, rang him and told him. He knew he had got on well with her, and had had several meetings with her since then and his attitude towards more junior people had once again proved fruitful. What he didn't know was what to do about it.

Then one of those chance encounter events intervened. He was at Stoke station with Janet the following Friday afternoon to catch a train to London for a long weekend. There was an exhibition at the British Museum and a film on new release that they both wished to see and while waiting on the platform who should be standing there but Roy Bacon who had been the Employers' side Secretary when Jack had been the Chairman of the Wholesale Grocery JIC. He had been visiting their Depot in Stoke and his car had blown a head gasket. Consequently, he was heading south on the train to go home in the expectation that his car would be delivered to him the following week—such are the benefits of a senior directorship!

They chatted about this and that until Roy asked how Jack had come to be in Stoke which Jack answered in somewhat brief manner. Picking up on this Roy asked him directly how things were going and Jack told him a little about his discomfort with what he was being asked to do but he also indicated that he didn't really wish to talk about that and, somewhat jokingly asked if he had any jobs going. Roy looked at him a bit peculiarly and said, "It's funny you should ask that. One of the reasons I was in Stoke was to interview a couple of short list candidates for a new role we are creating to be based in Stoke setting up a National Training Centre. Do I remember correctly that your title at Lintwoods was Personnel and Training Director?"

"Not quite, Service Director Personnel and Training, to be exact." Jack was then subjected to a number of questions especially concentrated on training and when he described the work he had done when he first joined Terry Linehams and the research, he had carried out into the sales force selling to the SPAR shops it became even more detailed. By the time they reached Euston Jack felt like he had attended an interview! They parted having arranged for Roy to telephone him on the Tuesday with a view to setting up a formal interview at some stage in the future.

In fact, when they got back on the Sunday evening there was a message on his answer phone asking him to confirm that he could attend one on the Tuesday. Roy explained that he had been so pleased with meeting Jack and especially with his answers about the work he had done with the sales force that he had rung the MD that night and told him. Although Jack had never met the MD the MD knew a lot about Jack from his role as Chairman of the Employers' Side of the JIC and, since there was to be a Board Meeting on the Tuesday, had asked Roy to arrange for him to attend and deliver a presentation about how their sales force could be improved.

Jack was delighted to confirm attendance and the presentation. He rang his MD on that Sunday night and told him he had a family emergency and would not be in on the Monday or Tuesday. He spent the Monday digging out his old notes from Linehams programme so that he was well prepared for the Tuesday. Situated in one of the Garden Cities, Letchworth, Jack arrived in plenty of time to set up an overhead projector and screen.

He knew that the Danish Provisions Company sold its products to mainly small independent grocers and concentrated on bacon products. It had been set-up by a Co-operative of Pig Farmers in Denmark way back before the First World War to sell their products to the UK. That trade had stopped during the Second World War, when Denmark had been occupied by the Germans, but had re-started in the late forties. The sales force called on all their customers weekly and took orders to be delivered the following week.

There were some significant differences between the two sales forces but enough similarities for him to talk their language. He said he anticipated that if he got the job, he would not start by running training courses but would want to identify precisely what the sales force actually did and the problems they experience doing it. He would do this by talking to two or three depot managers to get a feel and would then meet with each of the sales forces to explain the programme. In essence they would have to record how they had spent their time for two weeks using an agreed task dictionary and Jack would then analyse the results.

He took a chance and said to the Board that he anticipated that he would find that they spent a lot of time driving, a lot dealing with admin and not very much actually selling. He could tell from their looks that he had scored a few points. At the end of the meeting, he had gone on last, he was asked to wait in the MD's office and within five minutes he had been offered the job!

One matter which had bugged Jack which he had been able to do nothing about was the APD's policy on notice. The policy was that for all starters the notice requirement was one week either way after one month's employment. The original Contracts of Employment Act 1963 had introduced minimum periods of notice but they favoured employees in that the employer had to increase notice by one week per year up to a maximum of 12 while the notice from the employee to the employer, under the Act, remained at one week. It meant that leavers tended to hand in their notice, if at all(!) on a Monday and leave on the Friday.

Technically this was not a week but it was the norm across most industries. Salaried staff, who almost always took longer to replace, in all the companies Jack had ever worked in, operated on a month's notice either way until the minimum periods kicked in again and lifted it from the employer to the employee by a further week after five years, six after six and so on. Not everyone did give notice of course and Jack had tried to sue leavers on a couple of occasions for damages for not giving notice but with no success, but most did so, so that the company had a month or so to recruit a replacement.

For some reason he was never able to identify APD would not change their policy. Jack had always felt a little vulnerable that they could get rid of him with no notice at all or only one week after one month's service which was too short a time for him to find another job—at Lintwoods he had been on 12 months' notice either way which was wonderful because he had walked away with one year's gross salary, plus 15 weeks redundancy pay plus some accrued holiday pay! Now he was quite pleased that he had failed; it meant he would be able to walk in on the following Friday and give one week's notice! Which he did!

Chapter 35

Jack very quickly absorbed the functioning of DPC as it was so similar to that of Linehams he had joined more than 10 years before. The main difference was it was a much smaller company with a much smaller range of products—limited mainly to everything connected to bacon but therein lay the problem. The whole of the provisions trade was changing with major supermarket chains becoming larger and larger and gradually forcing out small corner shop type operations. Stores like Tesco could sell at a price cheaper than DPC could buy at and there was little that could be done about it. In particular bacon was becoming a packed product rather than fresh in the sense that sales of sides of bacon to grocers were plummeting off a cliff and being replaced by prepacked, sliced product and DPC did not do pre-packed bacon. Their depots were too small to carry a wider range of products, for example, in their current range they listed less than 7,000 items, even the smallest C&C in Lintwoods carried 11,000 and the largest something over 21,000 so unless they had access to almost unlimited funds to expand their Depots, (which they did not!) increasing their range was not an option.

This, to Jack's mind, gave only two options, stay the same or go smaller. One option might have been to build three enormous depots, North, Midlands and South and deliver with a huge fleet of lorries but they did not have the funds for that either which meant that it was smaller or stay the same. Once Jack had carried out the exercise of looking at how three of their Depots functioned vis a vis the Sales Force, they chose one of the best, an average one and one of the worst, but amazingly, the two week actions records for the Sales Forces came out pretty much the same.

The differences in performance seemed to lie mainly with the proficiency of the Depot. Jack, in selling himself to the Board, had quoted the 8% actual selling time of the Linehams Sales Force and the DPC figures were almost identical. Where they did differ significantly was in two tasks that the DPC people carried out that the Linehams ones did not; one was that they collected payment for the goods delivered the previous week which had to be paid into a bank before 3pm so that they could benefit by that day's interest and they also collected the order books for the next week's delivery on a Friday.

Jack found these last two functions absurd. From the time sheets he was able to identify that it took about half an hour to pay the money into the bank. Reps being Reps it meant that most of them used the opportunity to drive a distance there and a distance to the next customer so that the time 'off sales' could be as much as an hour and a half, or three possible calls lost for the sake of 'nothing' in the way of interest.

Interest at that time was running at about 8% so if he paid in a cheque (which didn't clear for seven days anyway!) for £100 the interest per annum would be £8 but for the one day it would be tuppence! They preferred the customer to pay cash and to that end all the Rep's cars had been fitted with little cash safes at God knows what cost, but it was still tuppence interest even if it was seven days sooner. All of Friday was lost to selling since they just functioned as a collection service.

Jack wrote his report simply setting out what he had found and where he felt changes should be made. He did not include what the solutions should be but waited for someone to ask, which they did in no uncertain terms in the form of the Operations Director who saw the report as a direct criticism of his running of the operation. At the Board meeting when Jack delivered his report the Ops Director was straight in as soon as Jack stopped speaking. It was abundantly clear from the sneering way he delivered his questions that he did not agree with what Jack had written. He started with one about if the Reps don't collect the money who would.

Jack responded with, do it by invoice and statement from a couple of little girls in the Sales or Accounts offices. When challenged with that wouldn't work Jack responded with 'it did in Linehams and they had three times as many customers as we do.' Jack also made the point that the Rep could always be the fall back to chase up non-payment on a routine visit but the current system was costing them a fortune in sales selling time lost, time, money and petrol for the journey to the bank and all for a pathetic tuppence per £100 of sales.

If they really wanted to carry on with the system then at the very least get each Rep to identify a bank within their area which had a night safe and stick it in there after closing time. The next attack came in the form of 'we can't rely on the Post Office delivering the Order Books on time so we will have no orders to assemble and the customer will not receive their delivery if we don't collect,' Jack responded with a few retired drivers with a little van can nip round collecting Order Books far cheaper than the salary of a Rep and more importantly, it will free up an extra day's selling for all Reps i.e. somewhere in the region of 75 days of potential selling in a month.

If you look at the time records you will see that 77% of the Reps made no potential new client calls whatsoever, in the two weeks, attempting to recruit new customers—just think what 75 days would achieve. He also suggested that there should be an in-depth look at whether they should have the Reps making calls for orders when that could be as easily and far more cheaply done by a telephone operation—most of their customers were small and if they bought extra one week because of a good price they almost always bought less the next week as their weekly sales varied very little; it was perhaps only the big ones who should have a Rep calling at all.

Each time he was attacked Jack had a devastating answer but he knew that he would have difficulties because when he had done his induction at Head Office, he had been staggered by two things; the shortest serving person of any seniority he had met had been with the Company for 27 years—a staggering fact—and, secondly, they did things the way they did because they had always done them that way.

Some changes were made, they did get the Order Books collected by van drivers and the Reps went on the road recruiting new customers but they were already too late and the Company was doomed. Two years and one week after Jack started Roy retired. One week after that the Operations Director walked into the National Training Centre Jack had been running for the two years, and fired Jack for redundancy.

Jack considered action at the Industrial Tribunal for failure to consult, no alternatives considered and a list of items but at Jack's level you were supposed to go quietly with the proviso that you were treated well and as they did pay more than statutory requirements Jack let it go and spent his time trying to move forward. He was not at all surprised when 18 months later he saw in the press that DPC had gone belly up.

Chapter 36

Jack was now 48 years old, the economy was struggling and, as usual, companies were looking to cut costs and one of the easiest areas to cut was Personnel or Training or both! Jack, with the knowledge he had, should have had no problem but he did—an indicator of just how bad things were in the country. Signing on at the Job Centre was a pain. In the nine months he did so they produced not one single job he could consider. He would have considered almost anything but they did not suggest anything at all. He continued to sign on because he needed his cards stamping for NI otherwise, he would not have bothered. He knew, from his work in Scotland opening the five new C&Cs as well as contact with them over the years as an employer, especially for disabled people, that they could be summed up as lazy, useless, jobsworths no use to man nor beast.

Jack retuned his CV every time he applied for a job so that it reflected the skills, they said they were looking for in their adverts but he couldn't get an interview let alone a job offer. As the 9 months out of work time point approached Jack sat down and reviewed his situation. His insurances against redundancy only had another three months to run although he did still have a considerable sum from his redundancy from Lintwoods plus he had the share option scheme money largely intact but from now the longer he was out of work the harder it would be to get one and after one year it would become a mountain to climb.

His CV, altered slightly to suit each job application, was indicative of a very senior person, director of this, chairman of the JIC etc and Jack wondered if it was too good, was he, in fact, putting people off? So, he went through it and remodelled it replacing Director with Head of… sat on JIC rather than chaired and so on throughout. No sooner had he finished that than he saw an advert for an Advocate. The company, Delta Management Services Ltd, described itself as specialising in Personnel Services, Employment Law and Health and Safety. The reference to Advocate explained that the role involved representing their clients in the Industrial and Employment Appeals Tribunal and involved travel throughout Great Britain.

Jack thought, *that's just the job for me,* and sat down to tweak his CV. He build up the section referring to representing his previous employers at Tribunal but without stating how many he had done. He handwrote the covering letter and sent them off the next day. He received a letter, almost by return, inviting him to an interview in Manchester a few days hence. He telephoned to confirm his attendance and to ask for directions. The secretary didn't sound too sure how to get there but it was sufficient for Jack to find his way at the appointed time— except he went to the wrong place! He had been told it was on the East Lancs Road and that was easy enough to find. He even found the bomb site car park he had been recommended.

As he walked back along, he spied a building on the other side of the road adorned with a capital D, stylised as the D on the letter head of their letter to him. The building ran along the road and then stopped at the side of a small square festooned with benches. As he was early, he sat on a bench until five minutes before his appointment time at which he got up and walked into the building. It was a tip and he wondered immediately what he was letting himself in for. Milling around were a bunch of students looking at notices plastered all over the reception area walls.

This can't be right, he thought. So, he asked a mature woman pinning up notices if this was the building for Delta to be told they'd moved out years ago! So, he asked the obvious question, 'do you know where to?' She told him, pointing further along the road, and saying they are about a 100 yards down there on the left. Jack made it at exactly 2pm and hoped the heat he had generated speed walking along was not showing as sweat! The interview, with the Advocacy Manager, Tony Attcliffe, went well thought Jack, as he left the building after an hour and a quarter. After an hour the Manager had excused himself briefly and had returned with the Director of Consultancy, Don Maybe, who asked a couple of question and then left. One issue which had come up was that as Jack lived in Loggerheads would it not be a bit too far to travel every day and would he prefer to be a sub-contractor rather than an employee?

Jack answered that, as he understood the role, he would be travelling all over the country and only visiting the office infrequently therefore the fact that he lived 65 miles away would not matter but if it did become a problem in the future he would always be prepared to move and he simply said he would much rather be an employee rather than self-employed to save doing all that tax, NI and stuff!

He was subjected to the third degree by Janet when he got home, especially as this was the first interview, he had had in nine months. He told her he thought it had gone well but he wouldn't know for a few days as they had other interviews still to do. At five o'clock the phone rang and Tony offered him the job. Although he had told Jack some of the terms and conditions the critical one of all which had not been mentioned at the interview, was salary which he announced would be £16,000pa. Jack was a bit stunned. He had been on £26,000 at DPC, which figure he had included in his CV, so such a low figure was a bit insulting especially as Tony had stressed the seniority of the role.

Thinking quickly, Jack simply said, "No thanks. You know what I was on, that's simply too low." He was greeted with silence. He kept quiet.

Eventually Tony said, "I should not tell you but the other four advocates are each on £14,000 but I felt you would probably not accept that, that's why I asked the Director of Consultancy to come in and meet you to persuade him to let me offer more. I probably should not say this either but you have been out of work for nine months and I know that it's very hard out there are you sure you will not reconsider?"

Whilst he had been talking Jack had been thinking the very same thing but he also knew that a few days earlier he had been looking at his finances in some detail including what was the lowest salary he could survive on at a reasonable standard. He had concluded that he needed at least £18,000, preferably more, but with what Tony had just said he didn't think there was any more in the kitty so taking his life in his hands he said, "I could not pay all my bills for less than £18,000, so it would be dishonest to accept any less than that as I would only do so whilst I looked for another job. That's not my way of doing business, so £18k and I'll start, £16k and I won't." Tony said he would have to consult with his boss and would ring him back in a few minutes.

When he did, he said, "Can you start Monday on £18,000?"

"Yes," said Jack and he did.

Jack wasn't to know it but he was to spend the rest of his working life at Delta. Initially he started as an Advocate. His first day, the Monday, was hectic. Beside the introductions, there were five Advocates, one of whom was leaving hence Jack's recruitment, who were all in the office—a rare occurrence for them all to be in at once—and who made him feel welcome. Advocacy was run by the

Manager, Tony, with a small office of three people, Tribunal Admin, answering to him who were responsible for responding to Tribunal Applications if the client had not done so or putting themselves forward as the future contact for the case if a response had already been sent in.

Tribunal work came to them in two forms, from existing clients receiving an Application which they were required to forward to Delta unanswered or an existing case where the Rep had been in and signed them up as a client part of the deal being that they would take over and conduct the case for them. Those cases were always difficult, firstly because they were routinely signed up only days before the case was to be heard (as Jack was about to discover!) and secondly because the response(s) already provided were normally poor saying too much about somethings and not enough about others.

The Office of Tribunals was bound by law to publish a list of all Tribunal Applications, so Delta, along with a few other companies, sent someone into the Tribunal Office and noted all the new cases. That information was immediately phoned through to Head Office where it was immediately passed to Telesales who would then ring the Respondent (no point in ringing the applicant they had usually been sacked and had no money!) and offered Delta's services. The offer included coming in and producing for the client a complete, up to date Personnel System, the same for Health and Safety and representation at the Tribunal.

In addition, they would have access to the 24hour, 7 day a week, Advice Line which they could ring any time they had a Personnel type problem or the H&S Line if it were a health and safety one. Provided they took advice before acting and followed the advice given, they would then be indemnified so that if a Tribunal did arise, they would be represented for free and further, if the Tribunal was lost Delta would pay the award. All they had to do was take advice and follow it. It was a fantastic deal and no wonder that Delta was expanding at a phenomenal rate.

On the Monday Jack was handed three Tribunal Applications, one to be heard that Wednesday in Manchester, one listed for London but in the event did not come to hearing for 18 months and one for the end of the following week so no pressure there! He was also given the keys to a Datsun 160 which had already covered 75,000 miles and had been used by the Consultancy Director's daughter up until the previous Friday. It was supposed to have been valeted but it was clear that that simply meant someone had only chucked a bucket of water over it without any sponging, shampoo or even leathering it off. It was dark when he collected it from the underground car park thus, he was unable to see that three of the four tyres were bald with one of them showing canvas through the rubber. He only discovered this on the Tuesday morning in the daylight. He had changed the worst one for the spare but the others were not much better, so, rather than drive on the motorway, which he had sped down the night before, he used the A road at a considerably more sedate speed! He shuddered at what might have happened!

The Manager of the Advocacy Department, Tony, apologised, and explained that he never used the garage across the road, which looked after most of their cars, because he felt they did not do a good job, but used a Datsun dealership a short distance away. He arranged for Jack's car to be taken there that morning and it was returned, properly serviced and with four new tyres, later that day. The previous young lady driver was caught drunk driving one morning a week or two later and lost her licence as a result. Jack thought it entirely proper that someone driving such a dangerous vehicle and prepared to drive still under the influence of alcohol should lose her licence. Her father was to commit an even more serious act of disloyalty and dishonour three years later, but that is yet to be related.

The Wednesday one was for unfair dismissal of a Waiter in a small restaurant specialising in sweets, puddings and cakes. The second case involved an unfair dismissal claim by a painter who the ex-employer said was not an employee but a subcontractor and the third one apparently just a straightforward unfair dismissal complaint following the employer telling the employee to fuck off!

Jack collected the first file from the set of filing cabinets outside Trib Admin and started reading. The first thing he did was to arrange the papers in date order with the oldest on top and the newest on the bottom. He was to learn the other Advocates had their own way of doing it but Jack felt that if he read the papers in this order, he would better understand how events had unfolded, if he did it the other way round, he would sort of be starting with the advantage of hindsight and that tended to distort things.

He had to use a time sheet to record the amount of time spent on the work on each part of the case which would form part of the claim for costs to the insurance company at the completion of the case; he also, on first read of the file, listed events by date and sometimes time to better understand how the situation had developed. This was quite often useful to show that the story being told now could not be true because at the time alleged the event, whatever it was, had not yet happened.

Jack also liked to detail the individual's details, age, length of service—it was amazing how often this one fact about service showed they did not have sufficient service to bring a claim, which killed it stone dead at that point. He also calculated the wage/salary so that he could make an informed guess at how much the Tribunal award might be—he was to find that was the most frequent question, 'how much is it likely to cost me if I lose?' he would be asked. As some awards were calculated on gross wage/salary and some on net he needed both figures and was to discover just how bad applicants were at recording the two figures as the IT1 required them to do (Industrial Tribunal 1 form—there was an IT2, a covering letter, and an IT3 which was the Respondent's response to the Application and these three forms were to become the be all and end all of Jack's life for the next three years).

Most applicants simply entered their net wage/salary—they always knew that because that was how much they received each week/month but few knew the gross figure as well, especially weekly paid people. As part of the routine, he would obtain the correct figures when he first contacted the client but since he anticipated that he would be asked the 'how much' question early on he used to estimate the gross, or missing net figure, when he compiled his facts list at the start of the file. He used a third or multiply by two calculation. He knew that, on average, what someone received in their pay as net pay was about 2/3 of the gross because of income tax and NI deductions. (Those part-timers working so few hours as to not earn enough to pay tax also probably didn't work enough hours to make an application to Tribunal but that was to change later.)

Thus, someone on £150 per week gross would receive about £100 per week net. If he knew their net was £100 then if he divided the net by 2 and multiplied by 3, he would arrive at £150 gross. He knew it was not totally accurate but it was close enough to work out the approximate figures he needed.

When he worked out the figures for the Waiter they didn't seem right. The gap was too big between the net quoted by the Applicant and the gross quoted by the Respondent so he made a note to check that. He telephoned the client and made an appointment to see him at his premises the following day at 10am. He went through what was to become a standard presentation for the next three years meeting clients. Firstly, a social pleasantry, introduction of himself and an explanation of how he expected the meeting to progress—many did not go to plan as he was to find! He always asked to see the individual's Personnel file and he would take that away with him to examine more minutely than he could in the meeting—some of what he was to find scribbled on the backs of pages was quite fascinating!

The Waiter had been employed for two years and three weeks thus only qualifying to be able to make an application to the Industrial Tribunal by three weeks. His age was 30 and according to the employer his wage was £143 gross. When Jack asked him about the Waiter's claim to receive on £80pw all he would say was he was mistaken. He was unable to produce the wage records because they were with the Accountant but he promised to obtain them and bring them with him to the Tribunal the following day. Jack asked all the questions he needed to, answered the client's and, having arranged to meet early at the Tribunal the following morning, went back to the office to prepare the bundle. When they did meet the client said he had been unable to get the wage details as the Accountant was off sick, so they would just have to wing it.

Although Jack smelt a bit of a rat it didn't seem important enough to pursue at this moment and he simply concentrated on briefing the client on what was to happen and what he expected from him. Unlike America where lawyers would practice and rehearse their clients, even filming practice interviews and having another lawyer from the practice play the other side to ensure their case was presented as well as possible, which gave enormous advantages to rich defendants, such practice was not allowed in the UK but Jack always ensured that his clients were always well prepared.

They were gathered from the Respondents' waiting room and were escorted into the Tribunal room with the Applicant and his Solicitor. The Tribunal were already seated with the Chairman in the middle of the three. He immediately started, with no social pleasantries of any kind, by saying, "It is my invariable practice to start by establishing the basic data of a case so Mr Smifff would you confirm that…" and proceeded to ask a series of questions relating to address, age, DOB etc ending with, "You've said that your net pay was £80pw but what was your gross?"

The Applicant said he didn't know what that was because of the £25 cash-in-hand for Saturday mornings. Consternation leapt around the room! Jack realised immediately that that explained the disparity between net and gross as per his formula. He also realised that the case was about to go belly up. The Chairman's face was a picture and he said, "Mr Jones, the Applicant's Solicitor,

I saw your face as that was said and I assume that was a complete surprise to you, is that correct?"

The Solicitor replied, "Yes, indeed it was, Sir." He simply gave Jack a dirty look.

"Right, both of you, I intend to adjourn for 15 minutes in order for you to take what actions you see fit but I must warn you that when we reconvene if you have not settled this case it will be my duty to strike out this Application as it has clearly been made relating to an illegal contract to defraud the Inland Revenue of the proper tax and NI contributions due to the Revenue and it will further be my duty to notify the Revenue of this case for them to pursue it as they see fit. An illegal contract cannot be brought before a legal court, so 15 minutes gentlemen." They withdrew and the two parties both withdrew to their waiting rooms.

In the waiting room the client immediately said to Jack, "It's ok, I have already been in touch with the Revenue and settled the amount they asked for, so there is no chance I'm going to pay that little shit anything to settle, I'm quite happy for it to be struck out." *I bet you are,* thought Jack. He said, "You knew this all along, didn't you?"

"Yes," he said, "I had another one a few years ago so I thought this would happen." Jack excused himself and went and spoke to the Solicitor, telling him only that his client was unwilling to settle so it was back to the Tribunal room when called and the case was duly struck out. The Chairman seemed to take great delight in saying he would be reporting them. Jack decided that since it had been struck out, with therefore no awards against his client that he would record his first case for Delta as a win. Whilst he would win many they were nearly all the ones where a Delta Adviser had been advising throughout; where the company had sacked them and come to Delta for help winning was much harder although they were often able to use the any difference test and contribution to reduce the award(s) to little or nothing.

Chapter 37

His second case wasn't to come to hearing for 18 months so it was on to the third. From what he could read Stephanie, the boss, had had a falling out with one of the Shop Assistants which had ended up with the boss telling Cyril to fuck off— so Cyril did—straight to the Tribunal. Having sorted out the file and listed the questions he wanted to ask Jack rang the client and asked to speak to Stephanie. When she came on the phone, she had the deepest manly voice that Jack had ever heard. Her phraseology and speaking were also very manly and, as he was talking, Jack looked around the open plan office and noticed that far too many people were paying attention to his conversation. Some of them were killing themselves laughing.

The conversation finished with Jack asking for directions as to finding them. The address meant nothing to Jack at this stage, as did almost every other one in Manchester, but when she said it was on the main shopping street Jack did know where that was. It was only when he put the phone down that several of the staff burst out laughing. Jack had to question several of them before he found out that Stephanie was a man who ran a shop selling women's clothes, shoes, handbags etc to men. Her shop was actually upstairs with an entrance between two shops on the high street at ground level.

It was very apparent what it was and Jack was not at all sure he wanted to go there—what if someone saw him going into a shop selling dresses for men, how would he explain it— 'on business' didn't seem to cut it! In the event, as had been said to him, it was all a 'hissy fit' and the two of them kissed and made up—well they made up anyway and the case was withdrawn, but Jack made it very clear that he would be very unhappy if he should receive another one involving that client—Jack was nowhere near the modern man.

On the Thursday, Jack went in the morning with one of the Advocates, Harry Bennett, who was a relatively young man but who had been trained by Tony to carry out the administration system that he required all Advocates to use who in turn was to show Jack. He had nowhere near the number of cases under his belt as had Jack but he did know the system of meeting clients to take instructions which Jack did not know—he could have done with it before his first case but there wasn't time. The first time he went with him was to a Tribunal in Manchester on that Thursday for a Directions Hearing.

Because the case was potentially complicated with a large number of witnesses on both sides a Chairman had directed the representatives of both sides to attend to go through the admin details including setting the number of days to be set aside for the hearing. The Chairman was in fact a woman and Henry was clearly scared stiff of her. Jack was puzzled because she seemed perfectly alright but Henry explained that in a hearing, she would be a very different character and woe betide any one not on the top of their game.

Jack was to see her in action a couple of weeks later and everything Henry had said was true but Jack was to enjoy his battles with her because, although she was a formidable chairman leaping on any mistakes by professional representatives, she was open to argument and would listen to what was being said unlike many others. One of her favourite tricks was at the very start of the hearing to rip out the first few pages of the Delta bundle. Normally comprising the pages of the IT1 and IT3 Delta ring bound those pages so that they were securely held in the bundle and easily to hand for reference to when needed. Miss Pelt would rip them out making a huge noise and terrifying the people in the Tribunal room which was probably her intention. Jack had warned his clients the first time he appeared in front of her—he found out who the Chairman was by looking at the lists in the foyer—and warned them when he saw her name.

Sure, enough she tore them out with her normal theatricality so Jack, when he asked the first question of whomsoever he was questioning first, asked them to refer to page 3 or 4 of the bundle and asked them to confirm the information at section whatever. The witness could do this because the pages were all still in the bundles of the documents all-round the room; the only one who couldn't do so was the Chairman because she had torn them out and thrown them in the bin so everyone had to wait whilst she found the paperwork in her file. In fact, this silly little scenario was to carry on between them for the next three years.

On the Friday, Jack arrived just after 7.30am having left home in Loggerheads at 6.30. The first 12 miles or so were on a fast, interesting 'A' road to pick up the M6 at Stoke South—Junction 15. From there it was all motorway whether he went up to the M6 and into Manchester centre that way or if he cut across to the M56 and in from the south. Although the M56 was marginally shorter the M6/M61 was marginally quicker but the main factor as to which he chose was what the traffic news on the radio said. This morning he came in from the south and had an easy ride, something which was to get less pleasant over the years as traffic built up as the economy improved. He would have to move eventually as the travel time became too long, but not yet.

This morning he arrived at the same time as the Consultancy Director, Don Maybe, who explained that he was getting married in a few weeks' time and Jack was invited to the stag night, details to follow. If they involved Amsterdam or something similar then Jack would not be going but he didn't say so then! He was to discover that the Director's fiancé was one of the Sales Force and a pretty unpopular one at that. Jack was not to meet her for quite a while but when he did, he could quite understand the ill feelings towards her, especially by the other Sales personnel.

He had only been at a desk (hot desking was the norm at that time—his empire amounted to a three drawer pedestal on wheels which accompanied him around the room to whichever desk he was currently occupying) when he received an urgent phone call. Sharing the space and desks were four other Advocates, itinerant occupiers of the space, an Advice Service Manager who had started a week before Jack and whose job Jack would have applied for had he seen it advertised. The Advice Department comprised the Manager, two full-timers and a part-timer who worked on Monday, Tuesday and Friday mornings.

As they permanently occupied the space, they had somehow acquired the best desks, chairs and pedestals on a permanent basis. Jack wasn't too bothered by this as he was to be out most of the time but it was annoying to be asked to give advice to a client, not because all of the Advisers were busy on the phone but because they were too busy chatting among themselves. Jack was to discover this was a sore point between his boss and the Advice Service Manager. It was a very sore point that the Advisers' advice was often slapdash making life very difficult for the Advocates in Tribunal trying to win cases which were insured when the advice given was crap!

It was also very expensive to lose. Relationships between the two departments were not good but over a period of time the Advisers, having heard Jack giving advice on a number of occasions, started asking him for advice on cases they were handling which, as he was approachable and willing to assist which, almost all the other Advocates were unwilling to do, did lead to a reasonable relationship with him although not, it must be said, with the Advice Service Manager who Jack thought was a lazy, incompetent clown.

On this occasion when he answered the phone, he was to discover a Rep, whose area was nominally Northamptonshire, was phoning from Cardiff! He was to discover this was quite a common practice as a lead could come from anywhere. In this case he had been given a lead by a client in Northampton whose brother owned a Rover Dealership in Cardiff and who had a Tribunal on the Monday. He understood Jack was the only Advocate who did not have a Tribunal booked for the Monday so could he do it? It would be a £100,000 deal for which the Rep would get 15% and he was offering Jack 5% if he would do it. Jack was only to discover later that the 5% was 5% of the rep's 15% not 5% of the 100,000 but the Rep wasn't nicknamed the Stalking Cat for nothing.

The brief description sounded simple enough, a Vehicle Specialist had fitted non-ventilated discs, instead of ventilated ones, to the front of a Montego Estate and when the MD had found out he had sacked the guy with no proper procedure at all. Jack asked for the IT1 and IT3, plus any other relevant paperwork to be faxed to him and he arranged to ring the MD in about an hour after he had received it.

In procedural terms the case was hopeless. The matter had come to light whilst the Vehicle Specialist was off sick with flu. When he returned the MD had given instructions, he was to be sent to his office straight away without starting work or even taking his coat off! When the Mechanic knocked on the door the MD shouted at him, "Did you fit new discs to a Montego Estate the week before you went off on the sick?"

And when the guy nodded that he had the MD still shouting said, "well you fitted non-ventilated not ventilated and nearly killed the woman driver; you're fired you bastard. Get out any money will be sent with your P45, get out of my sight now."

Jack asked a few questions of the MD when he rang him and then arranged for them to meet, along with the Foreman and a Clerk/typist on the Sunday at 10am. The drive down was easy, quiet and quick. He found the Dealership with no problem it was massive stretching along the main road into Cardiff.

He explained to the MD and the Foreman that in terms of procedures the case was lost but if they could convince the Tribunal that if it had been done properly, he would still have been summarily dismissed then there might not be an award. The MD, like most MDs, was not a happy bunny. Jack was never quite sure what made the Managing Director different to all other Directors, perhaps it was that they sat on the sharp point of the pyramid, but they were always convinced that they were God in the Universe and it wasn't until they were walking into the Waiting Room at the Tribunal that they seemed to realise that actually there was another God in the Universe and he had a bigger Universe and an even bigger hammer and it was at that stage they would suddenly decide they needed to be in the office and Jack would be ordered to settle it!

The MD was most indignant that a Mechanic who had put people's lives at risk might win just because of procedures. Jack had to point out that procedures were everything to lawyers and bureaucrats but the fact that lives had been put at risk was an extremely strong point for them and Jack wanted him to show how indignant he was about the danger when Jack led him to that point in his evidence. On that point he asked if they by any chance had the wrong discs which had been incorrectly fitted and the Foreman leapt up and shot out of the office.

He was back in moments with a filthy old sack the contents of which he emptied onto the MD's desk. What came out was disgusting. The two discs were scored and blackened. Also lying there were four brake pads which were chewed up, black and broken. Jack said, "Great. At some stage in the hearing, I will indicate that I want you to do just that again but this time tip the lot onto the desk in front of the Chairman in just as dramatic a fashion. I don't know which of you I will ask to do it but you will be sitting behind me with the sack on the floor between you so whichever one I indicate pick it up and dump it on the desk. Obviously, that's the non-ventilated ones, have you got a set of ventilated, new not damaged or marked that we can take along as well?"

"Yes of course," said the MD.

"We all know the difference between ventilated and non-ventilated but probably the three of them on the Tribunal, especially if one of them is a female non-driver, will have no idea and they may think it's an easy mistake to make. We need to show that the difference is so obvious that no-one in their right mind could make such a dangerous mistake."

(Dear reader, imagine a round, flat metal disc about 8 inches in diameter and a quarter of an inch thick—that's a non-ventilated disc. A ventilated disc is two discs one on top of the other but about 3/8ths of an inch apart. Because of the gap between them air can flow between them and cool them down; it is a very important difference and essential in a heavy car like a fully loaded estate if you need to slow it down quickly in an emergency!)

Jack took notes of what each of them said at to their individual roles in the meeting and then explained how he saw the hearing progressing. The company had admitted dismissal in their IT3 so unless something weird happened it would be for them to go first, so he would call the MD first as the dismissing officer and then the Foreman to confirm what happened. He stressed that if he asked a question that could be answered with a yes or a no to do just that, do not expand if he wanted anymore then he would ask another question, but it was the most important part of their evidence, in his experience witnesses said too much— don't do it.

He also stressed that they should try and avoid questions about the procedure of the meeting, it was their weakest point, so if asked something like that try and answer by saying something like, 'yes I understand what you're asking but what was going through my mind so strongly at the time was what would I have felt if he had fitted those wrong discs to my wife's car and that was all I could think about,' or something like that.

He was able to cobble together a reasonable little bundle although it was not ring bound but the Clerk was able to staple it down the left had side with a clear acetate sheet as a front cover and a plain piece of cardboard as the back cover. He used the time before they were ushered in to the Hearing Room to run through once again what he expected to hear when he asked a question based on what they had already told him. On entering Jack went and sat down on the left table at the front of the room and his two witnesses sat behind him.

The Applicant's Solicitor (Jack had asked the Clerk if he was represented) sat to Jack's right and the Applicant behind the Solicitor. The Tribunal were already sitting at the front but the Clerk handed the Chairman a note which he read and then left the room. In the meantime, the Solicitor opened his briefcase and took out just an A4 writing pad and a pen, nothing else. *Jack immediately started thinking, 'what's going on—he should at least have the IT1 & 3?' He's not prepared,* thought Jack. *He was expecting this to settle so he hasn't done any work! Right, he thought, change of plan.* Turning to his two witnesses he whispered, "change of plan. I'm going to call you first, to the Foreman and you second to the MD. Just remember listen very carefully to the question and only answer yes or no if you can."

He just had time before the Chairman returned and apologised for keeping them waiting and said, "Right, the Respondents admit dismissal so it's for you to go first Mr Hughes."

"Thank you, Sir, I would like to call Mr Evans." The Foreman went forward, stood at the witness table between the Tribunal and the two Representatives and was sworn in by the Clerk to tell the truth, the whole truth and nothing but the truth. Jack asked him is your name, role at the Respondent's company, have you been there for 17 years. Although these were technically leading questions the answers were clearly not in dispute so it was normal practice to ask these details in a statement form to save time. Jack then started with the meat of the detail. "Were you present at a meeting when the MD asked the Applicant for an explanation of why he fitted non-ventilated discs, instead of ventilated discs to a Montego Estate?"

"Yes."

"Did that take place in the MD's office immediately on the Applicants return from sick leave?"

"Yes."

"What explanation did he give?"

"He said the wrong parts must have been in the box from the Stores."

"What did you think of that answer?"

"It was rubbish."

"Why?"

"Parts are often put into the wrong boxes so there are notices everywhere saying it is the responsibility of the Vehicle Specialist to ensure they have the right part. He had just taken the old discs to the Stores to swap and he could not have possibly not noticed the difference, not possible at all, especially for an experienced Mechanic like him." *Great thought Jack, now's the time to produce the evidence.*

"Sir," said Jack, "I wonder if it would help the Lay Members if we showed them a disc and a non-ventilated disc to show the difference?"

"Yes, please, Mr Hughes (never suggest a Chairman needs help!). So, Jack picked up the sack which had been on the floor behind him and carried it forward to the Tribunal desk behind which the three of them were sitting and emptied it fairly carefully onto the desk (*I told you change of plan!*). He also emptied the brand new, pristine ventilated discs onto the table. The pile looked wonderfully disgusting, especially against the ventilated ones, oily, black, burnt, the four brake pads were all chewed up and one of them slid onto the floor which one of the Lay Members picked up with every show of disdain and dropped onto the pile. Jack asked the Foreman to describe what they were looking at and why it looked that way which he did getting in a couple of 'I have nightmares about that lot going onto my daughter's car' along the way. Jack then asked him as his final question, "The Applicant says in his IT1 that summary dismissal, given his long service was too severe a punishment. If you had made that mistake, would you have felt that instant dismissal was too severe?"

"No, I bloody wouldn't," he said, "I'd have deserved it, it's only a bloody miracle that nobody was killed."

"Thank you, no further questions, of this witness." *Now,* thought Jack*, we'll see the calibre of this Solicitor.* The Solicitor stood up and said, "I only have one question of this witness, Sir." Jack realised that he was so unfamiliar with Tribunal practice he had not realised that all the work was done sitting down, not standing up and down, even though Jack had not stood, so, like a Jack-in-the-box, he had leapt up!

"Mr Jones, here we do everything except the taking of the oath or affirmation, sitting down. Kindly sit down and ask your question." Jack only smiled inwardly.

"Bill never received any training as to how to change discs and pads did, he?" Jack had run several what could his one question be through his mind while the upping and downing was going on but that was not one of them. The Foreman said, "I don't know, he started about seven years before me so I don't know what training he had then, but I do know that he's changed many brakes over, old drums replaced by new, old discs and pads replaced with new and he done all them alright so he obviously knew how to do it."

"But you would agree that training is very important, wouldn't you and if someone hadn't had any then that would be very serious, wouldn't it?"

"Not half as serious as working for years doing a job knowing you didn't know what you were doing." The Solicitor then said he had no more questions, so Jack called the MD. After going through the usual identity rigmarole Jack asked, Firstly, you heard everything the Foreman said, is what he said a true account of the meeting the three of you had?"

"Yes."

"Clearly it is a matter of record that you summarily terminated his employment, why did you do that rather than say a Final Written Warning?"

"Just look at that (pointing to the burnt and scarred discs) I just kept imagining what I would have done to him if he had fitted those to my wife's car and she had been killed as a result of it, I would have done a lot more than just have sacked him."

Jack decided that that would be a good point to finish so he simply indicated he had no further questions and waited for the Solicitor to make a cock of it. And he did!

"What training did Bill have in how to change discs?" The solicitor asked.

Jack couldn't believe his luck when the MD not having answered immediately the Solicitor asked, "He didn't have any did he?"

The MD paused and just as the Solicitor looked like he was going to ask again the MD said, "For someone who you allege has had no training he managed to do the job for more than 20 years with no problems before this incident." Jack wished he stopped at no problems, the 'this incident' opened the door to a claim that something had happened to cause it but he was ok because the Solicitor immediately said, "But if he had no training surely that would explain the error?"

Saved by the Tribunal, the Lay Member sitting to the left of the Chairman suddenly interrupted and asked the Chairman if he might ask two questions to which the Chairman immediately agreed.

"What is this reference all the time to Vehicle Specialist, is that what I would understand to be a time served Mechanic?" The Solicitor started to answer but the Lay Member interrupted him and said, "No I'm asking him," pointing to the Applicant. The Applicant nodded.

"Then what's all this damn nonsense about training, a time served Mechanic with more than 20 years' service must know how to change things as important as brakes?" The Applicant looked down.

"Thank you, Chair," said the Lay Member. The Solicitor asked a couple more questions but it was clear his heart wasn't in it and when he tried to slip in a comment about training the Chairman simply shut him up. Jack had prepared a number of questions for the Applicant based around the problems routinely experienced with the wrong parts in boxes and the notices around the place regarding that situation and he had added a couple regarding how he could possibly have done the job over all those years without some training but he didn't get a chance to ask them because the Solicitor announced that he had no witnesses when instructed by the Chairman to present his first one.

That was the first time Jack was to face that situation and it only happened once more in the next 16 years when one of his witnesses refused to give evidence. Jack sat poised to add, delete or amend his drafted summary as the

Solicitor went first, Jack having had to go first with his case. His summary was abysmal. He could only say that summary dismissal was too severe for just one mistake by a true and loyal employee, that it should at the most have been a Final Written Warning for such a long service, especially as he had never received any training. That last upset the Chairman. He turned to Jack and said, "What do you say to that last, Mr Hughes?"

From the question and its manner Jack knew he was being asked to rebut the statement. He had long given up answering immediately, he always took a second or two to think, which he did, so he had no difficulty in saying, "Sir, we have heard no evidence about that. The two witnesses for the Respondent said they were unaware of any training because it would have been done before they knew him, (not quite true the MD avoided the question) and the Applicant could have said that in his own defence but he chose not to give evidence and the only way we know anything at all about that is because the Applicant's representative asked questions about training—that is not evidence."

"I am with Mr Hughes on that," said the Chairman giving the Solicitor the evil eye. He then asked Jack to summarise his case. Jack knew he had to keep it short, he couldn't afford for the Solicitor or any of the Tribunal to realise nothing had been said about procedures or appeals but he had to get out one EAT case decision to support what happened in case they did so he said, "I should like to start by referring to Khanum v Mid Glamorgan Area Health Authority 1978 an EAT case. That case defines natural justice and can be summarised as 'natural justice demands that someone should know what they are accused of, have the opportunity to defend themselves and should be dealt with fairly by the Tribunal considering the case'. Clearly the Applicant was asked if he had fitted the wrong discs and he admitted that he had. He was then asked for an explanation, i.e., an opportunity to defend himself, which he did, and his explanation was unacceptable for the reasons you have heard. There therefore only remains the issue of was it fair to dismiss him and since his actions could have resulted in the death of one or more people summary dismissal must have been a fair option. Look at the mess those are in (pointing at the burnt discs still in front of the Chairman) and seeing how easy it is to tell the difference between the correct and the incorrect discs I would submit that summary dismissal was fair. If I can help further, Sir, otherwise that concludes my case."

The Chairman thanked them and told them to wait where they were; the Tribunal then left the room. Jack was a little surprised, normally the parties

231

would be sent to their respective waiting rooms, but when they came back after only a few minutes Jack felt that the Chairman had decided before they left the room on the decision so he was simply saving time.

He announced, abruptly, "This application fails. You will receive our written decision and reasons shortly. Good day to you," and with that they up and left. Jack could not really believe it; he had expected an unfair procedure decision and to have to argue the any difference/contribution amounts but he had won so no need! The client was of course delighted – but not delighted enough to give Jack a free Rover; as also was the Stalking Cat. He rang Jack a couple of days later and was fulsome in his praise having, knowing a little about Tribunals, expected it to be lost on procedure if nothing else.

Although Jack wasn't to know it that result meant that Graham Black started to ask for Jack's help in a number of ways, he would ring Jack if he was with a difficult prospect and ask Jack to talk to him/them about the case and its prospects including the costs if they lost; he asked for Jack to attend with him to one or two very large potential clients and he asked Jack to speak at a number of seminar/sales pitch meetings he would organise. Jack started to acquire a reputation amongst the Sales Force and with the MD as someone who would willingly work with and for sales which was to stand him in good stead later on.

Chapter 38

Over the next three years Jack was to through put some 450 or so Tribunals. At one time he had 55 on the go at the same time but the number was more normally about 35. In his first year he drove almost exactly 52,000 miles. As he was the newbie as cases piled in so they were allocated to him but as time went on, he gradually took control of his diary and was able to stop the ultimate stupidity where he appeared in Inverness one day and Southampton the next! He evolved a system where as soon as he had organised and read the file, he would ring the Listings Clerk of the Tribunal concerned and ask them what period of time they would be likely to looking at to list it for hearing.

He would then ring the client having looked at the date that best suited him, Jack, in that time scale and tell the client to keep that date open for the hearing, most of them being dealt with in a day, and he would then ring the Listing Clerk back and tell them the date he and his client could make and the Clerk was only too glad to put that one to bed; thus he was able to bring some sanity to location and date such that his final year on the road he only drove 35,000 miles. About 30% of all cases settled or otherwise disappeared or he would not have been able to handle the number he did.

Jack was to establish a reputation as being very able but more importantly approachable so that he was regularly asked for assistance by the Advice Line Advisers, even including their Manager, and by other Advocates and Sales Staff, both out in the field and the Telesales people. Jack was unique in that during his time in Linehams and Lintwoods he had handled about a dozen take overs with at least nine of them governed by the Transfer of Undertakings (Protection of Employment) Regulations 1981 (TUPE) which had gradually influenced the process of takeovers becoming more and more complicated as time went on.

One early case Jack handled ended up at the Employment Appeal Tribunal setting the case law for the country and all future cases. *(Worry ye not oh readers there will not now follow a huge list of all the cases, just a few of special interest ones you will enjoy—I hope!)*

The Sales Rep had been in to see a potential client some months before but they had refused to sign up believing that they had a very good case and didn't need help. They did! The Company had been set up following the collapse of a civil engineering company which specialised in digging and laying sewer pipes, repairing, cleaning and refurbishing the same whenever and wherever they could get a contract. Most of the work involved laying the sewer and water pipes on new developments for industrial estates and for housing estates, both private and council. All the staff had been called together on Christmas Eve and sacked as the Company had gone bust.

Two of the senior staff got together over the Christmas and started up a new Company. They approached the various ex-clients who had unfinished work and obtained contracts to finish the job. They approached the landlord of the old premises and rented them as they did with the old company's vehicles which had also been rented. Since the old company name was painted on the vans and trucks, they approached the Liquidators and bought the right to the old Company name, Drain Diggers Supreme Ltd.

They then bought a company 'off the shelf' from Companies House and changed the name of that company to Drain Diggers Supreme Ltd; they contacted most of the old staff and offered them employment and were ready to start operating the first working day after the New Year—a truly remarkable performance. A couple of weeks after start-up they had concerns about one of the staff they had employed. In the old company he had been a good worker, why they had offered him a job, but in the new one he was terrible. Unreliable, late, absent and when he did deign to turn up the quality of his work was poor.

He was a massive bloke, big, strong and employed mainly to labour physically where strength was needed which could not be provided by machine. As they were a bit frightened of what he would do if they spoke to him about it, they decided to sack him by putting a P45 and an extra week's pay in his pay packet and gave it to him as he went out the gate on the Friday night. Problem solved! No, it wasn't. It came back in the shape of an Application to the Industrial Tribunal.

They took advice from ACAS (the Advisory, Conciliation and Arbitration Service) who advised them that since he had only been employed for a couple of weeks, he didn't have the service to bring a claim and that they should write to the Tribunal to tell them and that would be the end of it. Well, it wasn't although they did write. James Callaghan, the Labour Prime minister once made a comment which was to be attributed to him for ever and was, 'events, my boy, events' and well and truly did events step in. All the funds that the new company received were paid into the bank. Fine. All the bills they received were not paid because the bank, acting on the orders of the Liquidators froze all the money entering the account of Drain Diggers Supreme Ltd.

So, the landlord locked them out of the premises for not paying the rent; the van hire seized the vehicles because the rental had not been paid and the Post Office continued to deliver their mail to the locked premises they could not enter to retrieve. During this time communications were delivered from the Tribunal which, of course, they did not receive and to which they did not reply. So, the Tribunal went ahead and they eventually obtained entry to their premises the day after the Tribunal decision, that they had lost the case, was delivered!

It also included a notice of a hearing date for Remedy (how much they would have to pay) if they had not settled it in the meantime. Enter the Delta Rep and Jack. The Rep was the Stalking Cat again and he had told the client that in Jack they had the best Advocate in the country and he would be able to win that no trouble! Jack wasn't at all sure! Tribunal decisions were rarely overturned on appeal and once he had read the papers for this case, he was not at all sure of how to handle it. Appeal, obviously, but was that the best way? So, he went to see Tony and discussed it with him. Tony pointed out that since they had only received the decision two days before they were still well within the 14 day limit in which to ask the Tribunal to review its own decision.

Jack knew about Reviews but had never done one so Tony, who had done two, both of which had failed, explained how they worked. Clearly having heard all the evidence and witnesses the Tribunal considered its decision and then decided. To ask them to think again because you believed they had got it wrong was rarely likely to succeed. Tony related to how his two had failed and how Jack's might have a chance on the basis of new evidence. It was certainly worth a go because an appeal was a slow, long and costly process so Jack went for it.

At first Jack went all through the paperwork and listed a number of questions he needed to ask the client. He then rang him and asked them. Almost as an afterthought he said to the guy, this chap has a Barrister representing him, or at least he did at the Hearing, do you know how he could afford that?

"Oh, I expect he paid for her out of the redundo money."

"Redundancy money—are you sure?"

"Well, we all got these forms from the Social when we were sacked telling us that the company could not pay redundancy, notice or holiday pay and so we should claim on the forms attached to the letter."

Jack knew the system so did not need to ask about that but he did ask, "Are you sure he got it?"

"Well, it's the only way he could afford to pay that Solicitor and Barrister." Jack then asked him if he knew the office which dealt with them and he faxed the details to Jack about an hour later. Expecting to have a problem with confidentiality Jack did not expect to find out very much but he was very pleasantly surprised when, having explained the situation to the guy he spoke to he was very helpful. He confirmed that the forms had been sent to the Applicant, a Paddy Murphy, and that he had completed them and returned them.

The guy then asked if Jack would like to know how much he had received and, hardly daring to believe his luck, Jack replied yes and the guy told him. Holding his breath and crossing his fingers Jack asked the guy if he could put all that in writing and the guy said yes. Knowing he was up against it and the 14-day limit Jack thought he would chance his luck one more time and explaining the limit he asked if the guy could fax the reply as soon as possible. He received it later that afternoon and took back all that he thought about all civil servants, there was at least one good one in the country!

Jack fired off the request for a Review including most of his case but holding back the information that Murphy had claimed and received the redundancy package. He felt that the information about what had happened to the company and especially that they had followed the advice of ACAS, which Jack knew was wrong, so he had stressed that in his request, would mean they would try and cover that up by a proper hearing. Jack had also stressed that a party to a hearing had the inalienable right to be heard and the Respondent had been denied that right by ACAS and the fact they had been locked out of their building. He was therefore not too surprised to receive a notice of Review Hearing a few weeks later.

Jack took the client along with him in case something came up which Jack could not answer but it was mainly to be an argument by the Barrister and Jack in front of the Tribunal. Normally there would not be any witnesses giving evidence, hence just the Advocates. The Barrister was a young woman who tried to play mind games with Jack by coming into the waiting room and complaining to him that his application for a review was a waste of everybody's time because it was clear it would be refused. Jack simply replied, "I don't know why you are so bothered; you are being paid aren't you?" She did not like that.

When they were called in, Jack discovered that Paddy Murphy was in attendance and he immediately realised what an advantage that could give him if he could work it in alright. The Chairman immediately said to Jack, "Well, Mr Hughes, you have requested this Review so it is for you to go first but let me just explain that first, we will hear your arguments for a Review to be granted and we will then withdraw to consider that point. If we decide to grant a Review, we will then listen to the evidence supporting your request for the Review and we will then withdraw to consider whether that evidence merits a Review and then, if we decide it does, we will conduct a third Hearing to hear the evidence on which to decide the Review. Is that clear?" *As mud,* thought Jack.

"Yes, Sir," is what he said. So, he started. He started by defining the law relating to an application for a review and then said the key point was did the Tribunal have jurisdiction to hear the case in the first place. "Clearly," he said, "if there was no transfer of the undertaking then the Applicant only had two week's service and this did not qualify him to make an unfair dismissal claim since service of two years or more was necessary." He then referred to the events which led up to the creation of the new company.

As he did so he referred to a sequence of documents relating to the renting of the premises, the vehicles and two sample letters offering employment, one of them being to Mr Murphy. He then referred to some of the TUPE case law and described how although the name had been purchased from the Liquidator nothing else had, either from the Liquidator or the original company and so, he argued, there could not be a transfer of the undertaking since nothing had transferred from one company, which had ceased to exist two weeks before the new one even existed. He then referred to the letter the company had written to the Tribunal based on the advice from ACAS and he made much of the fact that ACAS knew, or should have known, that such a letter, unsupported by a witness swearing or affirming to its truth, was utterly worthless and that ACAS should have advised them to attend and give their evidence.

He had not been interrupted during this delivery apart from a few humphs from the Barrister which he had ignored and even up to that point he was not sure how he would introduce the redundancy payments issue. He paused and before he spoke the Barrister interrupted and said, "They could have said all of this at the original hearing. Nothing about the start-up is new and could have been introduced at the original hearing and we do not know that they wrote the letter on the advice of ACAS, it doesn't say that, and it could be this is just a sneaky way to have a second bite of the cake…" The Chairman shut her up at that point, saying she would have her opportunity later and asked Jack if he had any more to say. Jack said, "Well, Sir, apropos that last, the letter at page seven does say 'we have been advised' and my client, here, will confirm that it was ACAS which gave the advice…"

"Yes, very well," said the Chairman, "but you are pushing against an open door Mr Hughes," at which Jack immediately said, "In that event, Sir, I have nothing further to say." At that the Chairman turned to the Barrister and asked her to say why she thought they should not consider an Application for a review. She then launched into an entirely irrelevant load of old codswallop which said to Jack that she knew little about Tribunals and was practicing criminal law tactics of muddy the waters to create doubt and thus win. Certainly, the Chairman got fed up and cut her off with had she anything to say in contradiction of the events Jack had laid out to which she had to say no.

They withdrew a little surprisingly since Jack had not been offered the opportunity to counter her claims which would have been normal but he hoped that that meant he had convinced them and needed to say no more. In the event they were back in less than 10 minutes to say that they gave permission for Jack to apply for a Review and asked him to do so immediately. Which Jack did, saying more or less the same thing all over again justifying why they should be allowed a Review but again he said nothing about the Applicant's redundancy claim.

The Barrister said the same again and got cut off again. They then withdrew for slightly longer this time but came back and said Jack could now argue the Review which he did saying all the same things all over again but this time he added at the end, besides the argument about TUPE not applying that all the staff had been invited to apply for their entitlements and could he ask the Applicant through the Chairman whether he had applied. The Barrister immediately objected on the grounds of relevancy but Jack argued that it was extremely relevant, how could he claim continuity of employment if he had claimed a redundancy payment for the loss of his previous employment?

The Chairman agreed and asked the Applicant directly did he claim and much to Jack's pleasure he said he hadn't! Jack then asked the Chairman if the

Applicant could be sworn in since just answering the question meant that the answer wasn't technically evidence. The Barrister, of course, objected but the Chairman agreed and sent for the Clerk to swear him in. Once sworn Jack asked the question, "Now, Mr Murphy, you said just now that you had not claimed the redundancy package is that a true answer?"

"Yes," he said.

"Are you sure," said Jack, "because I would remind you, you are on oath and to deliberately lie is to commit perjury for which the Chairman can send you to the Criminal Court for sentencing…"

The Barrister interrupted to try to stop Jack but the Chairman, perhaps sensing something, allowed Jack to continue. So, Jack asked him again and again he said 'no'.

At that Jack reached down and opened his brief case and took out a sheet of paper. He asked the Applicant, "Does the figure £7,530 mean anything to you Mr Murphy?" The Applicant looking very uncomfortable and slightly shifty said, "No."

"Well, let me remind you," said Jack and he read out the figures for notice pay, holiday pay and redundancy pay totalling the £7,530, "and you still don't remember the figures?" The Applicant looked down and didn't answer. Jack said, "I apologise for springing this surprise, Sir, but I had reason to believe the Applicant was lying throughout this Application so I held back this piece of information to prove that fact. He could have told the truth when I asked him, twice, if he had received the redundancy package, but he didn't. Had he answered truthfully then I would have proceeded down a different route, but he didn't, he lied and I therefore ask you to rule that there was no transfer of the undertaking and therefore the Applicant has no continuity of employment and therefore lacks the length of service to give you jurisdiction to hear this case."

The Chairman looked straight at the Barrister and said, "There is nothing you wish to add is there, Ms Smifff?"

The Barrister could also realise that the door in her case was firmly shut and sensibly said, "No, Sir." And at that they withdrew. They were back in less than 10 minutes to announce that they had reviewed their decision, had decided that there was not a transfer under the TUPE Regulations and they did therefore not have jurisdiction to hear the unfair dismissal claim since the Applicant had insufficient service and the full details of their decision would be sent in writing to the parties in due course. Game, set and match.

The client was delighted but not half as much as Jack as he knew how hard it was to get a Tribunal to change their mind but for that he had the unwitting help of the Applicant whose lies had destroyed his own case. He wasn't, sadly, prosecuted for perjury.

But that wasn't the end of the case; just about six weeks later, just inside the time limit for appeal, notification arrived that Murphy had appealed the Tribunal decision. Representation at any appeal had not been included in the deal signed originally but within five minutes of opening the notification they were on the phone to Jack asking him if he would represent them. Jack referred them to Graham Black, the Stalking Cat, and he was on to Jack about 10 minutes later to Jack's boss saying the client would only sign up for the EAT case if Jack conducted it. That was all agreed between the client, Graham and Tony and Jack was simply told to do it! Normally new Advocates would have to work for Delta for several years before appearing at senior Appellate Courts but Tony knew Jack had appeared there before and was quite happy to agree—besides they wanted the business!

While it wasn't technically obligatory for the Respondent to be present at the Appeal, Delta always did so, so that they could ensure their case was forcefully presented. Jack prepared thoroughly presenting his case in two parts. The first was quite simply to say that they firstly relied on the Tribunal decision, who had clearly got it right, and then to repeat the reasoning of the Tribunal including quoting case law to support it. The bundle was 'professionally' presented, as usual, and it would be for the Appellant, Murphy, to go first at the Appeal.

In fact, they were listed as the second case with a due-to-start time of 11am but the previous case overran and they didn't start until 11.30am. Once again, the Barrister, the same young woman, started with the same argument as at the Tribunal but this time, instead of letting her have her say the Chairman, a Judge, kept interrupting with comments like, 'surely the Tribunal considered that and disregarded it'. This was damming for her because, following Jack's presentation at the Review Hearings when he had introduced all the new evidence, she actually had nothing to show the Tribunal had erred in law, and it was clear the EAT had realised that immediately.

Nevertheless, she struggled on until just before 1pm when she finished and the Chairman called a halt for lunch. When they reassembled after lunch, and before the Tribunal came in the Barrister started talking to Jack and saying things like, 'that went well—I've got this in the bag'. Jack couldn't suppress a smile

240

and replied with things like, 'you must be joking—you didn't win a single point.' They were called to stand by the Usher (not Clerks at Employment Appeal Court) and Jack remained standing when the Chairman told them all to sit, since he would be speaking and that was done standing up unlike the lower level Tribunals.

But the Chairman said, "No sit down, Mr Hughes, we have been able to reach a decision and will not need to call on you." Jack was immediately annoyed, the bastards weren't going to strike him down without him giving it a really good go, but the Chairman went on to say, before Jack could speak, "This Appeal fails for the following reasons…" and he then went on to read their decision. He finished by saying they would receive the written decision in due course, thanked them for their help and said goodbye!

Jack was amazed; pleased of course and even more pleased to say to the Barrister, "If that's what having it in the bag means then I'm very glad you did," with a very big smile on his face as he left with an equally smiling client.

Thereafter one of the Tribunal Admin Clerks in Delta, when a new starter started, would introduce Jack to them as, "And this is our famous Mr Hughes who won an EAT case without saying a word," and it was true, Jack had not spoken a single word to the EAT, not even a good morning. The case did establish a very significant issue of case law that a Tribunal must not go ahead and hear a case if the issue of jurisdiction is in doubt and Jack was to quote it in a case in Scotland a couple of years later.

Chapter 39

The next case served up a question Jack was to ask when interviewing for Advocates and Advisers when he was asked to do that a little in the future. The question is:

What is a year?

Think about it! The legislation, at that time, required that someone be employed for two years before they could bring an application to Tribunal. So exactly what is a year? If one thinks of it in birthday terms then 1st January to 1st January is a year; but if one thinks in calendar terms then 1st January to 31st December is a year. One of them can't be right. But which one is it? In the case Jack had just read the papers for the guy had started on the 26th October 1990 and he was called in off the road, he was a Rep, on the 25th October 1992 and sacked summarily. He was simply told, when he arrived at the office, at about 3pm, that his employment was being terminated with immediate effect and that he was to clear his desk and go.

No explanation was given to him and, indeed, Jack was never to receive an explanation as to why he was sacked, throughout the case. He was also given no right of appeal which Jack suggested to them they might consider so that he could argue that the appeal remedied any defect in the original dismissal, something he was able to successfully argue in a case in Scotland a few months later.

But the client, another one signed up by the Stalking Cat, with a promise to them that Delta had just the bloke to win it for them! Jack was to develop a strong love/hate relationship with Graham Black—he loved to hate him for all the bloody impossible cases he committed him to winning over the years. In this case Jack knew with absolute certainty that if they accepted the applicant had two years' service then the dismissal would be found to be unfair—you simply can't just call someone in and sack them without at least, as he had argued with *Khanum*, the basic requirements of fairness had been met.

He looked again at the IT1. The only hope was that the Solicitor did not know something that Jack did and the hope was that he/she didn't find out or the Chairman raise it at, or even before, the hearing. And what was that? It was a big worry—it was an absolute and meant an automatic loss for them if it came out. You will have to wait a while!

Jack carried out his normal preparations and in due course went to visit the client in Shrewsbury where it was listed to be heard. Jack tried to snaffle all the Shrewsbury cases when all the Advocates met every six weeks or so to divvy up the new cases, because the Shrewsbury Tribunal Office was just half an hour from Loggerheads where he was now living which meant little travel either to see the new clients or to the Tribunal Office. He was unable to get them to tell him why the Applicant had been sacked even when he detailed that in a worst case scenario, they could go down for something more than £10,000!

He did explain that he was going to fight on two grounds, the fact that he had insufficient service—which they explained was why they had sacked him when they did—and that he would also, if they lost on that point, he would argue that there was a clause in his contract which gave them the right to summarily terminate the contract, without cause or reason given, but which he felt the Tribunal would probably see as an attempt to get around the unfair dismissal legislation, but it was worth a try—it would have to be, it was all they had! He did not tell them about his big worry.

Nothing was said by the Tribunal or the Solicitor prior to the hearing so they all turned up on the appointed day for a Preliminary Hearing since Jack had challenged their jurisdiction to hear the case by virtue of his lack of sufficient service. The Chairman, sitting alone, looked extremely unwell; in fact, he was to retire almost immediately after the case. He was, in fact, the father of a Prime Minister, with a chequered history! He asked the Solicitor to go first to state why he felt the Applicant had the necessary service and the Solicitor was quite quick and succinct, he simply argued the 1st January to 31st December is a year and therefore 26th October 1990 to 25th October 1992 was two years and he therefore had the necessary service.

Jack, in turn, argued that 1st January to 1st January was a year, if the Solicitor's argument was correct everyone would have a different birthday every year since it would also be one day earlier every year. He also argued that the wording of the legislation was quite specific, it said, "…an applicant must have completed two annual years and an annual year was defined as 12 calendar months…"

Which must mean that the operative word was, 'completed'—the hand of the clock would have to get to midnight on the 25th of October and click past, it might only be a nanosecond but it had to click past and in the case of the Applicant he had been dismissed in the middle of the afternoon long before midnight, let alone past it. He therefore did not complete two years and cannot therefore bring this claim. The Chairman sent them back to their waiting rooms while he considered his decision. After about 30 minutes the Clerk appeared and asked Jack to accompany her.

When he walked into the room it was to find the Solicitor already there but no sign of the Chairman. He appeared after a couple of minutes and then asked the two of them to run their arguments past him again—something Jack had never experience before or would do again. Any event they complied and once Jack had finished, the Solicitor having gone first again, the Chairman said, "I am accepting Mr Hughes's argument that the Applicant does not have two years' service and therefore cannot bring this claim. I would point out," to the Solicitor, "that your claim for breach of contract can still go ahead since that is not dependent on length of service…" at that Jack interrupted and said, "Sir, regarding that last, may I refer you to page (x) of my bundle where you will see that there is a clause which specifically gives the employer the right to summarily terminate employment, with no reason necessary, and I would therefore ask you to issue a warning that should the Applicant continue with this claim it would be frivolous, vexatious or otherwise unreasonable and he will risk costs if he goes ahead and loses."

The Chairman wasn't having any of it and simply said, "No, no Mr Hughes, that is a matter for another day," and got up and left! Jack was of course delighted with the throwing out but he realised just how lucky they had been. He did warn the Solicitor that he would seek costs if they went ahead but that didn't deter him so that Jack found himself back in Shrewsbury a month or two later to fight the breach of contract claim. As normal they waited in separate waiting rooms and were eventually called in by the Clerk.

Jack wasn't quite sure who would have to go first and had prepared for both eventualities but he was completely taken aback when the Chairman, a different one, said, "Mr Smifff," to the Solicitor, "will you turn to page (x) of Mr Hughes's bundle, doesn't that clause (the one saying the company reserves the right to summarily terminate…) give you some trouble?" The Solicitor hummed and hahed but in effect said nothing. "I would assume that is the essence of your argument Mr Hughes?" An open door!

"Yes indeed, Sir," said Jack.

"No, no, we're not going to waste time over this. The employer clearly has the contractual right to summarily terminate employment. If the Applicant had two years' service, then we might indeed have needed to go further to decide if this was arbitrarily executed, but he hasn't and we don't, so this Application fails. Good day to you," and with that he was gone! Jack was a bit pissed off that he hadn't been able to ask for costs but since the original decision to deny the two years' service was wrong, he couldn't risk someone who knew what they were doing taking another look and changing the decision.

So why was it wrong? A clue. His two years' service occurred on the 25th/26th October depending on the 1st—31st or 1st—1st argument. That will be sorted out in another case later. There was a little known clause in the legislation which stated that for the purpose of calculating length of service, and only for that purpose, if Statutory Notice had not been given then Statutory Notice must be added to the termination date to get to the Effective Date of Termination (EDT). Just calling him in and firing him meant that he had not been given any notice so the clause applies. Statutory Notice is one week's notice after four weeks' employment rising by one week per year up to a maximum of 12 weeks after 12 years' employment. In his case, one week added to the 25th gives an EDT of 1st November so he had two years' service! (In fact, that one week takes him to two years so he is entitled to two weeks' notice—either way he qualified.

When Jack read the IT1 and sorted out the dates he immediately knew he was in trouble; but on close examination the IT1 had been completed by the Solicitor and as he had written the date of termination as being the 25th October, he almost certainly didn't know the law. Jack would have written the 2nd November and been prepared to argue the 1st/31st/1st figures if needed but either would get him past the 25th! He had expected all the way through for the Chairman to bring it up or the Solicitor discovering the clause at some time but no-one did and he got away with it. Further on is a case where Jack has to argue the opposite, i.e., the 25th qualifies as the necessary time and not the 26th—such is life!

Why did the Chairman not bring up the issue of Statutory Notice? Jack didn't know. If one of the parties was unrepresented (usually the Applicant) the

Chairman had a duty to ensure that their case did not go by default so Jack would have expected the Chairman to raise the issue, but when both parties are professionally represented then it is up to the representative to raise points of law, not the Chairman. In this case the Chairman retired on ill health grounds within days of the case so did he not care, did he not know? We will never know— what we do know is Jack won a case he should never have won thus helping to build a formidable reputation.)

Chapter 40

Although it does not fit chronologically the next case, happening in fact some 11 years after the one above, it fits here rather nicely. Jack was driving to Blackpool to meet one of the Sales Team specifically employed to recruit large companies when he received a call on his mobile. It was the Sales Manager for Scotland and he asked Jack if he would mind giving some advice to his sister who was being bullied by her employers, two Solicitors who owned a small chain of estate agencies which funnelled lots of lovely work to them, mainly regarding the purchasing, sale or renting of properties. He said he wouldn't mind at all but would prefer to speak to her direct rather than through him so that the story was as correct as possible so she should ring him whenever suited her. He didn't expect it to be two minutes later when he was exploring the top end of the rev range in his new (to him!) 4litre V8 Jaguar because he was late and the empty M61 provided a wonderful quick passage to Blackpool—he also had been waiting for an opportunity to see how fast it would go!

The two Solicitors, Smifff and Jones, owned five shops spread around Glasgow. Charity, the Sales Manager's sister, had started on the 8th April the year before and had started as the junior in one of the shops. Then two, more senior, staff had left and not been replaced, so she was now running the shop on her own. It had become too much for her and she had gone off sick, with stress the week before. Unfortunately, they wouldn't stop contacting her, the two Solicitors were staffing the shop with staff moved in from their other shops or themselves, but nobody knew where the files were, what stage(s) various sales, lets or purchases were at so they were having to ring her at home to find out— they had even rung her sisters and mother if she didn't answer the phone at home. Jack had some sympathy for the Solicitors, they had a business to run and some of the work was legally bound by time but Charity was ill with stress caused by overwork due to understaffing, which was entirely due to them exploiting her and putting two wages savings in their pockets each week; so, his sympathy was somewhat limited!

He dictated a letter for her to write to them asking them to collect all their questions together and phone them through at a time that suited Charity but not to contact her at other times because their so doing was making her more ill and delaying her recovery. That letter was delivered the following day, the 26th March. Charity's doctor had suggested she go away for a short break to help her recovery and Charity's partner had booked a long weekend away starting on the 27th, a Thursday.

On that Thursday, Charity took her son to school and then took a suitcase with clothes etc., to her mother's house who was going to look after him while she was away. Her partner collected her from her Mum's at 10am and off they went. The first night they stayed in Pitlochry and on Friday, they carried on to Fort William where they spent the next two nights before returning home on the Sunday. They stopped first at Charity's Mums to collect her son.

When she got home it was to discover a number of letters, two of which were from her employer. She did not sit down to read them until after getting her son to bed and it came as a bit of a shock to discover that both of them were the same letter, one marked 'Hand Deliver' and the other with a stamp, terminating her employment with immediate effect with one week's pay in lieu of notice. Jack received her phone call telling him this on the Monday morning at 9am.

Jack asked a number of questions, one of which was when did she start with them to be told the 8th April the year before. (The length of service requirement had been reduced to one year, from two, a few years before.) It was obvious immediately that they had dismissed her when they did to prevent her achieving a year's service—whether they knew that themselves or had taken advice was not known but Jack suspected they had taken advice because their experience practicing law was limited to commercial property law—as far as Charity knew they had never conducted a Tribunal or any other type of law, they didn't have a law office, they were based in the biggest Estate Agency in the centre of Glasgow.

From the questions Jack determined that the hand delivered one had indeed been delivered on the Thursday, the 27th, because her father had had to go to her house to get her son's favourite Teddy which had been forgotten and he saw it there although, of course, he didn't know its contents. He told Charity he would ring her back that afternoon as he had an order to comply with regarding another case and also needed to think about the next step. He did ask are you sure you read it on the Sunday; you didn't read it until the Monday and she was adamant that it was the Sunday. Jack had already done some number crunching in his head and wished that it was the Monday but it wasn't to be.

When he rang back the first point, he brought up was whether they should appeal or not. Not to do so would weaken their case as it would let the Solicitors argue 'she didn't even appeal'. Against that was Charity felt that it would be a complete waste of time, especially given their treatment of her, exploiting her and sacking her as soon as she went off sick. Jack listened and then said, "I understand how you feel but we need them to put in writing something about your dismissal. If I can persuade them that you have the necessary service…"

"But you won't be able to do so, will you? John, (her brother,) told me when I spoke to him before I rang you that they had clearly timed it so that I wouldn't make the year…" Jack interrupted her, "Well, let me see about that, your brother is a bloody good Sales Manager but he isn't a bloody good Advocate and I am, but I would strongly advise and ask that you send in an appeal I will draft for you. Will you do that?"

She agreed and in due course a long letter came back listing all sorts of events alleged to have happened whilst she was off sick, none of which had been put to her so that she had had no chance to defend herself. She didn't know what she was accused of, had had no opportunity to defend herself and certainly had not been treated fairly by being arbitrarily sacked! Khanum anyone?! They also refused her the right to appeal.

Jack responded to that letter by asking a load of questions in response to what they had said, for example, they had quoted failure to reprint photographs of a property when requested to do so. So, what photos, when, who was the client, what was allegedly wrong with them? Their letter was just over one page long, the one going back was just over four pages long and finished with the sentence, "…without the answers to these questions I cannot defend myself…"

They did not get a reply, which Jack expected, but he did not want one, he just needed the failure to reply. So, he submitted the IT1 Application Form two days before the end of the three month period allowed and sat back to wait for the objection to the Tribunal having jurisdiction based on insufficient service. The response took the form of a listing date for a Preliminary Hearing.

Jack took Charity and her father as witnesses and he had prepared a comprehensive bundle for the Hearing. He was not asked if he had a bundle by the Clerk before the Hearing which was better and better because his ability to ambush them was now complete. In the event the two Solicitors were there and one of them, Jones, answered the Chairman's questions by producing Charity's original employment offer letter which included the 8th April start date and the dismissal letter which listed the 27th March date and she simply said, "So, her effective date of dismissal is the 3rd April and she is thus 5 days short."

In preparing for the case Jack started by identifying that the critical issue was when the Statutory Notice started. As far as the Solicitors were concerned, and they did know about Statutory Notice because they added seven days to the 27th to get to the EDT of the 3rd April in their dismissal letter. The trouble was they had got that wrong. There were two issues, firstly notice does not start running until the next day, not the day it is served. Jack knew that and the case law that supported it, so the date would be the 4th, not the 3rd but for one further problem. You don't know you are sacked until someone tells you, you are, and he knew the case law for that as well and ironically it involved a Solicitor who had argued he didn't know he was sacked until he received the letter which he told the Tribunal he had received a day later than his employer thought he had received it. As there was no evidence to show he had received it the day earlier the Tribunal found for him but the important point was you don't know until you know which is why the first page of Jack's bundle was a letter from Charity's Doctor confirming he had advised her to go away for a holiday and then there were pages of receipts starting with one from the bank in Pitlochry on the Thursday night showing the withdrawal of £50 cash at 7pm, then receipts for the B&B for the Thursday night, some for meals on the Friday, Saturday and Sunday and receipts for the two nights B&B in Fort William.

All this clearly demonstrated that she wasn't at home until the Sunday night, the 31st, which was therefore the earliest time she could have known she was sacked. That case, notice not starting until the next day, also gave Jack the opportunity to argue, that starting on the 1st and adding 7 meant, 1+7=8, she therefore had the necessary one year's service. He hoped no one would notice that 1+7 did not equal 8 because starting counting with the first, second, third, fourth, fifth, sixth and seventh arrived at the 7th April, not the 8th! If anyone did notice then he was ready to argue that 7 days' notice meant 7 24-hour days which would take the time up to midnight on the 7th and, of necessity, go past for her to have had the 7 full days. Either way she qualified.

The day before the hearing Charity had rung Jack in a bit of a panic. She said she had heard something she thought Jack, should know. She started by saying that Smifff and Jones were partners, which Jack said he knew because solicitors could not form limited companies their practices were always partnerships although there was a proposal in the offing that they might be able to form limited companies in the future, when Charity interrupted him and said, no she didn't mean that, Smifff and Jones were partners outside of work and that Smifff had come home to discover Jones in bed with another woman, there had been a terrible row and now their partnership, in work and out, had been dissolved.

What was worrying her was that since their partnership, work that is, no longer existed would they avoid the Tribunal that way. Jack explained that all the liabilities incurred during the partnership were still their responsibility even though the partnership might no longer exist so no worry!

At the Hearing Jack presented his argument as he had planned and he told the Chairman that if necessary, he could/would call Charity's Dad to give evidence that the delivered by hand letter was in her flat when he went there in the evening to collect the bits and bobs and had not been there when he had gone in the morning to repair a fuse in the kitchen. The Chairman, reeling somewhat said that that would not be necessary. He did not offer the Solicitor the opportunity to rebut anything Jack had said and at that Jack smelt a rat.

The Tribunal withdrew for about 20 minutes and then came back to say they had not been able to reach a decision, they needed more time and therefore they were reserving their decision which would be forthcoming in writing in due course. That rat smelt even stronger to Jack and sure enough three weeks later they received the decision which stated baldly that as the employment terminated on the 3rd April the Applicant had insufficient service and the application was therefore barred.

Jack was not surprised. Prior to the hearing the Clerk had been upset about something and let slip that the Chairman was 'only a part-timer' which meant his day job was as a Solicitor and solicitors and doctors are the last two unions notorious for sticking together; so the chance of him finding against two solicitors was small to start with. So, he fired off the appeal within 30 minutes as he had already drafted it and only needed to insert the missing detail from the decision. The first bit that he needed was that they had decided the effective date of dismissal was the 3rd April when he knew for sure that it should have started with 7 days from the 28th—notice starts the day after the serving, for which he had provided the case law reference! He then simply listed the errors the Tribunal had made in ignoring the 'don't know you're dismissed until you're dismissed' case law and then referred to the evidence they had ignored as 'no reasonable Tribunal properly instructing itself could have come to that conclusion' and sent it off.

It was listed for hearing in Edinburgh, as the EAT sitting in Scotland, and Jack duly drove up ready for the hearing. He had never spoken at an appeal in Scotland and he was a bit nervous, especially when the Usher told him that the Chairman was in fact a Law Lord and should be addressed as Sir not your Lordship. As it was Jack who had submitted the appeal it was for him to go first. He half expected to be challenged at every point as the female Barrister had been at the drain digging lot, in London, he had won without speaking at all.

In fact, he found his Lordship nodding and appearing to agree with each of his points. When the Barrister for Smifff and Jones started attempting to destroy Jack's points he was faced with lots of 'oh really' and 'you don't say' which Jack interpreted as 'you must be joking' and when his Lordship said to Jack, once the Barrister had finished, "you don't really want to come back against any of that do you, Mr Hughes."

Jack realising, he was looking at an open door but not wanting to just let it go said, "oh I don't think there is anything to come back against, Sir, thank you" and at that they were dismissed. Jack expected to win and he did. The decision was scathing of the original Tribunal decision even to saying, 'it was hard to see how the Tribunal had come to any part of their decision when faced with the correct and proper case law quoted by Mr Hughes'. What Jack didn't expect was that the bastards appealed the EAT decision!

Such appeals in Scotland are to the Court of Session (and in England to the Court of Appeal) and Jack did not have the right of audience in the Court of Session only certain types of lawyers did. That was likely to be expensive but Jack thought about it and discovered a young Barrister who had carried out some law work for Delta, not in Tribunals, and who was prepared to take the case pro-bono (for free!) as it gave him the opportunity to become famous and create case law. In due course Jack trekked up to Edinburgh again to listen to the case. The Court of Session sat in a magnificent old building with three Law Lords, dressed in all their legal finery including red cloaks with crosses embossed all over them presiding.

This time it was a Barrister QC, with a junior, and an Instructing Solicitor sitting behind them, who started and right from the go the Judge in the Chair (not a Chairman!) who lit into the QC almost after every word he said. The Lord to the right of the Lord in the Chair also interrupted and gave the QC a good going over. As the case went on the young Barrister was going paler and paler and at one stage Jack thought he was going to faint when the Lord in the Chair really strongly attacked the QC. Finally, the QC referred to a case Jack had never heard of which apparently neither had the Lord in the Chair, because he asked the QC for the ICR reference.

The QC, slightly blasé said he hadn't that one but he had the IRLR reference at which the Lord in the Chair blew, "Mr Smifff, as a senior Barrister and a QC, aspiring to become a Judge, you know, or you should know, that all references are to ICRs not to IRLRs so kindly give me the correct reference." At that the Junior leapt up and ran out of the room. Everyone sat silent then as the Junior returned to the room the Lord in the Chair said, "It is alright I have it here."

Clearly, he had done it to put the QC in his place. He then turned to Jack's Barrister, who immediately leapt to his feet, and said, "Mr Jones, looking at your papers it would seem to me that the essence of your case is …" and he then shortly and succinctly described the case and having done so said, "is there anything else you would wish to add to that?"

The Barrister was no fool, he recognised an open door as well as Jack, and, perhaps fearing a savage attack from the Lord in the Chair or the Lord to his right said, "No Sir, thank you, I could not have put it better myself."

"No, you couldn't," said the Lord to the right which raised a quiet titter around the room. A few days later Jack received the decision the Court of Session had upheld the EAT's decision in equally strong measure so that Jack had proved that 1st Jan to 31st Dec is a year and 1st Jan to 1st Jan is a year! The law is the law and the law is an ass, or at least some of the lawyers are. But this was not the end of it!

Something over a year later Jack answered the telephone to be told that a Mary was on the telephone asking to speak to him. Jack couldn't immediately place a Mary but said, "OK put her on."

The woman said, "Hello Mr Hughes, thank you for speaking to me. I am Mary Jones, the Jones in Smifff and Jones in the case you fought about a year ago."

Jack was very surprised so, seeking time to think, he said, "Oh, yes, I remember it well. What can I do for you?"

She replied, "Well, we were extremely impressed with your ability to run rings around the two best employment law solicitors' practices in Scotland and I wonder if you would be willing to represent my partner who is being bullied by the Senior Partner in a practice where she works and she has just telephoned me to say that she has had to walk out because she is so upset?"

Jack was astounded, as much by the compliment as the request, but his answer was quite simple. "I'm very sorry, but we do not represent Applicants…"

"But you represented Charity in her case."

"Yes, I did, but Charity was the sister of our Sales Manager in Scotland, lucky for her and not so lucky for you, which is a bit naughty to say the least!" However, intrigued by what she had said, pleased, no very pleased, at the compliment he said, "But if you want to give me a brief outline of the problem, I might at least be able to point you in the right direction."

She instantly started by saying, "When my partner first started everything was fine but when the Senior Partner discovered that she was in a relationship with another woman he started criticising, making snide remarks about Lesbian queers etc. This morning he had a go at her that was nothing to do with her, someone else had made the error but he said it was what you could expect of bloody lesbos at which she shouted at him, I've had enough of your discrimination and walked out."

"Well," said Jack, "the first thing I would advise, were I advising you, would be to make an appointment with her doctor and complain to him of the stress she was under as a result of her treatment. Separately I would get a letter, hand delivered today (he couldn't help but smile at how useless that had been for her in Charity's case!) saying something like, 'for the avoidance of doubt I want to make it clear that I have not resigned or left, I have simply had to go home because of my ill health caused by the bullying and harassment I have suffered. I have an appointment with my Doctor and anticipate a sick note following in due course. I will also be submitting a formal grievance about the way I have been treated when well enough to do so.' Then sit back and wait. You will have thrown the ball into their court and it is up to them to take the next step."

She thanked him profusely and that was the end of the conversation. He did not expect to receive another telephone call late the next afternoon from her. She explained she knew he was not able to advise them but could she just ask him one question, just one. Jack agreed.

She then said that her partner had received a letter from the practice requiring her to attend a disciplinary hearing in two days' time, what should she do? Certainly, that was one question but the answer was likely to be quite long! So, he said, "Well, that's good news…"

"How can that be good news?" Jones interrupted.

"Well," said Jack, "you don't summon someone to a disciplinary hearing if you believe they have left or walked out, do you?"

"Oh, I see."

"Don't ignore the letter, acknowledge receipt, explain that she is too ill to attend at present and ask, I'm assuming the contractual terms will outline a grievance procedure and that if it is any good it will say something about grievances being dealt with before disciplinary matters, if it doesn't write something suggesting that you believe that to be so and ask for the grievance to be dealt with first. If she's successful there will be no need for the disciplinary anyway but more than that I can't foretell." He ended the conversation at that point and was a little bit disappointed that he never found out the outcome of that little rich tapestry of life.

Chapter 41

Jack was to conduct a number of Tribunals in Scotland over the next several years, the one in the previous chapter being perhaps the most important, but his first one was also important because it established how a proper appeal can overturn a very unfair dismissal. It started out quite simply. A customer, a regular, in a hotel bar remarked to the MD and half owner of the hotel, that he had just seen the Barman in the lounge bar zero the till. At that the MD shot into the lounge from the public and demanded of the Barman, "Did you just zed that till?"

And when the guy said he had he fired him on the spot. The guy then made an unfair dismissal claim to the Tribunal, the Rep signed up the client and the job landed on Jack's desk! He read the file; that didn't take long, the guy had just written that he was instantly sacked when he admitted he had zedded a till without any opportunity to defend himself and the MD simply wrote on the IT3 'I did not unfairly dismiss him.' The one thing that had been done right was that the wages figures and employment dates agreed on the IT1 and IT3—one less task to sort out. Jack rang the Tribunal, got the likely listing dates, about four months ahead and then rang the client. He had been given another case for hearing in Inverness and with Pitlochry on the way, even later still, so it made sense to combine a visit to the two of them which he did.

When he arrived, he met not just by the MD but his wife as well who turned out to be the Financial Director. After the introductions and the coffee in a very nice private room he started asking questions. From them he established that the other half of the hotel was owned by a Scottish Duke who ensured that any enterprise on his land (huge areas of Scotland were still owned by the aristocracy and it was common practice that any enterprise set up on the land was co-owned by them, albeit usually on a silent partner basis.)

As part of the Personal File handed to Jack was a letter received that morning from the Applicant appealing against his dismissal. Jack was a bit surprised by that it had never happened in a case before, where an Applicant had appealed after initiating a Tribunal, and he was never to come across it again but there it was and it actually helped Jack. He explained to the two Directors that the dismissal was pretty well 99.99% certain to be declared unfair and he quoted Khanum at them, no knowledge of what he was accused of, no opportunity to defend himself and unfair treatment by the 'tribunal'.

But he pointed out a case from shortly after Khanum which decided that a fair Appeal Hearing could remedy an unfair dismissal, especially involving procedure so he strongly recommended that they conduct an appeal. The problem was the appeal letter had been addressed to the Duke and the Duke did not get involved in the running of any of his businesses. Jack reserved judgement about what to do about the appeal and moved on to why he had sacked the Barman for zedding the till. (Zedding was the terminology for resetting an electronic till to zero, before or at the start of a shift, so that the total rung in on the till during the shift could be easily identified.) It turned out the MD had become suspicious of the honesty of the Barman shortly after he had started since takings seemed to have drooped. He had watched him like a hawk but had been unable to catch him at any dishonesty.

The very first time or two he had operated the Bar there had been the odd shortage in the cash against the takings shown on the audit roll at the end of the shift but when they had been queried the Barman had found the missing cash at the back of the drawer. He had taken to marking the spirit bottles by marking the level by turning the bottles upside down but the level in the bottle seemed to be right when compared to the till sales. Jack then asked, "Have you checked if he was watering down the spirits?" At which the MD jumped up and rushed over to shut the door.

Sitting down he actually whispered, "Yes, I did and I got a message back the day before I sacked him that it was about 10% too much water which for a 32-measure bottle meant he was stealing three tots, or thereabouts, from every bottle which would have been the best part of a fiver every time. But that is a secret if authority got to know I have been selling watered Scotch it would cost me my licence."

Jack tried to calm him down by saying that he would not be likely to sanctions because of a theft by one of his staff but he said, "You don't know what they are like."

Jack changed tack, "It's been my experience that we are very unlikely to catch these thieving bastards the first time they do it, so he's been stealing from you since he started, those notes going missing for example, if you hadn't queried it he would never have found them in the back of the drawer so the question is how was he doing it—you covered till shortages, watering is one way but that wouldn't have reduced your takings; he would have been selling the watered stuff which would show as a sale on the audit roll."

As he was saying it, Jack started remembering some of the training he had undergone in Lintwoods when they had introduced the electronic tills and then the thefts carried out by switching the tills to training mode by the management at one of the C&Cs and some of the other fiddles uncovered to see if any of them helped to identify this fiddle. "Just explain to me why you shot next door and sacked him for just zedding the till, what was so dishonest about that?"

The MD thought about it for a minute and then he said, "I don't know," with a bit of a sheepish grin on his face, "I was so mad at the watered spirits which had been confirmed the day before so when the customer told me about it, I thought *that's it, that's how the bastard is doing it* and I shot next door and sacked him."

"So, what was your suspicion regarding the dishonesty?"

The MD said, "I have been thinking that over and over and I cannot think of anything, it's just it must have been that!

"Have you got the audit roll?" Jack asked. At that the FD went over to a sideboard at the side of the room, unlocked it and brought back a small sack which she tipped out on the table. It was a pile of rolled up audit rolls, one of which had a red elastic band around it while all the others were brown. She handed it to Jack, as she did so she said it had obviously been jammed in the machine because of the mass of over printing. Jack immediately had one of those eureka moments as it came to him how the fiddle was being worked but to be sure he examined it closely. At the bottom of the roll was a long number.

"Can you find the one before this one and the one after it please?" In fact, it took the three of them some time to sort through to find the ones he wanted. He laid them out side by side and pointed to the long numbers at the bottom of all three and said, "What are those numbers?"

They didn't know and Jack knew his idea of how the thefts were done was right. "If you look there, across the three of them you can see that they run sequentially. I bet if you had not sacked him when you did, that one, the overprinted one, would have disappeared at the end of the shift and you would never have known of its existence. Let me explain. If you could go back to the first one ever put through the till, that number would be one and the one the next day would be two and so on. When he started, he started fiddling quite soon but on the standards, cheats such as money missing from the till, but you stopped those so he looked for others, watering and so on but at some stage he did what he did when he was caught.

"He stuck his thumb on the audit roll so that it couldn't wind up so it got over printed. He then zedded the till, and the first time he did it he probably tucked it in a glass along with the takings which would have been quite small so that if you spotted by checking the sequential numbers that there was one missing, he would have produced it claiming the till had jammed. But you didn't notice so he realised that you didn't understand the significance of the sequential numbering and then he was away. I suspect that the first time or two they were quite small and probably round numbers or as close as he could get, fivers, tenners but when you didn't spot them, he knew he was ok and probably increased his take. To see if I'm right you are going to have a lot of work to do…"

The FD said, "We're going to have to go back through all the audit rolls for the past three years and look for missing sequential numbers."

"Yes," said Jack, "but I'd start with the latest ones and work backwards. If you find that's what he was doing after doing say a dozen or so, you will have established that I'm right and then go back to when he started to see if you can find the first ones, say three or four, so that you will definitely have established the fiddle. You can then hit him with that at the Appeal Hearing and kill his application stone dead. I'll talk you through the way to conduct the appeal later, for now we need to establish that that was what he was doing; if we find all the rolls are there we'll have to think again and adopt a different approach."

Jack asked a few more questions and discussed a few issues including drafting a letter from the Duke to the Barman refusing to hear the appeal and nominating the FD to hear it—the MD couldn't because he sacked him there weren't any other directors—he'd have to deal with the issue of fairness vis-à-vis a FD overruling an MD's decision in her witness statement! He then said goodbye having arranged to stop in on his way back from Inverness two days later.

He had provisionally arranged that he would call in about 11am on the Thursday but in fact he was a little over half an hour early which, in the event, turned out to be fortunate. He had arranged it to see what they would have discovered, or not, from the audit rolls. The first words the MD said to him were, "Oh, good you're early—that gives us time for coffee before he gets here."

"Before who gets here?" Jack asked.

"The Barman, he'll be here at 11am, my wife is a bit nervous about conducting the hearing so we thought the obvious answer was for you to do it." Jack was a bit stunned, the situation of sitting in on a client's disciplinary meetings had never come up before and he simply didn't know if he should, so he said, "I'm awfully sorry but I don't think that's a good idea; I am not an employee of the company and shouldn't be involved, but what I can do is sit in, out of his sight line and nod or shake my head as appropriate if necessary…"

Just then the FD walked in and said, "Thirteen thousand and he's just arrived with the Vicar's wife as his witness." Jack simply looked at her, he needed time to think and advise.

"Thirteen thousand what?"

"Thirteen thousand pounds, it's what he stole from us—I have been through every audit roll and he was re-zedding two or three times a week making about £20, almost exactly, for every shift he worked although he didn't actually steal on every shift, only those toward the weekend when the takings were much higher."

"Bloody hell, what a bastard. Bloody hell! What's this about the Vicar's wife?"

"He wants her to be his witness."

"Right," said Jack, "that's useful—he doesn't have a right to that only a fellow employee but we can use it to show how reasonable we are and to justify me sitting in. Put it to him that he doesn't have the right etc but say you will agree if he lets me sit in to take notes but not to take part in the hearing." He then explained how to lead him into placing lies on record and he set the room out with a chair at the head of a very long table, one to its right side and two to the left. He set another one at the far end of the table for himself and they started.

The FD explained that this was an Appeal Hearing and she would listen to anything he wanted to say about why he felt his dismissal was unfair. Jack would normally advise starting by describing three reasons for an appeal, procedures not followed, new evidence or decision too severe but in this case that would only give him bullets to fire so it was just 'why was it unfair'. The guy started into a ramble about he hadn't done anything wrong, just re-zedded the till because it had jammed and that didn't warrant dismissal. The Vicar's wife was looking a little puzzled so Jack interrupted and asked her if she knew what zedding meant and when she said no, he explained the process to her. Having been 'trained' by Jack how to conduct the hearing the FD said, "Has it jammed before?"

"Oh yes, several times over the years."

"How many is several?"

"Och, three or four, maybe as many as five."

"Not ten?"

"Oh no."

"Are you absolutely sure about that?"

"Absolutely."

"Not 150 in a year?"

"You're daft!"

"Not 452 in three years?"

"You're mad!" Taking a couple of sheets of paper from her folder the FD handed them to him and said, "There is a list of all the z reads done on that till since you started three years ago. I compiled that from the old audit rolls but there are 452 which are missing and when I do the maths to identify the missing amounts it comes to almost exactly £13,000; and I bet each of the missing ones had a jammed mark on it just like this last one. Explain that to me?"

"Nothing to do with me, I didnae do anything wrong." He pulled a couple of sheets from his pocket but Jack couldn't make out what they were.

"Is there anything else you want to say?"

"No, I'll save it for the Tribunal."

"I think you do know about it; I think that you have stolen a fortune from us…" Jack was frantically mouthing coffee and miming a drinking motion. So, they broke for coffee. As soon as they did Jack explained that he thought she had done a brilliant job of getting the lies on paper but she couldn't let him go with something unsaid so he advised that when they reconvened she should say to him that if he knew something now was his time to say so, so that she could take it into account, if he didn't say then he would not, having been given the opportunity to do so now, be allowed to introduce it at the Tribunal.

When they reconvened the Vicar's wife was missing having had to rush off. They were only to discover why much later. The Barman had got a little job running the bar at the Bowling Club which was one of the few organisations which the Duke was not a part owner of, none of which would have employed him of course. She had rushed off because she realised that her tills at the Club might be the same kind, and they were, and yes there were audit rolls missing and he became unemployed from the Bowling Club the next day!!!!

None of this was known when they reconvened, just that the Vicar's wife had gone. It was put to him twice by the FD that he should say whatever he wanted to say so that she could consider it but he refused both times repeating that he would keep it for the Tribunal. At that Jack intervened and made it clear that having had three opportunities to say something and foregone them all he, Jack, would insist that the Chairman forbid their entry and invited him again to speak and again he refused.

The meeting then concluded with the FD reserving her decision to think very carefully about what had been said and to consider the appropriate decision. Once he had gone Jack asked a few further questions to understand the hotel and its functioning including numbers of staff and the pattern of staffing. That disclosed that the Barman worked across three bars, the lounge, public and a private bar in a function room which led Jack to ask could they connect to the Barman to the shift and till when the audit roll had gone missing each time. He was mightily relieved to hear the FD say that that had occurred to her so that she had gone through every roster and he was the only one of the potential seven staff who had been on duty on all dates. Jack asked her for a copy of the checking so that it could be kept ready to ambush him in the Tribunal if he tried to introduce a 'I wasnae there on that shift' defence.

Jack returned to the hotel, and stayed the night before the hearing—and jolly nice it was with the VIP treatment he was accorded. The Tribunal was actually heard in Dundee which meant a bit of an early start in the morning. By chance the Barman and Jack arrived at the Clerk's window—it was a bit like where you bought your ticket at the cinema—but with the Barman following Jack, Jack was dealt with first. He gave out all the details of himself and his two witnesses and handed in his bundles (actually called 'productions' in Scotland). He also asked the Clerk to inform the Chairman that as this was his first case in Scotland could he offer his apologies in advance if he should make any errors in terminology or procedures.

The Barman followed Jack and, when the Clerk asked if he had any productions, he said he had but 'yon' nodding at Jack who had deliberately hung around to hear what he would say, is going to object. The Clerk look confused so Jack stepped in and explained the situation to which the Clerk reacted by refusing to take the two pieces of paper the Barman had proffered and said that he would have to take that up with the Chairman when they were called in.

When they were called in Jack and the MD stood up in the waiting room but the Clerk said, "Not you" to the MD which Jack immediately queried. The Clerk responded that as the MD was a witness he would be kept out, as all witnesses were, and would only be called in to give his evidence when required. Jack was astonished. He knew the witnesses were kept out until called in, which he felt was actually a better system than in England where everyone was in together and everyone heard everything said enabling later witnesses to colour their evidence to match that gone before.

This couldn't happen in Scotland and they probably got closer to the truth that way so he was quite happy for the FD to come in later but the MD was his first witness anyway and he was also technically the Respondent since he, as well as the Company, had been named on the IT1. Jack argued but the Clerk was adamant so Jack insisted that she return to the Chairman and tell him that Jack wished to present an argument for the MD to be present from the word go. She did, and he was duly called in.

The Chairman referred to his apology about his first time in Scotland and the Chairman, absolutely charming about it, took some time to explain the differences between England and Scotland and that's why witnesses weren't in altogether was one of them. Jack thanked him profusely (laying it on thick with a trowel never did any harm!) but explained that the MD besides being a witness was also the Respondent and a respondent had the absolute right to hear everything said against him and if he was in the Waiting Room, he could not do that. The Chairman whispered to his two Lay Members and then agreed for the MD to be brought in.

Shortly after the MD started answering Jack's first question Jack learned another difference. Jack, watching the Chairman's pen could see that he wasn't apparently keeping up with the evidence being spoken so he interrupted the MD and said, "Would you slow down please to enable the Chairman to keep up?"

Jack had told both of his witnesses to do that when preparing them before the hearing but it was easy to forget when nervous. However, the Chairman interrupted and said, "We are more fortunate than our colleagues in England in that we are not required to record everything in Scotland, merely those items significant and important so we only take notes. If I can't keep up, I will tell you but thank you for the courtesy."

So, they carried on. The MD simply described the events as they had occurred and, in response to a specific question from Jack explained his suspicions and the eureka moment when told about the zedding by the customer. He came straight out with that he realised afterwards that he was probably unfair in the manner he had behaved and how he was pleased when he received the appeal letter since it saved him writing to the Applicant inviting him to an appeal which he had decided to do. He then confirmed that he had been present at the appeal and that he had told his wife that she must overrule his decision to dismiss in the event she disagreed with his decision.

Jack could see some doubt in the eyes of the three of them sitting in judgement but that disappeared when he said that she had actually agreed with his decision and therefore no contretemps between them had occurred. He also confirmed that the notes, taken by Jack and included in the productions, were an accurate record of the Appeal Hearing. Jack then pointed out that the Appeal Hearing evidence would be provided by the FD.

The Barman's cross examination was pretty limited. His first question was, "So you admit my dismissal was unfair?"

The MD replied, "I admit the manner of your first dismissal may have been procedurally unfair (it had taken him a while to learn to say the words in the way and manner Jack had advised him!) But ultimately, I believe your dismissal was more than fair."

"But at the time you dismissed me it was unfair?"

"Only in the manner, I know you stole thousands from me." The Chairman interrupted at that point with some questions about his employment dates and pay (In Scotland the Tribunal dealt with fairness and remedy in the one hearing; in England a Remedy Hearing was conducted if the Applicant established unfair dismissal. The Scots system wasted time in every Hearing because time spent re remedy data would turn out to be irrelevant if the Application failed, but in England everyone had to come back in the event of a win by the Applicant, so neither system was perfect more six of one and half a dozen of the other.) Having done that the Chairman then said, "You've no other questions, have you?"

The Applicant sensibly answered 'no'. In Scotland at that stage the Chairman might send the witness back to the Waiting Room to maintain their not hearing what other people say, just in case they might need to be called back to give rebuttal or further evidence but as Jack had established the MD was the Respondent he stayed. The FD came in and was sworn and she then described what had happened at the Appeal Hearing, prompted at stages by questions from Jack. The Chairman wasn't too happy when she dropped out in answer to a question from Jack about did she knew the reason why the Vicar's wife had not returned, she set it all out including the fact he had been sacked.

The Chairman interrupted and said what had happened elsewhere at another time was of no interest to them but Jack was happy that he had got it out. When it came time for the Barman to cross cross-examine, he only asked two questions, the first being the same as he had asked the MD that his dismissal was unfair wasn't it and his Appeal rejection was the same wasn't it? To both she, as tutored by Jack—if you can answer a question with just a no or a yes do so, don't elaborate, so she said 'no' to both and nothing else.

The Chairman stepped in, having a duty to ensure an unrepresented party's case doesn't go by default asked a series of questions the answers to which dug the Applicant deeper and deeper into the do-do! Jack was quite happy thinking he's on our side. The FD was released by the Chairman to go shopping if she wished—something very improper these days—but she elected to stay because Jack had told her that if she was released, she should stay for rebuttal purposes if the Barman's documents were allowed in and she needed to contradict something in them.

When the Barman was sworn, before he even sat down, he produced the two pieces of folded up paper from an inside pocket and said, "I want to introduce these but yon (pointing at Jack) is goin' to object."

"Mr Hughes?" Jack said, "If I may, Sir, can I direct you to page (x) of my productions at the bottom where it refers to the Applicant saying he would keep something for later."

Jack paused while the Tribunal read the pages and then said, "As you can see both the Financial Director and I made it very clear to the Applicant that he should raise any matter he wanted to but if he didn't having been warned I would object to it being introduced in the future since he had had his chance and had refused it—it would be quite improper for you to allow in something now which the Applicant denied the FD the chance of considering."

There was a long pause and then the Chairman gestured to the Clerk to collect the papers from the Barman. Jack was livid but he also thought *that's pretty stupid because he must know the case law and that by allowing these to be introduced, he's handed me an appeal victory on a plate.* As the Chairman was reading Jack could just make out that the two sheets appeared to be rosters and he thought *oh no, the buggers going to show he wasn't at work on those days.* The Chairman compared the Applicant's paper to a page in the bundle and then said, "But Mr Smifff this shows that you were on duty on those days?"

"Aye." He then examined the other page closely and said, "But this is the same, you were on duty then!"

"Aye."

"Well, why have you introduced them?"

"Because I had them." The Chairman was not at all pleased. He had allowed in documents he should not have and now he was in shtick, but he wasn't a Professor of Law for nothing and Jack, watching his face could see a solution arrive, he said, "I take it you'll no be objecting to these documents any more Mr Hughes?"

"No, indeed not Sir, in fact I think they do my job for me and, (looking at the Applicant) I would like to thank the Applicant for them," all said with a huge smile on his face. The Chairman asked the Applicant only a tiny number of questions, Jack thought just sufficient to justify that the Applicant's case had not been allowed to go by default and he then said to Jack, "I assume you will not have many questions of this witness Mr Hughes?"

"No, indeed Sir, just a tiny few," and he then asked him to look at the page in the Productions where the FD had recorded the attendances of the bar staff on the dates when an audit roll had gone missing, and asked him, "Can you point to any errors in that analysis by the FD especially as your productions confirm you were the only member of staff who was present on all those dates?" The Chairman gave Jack a bit of a look because the Applicant's productions didn't quite go that far, the only analysis having been done by the Chairman a few minutes before, but he let it go and the Applicant simply said, "No."

"So, leaving aside the manner of your dismissal for a moment what evidence, if any, can you provide that someone else had the opportunity to steal some £13,000 from the tills over three years?"

"I cannae, but it wasnae me that stole it."

266

"And were you not sacked from the Bowling Club for exactly..." The Chairman intervened with a do not answer that to the Applicant and a, "You don't have any more questions, do you?" Jack, having established the huge amount clearly in their minds, that he was the only one who could have stolen the money and the sneaky reference to the Bowling Club—Jack was there to win not to be nice or even obey the rules if he could get around them—said, "No, Sir."

Jack was expecting to go first but he did not expect the manner in which it was said to him.

"Mr Hughes as you are a highly competent professional and the Applicant isn't I am going to ask you to summarise your case, briefly, so that the Applicant will have the opportunity to see how it should be done and thus do it himself, you do not object do you?"

"Not at all Sir." So, he simply repeated as he had at the start that the procedure used to dismiss him might appear to be unfair but any such unfairness was more than remedied by a full and thorough Appeal at which all the evidence had been gone through with the Applicant being able to say and ask anything he wanted in his own defence. With a smile Jack said that he would pass over the issue of the withheld rosters as, in the event, they helped the Respondent far more than the Applicant. He repeated the huge amount of the theft to justify a Gross Misconduct dismissal and included a brief reference to the any difference test and contribution in the unlikely event that they decided the dismissal was still unfair after the Appeal. He only made those references because Scot's Tribunals dealt with remedy as part of the hearing and he could not let that go by default. When the Chairman turned to the applicant, he said, "What do you say to what you have just heard Mr Smifff?"

"I didnae do it and it was unfair to sack me."

"Well, that has the mark of brevity about it! Good day to you all; you will receive out decision in a few days," and with that they were gone and it was all over. Except it wasn't. The decision duly arrived and Jack had won handsomely; they had even said, somewhat obliquely, that they believed there was overwhelming evidence for the employer to believe he was the thief and that if there had not been an appeal the dismissal would have been unfair in which case, they would have had to consider the any difference and contribution tests which would have succeeded against the Applicant by 100%. As it was the Appeal remedied any unfairness and the dismissal was therefore fair. The applicant then had the cheek to appeal to the EAT sitting in Scotland but the MD did not ask Jack and Delta to represent them and Jack never did discover the outcome—very frustrating.

Chapter 42

Jack was to appear in front of the same Chairman again about three years later and after he had been promoted to Advice Manager. It came about because one of Delta's clients, a large fee paying one, insisted on Jack representing them as they had been so impressed with him when he had represented them before. Then he had taken over a case after there had been one day of hearing when the original Advocate had left. It was a real stinker of a case in more than one sense. The company started out life manufacturing frozen pet foods, which turned out not to be too successful so they had expanded into tinned and dried pet foods. The boss had lost his temper with a worker and told him to fuck off. The bloke did, straight to Tribunal!

Jack went to see them not having had the chance to talk to the Advocate who had left to see where the case had got to. Their premises in Edinburgh could be smelt miles away and the brief tour of the premises was equally unpleasant. At the resumed Tribunal Jack started to feel something was wrong. Every time he spoke Madam Chairman reacted badly but smarmed over the female Solicitor representing the Applicant. Jack deliberately didn't present much of a case to argue the fairness of dismissal but, when it got to the remedy part, asked to present the any difference and/or contribution argument and she refused to listen.

Jack pondered whether to let it go and then appeal or to fight her there and then. Not relishing the thought of having to return to the pet foods place he thought *right I'm not putting up with this, everything about the way she's been performing is that she's a part-time Chairman so threaten her with the Regional Chairman.*

"Mam," he said, "There are two ways to do this. You can adjourn for a few minutes and consult the Regional Chairman, if you are not sure, and discuss with him the issue of Polkey (the relevant case law) and the sections on contributory fault under the ERA (Employment Rights Act) or if you are so certain that you can refuse to consider the two matters, I can raise it at the EAT sitting in Scotland to prove you wrong."

If looks could kill Jack would have instantly expired but before she spoke one of the Lay Members leaned over and whispered something in her ear after which she said that they would adjourn for 15 minutes. Jack would love to have known what was whispered but it was never to be! When they returned, she simply said, "Say what you want to say." So Jack went through the two arguments and finished his summing up. The decision, three weeks later found the dismissal unfair but they reduced the awards by 75% for any difference and 100% for the contribution element so lost on unfairness, but no award.

The client was delighted hence the demand for Jack's services years later— not too many representatives were prepared to argue with a Chairman but Jack was to earn a reputation in that field! And he was to discover the evening of that Tribunal, as he was staying in Edinburgh that night for appointments the next day, why the Chairman was so nice to the Solicitor and not to him. Walking along the Royal Mile the two of them, arm in arm, came out of an entrance and started walking along in front of him; they did not see Jack, but Jack saw them and decided there is walking arm in arm and there is WALKING ARM IN ARM, and they were doing the latter! So, another mystery solved!

This later case was just weird. Jack recoiled when he opened the large envelope which arrived for him once Delta had agreed Jack would conduct the case; the smell of the place had obviously not improved but did travel well! Sorting the paperwork, mainly the IT1 but a few letters and notes as well, the first thing of significance Jack noticed was that the unfair dismissal claim had been submitted four months after the alleged dismissal date which was too late; it should be within three months. *This should be simple* he thought, *no jurisdiction,* but he read on anyway trying to see if a reason for the delay had been given. It hadn't, so he immediately fired off a letter challenging jurisdiction and, as expected, he received Notice of a Preliminary Hearing to decide the matter.

He went up the day before to discuss the case with the client and the basic story was very simple. The Applicant, who was a General Cleaner, including the most awful drains and pits where sludge from the offal etc accumulated, came in one day and announced he was leaving at the end of the week because he had got another job, a much better job, as a cleaner on the buses! That was the Monday. He didn't appear for work on the Wednesday and they never heard from him again until the IT1. The IT1 claimed he had been so bullied by the Forelady that he had felt he had to leave. He gave no details of the bullying and when Jack interviewed her, she denied any such thing. She did say that he was a lazy bugger and she was forever having to chase him out from the toilets, canteen, stores etc because he was always skiving off.

At the hearing the Applicant was represented by a Mr Carnegie of the CAB. Mr Carnegie was multi-disabled, his hearing loss and poor eyesight being the main two. He had obviously been to Tribunal before because the room was laid out such that his table had been moved to halfway between the Tribunal bench and Jack's table.

The Chairman started by asking Jack why he objected to their jurisdiction and Jack pointed to the two dates, both provided by the Applicant, of dismissal and on the IT1 and that they were some four months apart when the limit was within three. The Chairman, of course agreed with the dates and then asked Carnegie for an explanation. He simply said he would let the Applicant explain. He was therefore sworn and said that when he had gone to sign on, which was the Wednesday of the week he left, (*'left' noted Jack, not dismissed*), he told them he wanted to claim unfair dismissal; they had given him the forms, he had filled them in and returned them there and then and thought that was it.

It was only four months later when he asked what's happening to his claim that he discovered it had not been submitted so the very next day he filled in another one and despatched it. It was therefore not his fault that it had gone missing and he had acted within a day when he discovered something had gone wrong. The Chairman invited Jack to cross examine.

Jack started with, "you said you left, not that you were dismissed, isn't that the truth you left, you were not dismissed?"

"I didnae say that." Jack looked at the Chairman.

The Chairman said, "Oh yes you did." The Applicant looked down for a few moments and then said, "Aye well, I meant dismissed."

Jack pursued the matter, "But you gave in a letter of resignation on the Monday so how were you dismissed?" The guy looked uncomfortable.

"The woman in the Job Centre told me that I had been."

"How would she have known what happened?"

"I told her I had been bullied and had to leave and she told me that…" he paused and reached into a pocket and pulled out a piece of paper which looked like it had been torn off the corner of a larger sheet and reading from it he said, *it was constructive dismissal.*"

"What's that piece of paper?" The Chairman interrupted and told the Clerk to give it to him. He read it and then told the Clerk to give it to Jack to read. Sure, enough it said, 'constructive dismissal' and by the side of it was Flora Macdonald. The Chairman kept the piece of paper. He immediately gave his decision that the delay was not the fault of the Applicant and he said the case would be listed in due course— 'good day' and he was gone.

Jack now had a fight on his hands. Constructive dismissal was hard for an Applicant to prove; it was the equivalent of Gross Misconduct but by the employer not the employee. It had to be such a serious breach of the contract to entitle the employee to walk out as the contract had been so severely broken by the employer such as to entitle him to do so. Back at the client's Jack questioned in detail the Forelady and a couple of other staff who worked in the department and was quite happy that her chasing him up was no more than was proper.

He asked for the personnel file and looked at it and then asked where were the documents from the Job Centre—it being routine that when someone leaves and signs-on the Department contacts the employer (ex-employer!) and asks for the basic details to enable them to pay the dole etc, or not, as the case may be. The company denied ever receiving any which made Jack a little suspicious but at that stage he could do nothing about it.

He was back in Edinburgh a couple of weeks later and stuck in traffic. Obviously, something was going on somewhere up the front but he couldn't see anything. Glancing around on the offside of the road, one of the buildings had a stream of people passing in and out, most of them not ones you would want to take home to mum. Looking closer he realised it was a Job Centre and, knowing that he was in Leith he wondered why somehow a bell was going off in his mind—then he realised it was the one where the late Applicant had said he signed-on.

Just then the traffic started inching forward and a car parked on the left, just in front of him, put his blinkers on and started pulling out. His immediate reaction was to blow his horn but then he thought, *I'm not needing to be somewhere what if I go in and try it on? So*, he let the guy out and parked in the spot.

When he walked in, he stuck out like a sore thumb; dressed in a navy blue pin stripe suit, white shirt and blue tie he did not look like the people in there. When he had recruited years before in Scotland, he had been very impressed by the standard of the unemployed who had applied for jobs but this lot were different, was it a deprived area, problem area, whatever, he did not know? They had a General Enquiry Desk which he approached and when the woman looked up and did a double take, he felt sure something was odd.

When asked what he wanted he said that he was representing a client in a Tribunal case and his client had lost his paperwork; was there any chance he could get a copy? Clearly, she had never dealt with such a request before so he was passed up to her Supervisor who in turn passed him up to the Manager. He was even offered a coffee whilst the Applicant's papers were fetched. The Manager laid a clear, see through plastic wallet, on the desk, which although it was upside down, Jack could read some of the writing—he could see, in capitals:

POOR WORKING CONDITIONS, POOR PAY, POOR HOURS.

The Manager then said he could not actually show Jack the papers or give him a copy unless he provided written permission from the Applicant to do so. At that point Jack had to reveal that his client was the ex-employer not the benefit claimant. At that the Manager said that he would be delighted to help all he could but he would need an Order for Discovery from the Tribunal before he could do so as he doubted the Applicant would agree voluntarily and he said, with a very knowing look, he thought it would be a very useful exercise for Jack to do. He also added that they no longer wrote to employers asking for leaving details so he could not even give Jack a copy of the employer's paperwork. That comforted Jack that the employer had not been lying to him about not having any paperwork. Jack thanked him and went on his way. Driving to the hotel he kept running the words he had been able to read through his mind.

It was a couple of years since he had signed on before and Scotland was probably different anyway but it seemed to him that the words were in response to the question, 'why did you leave your last employment' which he was pretty certain would be asked in both countries. And if that was so those were the wrong words if he was telling the truth—they should have said something like 'forced to resign because of bullying'.

Once he got into his hotel room, he rang his Secretary and dictated a letter to the Tribunal seeking an Order for Discovery to the Job Centre to provide access to the Applicant's file. He half expected to be refused but he had included that 'evidence had come to light that the Applicant had lied at the Preliminary Hearing' and that was sufficient to get the Order. Once he received it, he rang the Manager of the Job Centre and arranged to see him first thing the day before the Hearing.

He was made to feel very welcome when he arrived, offered coffee and biscuits and the Manager had already copied all the main documents. Jack briefed him on the claim and told him about the constructive dismissal claim explained to the Applicant by Flora MacDonald. The Manager immediately said, "I have been here for 15 years and there has never been anyone of that name here." Not a lot could surprise Jack after so many years of dealing with people but that did.

The guy looked at the paperwork and said, "He was dealt with by Sue McGregor throughout, would you like to speak to her?"

Jack gave the obvious answer. Sue joined them and Jack explained the events at the Tribunal and she flatly denied him every having raised bullying or being forced to resign; he had simply repeated what he had written about poor conditions etc. She was happy, indeed very happy to agree to give evidence to that effect the following day. The Manager volunteered to come to give what evidence he could. Jack was intrigued at the willingness of both of them and an off the record chat with the Manager quickly established that there was no love lost between the staff and some of their clients who were expert at not working and screwing the system for every penny they could.

Jack had detected something like that at the five Job Centres he had regularly used throughout Scotland when opening the cash and carrys years before so he wasn't entirely surprised. He didn't actually need the Manager because Sue could give all the evidence, he needed but because the guy had been so helpful Jack said he would welcome him coming if he had the time but he might not be called once Sue had given her evidence. His face lit up and he said, "Spending a day watching one of these thieving, idle, lying bastards get their comeuppance will be well worth it."

When Jack logged in in, he explained to the Clerk that he wanted to address the Chairman on the issue of jurisdiction before the case started and he was asking the Clerk to warn the Chairman of his intention so to do as a courtesy.

They were taken in with Mr Carnegie's desk being placed halfway forward as before. That was not a surprise. What was a surprise was to discover the Chairman was the same one he had appeared in front of for the Barman stealing by zedding the tills. The Chairman opened with, "Mr Hughes, how nice to see you again in Scotland. Your last case in front of me was extremely interesting and from the message my Clerk has passed me this one would seem to be lining up to be the same but I hope you are not just going to complain about the Preliminary decision because you know very well that you cannot do that?"

"Good morning, Sir, and what a pleasure it is to appear before you again. (Jack could serve up crawling along with the best of them!) Indeed, I do know, but I also know that I can challenge the decision if I have new evidence that the Applicant lied and I have an EAT case to quote in a moment in support of that."

"Indeed, what is your new evidence?"

"May I ask you to look in the file, Sir, and see if there is a small piece of paper, torn from a larger piece, with 'constructive dismissal written on it along with the name Flora Macdonald'." The Chairman started going through the file and then produced the piece of paper. Jack then explained that the Applicant had produced it in response to a question from Jack and had said that Flora Macdonald was the lady in the Job Centre who helped him fill in his Tribunal claim and had explained that since he had been forced out that that amounted to constructive dismissal.

It was based on that evidence that the Tribunal had waived the three month time limit and it was all based on lies. He then said that he had in the waiting room a lady from the Job Centre, who would say in evidence, that she had dealt with the Applicant when he had signed on, that her name was not Flora Macdonald, and that he had told her he had resigned for poor conditions, poor pay and poor hours, which he Jack had seen written on the form and of which he had a copy ready to show the Tribunal. But before he asked to call her, he invited the Applicant to withdraw his lies and tell the truth to save them all the time that would otherwise be wasted going through the process.

Mr Carnegie then interrupted and said that what Jack had said was a total pack of lies and his client would not be changing his story to which Jack said, in that case I would wish to draw to the Chairman's attention forcibly that I have given him this opportunity and as he refused it, I will equally forcefully ask the Chairman to refer the Applicant to the Criminal Court for sentencing for perjury in due course once the evidence has been heard.

"Before we go any further Mr Hughes might I ask what made you suspicious of the truth from the original hearing?"

"Sir, of course you may ask. My suspicions were aroused when I saw that piece of paper. Firstly, it was too convenient. Secondly, although I know almost nothing of Scottish history, I do recognise the name of Flora Macdonald, a heroine who aided Bonnie Prince in his escape from the English after Culloden and it didn't seem right. Thirdly, the writing on the paper was large, untidy and unformed, more like that of a poorly educated man rather than an educated woman so I checked his writing on his Application Form to work at my clients and it seemed to be the same.

"Separately, my client had no paperwork from the Job Centre which I thought to be odd; I have held Personnel roles in the past and am familiar with leavers' paperwork so I went to the Job Centre and asked for copies. During the meeting the Manager had on his desk a plastic wallet through which I could read 'poor conditions, poor pay, poor hours' all apparently in the same handwriting as on that piece of paper you have in front of you so I asked for the Order for Discovery and the rest, as they say, is history."

"You have, I must say, a very remarkable Advocate representing you, Sir," said the Chairman talking to the Respondent's MD sitting in the Court. After that it was easy. Jack called Sue and she gave absolutely damming evidence that she had 'served' the Applicant, there was no discussion about being bullied just the three 'poors,' the subject of a Tribunal application did not come up at all and she had not written anything on anything for him. Jack called the Manager, mainly because he wanted to have two people saying, 'white' against one sayings, 'black' but also to confirm there had never been anyone of the name of Flora Macdonald working at the Job Centre Job Centre in the last 15 years.

Jack did not know what to expect from Mr Carnegie to prove that his two witnesses were liars, but all he did was to ask both of them the same question, and only one question, namely that your evidence has not been true has it to which he received a 'oh yes it is' in both cases.

Jack had to sum up first as he was challenging the previous decision. He did not want to bad mouth the original Tribunal, not good practice, so instead, he praised them with, given the evidence they heard their decision was obviously correct, but given that the evidence they were given was false then their decision had, through no fault of their own, to be false too. He just said I will not go through all the true evidence you have heard here today again; I am sure you remember it all, I will just refer you to the case of, and he produced from his brief case the actual EAT decision of his case involving the drain company which had decided that a Tribunal must not go ahead if there is any doubt as to their having jurisdiction. (Jack carried a file cover with about a dozen key EAT decisions with him which he commonly needed.)

The Chairman took the decision and read it and then said, "I take it your familiarity with this case has something to do with your name appearing on it, Mr Hughes?" Jack laughed and simply said 'yes Sir'. Turning to the CAB guy the Chairman said, "A very short summation I think Mr Carnegie." And it was.

They didn't reserve their decision, they didn't even withdraw, the Chairman said, "It is clear from the evidence, the very compelling evidence, we have heard here today that we have no jurisdiction to hear this case. In addition, Mr Carnegie, your client should be in no doubt that his evidence at the Preliminary Hearing will be referred and he will face prosecution for perjury and almost certainly a prison sentence. Good day." And they were gone.

Jack expected his client to be happy but he was surprised at how happy the two Job Centre people were, they were absolutely delighted that one of the scroungers had got his comeuppance and might even be sent to jail.

Chapter 43

Jack had two cases where he ended up, not through choice, arguing with the Chairman. On the basis that, whoever upsets the Chairman first loses, this was not a good idea, but in both he had no choice. The first one was one of the three cases he was allocated on his first day at Delta. The second was one about two years after his start and involved his old adversary the ripping out the IT1s and 3s Madam Chairman. The first involved a self-employed painter and the second a Quail Farm. Not a lot in common you would think but both involved not only a bolshie Applicant but a bolshie Chairman too!

In the first case the Painter had, according to his boss, been a self-employed for, he claimed, 27 years and when on a Friday the boss said to him that 'he was very sorry but he had no work for him so don't come Monday and goodbye' he immediately made an Application to Tribunal for unfair dismissal and a redundancy payment. The client was apoplectic.

As far as he was concerned the guy was self-employed, he had been paid gross, on invoice, over all the years and now wanted to claim he was an employee all that time; and anyway, it hadn't been for 27 years because he had had a break in service of three years during that time. Jack ascertained those details and juicy they were! Jack carried out all his normal preparations and then challenged the jurisdiction of the Tribunal to hear the case. He expected to receive notice of a Preliminary Hearing but instead received notice of a hearing which had added to it the words, 'the issue of jurisdiction will be dealt with as a preliminary issue at the hearing'. This was the first time he had come across this way of dealing with the issue and he was a little uncomfortable with the unknown. He wondered if they had actually already decided that issue or whether they were just lazy, either was possible or, of course, both!

Since Jack was challenging jurisdiction, it was for him to go first and he called the client to give evidence first. He had deliberately coached him to keep short answers which the guy did very well. He simply said that the guy had not worked for him for a period of three years from 1989-1992 so whatever the relationship was it was only for two and a half years. Jack had deliberately told him not to say anything about the reason for the gap.

The Applicant tried to get the Employer to say that the original conversation, 27 years before, was all about him being an employee but the Employer was adamant that the Applicant had turned up one day looking for work and had been told that he was not hiring but he was looking for subbies and the guy said, 'I'll do that' and that was what had been agreed. When the Applicant gave evidence, it was simply to say that the first conversation was that he would be an employee but even if it wasn't over the 27 years the relationship had changed to that of employee. Every alarm bell started ringing when he said that because that told Jack he must have had advice from someone who knew what they were doing because it could indeed mean he had become an employee by virtue of the relationship changing over a period of time.

When Jack got his chance to cross examine, because there was now a chance that they could find he had become an employee over time and because the way the Chairman was behaving indicated to Jack that he was anti-employer as many were in some Tribunal offices, so he felt the best way forward was to establish first that there had been a three year break which would apply to employment as well as self-employment so Jack asked, "You do not have 27 years of service of whatever kind do you, it is only two and a bit?"

The guy didn't answer so Jack asked again and again he didn't answer. "Look," said Jack, "I know what the gap was for but there is no need for the Tribunal to know, all you have to do is to say 'yes' to my question, there was a break of three years wasn't there?"

Again, the guy refused to answer so Jack turned to the Chairman and said, "Will you please direct him to answer the question, Sir."

The Chairman paused and then said, "No, just carry on Mr Hughes."

"Sir, I can't. The issue of length of service is a crucial one to my case it goes to the amount of an award should your decision go one way and it is extremely germane as to the credibility of this witness."

"Move on Mr Hughes." Jack paused, *no he thought either this bugger answers or I'll let his dirty little secret out.* Speaking directly to the Applicant he said, "I will give you one last chance to answer or I will ask for your employer to be recalled to answer." The guy stayed quiet but the Chairman intervened and ordered Jack to move on but he had had enough. "I have offered you the opportunity of saying yes or no several times but you have not taken advantage of that, so I put it to you, you were sent to prison for six years for throwing the husband of a woman you were caught in bed with, out of the bedroom window and seriously injuring him, weren't you?"

The Applicant's face had been getting redder and redder and as Jack stopped speaking the guy launched himself from the witness table and dived over Jack's table to grab him round the throat. He then proceeded to try to strangle Jack. There was uproar with the Chairman shouting to stop that and pushing the bell to summon Security in the meantime Jack stopped trying to pull the guy's hands off his throat and reached down to his balls, grabbed them and proceeded to squeeze with all his might.

Perhaps not surprisingly he let go of Jack's throat and reached down towards Jack's hands but Jack squeezed even harder then let go and punched three quick punches into that area, two of which landed on target. For the next 10 minutes or so all the Applicant could do was hug himself and moan. Jack straightened out his clothing, looked at the Chairman and said, "If you were any good at your job, you'd have ordered him to answer and this could have been avoided."

"You will treat me with respect…"

"I'll treat you with respect when you've earned it…" At that moment Security rushed into the room at the speed of a slow tortoise and spent the next few minutes comforting the poor little diddums whilst throwing evil looks at Jack while they did so. The Chairman squeaked that we are adjourned until 2pm as he left the room. One of the Lay Members gave Jack a surreptitious wink as he walked out and Jack got bought a decent lunch by the client—something which happened very rarely!

They were back in the waiting room a few minutes before 2pm but the Clerk didn't fetch them until nearly 2.30pm. When they entered the room, it was to discover the Applicant sitting at the Witness Table but with a Security Guard standing either side of him. The Chairman read out to him Jack's last question and asked him if it was true, he had been in prison. The guy simply nodded his head. Although Jack had been allocated this case on the day, he started with Delta it was now some 18months later and Jack had handled a number of self-employed v employee cases in the meantime and had noticed that Tribunals in general got a bit agitated at someone being paid gross when they, the Tribunal Members were never paid gross but net, so he had evolved a strategy of playing on that.

Consequently, he quoted the gross figures as shown on the invoices he had submitted going back for 13 years, the longest the Company could go back, and then quoted the net figure he had had the Accountant calculate as to what he would have received as an employee. The figures for gross were around £208,000 and for net £135,000 a difference of some £73,000 so he quoted that twice as the benefit he had received from being self-employed. He also brought out the other key factors Tribunals looked at such as giving notice of taking holidays rather than asking for time off, worked whatever hours he wanted, had turned a number of jobs down over the years because he had been offered work by other companies which was more profitable etc.

During these questions the bloke started to shift about and take his time answering so immediately he started Jack said, "You would be well advised to answer my questions promptly and not piss me about because I have not yet made my mind up as to whether I report you for assault and since you have already done time for that you would be looking at a much longer term next time, so…"

The Chairman interrupted to say move on again and Jack, under his breath just muttered *that's all he can say like a fucking parrot* but from the look on the Lay Member's face who had winked at him, he was thinking along similar lines! There was no summing up by either party, the Tribunal simply got up and left. They were back in less than 20 minutes and announced that according to the evidence the Applicant had been self-employed, albeit on two separate occasions, and consequently they had no jurisdiction. The Chairman hurrying out, called over his shoulder, "the Regional Chairman would like to speak to you Mr Hughes if you would go with the Clerk," so he did.

The Regional Chairman had a suitably regal office for his highness and initially he was very nice apologising profusely for the assault on Jack but he then started to say that, of course, if he had moved on as the Chairman instructed, *aye, aye he thought I am being told off and blamed for the incident here if I am not careful.* Jack interrupted and said, "Sir, I accept your apology but there would have been no need for it if your Chairman had done his job properly and instructed him to answer after any of the four or five times, I asked him to, especially as I indicated the importance of an answer for my case."

After a pause the Chairman said, "That's as may be, but be assured that if you ever speak to one of my Chairman again as you did you will regret it."

Jack paused even longer, giving him the evil eye and then said, "And be assured, Sir, that if I ever come up against chairmanship like that again it will not be a pleasant experience for your Chairman."

At that Jack got up and walked out calling over his shoulder, "I think I will be referring this to the police." *Let the arrogant bastard sweat he thought.* He never did complain but he hoped the Regional Chairman had a bad day or two as a result.

The other case which enlarged his reputation for being willing to argue was in Manchester in front of the rip-em-out female Chairman. That case involved an Applicant who claimed his dismissal was not for redundancy and thus was unfair. He had been employed on a Quail Farm where there were around 120,000 birds—no one knew exactly how many there were because they never stayed still long enough to be counted! An epidemic of bird flu swept the country and the owners were ordered by the Min of Ag and Fish to separate the egg layers, of which there were about 20,000, from the birds sold for their meat, about 100,000. The meat birds were removed to a site about seven miles away.

The Applicant had been offered work at that site but as it was in rural Lancashire with no bus services between the Applicant's home and the farm located to, so he could not get there which had resulted in his dismissal. He had received all the payments he was due plus a small ex-gratia gratuity on top. His Application claimed unfair dismissal because it wasn't a redundancy situation in several places.

Jack did his normal thorough preparations including asking the client if he knew any reason why the lad should claim it wasn't redundancy like had he had a falling out in the past, was he courting the boss's daughter and thought to be an unsuitable match etc but the client just laughed and could come up with nothing.

At the Hearing Madam Chairman did her usual of tearing out the IT1 and 3 and Jack did his normal of asking the client to comment on something on the IT1 and 3. He got him to explain that he had been ordered by the Ministry to separate the two types of birds which he had done by moving about 100,000 to a site seven miles away. He had had a meeting with his eight staff and explained the situation and asked for suggestions—there were none so, using last in first out, their policy in a potential redundancy situation, he had chosen seven of them, the last seven starters to move to the other site. The ones he had retained as well as being the longest serving were also all family members.

The Applicant had, once told that he would have to move, refused on the basis that he could not travel. The employer considered whether one of his family could be moved but the two children did not have transport either so, reluctantly he had terminated his employment. He considered that, as he had offered him alternative employment whether he should pay the redundancy pay and ex-gratia but decided that, as he had been a good worker and had a genuine reason for refusing the offer, he paid him anyway.

When given the opportunity to cross examine, the Applicant representing himself, he asked no questions so Madam Chairman, following her duty to look after unrepresented individuals up against a professional on the other side asked a few admin questions of no particular significance and since neither the Applicant, nor the Chairman, challenged any of the facts stated by the employer Jack did not call his second witness, he had ready, in case of challenges. The Applicant then gave evidence and confirmed what had been said about the process was true but it was not a true redundancy situation and stopped.

So, Jack asked the obvious question first, "Why do you say it was not a genuine situation?" The lad didn't answer. "Let me define redundancy, and I am sure Madam Chairman will correct me if I am wrong, but the simple definition is *the need for work of a particular kind has ceased, or will cease, has diminished or will diminish, at that site.* So which bit of that do you challenge? The work of a particular kind? No answer. "What about has diminished?" No answer. "What about at that site?" No answer, at which Jack turned to Madam Chairman and said, "Will you please direct the witness to answer Mam, I have asked at least five questions none of which he has answered."

"Move on Mr Hughes."

"Mam, I cannot. You have not challenged or contradicted my definition of redundancy and since the Applicant's case is that there was not a true redundancy situation, which is the crux of this case I cannot move on unless I know the path to follow so will you please direct him to answer."

"Move on Mr Hughes." *Shades of London Central,* he thought—*I hope this bugger isn't going to try and strangle me.*

"Mam, I can't."

"Move on."

"Mam I can't, with great respect *(i.e., none at all!)* I do not know what to ask." The two Lay Members were starting to look uncomfortable which was nothing like as bad as Jack was feeling.

"Move on for the last time."

"Mam, I cannot and will not. May I suggest a short break so that you may consult your Lay Members or perhaps the Regional Chairman if he is available to avoid the inevitable overturning of any decision you might reach on appeal." Madam Chairman looked as though she was going to leap over the bench and strangle Jack but, perhaps just in time, one of the Lay Members leaned over and whispered something in her ear, *thank God for Lay Members,* thought Jack, after which she said, "We will adjourn for 15 minutes," and they were gone.

His client was looking at Jack in shear amazement and the Applicant was goggle eyed. Jack whispered to the client that he hoped his number one rule that whoever upsets the Chairman first loses was not about to become true! The Tribunal returned promptly after 15 minutes, the longest 15 minutes of Jack's life, and said, "Mr Hughes, if I said to you that as far as the Tribunal is concerned it was clearly a redundancy situation and we reject the Applicant's assertion that it wasn't would that help you?"

"Yes, indeed it would Mam, and that being the case I have no further questions of the Applicant."

"That being the case Mr Hughes as the Applicant is unrepresented and you are a professional, I would ask you to sum up first, are you ready for that or would you like a few moments?" *Oh wow,* thought Jack, *I don't know what was said when they withdrew but she is clearly trying to make amends,* but he didn't really need any time so he thanked her for the offer but said he was ready and he went ahead. All the Applicant could do was to say again that it wasn't a true redundancy situation and that was that. They only took 20 minutes to find that it was a redundancy situation and his selection for dismissal was fair.

Jack never did find out what the lad's real gripe was but he did increase his reputation for fighting Chairman although, as it was to happen, he never did appear in front of Madam Chairman again.

Chapter 44

Only another 645 cases to go! No, seriously, just one more and then, promotion. Jack had handled every sort of case one could imagine, sad, funny, ridiculous, involving a husband sacking his wife (two of them and both husbands lost!), involving print unions, one involving 350 Applicants which Delta had advised on sacking in the first place and one for a private hospital which was the last one as an Advocate before moving on—although he did do one from time to time to keep his hand in so to speak including the biggie in Scotland for what is a year.

A private hospital recruited a new General Manager to help them fight another private hospital which was to be built across the road from them. He looked, analysed, planned and acted. The basic problem he believed was the way they functioned. Reception opened about 9.30am and closed at 8pm, although with most patients discharged from the hospital by 4pm there was very little work for a Receptionist after that time. That was long enough, with some time left over to get the patients in during the day, operate and get them out again. He felt that if they opened earlier and closed later, they could process one group of patients in the morning and another group in the afternoon.

He started with the Porters explaining the serious threat to their continued future when the competitor opened and explained what he proposed and why and told them how he saw the Portering function operating. They agreed. He then spoke to the six Receptionists and produced a roster which meant 10 days on and 10 days off working a mix of earlies, middles and late shifts staffing Reception from 6am until 10pm. They flatly refused to accept the changes so he went back to the drawing board and developed a roster of 6 days on and 3 off again working a mix of earlies, middles and lates. Again they flatly refused and at the end of that meeting he asked them if there was any point producing another roster and they said, 'No,' so he dismissed them all!

Jack went to see the client, a new one, as usual and was impressed with Reception—he wondered if the original Reception was as good! He met with the

General Manager and the Personnel Officer. He asked a few questions of the GM to establish the economic arguments to justify their actions although an employer has the right to run a business and change it around how he liked providing he goes about it reasonably, even without an economic justification, but an economic justification helps, indeed might be essential, in a redundancy situation.

The one thing Jack established with them was that he did not think it was a redundancy situation, there would be more hours being worked in Reception after the changes than before so why were they claiming unfair selection for redundancy? Neither knew, although the PO did think it was for the money since four of them were quite long serving and they had been dismissed with notice so that effectively when they walked out the door for the last time, they only had a few pounds in accrued holiday pay to their credit. Jack, having asked all he wanted of the GM and answered his immediate questions, asked to spend some time with the PO to go through their Personnel files. That took several hours but, in the event, turned out to be time well spent.

The Chairman in Leeds turned out to be a sitting Judge which was unusual especially as he bowed his head to the room when he entered on telling them to sit! Jack had a huge pile of files/paperwork on his table to his left and a smaller one to his right. He intended, as his first point to try to challenge the issue of redundancy and get that ruled out before starting the hearing proper but the Chairman spoke first to the Barrister representing the four Applicants, two more having too short a service to apply, and said, "Miss Smifff, isn't the issue of redundancy going to give you some trouble as reading the papers of both parties it would seem that the workload was increased rather than ceasing or diminishing?"

"Yes, Sir, I have given that some thought and I believe it appropriate to withdraw that element of the applications."

"Quite right. I assume you have no objection to that Mr Hughes?"

"Indeed not, Sir." At that Jack picked up the huge pile to his left and dropped it on the floor at the side of his table. Although a little pissed off at all the work he had done preparing to argue the redundancy issue he was nevertheless pleased that his interpretation had been right and he would not now have to argue the issue. As the Respondent admitted dismissal it was for Jack to go first so he called the GM who described the competition they were about to face, how they decided to fight it and how he had gone about doing it.

He particularly emphasised, because Jack had advised him to do so, how having spent a lot of time recalculating the second proposed roster, the first having been rejected out of hand, how he was perturbed by the flat refusal of the second one and how, having asked the question 'is there any point in producing yet another one' they had said a unanimous 'no' leaving him with the only alternative of dismissing all of them for some other substantial reason.

On cross examination by the Barrister, dressed in a hippy dress, no shoes and dirty feet, he did very well. She was unable to push unfairness in their treatment other than to stress was that the way to treat such long serving, loyal, staff. Prepared by Jack for just such a point he responded with the Hospital was facing such severe competition from the new one that their very future was threatened and they had shown no loyalty or willingness to fight to save it so why should he fight to save them. She could only reply that it was her job to ask the questions and his to answer them and not the other way round!

The Personnel Officer gave evidence just to support the General Manager's evidence as being accurate, there being four Applicants who might disagree, but the cross examination was non-existent other than a simple challenge that their dismissal was unfair to which the Personnel Officer disagreed quite forcefully.

Jack had no idea beforehand as to which of the Applicants would go first but in the event, it was one who was a single mother, a Justice of the Peace in her spare time i.e., she had to be allowed time off for such duties with pay and one who presumably, they thought, would be able to handle any mere Personnel Consultant. Her evidence was that she was a single parent, had two sons, one 16 and one 18, who were about to take their GCSEs and for whom she had to be there in the evenings to ensure she could help them with their homework and exam preparations so she could not possibly work all the evenings in succession required by either of the rosters proposed by the GM.

Hm, thought Jack, *going for the sympathy vote and sex discrimination indirectly as a single mother.* She also stressed that she had been there for more than 15 years and it was unfair to dismiss such a long serving and loyal member of staff.

Jack started with could she suggest how she could have been kept on working the hours she had previously worked without completely wrecking the roster system, either one, proposed. It was clear that that had not been considered to be a likely question and prepared for it, by the stumbling way she eventually said she could not. Jack then asked her to turn to page (x) in his bundle (unlike as to what was to be the practice later, he had produced his bundle to the Clerk just before the start of the Hearing and they would not have had time to read it all, all 112 pages, before the Hearing started).

The page showed attendances by an un-named person at work where 73% of the attendances were between 4pm and 8pm. Previous management had really left the Receptionists to organise themselves as to who worked when but they had ensured that accurate records of attendance were kept. So, Jack said, "This attendance record shows that 73% of this person's time was worked in the evening and the remaining spread over mornings and afternoons in pretty well equal shares. That record continued up to the date that person left. Will you please note that the person is named as employee 2. Now will you please turn to page (xx). There you can see the numbers 1-6 with a person's name against each number. Would you please read out the name against number 2?"

She read out her own name. "Now, how does that fit with you saying you could not work evenings when that is primarily the pattern you were already working?" She at least had the grace to look guilty before mumbling about shifts would have meant problems with her daily life to which Jack said, "But the GM said that if a particular shift would pose a problem an individual could change with someone else if they needed to, didn't he?" And she had no option other than to say 'yes'?

Jack finished with, "You made much of your 15 years' service and loyalty but when you were needed to show such loyalty by agreeing to a plan to save your company you refused for no good reason how does that indicate loyalty?" Jack was happy for her not to answer. He finished with, "Just one last question, your GM did, after the second roster was rejected, offer you the choice of more or would that be a waste of time and you, and all the others, agreed it would be —is that not so?" She nodded yes.

The second Applicant took the oath and described how she had been employed for 15 years with no disciplinary warnings of any kind and she had always been loyal but she couldn't work either of the rosters because she had an elderly and infirm mother who lived on her own and who she had to call in on every day to ensure she was alright, get her shopping, help with household chores etc. If it had not been for that she would have happily worked the rosters but simply couldn't. Jack started, "Please turn to page y. There is a copy of the first roster is there not?"

"Yes, that looks like it."

"Right, that shows the earlies, middles and lates for 10 days and then 10 days off, doesn't it?"

"Yes."

"So, on which of the 10 days off would you not be able to look after mother as you allege you were doing before?" She looked at him as though he was mad.

"None of them, of course."

"Right so that wouldn't affect you in any way, would it?"

"No."

"So, on the mornings you worked earlies what effect would that have?"

"Well, I wouldn't be able to see her."

"But you would be able to see her after your shift finishing at lunchtime, wouldn't you?"

"I suppose so."

"And I suppose that you could see her before or after the middles, or only before the lates?"

"Yes."

"So how would that roster or indeed the recalculated one have prevented you from looking after your mother?" She didn't answer and Jack was content with that because of where he was going next. "I understand you are quite successful with your dogs at various dog shows and even once an appearance at Crufts, is that correct?" Her face lit up.

"Oh yes, we got a third in class in the appearance at Crufts."

"Jolly good. But I think this takes quite a lot of your time does it not?"

"Well, not too much."

"As I understand it you spend most weekends from the early summer until the autumn attending dog shows and competitions from as far apart as Plymouth to Carlisle. Is that not right?"

"Yes."

"And that means going away, in your Campervan from Friday night until returning on Sunday, sometimes not until Monday. Is that not right?"

"Yes, sometimes."

"So, who looks after mother while you are away?"

"Well, sometimes a neighbour looks in."

"But you are able to go away virtually every weekend for months at a time without worrying about mother?"

"I do worry about her while we are away."

"I'll rephrase that then, as I am sure you do worry about mother. You are able to go away virtually every weekend throughout the summer without visiting your so dependent mother at all from Friday to Monday?"

She didn't answer. "Did you enjoy your three weeks in the Maldives last summer?"

By now the woman was hating to answer every question so she said, "What's that to do with you or this case?"

"Well, if you do not want to answer that, answer this, did your mother go with you?"

"No."

"So, who looked after mother for three whole weeks while you were unable to call in for every one of those 15 days?"

At this point the Chairman interrupted and said, "I think you have made your point Mr Hughes, kindly move on."

Jack replied, "Yes of course, Sir, I have just one more question. I think it would be true to say that you could not work the roster patterns is more that you did not want to; is that not true?"

"No."

"But you could have worked either of them if you had had to, couldn't you?"

"Yes."

"One final question, you did say 'no,' along with all the others, to your GM's question as to whether there was any point in producing yet another roster didn't you and she agreed that she had."

The third Applicant was already flustered when she took the oath and Jack hadn't said anything to her yet! *He thought I need to seem nice to her, because I hammered the last one so how can I start?* An idea came to him; after she had given her evidence in chief which was mainly that she was occupied in the evenings with work for her charity but she neglected to mention her dancing giving Jack the chance to start gently.

"I understand that although you didn't mention the charity's name it in fact specialises in helping deaf children, is that right?"

"Yes," she said.

"Well, I am the father of a deaf child, although she is an adult now, and I was involved with that same charity myself as a collector with a tin on a Friday night going around the pubs trying to beat the Salvation Army, does that still go on?"

"Oh, yes," she said, "very much."

290

"And is it still difficult to get people to help with everything and anything; at times I was the only one on the Education Sub-committee that turned up?"

"Yes, nothing has changed."

"Well, may I say how much I admire the work you do in that field but I have to now move on and ask you some questions. How much of your time does that work take up?"

"Quite a lot, it varies from week to week."

"One night or two or three?"

"Yes, sometimes."

"Anything else which would have prevented you from the roster system?"

"No, not really."

"Oh, that surprises me. What about your dancing? Doesn't that take up quite a bit of time, something like two nights a week, Tuesday and Thursday, and then the competitions on the weekend," and he turned to page (x) in his bundle, "can we turn to page (x)," which was from the local paper reporting on the success of a local dance team at Blackpool in a regional competition. She just nodded. "So, isn't this another case of your loyalty to your past-times was much greater than to your employer?"

She didn't answer and Jack was content to say, "I have no further questions of this Applicant, Sir. Oh sorry, one more, you did say 'no' to the question from your GM about it being pointless to produce another roster?" She nodded. The Chairman said that as it was just about 1pm they would break until 2pm, he bowed and was gone along with the two Lay Members.

They were all taken in by the Clerk just after 2pm who handed the Chairman who was already seated, a note. The Chairman read it and said for them to wait whilst he sped out. As they stood up when he left the Applicants, the GM and PO started talking to one another, how are you etc and one of the Applicants, the one who had not yet given evidence and was due to next started handing around Polo mints from a roll.

When she got to Jack, she said, "I don't know if I want to give you one if you are going to dissect me like all the others," but she did proffer one. Jack smiled and refused saying, "I thank you for your offer but I won't in case he comes straight back and I can't ask the questions I intend to because I have a sweet in my mouth." She looked a bit pale at that but just then the Chairman returned and she was called to give evidence by her Barrister. It didn't amount to much more than a litany of routine family duties. Jack didn't really have any knowledge of her like he had of the others but something was clearly bothering her.

Her evidence in chief didn't take much more than 10 minutes but as she did so she was clearly becoming more and more nervous, stumbling over her words and even wringing her hands. *She's hiding something he thought but I haven't a clue what it might be.* So he decided on a bluff, something he rarely ever did. He reached down to his brief case at the side of him, picked it up, opened it and extracted a piece of paper with printing on it and placed it on the table in front of him. He then made a bit of a show of closing the brief case and replacing it on the floor. He then said, "I do have one or two points here I would like to ask you about and I would like to start with you did not want this plan to go ahead, did you?" She was clearly very agitated but said, "Well, we didn't think it would happen…"

"What would happen, the competition from the new hospital?"

"No, we thought that if we all said no to the roster then the GM would not go ahead and we would stay as we were." Jack's brain exploded. What she had said was dynamite but it was a question of what to ask next to prove it. He needed to get out that they had conspired to attempt to defeat the proposal, but what to ask? "So, you did all discuss how to react to the GM's proposal?"

At that the Barrister interrupted with a "I fail to see where my friend is going with this, Sir." As she said it, she was shaking her head strongly from side to side and Jack thought *Fuck, fuck, fuck, that's a prearranged signal, agreed beforehand, to tell her to stay away from answering that or even to say no.* The Chairman simply said she can answer but it was too late, but he had to give it a go.

"I note you said 'we' not 'I' how many wees was that?"

"I don't understand." Yes, definitely she was staying away from answering. "Well, did you just discuss it with one other colleague or two?"

"I don't remember."

"Well, it can't have been more than six could it, as there were only six of you, or did you discuss it with others besides those six?"

"Oh no, we didn't discuss it with anyone else."

"So, six of you in total, that means you discussed it with the other five?" She was stuck so she said nothing. "So, however many it was who discussed it, probably six people, were you all in agreement or did anyone disagree?"

"No-one disagreed." Jack turned to the Chairman and said, "I think you have heard enough, Sir, to understand that the four Applicants plus the other two Receptionists who have insufficient service to bring an application, in fact conspired to defeat their employer's attempts to fight off competition they knew was coming and that by so doing they were, in fact, taking part in industrial action.

"That being the case, with respect, this Tribunal has no jurisdiction to hear this case and you must stop this hearing now. He then withdrew his drains company EAT case from his folder and passed it to the Clerk asking her to hand it to the Chairman. The Chairman turned to the Barrister and said, "What do you say to that Ms Smifff?" Ms Smifff was quite quick responding but she was clearly thrown by Jack's demand.

"Sir, it is of course well proven law that taking part in industrial action which results in the termination of the employment of those taking part, is without the jurisdiction of a Tribunal but I would argue that discussing what might happen if they took action, in this case refusing a roster, amounted to industrial action; discussing something cannot possibly amount to action, surely they would have had to do something like threaten to strike or even strike for it to amount to action."

"What do you say to that Mr Hughes?"

"Action is a very wide word, Sir (get in as many sirs as you can when begging!) Obviously as my learned friend says strike action or even to threaten a strike is clearly action. But saying no to a proposal to produce a further roster is action, they were saying no and that must amount to action. If they had said what will happen if we say no is not action, it is merely a question and a reasonable one in the circumstances but they did not do that they said an emphatic no and that was action."

"Wait there, we will not be long." And they were gone. This time the two parties did not mingle! Jack felt he had probably been crossed off their Christmas card lists but he wasn't sure. It was over half an hour before they returned and the Chairman said, "We are divided on the issue but the majority, by a very narrow margin believe that the actions of the Applicants and the other two Receptionist came close to industrial action when they refused further discussion about further rosters but it was not quite sufficient to amount to action as required by the Act. Now Mr Hughes, unless you have any further questions of the last witness we will proceed to your summations."

Dam, thought Jack, nearly got it, but there you go. Have I anything more with this one—the answer must be no, I had nothing in the first place so he said, "I have no further questions, Sir, thank you and I am prepared for my summation as soon as you wish."

"Well, normally it would be for the Respondent to go first but it is our wish in this case, for you to go first Ms Smifff, so are you ready?"

"Yes, indeed, Sir." He nodded at her and she started but as far as Jack was concerned, she didn't have much so she resorted to the norm for a Barrister steeped in criminal law, she blurred the issues attempting to muddy the waters to prevent a beyond all reasonable doubt decision. However, as Jack was steeped in Tribunal law all he had to do was to work to a reasonable doubt a much easier decision and he had good facts to work with.

The employer having found a very difficult problem on the horizon, came up with a plan and explained the situation and the proposed solution to the staff. They had raised issues which had been dealt with by a revised roster but had rejected the revised roster and the offer of yet another one, indicating quite clearly that they were not prepared to assist the employer in anyway. Their reasons for failing to do so, Jack said, you might feel were selfish but they were their reasons and they were entitled to them.

But they amounted to that they did not want to work a roster system not that they couldn't as his cross-examination had clearly shown, and therefore their dismissal, for some other substantial reason (one of only five potentially fair reasons allowed in law) must be fair. The Chairman reserved their decision and that was that apart from the waiting.

The decisions for the four cases came through about six weeks later and all found that the dismissals had been fair. The client was delighted, so much so he wrote quite a detailed letter of thanks and praise to Delta's MD praising Jack and lauding how his detailed and precise research into the Applicants' backgrounds had destroyed their case. He said he had had some reservations before the case because Jack, who was only an Advocate, was up against a quite famous Barrister in the area and he had worried about was he, the client, under gunned, but he had never seen someone so comprehensively destroyed as Jack had her.

But that was not the end. Some three or so years later the GM contacted Delta again. He explained that he now worked, as a Director, for another company in the medical field and would like Jack to come and see him with a view to signing that company up with Delta, but it had to be Jack. The MD called Jack to his office, gave him a copy of the letter, a blank contract sheet, a fee calculation sheet and said, "Go sign him up."

That was amazing but the most amazing thing was, when Jack rang him to find out where they were he said that they were in St James's Road, Surbiton at which Jack said, "Oh, that's just across the road from the station," to which the GM said, "Christ, I knew you were bloody good, but that's incredible, how does someone in Manchester know that?"

Jack laughed and replied that as he had been born and brought up there it would have been a surprise if he hadn't known because the cinema was on that street. Jack agreed a time and date to go there and successfully signed them up. He also managed to time it that he went to see another client in Esher the following day so he spent the night in Surbiton and had a nostalgic little trip around to see the house where he had lived, his old school, no longer a grammar which had moved to near Esher, and one or two other familiar places. He had gone off to join the Army in 1963 and here he was back for the first time (and as it turned out the last time!) in 1999, only 36 years later!

The one thing that did surprise him was how small the area of his world had been then. It was about three miles from his old home to school, about the same to his best mate's house, the same again to his dad's factory and the office building where his mum worked. His two uncles lived a bit further apart, one in Twickenham and one in Tolworth but nevertheless it was a tiny world in retrospect although it had not seemed that to him at the time.

Chapter 45

About two and a half years after Jack joined Delta the Manager of the Personnel Department suffered quite a severe heart attack. The Personnel Department's Personnel Consultant's job was to visit a new client, talk to them about how they functioned the department in their company and gather together copies of all the documentation they used to carry out the personnel function.

Quite often, especially in the early days, this amounted to little more than odd scraps of paper with bare minimum details regarding their employees. They would return a short while later with a complete set of documentation starting with a few sample adverts, application forms, employment record forms, sample job descriptions, a model contract of employment statement and a handbook to support it. They would take the client through the whole system, make any alterations, legal alterations that is, that the client wanted and then leave them with the system.

At the same time as they were signing up for the Personnel System, they became entitled to use the Advice Service. Although some did still call the Personnel Consultant because clearly, they knew them rather than some faceless Adviser in Manchester, they were discouraged from doing so as the Personnel Consultant was probably in with another new client, when they rang, and could not be interrupted but the Advice Service was available at the end of a telephone 24 hours a day, seven days a week, 365 days a year. (And a quarter!)

If a particular situation ended up in a Tribunal Application, then Delta would have one of its Advocates (Jack for instance) represent the client, for free and would even pay any award(s) if the case was lost; the only condition being that the client had taken advice and followed it. Simply it was a three department consultancy operation Personnel having written the contracts, Advice having given advice based on the contract and the law and Advocacy fighting the Tribunal if necessary. (There was a mirror image function if they had signed up for Health and Safety as well.) At the time Jack joined there were two full-time and one part-time Advisers and this had grown to six three years later. Of the three departments the weak link was Advice. The Advisers were making mistake after mistake which made it almost impossible for the Advocate to win in Tribunal, it was also costing the company a lot of money!

It became apparent quite quickly that the Personnel Department Manager would not recover sufficiently to return to managing the Department and it was a bit of a surprise when the appointment of one of the Advocates in his place was announced. Jack wasn't bothered because he would not have wanted the job anyway.

However, only a few days after the appointment he was in a meeting with his boss about a particularly difficult case when he asked Jack what he thought of the appointment. As it happened Jack thought that the guy appointed probably would be able to do the job very well but he didn't really think that his boss should be asking him that. So, he said, "I don't think you need to worry about him so much as all the others who didn't get the job and would have liked it."

"What do you mean?"

"Although we are growing, growing very quickly, the opportunities for promotion in the two and a half years I have been here have been precisely nil. It would have been nice to see a little advert for the Personnel Manager's post and the opportunity to put my hand up—not that I would have done I wouldn't have wanted it—but that is the view of a lot of my colleagues and they didn't get the chance so they are pissed off, some of them very."

Tony did not respond so Jack carried on, "It's not as though they had to give it to anyone that applied, they could have known who they were going to give it to from before the advert, only they would know that, everyone else would feel that at least they had had the opportunity to apply and those that did, whether they got an interview or not, would know they gave it a go. That way only the one or two who felt they were the best one for the job and better than the successful one would feel pissed off, as it was, they all do! And let me say again I would not have put my hand up."

"Why not?"

"I'd be bored out of my mind producing and updating systems day in day out—no thanks. Besides I am happy having no responsibility other than for myself, taking on a department as well isn't something I fancy." Tony let it go at that. About six months later Jack arrived at the Tribunal offices in Liverpool and happened to meet one of the other Advocates who was also appearing there,—

something that happened! She was all agog, "Did you hear, Dons gone and all his tribe!"

"What?"

"Yes, he's gone and his wife. Had some sort of problem with the boss and so he's gone." He had been the Director of Consultancy but Jack had had little contact with him. He had produced, at the guy's request, a draft training plan following a discussion about training which Jack had described as one he had used in a previous role. The Director had seemed very interested and had asked Jack to put it in writing but that had been months before and nothing had come of it.

Don's wife had originally been a Field Sales Person and had been very successful, mainly it was believed because he was feeding juicy leads to her from the Telesales people. The one fact that was indisputable was that she popped up all over the entire country, even more than the Stalking Cat, and the rumour was that it was leads for bedding, but salacious rumours were one thing, evidence another! Whatever the truth he had married her only a few months after Jack joined Delta. He had been sent to help her with potential clients on a couple of occasions but after the first one would not have gone to any others voluntarily—she was as tight as a duck's arse and that's watertight!

Every other Rep that Jack helped to get a deal ensured that Jack got a little something in recognition, but from her, nothing. He also simply did not like her, she was rude, apart from when fawning around a prospect, unkind and sure of her own supremacy. Jack just thought she was a Meadow Lady (cow!). He had no feeling either way about Don but he was glad to see the back of her if she had, indeed, gone.

It took a while for the whole story to come out and Jack was sure that some of the 'facts' were probably conjecture, but the two of them had been setting up a company to be in competition with Delta, having done so because he was only on £50,000pa while the MD was paying himself £500,000pa. She felt that was unfair and had egged him on to ask for a pay rise and when that was refused had led the way in creating the new one to compete with Delta. Don's daughter, from his first marriage had gone with him but his son, a Senior Clerk in Advice had stayed. Soon, several other staff started handing in their notices, one of them being the Advice Service Manager.

People being people, word soon spread that they had all gone to the new company. It also came out that the MD had discovered what was going on and had got Don in and told him he knew about the new company and that if he would stop it, he could stay where he was, but when this was refused, he was fired. Of course, all of this created all sorts of mayhem and rumour, most of which Jack took with a pinch of salt but it was indisputably true that Don, his wife, daughter and 17 staff had left.

Within days of Don going Jack's boss, Tony, was appointed Director of Consultancy in his place. There had only been four possible candidates in practical terms, Tony, The Manager of Advocacy, The Advice Service Manager, now left, the Health and Safety Manager and the new Personnel Services Manager, but he was too new, the H&S one had no personnel, employment law or tribunal knowledge leaving, in reality, only Tony. In the event he was to, in less than three months, achieve more than Don had achieved in the previous eight or so years.

One of the first things he did was to put around a short advert for the vacancy of Advice Service Manager which when Jack saw it thought, *ah well, my little lesson about how to handle promotion opportunities a few months ago went home although they didn't advertise the Consultancy Director's post!* Jack saw the advert on the Tuesday and, although he did think about it, he had done nothing about it when he went into the office on the Friday. Tony called him into his new office and spoke to him about a Tribunal that was in the pipeline which he wanted Jack to handle—it was for a friend of the MD's and needed especial handling. As the meeting finished and Jack was walking out, Tony asked him when he would be submitting his application for the Advice Service Manager's job. Jack stopped turned round and looked at him. "What?"

"When can I expect your application for Swinton's job?"

"I'm not sure I want it and anyway the closing date is next Friday, isn't it?"

"Yes, but I want you appointed before then. The only other two who are going to apply have already submitted their applications and I am seeing one of them on Monday and the other on Tuesday. I'll see you on Wednesday and announce your appointment on Thursday."

This all said with a huge smile on his face, "You did advise me to do it that way didn't you?"

Jack laughed and said, "Monday if I apply. I am quite happy being responsible just for myself and I will need to give careful consideration as to whether I want to take that lot on." And with that he walked out. He talked it over with Janet over the weekend and thought very carefully about whether he wanted the job. He was now almost 52 years old and the long days, high mileages and nights away were starting to be a bit of a drag.

As against that he would still have long days made up of nearly two hours' drive to Manchester in the morning and back again in the evening with a real task in front of him to sort out a Department that was definitely not functioning very well. Although he had quite good relationships with the six Advisers plus indeed the Manager, all of whom had sought his advice about problems they faced at some time or other – some frequently-, but actually managing them, as against advising them, was a very different ball game; if he had known just how much and what was to face him, he would never have written the application, but write it he did.

On the Wednesday when he presented himself for the interview it was not what he expected. Tony wasn't one to dwell on social pleasantries he simply opened with, "I am going to create an Assistant Manager post," *Oh no I'm not falling for that, thought Jack, there is no way I'm going to take that position but it was ok because Tony went on to say*, "I'm sure you are as aware, as I am, that there's a bit of 'us and them' between Advice and Advocacy and putting you in as Manager will only cause them to close ranks against the outsider feeling that one of their own, namely Bill Jones, should have got the job; so by making him Assistant Manager, particularly as you won't be around much for a while, while you run out your Tribunals, will give him a job to do and let them get used to the idea. I will announce your appointment tomorrow when you are in Shrewsbury so by Friday, when you're back in, it should be yesterday's news." Jack was a little stunned to say the least so he responded with, "Do I take it that the interview has finished?"

"Yes, the interview has, but I want to go through a few things with you about what I see as needed to be done and to make it look like a proper interview to all those eyes out there watching you coming in and going out, so don't look to happy about it when you go out will you?"

Jack laughed and they spent the next hour and a half going through plans for the future. He made a point of looking harassed when he left but he didn't think he would have got an Oscar for it! What is that Scotsman said, *'the best laid plans of mice and men have often gang aglee!'* Well, they did! The following day the announcements were made of Bill Jones as the Assistant Manager and Jack as the Manager. At lunchtime Peter Swinton, the Advice Service Manager went to lunch and never came back. He had given three months' notice to leave, and although he had refused to say where he was going word came through from another source that he had gone to join Don and his wife at their new company.

His actions breaking his contractual notice fitted in well with the new company's ethos, although they didn't discover that for another month or two. For Jack, when he arrived on the Friday it was the worst possible news. Bill Jones had made it known to all and sundry that he had only taken the Assistant Manager post whilst he looked for another job, he feeling so slighted that he had not got the top job because he was clearly better suited for it than was Jack.

Jack could have easily lived with that, he would probably felt the same in his place, but all six of the Advisers were vociferous in support of Jones's view, despite the fact that all of them including the departed Manager had gone begging to Jack for help in the past. It was also a problem for Jack since he had to take over managing a crap performing department whilst running down a list of some 35 Tribunals. A short conversation with Tone resulted in 20 of them being taken away but that still left him with 15 the biggest one involving 350 Applicants and listed for 10 days of hearing which would involve an enormous amount of work.

It involved a transfer of undertakings claim by the 350 arguing that their employment should have been transferred to the new company taking over and since the new company had denied a transfer took place all 350 were claiming unfair dismissal or in the alternative redundancy payments, notice pay and holiday pay. There were a few other claims as well making the award of a fortune if the cases were lost! It didn't help that the advice to the client had been given variously by the ex-Manager and Bill Jones meaning that the bill would have to be paid by Delta under the guarantee procedure, Delta having given advice throughout.

Jack checked very carefully as his first action to make sure they had followed the advice because failure to do so rendered the guarantee invalid but no such luck they had done exactly as they had been told—the problem was the advice was, a legal technical term you understand, crap! In the event Jack had to speak to Bill Jones a lot about the advice given, Peter Swinton no longer being available.

Jack saw an opportunity to demonstrate the difference between them and as he asked questions so Jones shrank into his chair as question after question that Jack asked couldn't be answered but he should have been able to and would have if he had done the job properly in the first place. Jack also made him sweat by reminding him of a clause in his, and everyone else's contracts, about the

Company's right to claim damages caused by negligent actions on the part of any member of staff, and he made sure that Jones realised he had done nowhere near a good job especially as the two of them knew that 350 staff were involved.

In the event Jack went to the company, withdrew the notices of dismissal and ran the consultation as it should have been done in the event that there was a dismissal for redundancy as a defence against failure to consult if the Tribunal decided that there was not a transfer under the TUPE Regs. He then ran the Tribunal case and persuaded them that there was indeed a transfer of the undertaking and the responsibility for taking the staff on, and then dismissing them if necessary, sat with the taking over company. Bill Jones, of course, showed no gratitude for Jack saving his bacon, but worse, he did not understand that Jack had thereby demonstrated that Bill Jones was not the man for the Manager's post and that he, Jack, very much was.

In the event Jones was not to last long by his own choice. Jack had heard the odd word that Bill had shouted at clients who wouldn't follow his advice but, as he had never witnessed it, wasn't too sure that it was true. But it was! He had popped in on a Friday morning, before walking over to the Manchester Tribunal Office, and, as he was leaving, Bill started shouting at someone and it really was shouting, not just a somewhat raised voice. I'll have to speak to him about that he thought but for now I must not be late or the Chairman will have my guts for garters—remembering whoever upsets the Chairman first loses!

Jack was in the Saturday and Sunday mornings because they were building new work stations. As the Company had grown all sorts of furniture had been bought, most of it second hand, with no two desks matching. They were also overcrowded. They had managed to gain possession of the floor below and Personnel Services and Health and Safety moved down there as part of the reorganisation. Advice and Advocacy stayed where they were but units were emplaced over the weekend.

Essentially, they were trapezoid in shape with four units making up a circular unit. They were cleverly designed with a shelf, overhead cupboard unit and a VDU with space for the keyboard and space to the side to write notes when on the telephone. Jack had worked with the designers and had one of the Advisers go with him to their factory to ensure that it would enable someone to do the job. Yes, it was small and one had to be tidy or it rapidly became a cluttered tip.

On the Monday morning when the Advisers turned in it was to an entirely new office; one Jack thought was far better because it was purpose built and, although the Advisers were close together and could ask round the corner if they needed help, it was not so open that two or three of them could sit there chatting rather than working. Bill Jones took one look, threw his brief case (which only ever contained his sandwiches and drink!) onto the unit and started shouting, "This is no bloody good, it's a." and he relapsed into full flow Anglo Saxon. Jack stepped in and said, "Bill, that's enough. I get you don't like it but I will not tolerate such language. Cut it out or leave." So, he did!

Then next Jack knew was a call from the MD to go up to his office where Tony was also waiting. "What happened," he asked. Jack told him and he said, "Well, he's obviously not a happy bunny, he's asked for a meeting with me at 5.30pm to which I have agreed, but I would like you both to be here then." And they were. The first thing Bill said was that he wanted to speak to the MD alone without Tony and Jack present.

That was given short shrift by the MD by him saying that if he was going to bad mouth them, they had a right to hear what he had to say and if he wasn't prepared to say it in front of them, he certainly wasn't going to say it just to him. So, he started by saying the two of them were the worst two Managers he had ever known, they were useless, had no idea how to manage and should be immediately sacked.

The MD looked at him for a moment and said, "Well, I don't. I consider them to be two of the best Managers I have ever known and I am certainly not going to sack them on your say so." At which Jones stood up, reached into his inner suit pocket and pulled out three envelopes, one addressed to the MD and two unaddressed. He handed them to the three of them and said, "I thought you would say that," and turned and walked out. The letter to the MD was his resignation and the ones to Tony and Jack, identical, were rabid religious tracts quoting from the Bible and condemning both of them to the lowest levels of hell, there to burn in Hellfire for eternity. Tony and the MD both laughed.

"Did you know he was like that?" The MD asked.

"Well, a bit. I knew he was a staunch Roman Catholic and was studying for the priesthood in his spare time. He had had trouble keeping up with his studies, which we talked about, and I asked him if he would wish to go part-time to give him more time to study but he declined. I think he wants to become a Deacon, whatever that is, but judging by his treatment of clients who won't do as they are told I imagine the penance he would give some poor bugger for sinning would be burning at the stake as they did with John Huss in 1415!"

They both laughed and Tony said, "Better advertise the vacancy and get someone you want as soon as you like." That was, of course, not the end of it. Jones submitted a Tribunal Application which Jack fought and easily won.. To win a Constructive Dismissal claim is very difficult for an (ex)employee; they have to show that the employer in some way committed a gross misconduct action so shattering the contract to enable the employee to regard it as at an end with immediate effect.

His problem was that the employer had not broken his contract in any way. To provide new, better work stations was not a substantive breach and to allege that the staff were not consulted was blown apart by Jack describing the involvement of the member of staff coming with him to see the new units under construction and indeed she had made a couple of suggestions for improvement, both of which had been incorporated.

For Jack, the finding of a replacement would turn into a nightmare which would affect him for years to come, indeed even 30 years later he still bore a hate for the people involved. The MD came up with the idea that they would provide a premium employment law advice line that anyone could ring a get advice on an employment matter, employee or employer it didn't matter all were welcome.

The rules to operate a high cost premium rate line were strict and complicated starting with the 'expert' had to answer the phone, it couldn't be a Clerk because all the experts were busy as the caller would be paying a high rate for being on hold. Partly for that reason and partly so that their own clients didn't discover that this was a lot cheaper as a way of getting advice, the adverts used a different company name and a completely different telephone number and a different set of telephones were to be used. This was all being set up at the same time as the Jones nonsense was taking place.

Jack placed an internal advert and only one member of staff applied. A woman called Christine Jones (no relation to Bill Jones!) applied. Before the new office layout was constructed her desk was immediately in front of Jack's and as she started at 9.30am so as to finish half an hour later than the others, at 6pm, Jack was often the only one left with her. If there were no calls, she would often start a conversation with him so that it could be said that he knew her better than any of the others.

He had wanted a relatively new person, who he had just recruited as part of their expansion plans to apply but she didn't. She said she didn't feel ready for such seniority yet. Jack was a little surprised because she had held a far more senior role before being made redundant when the organisation closed down. Obviously, he couldn't promote someone against their will so he talked to Tony about the only applicant.

He explained that he had no reservations about her knowledge, she had worked for ACAS for more than 20 years but she had never held a managerial position. The closest she had come to that was she had been a Trainer for her last two years at ACAS. Management as a Trainer came more from knowledge than management leadership so, as she was in her late 50s, early 60s, he proposed to appoint her on a three month trial basis. That way he could demote her if she failed; if he simply appointed her and she failed he could not demote her only sack her and that he did not want to do.

Then the problem started. She was on holiday for two weeks and the Monday she returned Jack started a two week one. So, he spoke with Aileen Keeler, who would have been his first choice for the job, and explained that he would like her to tell Christine Jones that he would like her during her first week back to produce a roster for the Advisers to man the Premium Line phones, three of them, if calls came in, as the calls could be expected from the start of the second week.

How well she did that would then be a subject for discussion at the interview with Jack when he returned from holiday. Best laid plans etc, Jack received a telephone call in Greece on the Friday of his first week away that his father had unexpectedly died so that he and the family returned early. The funeral was the Wednesday of what would have been his first week back and that threw his itinerary out as to attend meant three days away, he living in Manchester area and his father in Arundel way down in the south.

He did have a brief word with Christine saying he hoped to speak to her that afternoon, the Monday, at which she complained she had wanted to tart herself up in all her glad rags for the interview. Jack laughed and said he would much prefer to see her as she really was than some tarted up Dolly Bird—this a woman who was obese, old looking beyond her years and never smartly dressed—in fact Jack already had in mind that if she had to go and see an important client, he would have to speak to her about her appearance, something not practiced by any of the ACAS officers Jack had met.

Unfortunately, he was unable to speak to her as planned as the MD landed a special task on him that had to be done that day before he left for the funeral; so, he sent for her and apologised saying that he had booked a room for the following Monday at 9.30am so she would have as much time as she needed to tart herself up, mini skirt, low cut blouse whatever! (She had a tattoo between her breasts which she was inordinately fond of showing off, which everyone else was inordinately pleased if she didn't—it was not a pretty sight!). She roared with laughter and said he'd better have some smelling salts with him because he would need them to get over the shock, she was going to knock him out!

In the event she turned up quite smartly dressed in blouse and skirt and said that she had considered the mini skirt, even a see through blouse, but thought that might be too much for his heart so she had toned it down a bit. Jack started the interview by apologising for the delay in seeing her and then asked her how she had got on organising the roster for the Premium Line. She looked at him a bit peculiarly and said, "I didn't, when I came back on the Monday Aileen had already done it."

Jack looked at her and then said, "That's a pity, I actually asked Aileen to tell you that I wanted you to do that, but I didn't tell her that it was a little bit of a test to see how you got on with your first bit of management, but she must have misunderstood me and…" and at that she got up, threw her pen onto the desk and stormed out! Jack was absolutely stunned, *what the hell was that all about,* he thought.

He sat there running through his mind all that had been said trying to pin point what he could have said to cause her to behave in such an extraordinary manner. The phone rang and it was Tony asking him to come up. In his office Tony asked him what had happened as she had come flying in to his office shouting that he, Jack, wasn't taking her application seriously and she wanted to raise a grievance against him. Jack explained what had happened, after all the whole interview hadn't last five minutes, and Tony ended the meeting with he would deal with the grievance once he received it.

Jack was never to really discover the truth of what had driven her behaviour. He put it down to nerves prior to the interview, it had taken rather a long time, and that given the antipathy between Advice and Advocacy it had somehow built up in her mind such that as soon as he said 'that's a pity' and the words that followed it, it must have triggered some switch in her mind to convince her that she wouldn't get it, not because she was not good enough but because she wasn't an Advocate and only Advocates were getting promoted because Tony was an ex-Advocacy Manager and was, of course, biased. She did not attend work the following day but sent in a sick note stating stress as her illness. She remained on the sick for some time but she wasn't so sick that she wasn't able to send in a series of complaints to add to the first one.

Tony asked Jack about each one and Jack was able to provide a complete answer to each. For example, she complained that he had teased Sean Bartly about going bald which had upset her as Sean couldn't respond because Jack was a Manager. When Tony asked Sean if he had been teased by Jack about going bald, he said no he hadn't; in fact, Jack had given him a client to particularly look after who ran a wig and hair transplant business so he, Sean, had been teasing Jack about needing their services, to which Jack had agreed and laughed.

In all she raised 26 complaints all of which fell into a similar category, baseless. She then brought out the H-bomb! Having had all her complaints roundly rejected she complained that Jack had put his hand up her skirt in the office in front of everyone. The day she made that complaint Jack, who had been working virtually seven days a week totalling 70+ per week had been down in London for a particularly harrowing Tribunal where he had been physically assaulted by the Applicant (another one!) and didn't get back home until about 9.30pm. Tony rang, just before 10pm and said, "She produced another claim and this time I think you had better sit down before I tell you." Jack's phone was in the hall and there was no chair but he laughed and said, "OK, go ahead."

"She says you put your hand up her skirt in the office in front of everyone and she was so shocked she didn't say anything at the time but she now wants to report it." Jack said, "For the record I did no such thing. When does she say that happened?"

"She can't be exactly sure because she was so shocked but it was in March sometime."

"I was an Advocate then and out of the office most of the time." Jack could feel pressure building up and he said, "I can't say anymore at this moment other than to deny it utterly. I would never do such a thing; I wouldn't even put your hand up there. I shall be in tomorrow and I…" at that moment all the long hours (for years) the high miles, stress of sorting problems with a million possible solutions but only one correct one, with frightening penalties if he got it wrong and his father's recent unexpected death combined together to say enough is enough, and Jack passed out collapsing in a heap to the floor. Janet, who had been listening, grabbed the dangling phone and shouted down it, "Jack has passed out I need to phone the Dr, get off the phone."

Jack came round sometime after 3am with the Dr hovering over him. Janet and the children had managed to move Jack into the lounge and get him up onto the sofa but getting him to his bed was beyond them. A Mental Health Nurse Specialist attended the house every day to help with his recovery and to monitor the Valium, Librium and Prozac he was to take, the Prozac for more than a year; she attended daily for a fortnight and that then was gradually reduced to every other day and then stopped altogether after three months. Jack was off work for more than five months. Initially he was heavily drugged to keep him sedated and rested.

He was in the future to describe the event as being a bit like most motorists had experienced. His battery had gone flat and the engine wouldn't start and although the battery had been recharged, with the drugs and the rest, the battery never came back quite to full and so he needed to make sure that he didn't overdraw the energy in the future. (In fact he was to have two more breakdowns, 'his battery never quite coming back to full' and him drawing too much from it!) It was also amazing how quickly Jones recovered and returned to work after her company sick pay ran out just as Jack went off!

During the time he was off Tony carried out a thorough investigation and could find no evidence whatsoever to support Jones's allegations, but there was plenty to show that Jack had not done anything wrong. When Tony spoke to her to tell her that, she threw another tantrum and demanded to be moved to the Personnel Services Department. At the time there were no actual vacancies but Tony knew that they were intending to expand the department shortly thus creating some, so he arranged for the transfer. She then refused it! Tony spoke to Jack throughout his illness on a purely social and caring basis but once Jack indicated a likely return in two weeks' time Tony asked him how he felt about coming back with Jones in the department.

Jack thought about it for a couple of days and then the next time they spoke he said, "I cannot return if she is there. She is such a liar I would be frightened that if we passed on the stairs she would, if there were no witnesses, suddenly start screaming and yelling that I had touched her again or hit her or sworn at her or something. I just couldn't do it."

"Ok," said Toney, "you won't have to, she won't be in your department when you come back." Unbeknown to Jack Tony got Jones in and said to her, "You have already indicated to me that you will not work with Mr Hughes after which you asked to be moved to Personnel. When offered a post of more money plus a car you refused, is that still your position?"

She nodded immediately. "Mr Hughes has indicated he will not have you in his department because you have made an enormous number of unfounded allegations against him. Allegations I have personally investigated and found to be untrue. That leaves me in the position that one of you has to go and since Mr Hughes has done no wrong and you clearly have, it must be you. Consequently, I am terminating your employment with immediate effect. You will be paid in lieu of notice and any other monies due to you, such as any accrued holiday pay will also be paid. Please collect your personal belongings and leave now."

She should have looked surprised at least, she should have protested or something but she stood up and said, "I have already removed my personal possessions because I knew you would stick with him." And she walked out.

An application to the Industrial Tribunal arrived at the Tribunal the next day and it was 78 pages long, so long it must have been weeks in the preparation. So, her comment that she expected to be dismissed must have been true—in the event the only true thing she was ever to say over the next seven years which it would take to go through the Tribunal and Employment Appeals Tribunal!

The first problem was the first Chairman. Delta personnel always tried to find out who was to be the Chairman for any hearing. They discovered that the one nominated to hear the Application by Jones was a part-time one well known to them. The fact that he was a part-time one was not a problem. The fact that his normal day job was that of a solicitor was not a problem. The problem was that he was always in the press, media generally shouting off about how unfair it was that non-solicitors were allowed to represent clients in the Tribunal System.

Nobody in Delta felt that they stood a chance of a fair trial with him as the Chairman. Least of all Jack who had appealed three cases against him and had won all of them at the EAT. Tony had instructed an ex-Delta Advocate, now employed by a leading solicitor specialising in employment law, to write to the Tribunal asking the Chairman to recuse himself because of the danger of the appearance of bias against Delta. His name was Henry Bennett who had left to join a prominent solicitors' partnership when he had qualified as a Solicitor in his spare time. He was the chap who had shown Jack the ropes as to how Delta worked when he had first joined and Jack had a high opinion of him.

The Chairman refused so Delta submitted a complaint to the Regional President and an Appeal to the Employment Appeals Tribunal. The Regional President refused to allocate the case to another Chairman so it went to Appeal. It was 18 months before that was heard. The EAT did as it so often did which was to try to protect one of its own, but as Delta had made it discreetly known that a rejection of their appeal would result in a further appeal to the Court of Appeal, they produced a decision covering two pages of A4 as to why there was no threat whatsoever to the partiality of the decision by the oh so wonderful Chairman with an impeccable record—this despite Jack having won three appeals against the wrong decisions by this Chairman—they finished with one line that they could understand Delta's argument that his appointment could be seen by some as potentially biased, they ordered a hearing by a different Chairman!

By the time the hearing was held all six of the original Advisers had left and gone to join their previous Director of Consultancy. Shortly after Jack returned to work something started happening with all sorts of hurried meetings with the MD, Tony, an unknown person and a policeman! It turned out that the MD had managed to obtain a complete set of manuals being provided to clients by the ex-Director of Consultancy, from his new, in competition with Delta, company. Those manuals were copies of Delta's down to the last comma, full stop and a typo! Delta had therefore obtained a nuclear bomb and thrown it at him. It was called an Anton Piller Order.

The injured party to a case on obtaining an Anton Piller Order could enter the premises of the Defendant (the accused) with the police and a Solicitor and remove from their premises any items necessary to their case against the accused. It really is the atomic bomb of legal actions; it is issued without the other party being aware of it—to prevent them from removing or destroying the evidence. The MD took with him Tony, the policeman, his Solicitor, the Manager of Tribunal Admin, the Credit Control Manager, the last two both computer experts and the Personnel Services Manager.

They arrived just half an hour before closing on a Friday and spent the entire weekend examining all of their competitor's documentation system. They removed three van loads of documentation including computer discs such that once they had gone absolutely nothing was left, the dishonesty of the pair being such that they had stolen the whole Delta system for Personnel Services,

Advocacy, Advice and Health and Safety. They had even stolen all the computer programmes that Delta had just started to develop for their unique business.

When it eventually arrived at Court their defence was that, as he had written all the documents in question when at Delta, he had simply sat down and written them again at his own company. He was totally unable to explain how thousands of words, dozens of manuals, and hundreds of sample documents were absolutely identical, literally word for word including an embarrassing typo where 'the cart before the horse' had been typed as 'the fart before the horse'. He also could not explain how he had managed to write all these documents within two days of being fired from Delta, his financial records showing the first client, with those documents, being signed up on that day, nor was he able to explain how he had managed to write at least 14 different computer programmes when he couldn't even switch on a computer! It cost him and his wife thousands, justifiably.

Jack didn't think it was worth it to raise that Don had asked him to write a training programme for Advocates just days before he was fired and Jack identified it amongst the documents, he subsequently saw recovered from them. One thing Tony did comment on was how amazed he was that 19 of the 20 staff there were all ex-Delta, including. Of course, Peter Swinton, Delta's original Advice Service Manager who had left Delta breaching his notice period, which of course fitted very well with the way they did business!

By the time the Tribunal was heard Jack had recruited 12 new Advisers who were averaging 150 calls per week. When he took over as Advice Manager, he was surprised to discover that there were no known statistics to measure the performance of the department. There was a lot known about the Tribunals that had been lost because of bad advice, but nothing about performance. He knew that there were originally five Clerks entering details from the call log sheets but not what was done with the information. It turned out nothing!

No-one had ever asked IT for information, so Jack did. The average call rate was 75 per week per Adviser. Just by sitting in the department for a few days whilst running out the Tribunal cases and odd jobs for Tony and the MD during the three weeks over which those days were spread the call rate went up to 95. When he saw the figures for that period, he put the improvement down to his presence sitting amongst them meaning they had cut down on the chatting and sped up on the call answering as every time he heard a phone ringing for more than a few rings he would look up.

Also knowing that their advice was poor on occasions he had handed out to each of them a call log sheet which he had had amended. Alongside the subject matter, Conduct, Capability, Redundancy etc he had had typed two columns headed, 'Feel competent' or 'Would like further training' and had handed them out for them to assess their own knowledge. He did add that if anyone ticked 'feel competent' and they gave bad advice resulting in a loss at Tribunal they would be having an embarrassing interview with him. He had been taken ill before he had assessed those sheets and done anything in the way of training. In the event he was glad about that because he would have hated to have handed six well trained traitors to the opposition!

When the Tribunal did eventually start, more than two years after the Application had first been submitted, it was a nightmare for Jack and he had trouble sitting and listening to witness after witness telling lies about events that had never happened. One of the witnesses was Bill Jones, who when asked about what position he had held at Delta, started an absolute rant about Tony and Jack; he didn't answer the question and even when directed by the Chairman to do so continued his rant, so much so that the Chairman ordered him to stop, ordered the Clerk to escort him out of the building and instructed the two Lay Members to disregard everything he had said as 'he clearly had his own agenda'.

Well done Bill, thought Jack, as he was escorted out, *that helped my case a lot!* During this time the trial of Lord Archer for perjury along with one other was taking place. As history shows he was found guilty but the man charged alongside him was found to be innocent. Purely by chance Jack happened to see an interview with him and he used a term that was to resonate enormously with Jack. He said that as the trial had proceeded that although he knew he had not done the things, of which he had been accused, he started 'to feel the guilt of innocence'. The guilt of innocence, Jack knew exactly what he meant, he, Jack, knew he had not done the things of which he was being accused but there were so many people saying he had that he started to feel guilty for being innocent!

Because Jones had made allegations about sexual assault amongst others she had had to go first. As her witnesses told their tales, always with two of them to confirm the event, the looks directed at Jack deepened. That was until evidence was given about the Appeal heard by the MD about her sacking. Aileen Keeler, the one Jack would have liked to promote, was Jones's witness at that hearing and had taken notes. They were produced to support what was said. All the copies used in the Tribunal were copies.

They were written on a small ring pad commonly referred to as a Reporter's Notebook and the writing, grammar, punctuation etc were absolutely perfect. Far too perfect to have been scribbled down as notes in a meeting but she maintained that she had written them exactly as they had been presented to the Tribunal. As the conversation between the Chairman and Keeler, Henry Bennett representing Jack, had had a much closer look at the notes and as soon as the conversation stopped, he interrupted and asked, "Sir, following on from that conversation, may we please have a look at the original notes? As I am looking at them there are some normal paragraphs and some very long ones which is a bit unusual, especially as the long ones contain the defamatory comments in the middle of them. Looking at them very closely those defamatory, and untrue, (good one Henry!) comments seem to be very lightly written in thinner writing so I believe there may be something wrong with them that the originals can easily clear up."

The Chairman looked at the notes, holding them up very closely to his eyes and said, "I take your point Mr Bennett; where are the originals?"

Both Jones and Keeler looked very uncomfortable. Jones answered saying she did not have them and then Keeler, looking very uncomfortable, said, "They are at home."

It was obvious the Chairman was not best pleased. All of the people there, unusual to a normal Tribunal, were all experts in Tribunals and employment law and knew, or could be expected to know, that all original documents should be there to support the accuracy of the photocopies.

Before he could say something, Henry Bennett interrupted and said, "Sir, I am concerned that if the witness is ordered to bring those notes in tomorrow, she might feel tempted to lose them or re-write them over again; so, might I suggest that the MD's driver, who is present at the back of the Court, take her home now, along with the Clerk as a witness to collect them. It is only 10 minutes or so until we would break for lunch anyway and they could easily be back for the restart at 2pm."

"That's a very good idea, Mr Bennett, so ordered."

When they returned and the notes were produced the bombshell exploded! Whilst most of the notes were written in black ink, the defamatory notes in blue had clearly been fitted into the two line gaps left between all the paragraphs. When questioned all Keeler could say was that those words had been said but that she couldn't quite keep up so had had to write them in later! That clearly did not go down well with the Tribunal!

The rest of that afternoon was taken up by the last witness for Jones. Her evidence was particularly damming. It came from a Personnel Services Consultant who happened to be visiting Head Office on the day in question and had witnessed a conversation between Jack and Jones. Jones had been to visit a client, one who produced a particularly risqué newspaper featuring lots of pictures of topless models. She said she heard Jack say to Jones, did they agree to put you on page 3 and 4—a reference to Jones being very large in that area, so large in fact that she would have to be spread over two pages. In response to this Jones had said that she had told him, Jack, before that she did not like comments like that and was asking him again not to do so.

One of the pieces of advice that ACAS, and other experts always gave, was at first to ask the person who had said or done something to upset you, to stop whatever it was. That evidence did two things, it showed that she had asked him to stop in front of a witness and that she had done so before.

Rose West, the Personnel Services Consultant, was vehement in her evidence and contained lots of detail about how tears sprung to Jones's eyes when Jack spoke to her; how he was arrogant and domineering, he was power dressed in a formal, blue pinstripe, business suit, white shirt and red tie, how he stood close and domineering with his elbow on top of one of the filing cabinets and on and on. On cross examination she gave nothing away, just repeated the allegations word for word. As usual at the end of her evidence the Chairman asked the two Lay Members if they had any questions and they hadn't but he had one, "Why is it that you can describe Mr Hughes's actions in the minutest detail, you can describe what he was wearing, where and how he stood but you can't tell us when this was?"

She said, "I can," and she reached into her brief case and pulled out a diary. "It was the 6th June."

The Chairman said, "Thank you." Jack and Henry heard an atomic bomb burst as she said that. As far as the Tribunal was concerned, they heard nothing, but Henry said, "Sir, as it is just a few minutes to four o'clock I would like to start my cross examination of this witness tomorrow, rather than go part heard tonight."

The Chairman agreed and they dispersed. Jack almost ran back to the office and into his own. He kept all his old diaries in a cupboard behind his desk under lock and key. His hands were literally shaking as he unlocked it. Sifting through to find 1996 he rapidly, if shakily, opened it to the 6th June. He was out!!!! He had listed a visit to a company in Newcastle and as he read it all the details came back to him. He immediately made his way to Tony's office where Henry was describing the day's events and had just described the date as Jack walked in.

"Geroni-fucking-mo! I went to Newcastle to those Care Homes who were trying to say that the residents were the employer and not them, remember it?"

Tony smiled, "Yes, I do." The significance, Dear Reader, is that in the build up to the case Delta had sought Tribunal Orders three times where Jones had been ordered by the Tribunal to provide additional details about allegations including THE DATE(S) of the events. In all three cases although she had provided more details, always more damming, she consistently failed to provide a date as ordered claiming she only knew it was in March or April or something similar.

Delta had challenged this each time claiming that as an ex-ACAS Adviser she would have given advice about the importance of recording dates of significant events; for her not to have done so was simply unbelievable. Delta believed, of course, that she was deliberately hiding dates because she would have known, as well as Jack and Tony did, that Jack was out a lot, running out Tribunals, visiting clients etc at that time and if she quoted a date, it might be her undoing. She also said she was so upset at the time she could not make a note.

As far as Delta was concerned, she couldn't remember the date exactly because the event never actually took place, they were all lies. Jack was pestered by the police for an interview almost from day one of his breakdown because she had gone to them and made a formal complaint about the skirt incident. Jack had refused to speak to them, with his Doctor's support until a week before his return to work.

He had to attend a police station in Hyde, NW Manchester and had taken with him an Advocate who was a qualified Solicitor. She had pointed out to Jack that she did not currently have a Licence so could not represent him, but Jack explained that he wanted to get her into the meeting as a Solicitor witness and he did not want her to speak for him; just to be there as a witness because he simply did not trust the police. At the meeting was a female Detective Constable, and an old, dour, Detective Sergeant, who had obviously seen it all and heard every excuse under the sun. He explained that the interview, not under caution or arrest, would be conducted by the DC and he was merely there as a witness. The DC started with, "What have you got to say in your defence?" *Hm, she's the bad cop he thought or she has already decided I'm guilty!*

315

"My defence to what?" asked.

"You know why you are here."

"No, actually I don't. None of the telephone calls harassing me and demanding that I attend an interview explained why, each person simply said they wished to interview me about a serious allegation that had been made against me. They never said what it was. If you were one of them then you know that is true." She at least had the grace to look uncomfortable. She said, "A Mrs Jones has made a serious allegation that you sexually assaulted her by putting your hand up her skirt in the office in front of witnesses."

"And when was this supposed to have happened?" She looked uncomfortable. She clearly did not know so she had to examine her notes. Having done so she said, "April 1996."

"Ah," said Jack, "Since she told my boss that it was March and she has put May on her Tribunal application am I to understand that I am alleged to have done this terrible thing three times or is she so incompetent that she doesn't know which it is because it didn't happen?" Making it up as she went. The DC said, "She was clearly very upset by it and probably was a little confused."

"She was a senior ACAS Adviser for more than 20 years and must have advised thousands of women during that time to record the date of an event. How can she have possibly not have followed her own advice?"

"Is there anything else you wish to say," asked the DS?"

"Just for the record, it didn't happen in March, it didn't happen in April, it didn't happen in May, it didn't happen ever. She's a liar and has made the whole thing up. You," looking at the DC, "said in your opening remarks that I did it in front of witnesses. Who are they?"

She simply looked at him. "No, I thought not, there aren't any of them either because it didn't happen." The meeting ended.

"That was quite a performance," said his Solicitor. In the event the police contacted him six months later to tell him no action was to be taken about the complaint. He discovered a little while later that Jones had been told three weeks after the interview. The delay telling Jack he put down to a certain pissed off DC. But Jack knew halfway through the interview that they were hoping he would convict himself out of his own mouth which is why if you should be interested enough to re-read the above you will discover that he asked questions, AND THEY ANSWERED THEM, telling him all he needed to know so that he could challenge their evidence and formally state for the record, not me governor, not guilty!

He wondered then and gradually more as the push to recruit more women and ethnic minorities into just about every Government position, whether that female CID Officer had earned her place against male competition or whether she was the compulsory female chosen over better male Officers simply because she was a female.

As Jack, Tony and Henry considered the implications of the now named date and discussed it a plan formed. Jack was tasked with producing two bundles for them to use the following morning. Henry planned the questions for Tony and Jack to make the most effective use of them. When they started Henry told the Chairman that he did wish to cross examine Rose West so she was ordered to the witness table and reminded that she was still under oath. Henry then attacked her strongly about the date. She was sure she had the right date. He challenged it every which way but loose—was she sure it was a Thursday?

Was she sure it wasn't Wednesday? Was she sure it wasn't Friday? Was she sure it wasn't in the morning rather than the afternoon? Was she sure it wasn't the Thursday of the week before? Was she sure it wasn't the Thursday of the week after? Gradually she got angrier and angrier until Jones interrupted and complained that her witness had answered the question more than enough times and Henry should move on. The Chairman ordered him to do so and he said, "In that case, Sir, since the witness is so adamant about the date and the Tribunal issued three Orders ordering the Applicant to divulge the dates of any events and they failed to comply with any of the Orders I must ask that this Application be struck out."

Jones and her mob went daft and the Chairman ended up banging a gavel loudly and continuously until he got silence. He then said they would withdraw to consider the demand. They were out for more than half an hour and when they returned the Chairman announced that by a majority, they felt that, although the Applicant was indeed in breach of an Order, so much time and effort had been invested in the case that it should continue. They did, however, note the failure to comply with the Order and that would be taken into account if the Applicant were to win her case in the calculation of any award. In discussing this the day before they didn't believe it would be struck out for the very reasons stated by the Chairman and had planned what would come next in that event. However, they were delighted with the decision being a majority one because it meant that one at least on the Tribunal was on their side!

Henry then, in a very disappointed and downbeat voice said, "That being the case, Sir, I must beg leave to introduce an additional bundle." Jones immediately objected saying she had not seen a copy and it should have been produced weeks before. Henry then said, "Indeed, Sir, but until late yesterday afternoon we did not know the date of the 6th June so we could not have produced it before. It would be my intention to call Mr Attcliffe, the Director of Consultancy, to give credence to this bundle."

Tony took the stand and the oath and then sat down. At that stage Henry handed four copies of the new bundle to the Clerk who gave three to the Tribunal and one to Tony. Henry slid a copy along the table to Jones. Please tell the Tribunal what this bundle is."

Tony explained, "Mr Hughes and Mr Bennett came into my office yesterday afternoon shortly before 5pm and told me of the 6th June date. I immediately telephoned Reception and ordered the Receptionist to bring me the folders containing the Visitors Logs for the period September 1995 until December 1996 which are kept in a cupboard in Reception. Every visitor, even a member of our staff who are not based in Head Office, are required to sign in—primarily so we know who is in the building in the case of fire or some other emergency.

"I asked for that period because it starts with the time Mr Hughes was promoted to Advice Service Manager and for 6 months after the alleged date of 6th June. I checked all the sheets to see if Miss West had signed in on that date or some other. I only found one entry for her near that date and that was for the 6th June as she apparently claims." At that point everyone with a copy turned the pages to the 6th June and indeed there was West's signing in at 2.55pm. All of Jones's mob were by then smiling and high fiving.

"What did you do then?" I directed Mr Hughes to search his diaries, which I knew he kept in the event of queries by clients, or whomsoever, about where he was at that particular time or date. He went to his office and then came back about 20 minutes later. Besides going to his office, he had also been to the office of the Financial Director and showed me a bundle of documents."

At that, he reached into his brief case and produced a second bundle of documents. He said, "I should further like to produce these documents which we could not have produced before because of the Applicant's breach of the Order to tell us the dates." The Clerk took them from Jack and handed them out as before whilst Henry slid another to Jones.

The Chairman looked at the bundle and asked Tony, "Has the Applicant seen these?" And before Tony could answer he added, "No, of course she hasn't you have only just produced them. We will retire for 15 minutes to consider them. Stay there please," and they were gone. Jack couldn't resist, he looked at Jones and all her motley mob and gave them the biggest smile he had ever produced.

The Tribunal were back in less than 15 minutes and the Chairman said, "Unless this is the most fraudulent document in the history of the world it shows that Mr Hughes was not in Manchester on the 6th June, he was in Newcastle. You don't intend to challenge that do you Miss Jones?" The tone in which he said the last sentence was a clear indication to her that any such challenge would receive short shrift and she sensibly recognised that and agreed she did not challenge it.

Once Jack had identified the date in his diary for that year it was simple to produce the incontrovertible evidence seen by the Tribunal. The first page was a copy of a little notebook he kept in his car in which he recorded the day's date and his starting mileage each time he went on a business trip. That page showed not only the starting mileage but a mileage recorded in Newcastle and back home. For years driving from home to wherever meant that to get from SW of Stoke to anywhere in the NE he had three choices of route.

He could travel east to just past Derby on the A50 and then travel north on the M1, or he could go north up to the M62 at Manchester and then east to meet the M1 or he could go right up the M6 to just north of Penrith and across east to Newcastle—a sort of two sides of a rectangle to return the same two sides or the other two sides. In all the years he had never taken the Penrith route. It had a fearsome reputation in the winter and therefore well avoided if possible.

But this was summer and he fancied trying it. He knew his timings for the other two options, but not for the new one so he had deliberately recorded the distance on the new route and the time it had taken and then came back down the M1 to Derby and west to Loggerheads. Going up was 7 miles further and 30 minutes longer and that was recorded in his little book. The times were useful to prove his non-presence in Manchester.

The second document in the bundle was the receipt for his breakfast at the Preston Services showing him as being there at 7.20am having left home at 5.30am.

The third document was the notes he took at the client's. It was a Care Home set-up which tried to argue that the residents of the homes were the employer of the staff at each home, not the Agency, which owned the homes and provided the staff. Jack had warned them this was unlikely to fool a Tribunal. (Indeed, by the time Jack's case came to Tribunal the Care Home one had been lost Jack having been proved right!).

Following the visit Jack had written a long report which was also included. His stay in Newcastle had lasted until 2.45pm and since they had not provided lunch, he stopped at the Washington Services on the A1M for a burger 30 minutes later and home 4 hours 10 minutes after that i.e., at 7.55pm—all nicely recorded.

As the final document he included his expenses claim sheet for the meals and petrol—a document bundle impossible to forge or disprove and the very reason Jones had refused to name dates because of the danger to her pack of lies.

From that moment the attitude of the Tribunal changed from anti-Jack to anti-Jones. Before Jack could move to the witness table the female Lay Member asked the Chairman if she could ask a question of Jones. Jones was sitting at her position at the table for Representatives so the Chairman reminded her she was still under oath but could remain where she was to answer the question. The Lay Member then asked her, "Why did he put his hand up your skirt? Had you led him on in some way?

"No."

Did he fancy you?

"You'd have to ask him that."

"But he had never asked you out or asked you for a drink or anything?"

"No, never."

"So why would he put his hand up your skirt in front of witnesses?"

"I don't know."

"Why have you not called any of these so-called witnesses, you've called just about everyone else?" Silence. The Lay Member looked at the Chairman who directed her to answer.

"I don't know who saw it."

"So how do you know anyone witnessed it?" A long pause and just before the Chairman ordered her to answer again, she said, "I don't."

"So, your statement that it was witnessed cannot be verified despite the fact you said there were witnesses, a statement you made under oath earlier?" Jones didn't answer, there was no need, it was clear to everyone in the room it was a lie.

Having taken the oath Jack said, before Henry could ask him anything, "I should like to state for the record that I did not put my hand up Jones's skirt in the office, outside of the office or anywhere, the whole idea disgusts and appals me. I would add that I have here, (removing from his briefcase) a bundle of papers clipped together which are the originals of the copies submitted in the second bundle by Mr Bennett a few minutes ago. Unlike the altered and fabricated notes submitted by Keeler, they are original and unadulterated and I specifically ask they be admitted to the record as evidence of the authenticity of them to counter the falseness of the evidence given against me yesterday by West."

The Clerk collected them and handed them to the Chairman who took a few moments to look at the various till receipts, handwritten notes, typed report and mileage notebook.

"So ordered," he said, saying, "Thank you for these Mr Hughes, they will be returned to you in the fullness of time since I imagine you may need them if the Revenue ever want to audit Delta." This he said with a big smile to which Jack could only say, "Yes indeed, Sir, thank you very much."

At that point some of the Delta staff who had given evidence against Jack realised that Jones's case had just fallen apart and fearing for their own futures started to chicken out. The first one was a young man, the Senior Clerk, replacing Don's son who had left when the Anton Piller Order was served on his father who had given evidence of how upset he had been when Jack joked about the knob coming away from his desk draw in his hand. Prior to the new units being built, to which Bill Jones had taken such exception, all the furniture was second hand and some was quite dilapidated.

In this lad's case the old fashioned round knobs kept coming out of the wood when opening the drawers. Jokes referring to his knob were frequent and funny when that happened but according to the witness statement, he had read out he had been very offended by Jack's joking and it had upset him so much he had complained about it to Jack but it had not stopped. They had planned to attack his evidence by making the point that there was no difference between Jack's joking and the other staff so there could not be any value to his complaint. In this lad's case he stood up and called out to the Chairman and asked, "Can I say something please?"

The Chairman looked at him and turned to Henry and asked if he objected. He didn't, so he warned the lad that he was still on oath and said to go ahead. "I didn't actually write my witness statement, she did," and pointed at Keeler, "and I was bullied into signing it." He sat down. The Chairman looked at Keeler, but before he could say anything, two others stood up at the same time and said theirs had been too.

When the Chairman asked the lad if the statement was true, he said more or less but he hadn't been as upset as it made out. The Chairman whispered to the two Lay Members and asked Henry to move on. At which he asked Jack, "Would you like to make a general statement about the allegations made against you?"

Jack answered, "Every single one of them is a lie. I ask the Tribunal to believe what I say even though there are frequently two people making the same allegation because I have proved beyond any reasonable doubt by my evidence proving I was not in Manchester on the day the Applicant and one of her witnesses described an event that was patently untrue; all the other allegations are as untrue and a collusion between a number of people seeking to get rid of me in the hope they could return to their comfortable little chat room."

At that, Henry said to the Chairman, "Unless you direct otherwise, Sir, I do not intend to ask Mr Hughes to reply to each of the allegations which would take some considerable time, wasted time which could be better spent differently and so would ask you to accept his denial of all the allegations unless you wish a specific denial against each one?" The Chairman whispered to his two Lay Members and then said, "We are quite happy to accept Mr Hughes's well founded denials of those allegations."

"Thank you, Sir, in which case I have no further questions of Mr Hughes." Jones, of course did, but she was not good enough or quick enough to alter or adjust her pre-prepared questions and her first one was, "You heard Rose West say she heard me say to you that I didn't like suggestions that my breasts were so big that they should be on page 3 & 4, didn't you?"

"What, from more than 200 miles away—they're not that big!" The room erupted in laughter even the two Lay Members but excluding the Chairman who managed to keep a straight face but there might have been the slightest glint in his eyes! Thereafter, for her, it went from bad to worse as Jack simply kept saying to each allegation that it was as true as the one about her large breasts. Jack was sure she gave up after about half of her questions and said she had no further questions.

As Jones had had to go first Henry had to sum-up first which he did quite shortly and succinctly relying heavily on Jones having been shown to be a liar and so had at least one of her witnesses. He also made great play of the altered notes of the Appeal Hearing with the MD by Keeler. Of the other witnesses, at least three had changed their evidence so that their original allegations could not be trusted, indeed in view of the complete destruction of their evidence the Tribunal should disregard it all and accept Jack's which had been proven to be truthful. He also drew attention to the disobedience of at least one of the Tribunal Orders because she clearly could have provided at least one date.

Indeed, if she had done so the case might not have gone ahead and wasted years of time and money since the Respondents would have been able to show, at a Preliminary Assessment, that they would surely have asked for, that the entire case was without virtue since Mr Hughes was not there! If that had happened it was quite likely that the Tribunal would have issued a costs warning and that being the case, he asked the Tribunal to consider awarding their costs in the event they found for the Respondents. Jones looked like she would faint at that last and, consistent with the quality of the rest of her performance, her summing-up was poor and clearly made no impression on the Tribunal.

Not surprisingly the Tribunal reserved their decision which came through some six weeks later. Normally a Tribunal faced with one party saying black and the other white simply describes both cases in short or in detail and then states 'we prefer the evidence of'. They did not do that in this case. They took each of her points and destroyed it finishing up by actually calling her a liar. This was the strongest condemnation of a party that Jack had ever read. He, of course, agreed with every word of it! Unfortunately, they remained silent on the subject of costs!

Tony sent for Jack once they had both read the decision and after a very jolly discussion of it Tony said, "Jack, I have a request to make of you. If you asked me to sack Rose West because of the proven lies she told about that never happened meeting, I would do so like a shot, today if you like, but I am asking you not to do so. This case has gone on for more than five years and has done a lot of damage to everyone involved, you included. To sack her would probably result in another Tribunal and the attendant adverse publicity so I am asking you not to ask me to sack her."

Jack thought about it and then said, "I am very grateful for the support I have received from you and the MD when all the evidence was stacked up against me;

but I am also aware that she will be around the place from time to time which poses danger to me. Therefore, I would ask you take disciplinary action against her, a Final Written Warning would seem appropriate as she could clearly not do something like she did again and survive, so yes, no dismissal but a Final." Which is exactly what happened and on the few occasions he did see her she must have wondered why he had a smile on his face whilst passing.

Chapter 46

Over the five or so years Jack was to manage the Advice Service it grew from six Advisers when he took over to 35 when he moved on. From an average of 500 calls per week to 5,250. The rate of 'bad' advice given dropped from 2-3 per month to none for the last six months he managed it. He started by making sure that the new staff were properly trained.

He developed a training course at the start of which to absolutely disbelief he would say that he was going to teach them more in the five days (extended to eight eventually as the amount of law increased) than they had learned so far in their working lives—as most of the new people were well along in years—Jack and Delta were fortunate that the economy was failing so that the first people dismissed to save money were Personnel experts, just the people Jack wanted. It came as a surprise statement but at the end of the course Jack would refer back to that comment and ask them was it true. Never did anyone disagree!

As Delta initially was a small company when extra-curricular problems arose the MD tended to give the problem to the first Consultant he saw. Tony faced with problems in Advice with the Manager leaving to join the ex-Consultancy Director without working his notice, and with problems in the Health and Safety Department solved one of them by appointing Jack to manage Advice but this caused problems in Advocacy with the loss of a Senior Advocate to Advice!

As both departments were growing advertisements had been place for job vacancies in both Advice and Advocacy and indeed interviews had already been set-up for applicants for both departments. With the work going on from the Anton Piller Order and the problems in H&S Tony couldn't do it all so he asked Jack to carry out the interviews for both Advice and Advocacy since he had worked in both of them. This little, just do this for me, ended up being part of Jack's job for the next 13 years!

Jack became famous for his interviews which were substantially the same for Advocates or Advisers. Lasting on average one and a half hours apart from a relaxing, how did you find us/any problems getting here/hot today isn't it type of question to start with Jack only asked three questions. The first two, and they were always in that order, sought to test knowledge, the third was the lulu. The first was, 'what rights does someone have before they are even an employee?' The second was 'what additional rights do you get once you start?'

Both those tested knowledge of employment law with, mainly, the answer to question one being the discrimination rights, sex, race, religion, trade union, disability (after 1997) and age, the last one of which disappeared again quite quickly! For someone who looked as though they were struggling to relax at that point he would often introduce as his answer to the question that he thought that placing an advert for a job which said, 'no black, female, disabled, pregnant trade unionist with a limp need apply' pretty much said it all! It almost always produced a smile; when it didn't, he started to feel worried! (In later years more and variations would be added such as gender reassignment, marriage and civil partnership.)

To the second question there were literally dozens of rights gained on starting employment, far too many to list here but he expected the interviewee to be able to rattle off at least half a dozen. If they couldn't he would also start to feel concerned that they didn't have the knowledge needed for the job, but the third one was the killer because that one failed or passed them. It was, 'what is a year—if someone started on the 1st January on what date would they complete a year?'

The answer would normally be the 31st December or 1st January. (The guy who actually said the 31st October didn't get the job!) Whichever answer they gave Jack would use the other one to contradict them and get them to argue that they were correct. If they couldn't they didn't get the job. It was a test of thinking and arguing and rarely failed him.

After a few years Tony relinquished the direct managing of Advocacy and the new Advocacy Manager came to Jack and said he wanted to do the interviewing for his department at which Jack was delighted to get rid of that work load which had been pretty continuous because of their expansion. The workload for Advice was also pretty heavy for the same reason so when the Manager of Advice came to him, a few years after Jack had moved on, and said they wanted to do their own recruiting he did not object at all, he was delighted to get rid of the work load because all sorts of problems were being added to it anyway.

He wasn't so pleased when they came back six months later and asked him if he would mind restarting it because they had made several bad appointments whilst Jack had never recruited one bad one so would he help please. He did!

The Company decided to produce a magazine to go out to all clients. Produced in four editions a year the first one in draft form arrived at Jack's desk for him to check the article in it which he had written. It was fine but when he read, out of interest, the others in it he could not believe the number of mistakes of grammar, punctuation, spelling and missing words; the most common missing one was 'not' making a nonsense of the sentence! He could not resist marking each error in red ink and returning it to the Editor.

He immediately received a new job, checking and editing every document the company produced for publication irrespective of which department it was from—if it was to be published then it went to Jack first. There were quite a few occasions over the years that he was to regret his English 'O' Level distinction pass!

As word of this spread around the Chairman of the Insurance Company, one of the group which included Delta and situated in the same building, came to see Jack with a bulky document. He explained that the MD, who was also a Director of the Insurance Company had suggested he let Jack have a look at it so he could spot any errors there might be. Jack protested that he knew nothing about insurance law so felt he could not contribute but that got him nowhere. "Just check it for English," was the request! So he did, and again he could not believe what he was reading.

The Chairman said it should be straight forward as it had only been up-dated by specialist insurance Solicitors a couple of months previously, at considerable cost, and should be perfect. It wasn't! It was the furthest from it that Jack had ever seen. It was quite frankly unbelievably bad. Spelling mistakes on almost every line—given that it was clearly produced on a word processor there should really have been no spelling errors at all, but if they had used a spell checker, they had clearly not responded to what it was telling them.

There were paragraphs repeated two or three times and he found four paragraphs where one contradicted the other, twice! Jack knew the policy in the sense that it provided payment for cases which went to Tribunal where the client had taken advice and followed it—they were thus covered by the guarantee which paid for the representation costs and even the award(s) if the case was lost. What he was reading did not cover some of those items and covered some that were routinely refused by the insurance company. By the time he had finished marking errors, writing this is repeated at para x page y, writing this contradicts para x at page y, this refers to para x at page y for details but there is no para x at page y and all the other incorrect commas, full stops, lack of or extra, not needed capitals, his comments were almost as long as the original document!

He didn't see the Chairman when he took it upstairs and was quite glad to leave it on his desk! He could not resist using a post it note to say, 'I would send a copy of this to the Solicitors and ask for your money back!' He gathered the Chairman approved of his comments because he got the job of checking the letter to them too!

Chapter 47

Jack caught the flu! Not man flu, but the proper villain; he went down with it on the Saturday—typical to lose the weekend—and was off the whole of the following week and was only just recovering on the Wednesday of the second week when he received, at home, a telephone call from the PR guy. He had written a few pieces for him for publicity blurbs and had even been on Radio 4 at Drive Time talking about forthcoming legislation on disability. Coming out of the BBC Studios on Oxford Street in Manchester just after 6pm he was surprised to discover two young girls with autograph books running towards him. Wow!

No—he thought they can't be for me! And they weren't! They ran right past him into the building. Just for a moment he thought, just for a moment! The PR bloke had carried out a survey regarding the oncoming legislation and some of the figures caught the attention of the press, not as much as was to come the Christmas the year later but very considerable nonetheless. In his phone call he was wanting Jack to fly to London the following morning to do an interview on SKY about the survey.

Jack was already due to speak at a meeting of Personnel professionals that Wednesday evening and he had been fighting to get better to do the presentation to what was to be quite a large group. Delta had been recruiting many small companies as clients; mainly ones without a Personnel Officer, Manager or Director on their staff. Many of those professionals saw Delta as a threat to their jobs and it was Jack's task to persuade them that rather than a threat Delta was a benefit to them in their role.

This engagement had been set-up by PR so he wasn't surprised to find him at the end of the telephone, but he was surprised at the request he made, both to fly to London and also, he was asking Jack to travel into Manchester that morning to be interviewed again by the BBC, about a different subject, at their Oxford Road Studios. Jack had to point out that he couldn't do it. At that time of day, he would need at least two hours to get to Manchester, do the interview maybe an hour all told and then drive back home, about five hours or so and then he would need to get ready almost immediately to drive to Shrewsbury.

It was asking too much given the present state of his health so he refused the Manchester one but said he could probably do the London one as he would have been able to have a night's rest. Fifteen minutes later PR were on the phone again asking if he could do the interview over the telephone in 10 minutes time! He did it.

He drove to Shrewsbury and received a polite but less then friendly welcome. I need to break the ice here he thought. *How can I demonstrate to them that they do not have anywhere near enough knowledge? I will ask them two simple questions and I bet they don't know the answer.* Having got through the initial good evening—thank you for this opportunity etc he took a tenner out of his wallet and put it on the rostrum saying, "This is for anyone who can answer two questions. They are, your secretary comes to you and says, 'it's good news I'm pregnant', Jack slipped in a 'it might not be such good news given who the father might be' which raised a good laugh and improved the atmosphere no end. He carried on, 'I understand that I am entitled to time off for ante-natal care and that it's paid. Is that true and how much is it?'"

"Well, who can answer both?"

Not one hand went up from the 120 or so people present. Jack let the silence go on for a short while then picked up the tenner very obviously and said, "Right you can each give me the tenner you owe me as you leave later. I did mention it was a bet, didn't I?"

He got a good laugh for that. Then he said, "I suspect everyone knows that she is entitled to time off for ante-natal care but you are less sure about the pay. So, first part of the question, is time off paid? Put your hand up if you think it is?"

Hands shot up with some of the sheep following the flock. "Yes it is, but the second parts the hard one, how much. Anyone prepared to answer?"

"All of it came," came a voice. "Who agrees with that?" A forest of hands shot up with a few ditherers deciding to join the flock. "Wrong," said Jack. "Any other answers," asked Jack.

None came. "Well, the correct answer is in two parts. The first appointment with the Dr or hospital or whatever is not paid as it is not technically an ante-natal one, the others are, so every other one is paid, even to the extent that if a

Dr says a woman needs to have an hour's rest every afternoon for ante-natal care then she gets paid for that hour and as many of them as the Doctor says."

"So, let me demonstrate my knowledge further compared to yours. Has anyone got a problem at the moment that they just don't know the answer to? If you have and you were a client of Delta you would ring me or one of my Advisers, and tell them the problem seeking, of course, advice. So, here we go, ring, ring, hello Delta here how can I help?"

Silence, and then the questions started coming thick and fast. Instead of his prepared speech Jack used most of his time answering the questions. Some of them were pretty obscure so instead of answering them he threw them back to the audience betting that they didn't know and only one of them received a more or less correct answer.

He finished his presentation by using a set of words he was to come to use frequently, wouldn't it be nice if faced with a problem to which you do not know the answer, and which might cost your company a lot of money if you get it wrong, wouldn't it be nice to be able to pick up the telephone and phone someone who will know. Further you can ring and ring again because rarely can a problem be resolved with one call and then if the worst does happen and you get dragged to Tribunal screaming and kicking there is a nice friendly Advocate to represent you free of charge, and who will amazingly, even pay the Tribunal awards, should there unfortunately be some, it will cost you nothing saving only that you took advice and followed it? How do you do that? Well, my colleague at the back will be only too pleased to arrange a meeting, with no obligation and no charge, with you at your premises or anywhere you wish. Thank you for your attention."

The Rep said afterwards that he knew Jack knew his stuff but what he had just seen amazed him. He was even more pleased that he signed up 15 new, high value clients as a result!

In fact, Jack being asked to speak at meetings arranged by Reps grew and grew until the Company developed a full blown day to which businesses were invited, free of charge, and the last one Jack was to do was in Edinburgh with more than 250 people in attendance. The speakers were Jack and his boss and Jack also chaired the event.

As Jack drove back home from Shrewsbury, just after 9pm his mobile rang. It was PR to say that the BBC had been on the line and there was a problem with the recording tape, so much so that it was unusable— could Jack drive into Manchester and redo it? Jack deliberately let a few seconds go by so that he could temper his language; then he said, "Could I fuck. I am about two and a half hours drive from Manchester so I wouldn't get there until about midnight; at least an hour to do the interview and then about two hours home—say three am. I have to be up at 4.45am to be able to catch the flight to London."

So, he added, "How can I put this succinctly, no fucking chance" and rang off. Clearly it didn't wholly work because, just after he turned the lights out and settled down to sleep, the phone rang. It was the BBC ringing him directly. They explained that without his interview they would have an unsatisfactory hole in their programme so could he go to their studios in Heathrow, once his plane landed, and do the interview then? Although Jack was more than pissed off by this time, it was after all their fault that they had somehow buggered the first tape and now he was being put under a lot of pressure at a time when he should really have been in bed; and to work against being signed off by his GP as fit to work he was technically breaking the law!

But he also understood the importance of the appearance on the BBC and Sky to Delta so he agreed. Fortunately, for all concerned the guy gave Jack his mobile number because, when Jack agreed reluctantly to do it, he delivered the caveat that he was recovering still from the flu and having done what he had done that day he might suffer a relapse and be unable to do it. Never had bed been so welcome!

Jack was booked on the 8.30am flight which meant being at the airport by 7.30am for check in. That meant leaving home at 5.30am to get there and park. That meant getting up at 4.45am but what about breakfast? There would be the nearly one hour wait after check-in to grab a meal at one of the food stalls so he didn't need to get up any earlier to allow time for breakfast—yippee!

The getting up, travelling, parking and checking in went as planned and then the rest of the day was a shambles. He checked in at 7.20am and the Agent said to him that if he wished they could get him on the 7.30am flight but he would have to hurry. As he knew he would be pushed at the other end he seized her offer which meant almost running to the Departure Gate. By the time he got there he was regretting it—he was nowhere near recovered from the flu and he started to feel hot and cold and quite unwell.

To add to that the heating wasn't working on the plane—something to do with ground generators being u/s but weirdly this suited Jack because he felt so hot, he took his overcoat and jacket off. His head started going round and he suspected that was low blood sugar as a result of no breakfast and the exertions to catch the plane. In fact, he started to feel so ill he started to put his jacket on to get off the plane but at that moment the Stewardess shut the door and started the announcements. Jack was feeling awful but once they handed out a bacon roll and he ate it he felt a bit better; when the guy next to him declined his bacon roll and offered it to Jack, he felt even better!

At Heathrow there was no-one to greet him with a message board as he was on the wrong flight! He followed the directions he had been given and found the BBC Studios without too much trouble. He rang the bell. He rang the bell again. After no-one answered the third time, he rang the mobile number the guy had given him the night before and fortunately he answered. Jack explained there was no-one at the Studios to meet him and the guy asked him to hang on. When he came back, he asked Jack if there was a number pad at the side of the door. Jack found it and told him 'Yes'. The guy read out a number and asked Jack to input the four digits. He did and the door opened.

Jack then followed a sequence of instructions which ended up with him turning on all the power at a master switch, turning on the building lights, turning on the studio lights, turning on the microphone and doing the interview. He then turned everything off in the reverse order and left the building! He made his way back to the Arrivals Hall in time to find a bloke standing with a big board for Mr Hughes!

Jack introduced himself and they started walking to the car park. In the conversation the previous day the PR guy, in an attempt to persuade Jack to do the interview, said that he would be picked up in a limo at the airport so Jack responded with "Yes, a bloody Mini!" but he was assured it would be a limo. As they walked further back into the multi-storey car park so the cars thinned out until they were walking past nothing but empty spaces and there, at the far end of the car park, was a single, solitary car, a Mini!

I don't believe this, thought Jack. But he was wrong, the guy walked past and down some stairs to the lower floor and the first car they came to was a Vauxhall Senator, 3 litre top of the range, a limo indeed. It was just as well because although the bacon rolls had bucked him up a bit, he was still very fragile and bouncing along in a Mini in heavy rush hour traffic on the M4/A4 would have done him no good at all.

When he arrived, he had to process through Security and then was taken to make-up! Three chairs were in use with all of them occupied with two men and a woman being made up. One of the men was finished almost immediately so

Jack was able to sit down but then he had to stand up again as the guy was introduced to Jack as the one who was to interview him. After the introductions he said to Jack, "As I understand you are an expert on employment law could I ask you a couple of questions?"

Jack nodded. "Sky has recently got a new boss and I, and lots of others, are worried about our futures as we are not actually employees; can he just get rid of us or do we have any protection from the legislation?"

Jack looked at him and thought for a second and then said, "There are basically three types of relationships in situations like this, a full employee, such as me, paying PAYE etc, a full contractor or sub-contractor like someone who comes in and builds your extension on your house and then goes who is obviously self-employed and then there is someone in the middle between those two technically a worker. I assume you are not self-employed like my builder example because you don't employ people and run a business; you are probably called free-lance, is that correct? The guy nodded. So, can you send someone else in in the morning to do your work if you feel like it?"

The guy shook his head. "You are therefore committed to providing the work you are contracted to do personally, you can't send someone else, which makes you a worker. In which case you have seven rights (increased since then!) the same as employees, such as the right to the minimum wage, the right not to suffer deductions from your pay, the right to paid holidays…"

At that the guy interrupted him with, "Paid holidays, I'm entitled to paid holidays?"

Jack replied, "If I am right about you being a worker, and I would need to ask a bit more, but then yes you are. You might even actually be an employee by another name, for example can you just come and go as you please or do you have to submit to work place rules, do you tell them you are taking holidays or do you have to ask? But if you are a worker, you are definitely entitled to paid holidays."

The guy looked at him stunned but with a big smile on his face. He said, "Fine, thank you; we must speak again later," and walked away.

One of the make-up ladies immediately said, "Can you explain that to me again about paid holidays please?"

Jack looked at her and smiled and briefly explained why he thought free-lance people might be workers and thus entitled to paid holidays as well as other employee rights. As he did so he realised that everyone, about seven people, were hanging on his every word! As soon as he stopped talking, he was whisked away to be introduced to the Producer. He explained the set-up of the Newsroom and then asked about paid holidays. Jack laughed and explained. He was led to a small area to the side of the Newsroom—if you have ever watched Sky news, or indeed any of the other channels, in the background, visible is a room full of people and its chaos! People moving around, shouting, yelling, a real hive of frenetic energy. Jack sat quietly, in the Green Room, drinking the water he had asked for and feeling quite frail.

A young man approached him and asked him if he would like a coffee or something. Jack asked for some more cold water which was duly delivered in a polystyrene cup. As he delivered the water the young man asked if Jack was the chap who knew about paid holidays. By this time, he was wishing devoutly that he had kept his mouth shut! He was taken into the Studio by the same young man a few minutes later. He was settled at the end of an arcing table and was fitted with a microphone attached to his jacket by a hand that appeared from under the table!

Then, to his enormous dismay, the hand re-appeared and removed the cup of water Jack had placed in front of him on the table. Panicking somewhat and feeling very frail Jack didn't know if he could speak without it being broadcast, so he gestured placing a cup to his lip and mouthing water at the male interviewer. He laughed and said, "It's ok—we don't like the viewers to see plastic cups so you'll receive a nice glass in a minute, but please don't break it as it's the only one we have!" At that the hand reappeared with a lovely glass full of water.

Jack asked, "Can you give me an idea of how you want to play this, what questions etc?" The guy replied that if Jack looked at the camera immediately in front of him, there were three or four in an arc across the front of the table, he would see the questions there. In the old days the script for the newsreaders etc would be projected on a separate screen to the side or above the camera; as Jack looked a question appeared across the rectangular screen of the camera lens and before he could say or do anymore a voice announced a count down and he was on!

He was on and the interview proceeded smoothly with Jack answering competently and well until the last one. He had religiously looked between the interviewer and directly at the camera to project openness and directness when a voice in his ear peace warned of a countdown which left one question to be answered; it was very straightforward and obvious as the last one but here was one minor problem, he didn't ask it but instead asked, "Well, Mr Hughes isn't all this fuss employers are making simply just a fuss to try to prevent very worthwhile legislation for some of the most unfortunate disabled people in the country?"

As he was asking Jack took in what he was saying and put on his most serious face ready to answer which he did *whist thinking you bastard I've just got you paid holidays and that's how you thank me by ambushing me like that.*

"No, not at all, the Government brought in an Act before which was a shambles, they didn't publish it until just two weeks before it was due to come into force; an Act which required major negotiations with, especially, the trade unions which took the best part of six months. There were so many problems that the Government apologised—a very rare thing indeed and promised it would not legislate in haste and repent at leisure in the future. This time the legislation came into force two days ago and they have not yet published it; further they don't know when they will. It's a complete and utter shambles."

The Producer cut to a recorded piece and Jack was out the door looking for his Driver, clutching his coat and briefcase before he knew where he was—talk about the bum's rush! He found his driver waiting in the car park who asked him where he wanted to go, he pointed out that he had been booked for the day and he could take Jack to the West—end for Christmas shopping if he wished—before running him back to Heathrow.

By this time Jack was only just hanging—on by his boot straps and said, "No, please take me straight to Heathrow," which he did. Jack was not booked on a flight until 4.30pm but he hoped he might be able to get an earlier flight as he had in the morning. When he arrived at Heathrow, he couldn't see a check-in desk for 'normal, i.e., outside lavy class passengers' only for Gold and Silver. One of those desks was empty of passengers with two women sitting there, so he walked over, speeding up to beat someone else who was also heading to the same one and, just beating him, asked one of the women where he should go to change to an earlier flight.

She gave him quite a peculiar look, which he put down to his race to get there, and she said, "Oh, we can do that here, Sir." She did the necessary and then said he needed to be quick getting to his gate number as they were just about to board. Feeling a little like death warmed-up Jack hurried to the seating area by his gate and gratefully sat down. He was on the end of a row of seating and sitting opposite him on the end of a facing row was an attractive young lady. Next to her were the family from hell. Two children somewhere around 12-14 years old, with two parents beyond them, were arguing and shouting. The boy shook a can of Pepsi and opened it spraying pop everywhere. His sister tore open a bag of crisps which scattered everywhere. Jack caught the eye of the young woman and did a look with his eyes at the family and then upwards to indicate, goodness gracious me and she responded by getting up and walking away!

Jack was more than surprised but only for a moment because a man who had been sitting on her equivalent seat, but a row further away got up, came over and sat down opposite Jack and said in a very camp voice, "Hello." As he was wearing a pale pink suite with a dark pink shirt and a yellow tie Jack became slightly worried at what was to come next. Fortunately, the tannoy sprang to life announcing Jack's flight. He leapt up, called out, "that's my flight," and shot away as fast as he could! Standing in the queue to hand his ticket to the Attendant he glanced in the mirror by the side of him and was horrified to see that he was still wearing the exaggerated make-up applied for his interview at Sky! He spent the entire time on the flight hunched in a window seat scrubbing his face with his handkerchief.

Arriving at Manchester he hurried to his car and sped off towards home. His mobile rang and answering it he found PR on telling him what a wonderful job he had done and asking if he was coming into the office. He told them no because he felt so unwell and was going home to bed at which the MD came on and congratulated him on his performance and wished him a quick recovery. In the car Jack could see in the mirror that he had not managed to remover very much of the make-up at all and going into the office in such a state was a real NO-NO!

After that Jack became the go-to-man for latest employment law news for the media for the next ten years. He wrote a 'Dear Doctor' article answering a written in question on employment law issues for the Sunday Times virtually every weekend for the next ten years. During that time, he, or the Sunday Times, only ever received two complaints. In one answer he had written a 'how to recruit' for yourself article to which a female complained that he had not included in his answer that employers could always use Recruitment Consultants. Speaking to her on the telephone Jack asked her if she had the article in front of her. She said she had, so he asked her to read the first sentence of it to him. She started reading it out and then stopped. Jack let the silence run and then said, "So that's why" and hung up.

The first words were, 'I am fed-up with the poor quality of Recruitment Consultants and want to do my own recruiting, what should I do?' The other complaint came from the Disability Rights Commission (DRC, as was!) Jack had answered a question from an employer asking if he could advertise for, and recruit, only disabled people. The simple answer was 'yes' but Jack had to fill a 500 word spot so, besides saying, 'yes,' he expanded his answer to advise that if he employed able bodied staff he needed to be careful because positive discrimination for one group was automatically negative discrimination against every other group—a reason why Jack disagreed with positive discrimination in principle—so he advised that the employer should meet with his staff and explain what he wanted to do and why.

He should give them the opportunity to say what they thought and ask if there were any objections. If there were he should consider what they were and what could be done to remove them. It was a bit difficult always to give in-depth advice in just 500 words but he did his best. He was staggered to get the Sunday Times on the phone saying that the article was wrong, it was against the law to do as Jack had advised. Jack asked who exactly from the DRC had been on the phone so he could contact them. After he had put the phone down, he considered what to say and then thought, *no*, I am going to put this in writing. So, he wrote to them, copy to the Sunday Times saying,

I am in receipt of your complaint about my answer to a question in the Sunday Times on (date/etc) and am staggered at your ignorance and cheek. Section (quoted) specifically states, unlike all the other anti-discrimination laws, that positive discrimination is allowed. One of your own publications even advises, as did I, that it would be best practice to ensure your other staff know what you propose and are consulted on it. Why does your right hand not know what the left hand has written? I expect a written apology by return, to me and the Sunday Times, and I am quite prepared, at a fee, to come along and teach you what you should already know.

Yours etc

He never did receive one, Government quangos are notorious like that but he did get a nice note from the Sunday Times thanking him for his answer to the complainant!

It became a standing joke with PR that if Jack was to attend a radio interview he would only do so if he would receive the services of a make-up artist.

He carried out one interview with Granada in his own office well he actually did quite a few but one of them stood out in that as they were setting-up the Cameraman, looking at Jack's eyebrows, long, bushy and quite white said, "Well, at least we won't need the reflection screen with those eyebrows." (A white screen used to reflect light onto the face and eliminate harsh shadows.) Jack spun his back to him on his chair, curled both eyebrows up into a Devil like curve and spun back saying, "You mean these!" It got a laugh but he did the interview just like that with these two long, arched eyebrows prominently displayed!

Chapter 48

Jack ran Advice for more than five years and it grew from six Advisers to 35 in that time. He introduced a management structure starting with just an Assistant Manager, Malcolm George, who he had originally interviewed for an Advocate's role. A mature man who had retired relatively young from the NHS he wanted to try the role. Jack, having read his CV and interviewed him wanted to appoint him as his Deputy but he declined Jack's offer.

Jack, knowing how he had started to struggle with the very long hours and high mileages suspected that he would become disillusioned with the role quite quickly so he offered him the role of Advocate and that he could change his mind at any time, but not after too long a time, and join Jack instead. Jack was right, Malcom joined him quite quickly and the two of them made a tremendous team developing the department.

But during this time Jack had handed to him other duties which expanded his roles enormously. He had started to become in involved in sales. He was invited to attend the first Sales Conference after his appointment as the manager of Advice. In taking over he was appalled to discover how little management information existed and had put in place a system to tell him the numbers of calls handled by Adviser, the subject matters covered and any problems identified as bad or inadequate advice. He was also appalled at the paperwork that arrived from the Reps' deals.

They only had to complete one form, to contain quite basic information such as the Company name, address, phone number, name of primary contact and any matters to note. He heard one of his Clerks complaining to the Senior Clerk that there were three companies of the same name but as the Rep had not given the address or phone number, she could not identify who was the real customer. Jack stopped and asked a few questions and was shown every single contract, about 24, that had arrived up from Accounts had essential information missing.

He was angry, very angry, those lazy bastard Sales staff were paid, with commission etc, more than three times his salary and they couldn't even be bothered to fill in a simple form. He took all 24 with him to see the MD and said he intended to change that at the Sales Conference in a week's time—as the Financial Director was with the MD at the time and whose department also suffered with no love lost for Sales people, who did manage, however, to complete their commission and expenses claims properly—was quite happy to agree.

So came the big day, Jack stood up in front of nearly 200 people and introduced himself by standing up with an A4 folder on the front of which he had had printed, 'How to talk' in large capital letters. As he held it up for them to see he said, "In here it says that I should start with a joke or funny story but I don't know any but I can tell you a true story of a problem we are having to advise on at the moment to illustrate the sort of thing Advice does. Those golfers among you cannot fail to have noticed the large, high walled old mansion at the far side of the course surrounding this hotel. It is, in fact, a Nunnery. Their Doctor, an outsider who comes in to treat Nuns in need, became very concerned about their regime causing health problems. Poor diet, not much more than bread and water, long hours on their knees causing housemaids knee in almost all of them, lack of sleep because of prayers through the night and hard physical work in the gardens growing their own food etc.

"To cut a long story short he approached the Health and Safety Department Manager who ended up contacting the Pope because of the refusal of the Mother Superior to act on any of the recommendations he made. The reference to the Pope raised a few giggles and maybe a suspicion that this wasn't quite a true story. The Pope ordered and the Mother Superior obeyed. One of the recommendations was for exercise or sport. Sister Maria decided she would like to play golf, having glimpsed golfers over the wall and despite every effort of the Mother Superior to dissuade her she insisted that was what she wanted to do.

"Come the big day she was back in less than an hour in a dreadful state— upset, crying and shaking. The Mother Superior asked her whatever had happened and she wailed that golf was a terrible sport it had made her swear and throw her club down. The Mother Superior again asked her what happened. Sister Maria said she had been on the first tee and had hit the ball very well— she knew that because the Professional, a woman insisted on by the Mother Superior, had said she could tell by the solid thwack of the hit. Unfortunately, the ball only went about 20 or 30 yards before hitting a pigeon flying by. 'Ah, that's why you swore' said the Mother Superior. 'No, no' said Sister Maria, as the ball dropped on the course a squirrel ran out, grabbed it and ran off with it. 'Ah, so that was when you swore.' 'No, no,' just as the squirrel ran off a Bustard swooped down and grabbed the squirrel and flew off with it. 'Ah, so that was when you swore.' 'No, no,' because as the Bustard, Bustard repeated Jack, emphasising the 'u,' the squirrel dropped the ball and it rolled onto the green about a foot from the hole. The Mother Superior looked at her for long seconds and then the Mother Superior said, 'You missed the fucking put, didn't you?'"

It took a few seconds before the audience roared! Jack was to become famous for his I don't know any jokes/funny stories introductions.

He then spent some time explaining his role and how he could help sales. He offered that if they were with a difficult potential client they could demonstrate the service, if the client had a problem, by ringing Advice and getting someone to demonstrate the service. Jack pointed out that there was little danger to this because rarely could a problem be solved by one piece of advice so it may well hook them into the system for the further advice necessary—which would not be free!

He also pointed out that with so many Sales people on the road, it would be impossible for his Advisers and Clerks to remember all their names so when, and if, they rang in if they simply said this is Graham Black it would not mean a thing to the recipient, they needed to clue them in by saying something like, 'high this is your happy Salesman from Manchester or wherever' otherwise in front of a potential client one of my staff might say 'who the hell are you'!—not a good start!

He also pointed out that it might just be that all the Advisers were on the phone when you call—he hoped they would be—so a Clerk would probably answer and he had set-up a system that the Clerk would give the message to the first Adviser to come off the phone, they would therefore be the priority to ring back. All this went down very well as his predecessor in the role had seen Sales personnel as a pain in the arse and did everything possible to avoid and hinder them.

He then hit them with the cost of this service to them. He projected onto the screen a copy of the Sales Contract that he had seen with the Clerk. He said nothing. He then showed 11 more saying nothing. Every one of them was equally appalling and missing almost all information. He then took from his briefcase 12 envelopes containing the 12 orders which had the Sales person's names on them. He called them out one by one and handed them their envelope.

He then said, "I have stopped all those contracts; we will not be processing them, we will not be contacting them if they have an urgent Tribunal and you will not be getting any commission until they are completed properly. You only have one form to fill in, one fucking form, and you can't be fucking bothered to do that. So now you know the penalty. Those 12 came in on Tuesday. Any since will be posted back to you and none, I repeat, none will be processed if they are not completed properly." There was dead silence in the room.

He let it run—silence can be good—and then he said, "I have said all I want to say and I mean every word of it including what the Mother Superior said and although my book, holding up the How to talk says I should finish with a joke or funny story I cannot do that as I do not know any but I can tell you of another problem we are dealing with for a golf club. They needed to discipline a member of their staff but didn't know how to do it so one of my Advisers helped them."

Apparently, the Chairman was about to play a stroke when the tannoy burst into life and a voice said, "Would the gentleman on the first ladies' tee kindly move back to the first gentlemen's tee please."

The Chairman ignored the voice and continued to address the ball. At which the tannoy clicked on again and the voice said, "Would the man on the first ladies' tee move back to the first men's tee."

The Chairman again ignored the tannoy and practiced a swing at which the tannoy burst into life again with the voice saying, "Oy, you, move back from the ladies' tee to the men's one," at which the Chairman threw down his club and screamed at the top of his voice, "Will the fucking prat on the tannoy shut the fuck up and let me play my second shot!" Some of the audience had twigged quite quickly that this was a joke too, but at the punchline it brought the house down. Jack finished by saying we advised sacking the Chairman! He also almost never received an incomplete contract in the future.

Jack was to speak regularly at every conference for a couple of years and then was asked to chair them when the original, retired salesman, who had done the job for a number of years including the Induction Training of new Sales personnel, had to fully retire on health grounds. Jack also took over planning the, and delivering of, a lot of the Induction Training, updating it to include more knowledge of the product the Sales person was selling.

A year or two after that he was asked to take on, in addition, the role of Compliance Manager. There had been a lot of miss-selling of insurance as well as the selling of individual's data, in the country as a whole, and the Government had stepped in to legislate. As the guarantee to provide free representation at Tribunal and even to pay the award, if lost, was insurance-based Delta came within scope and Jack was stuck with it! He also sifted applications when Sales roles were advertised and selected the ones for initial interview. He would then discuss the best candidates with the MD and sit in on the final interviews with him. It was a huge workload and great responsibility.

Jack also gradually became overwhelmed and unable to cope. With all of the aforementioned as well as the work involved in managing, growing and developing Advice he was becoming inundated with this other work amounting to an entire job in its own right. He was still the go to man for the PR department who were calling on him every week, usually at very short notice. He was committed to writing a 500 word, 'Dear Doctor' column in the Sunday Times, every week, answering employment law questions sent in. PR one Christmas published a survey showing that some 80% or so of employers intended to ban Christmas decorations and festivities because it might offend other religions!

Jack did his first live interview on Drive Time for Radio Essex at 6.50am and then 26 more during the day—a mix of radio, TV recorded interviews on the telephone or in his office. He finished with a call from Radio New Zealand at 7.10pm as he drove home—hands free of course! He was absolutely shattered. The following morning, he assured the PR Manager that if he ever had to do that again he would take the survey and insert it so far up his fundamental orifice that it would damage his surveys for ever!

Eventually Jack felt overwhelmed. He had never fully recovered from his original breakdown and he could feel the stress building up to a level he could not reduce. He was also starting to struggle with some other health issues which the Doctors were unable to immediately diagnose. So he went to Tony, shut the door, and told him. Tony's response was to say that the only thing that surprised him was how much longer he had coped than he had expected! It was clear that there was a need for someone of Jack's enormous experience to carry out a new role the Board had been considering.

As the Company had grown so to Tony himself was struggling with multiple demands particularly to deal with the amount of new legislation being proposed and introduced. So, Jack became the Senior Employment Law Development

Manager and Compliance Manager giving up managing Advice. Jack had hoped, and recommended, that his Deputy, Malcolm, would take the role but he didn't want it and took retirement again having retired once before! Jack and he continued to meet for lunch for many years.

In his new role he continued his involvement in training new Sales people in Compliance and assessed their performances by random monitoring. He was also still very much involved in training new Advisers and Advocates—his course had grown from five to eight days and was showing signs of needing to be increased by a further day, especially the law and case law appertaining to the Transfer of Undertakings, Protection of Employment Act (TUPE) was coming under the influence of the EU, and not for the better. Disability was also becoming a major issue. He started receiving the proposed Government Green Papers and assessing their impact as to whether they needed to respond or not.

One issue which was causing major concern to the Company related to a proposal to remove the address of Respondents from Tribunal Applications when they were released to the public as this was a major source of leads for the Company.

An employee went into the Office of Tribunals every working day and noted the new cases. That was telephoned to HO and the Telesales Team immediately started contacting the Respondents to try to set-up an appointment for the local Sales Rep to go in and attempt to sign them up. In the very early days almost 100% of new customers were obtained that way and whilst they had moved on somewhat with other methods of finding leads the Tribunal system was still a very significant part of their attraction of new clients.

Jack responded to the Green Paper pointing out that the withholding of the private address of the Applicant was sensible—they would find that out if they needed it once they signed up the employer—but the Respondents were businesses who advertised their services openly and to hide the address from another business who needed to contact them as part of their business was plainly wrong.

In time, the Government published the results and claimed that there was pretty well universal agreement to hide the addresses of both parties. Both Jack and Tony felt that this was a downright lie and they considered what to do about it. It ended up with Jack travelling to London and asking to see the responses to the Green Paper, the consultation document, in the library of the Department responsible. He was eventually handed 165 responses—not very many considering. He actually wrote down the name of everyone who had responded and a brief note of what they said. One reply was from a Labour MP who simply wrote 'don't do it' to six Citizen Advice Bureau Companies, one of which was for the proposal, and five against. He even found a copy of the response he had drafted which had gone out under Tony's name and upon which someone had scrawled 'ignore'.

The analysis that Jack carried out when he got back was that the numbers against hiding the address of Respondents was considerably more than those in favour—about 65-35%! So, the MD wrote to their MP complaining about the Government's dishonesty. Since their MP was a Labour Minister, they did not expect to get a reasonable response but she replied she would like to visit them and sort the matter out!

Jack was warned that he was to attend the meeting but not to speak unless either the MD or Tony asked him to. The Minister was all sweetness and light—clearly, they had decided that charm was the way to deal with these upstarts challenging them. She even asked that they address her by her first name rather than 'Minister'. She started by explaining that she had looked into the matter and was certain that the announcement they had made was a correct analysis of the returns they had received, for example the TUC, their paymasters of course, were against publishing the addresses.

The MD looked at Jack and nodded so Jack said, "Minister," she interrupted to ask him to use her forename, Jack continued, "Minister, that isn't quite true; the TUC did say that Applicant's addresses should not be published but they had no objection to the Respondents' being published as they were businesses—which is exactly out position."

She looked flustered and Jack thought, *I bet she's wondering how I know that and if I am right.* She did not reply to that but said that the CAB did not agree with it either and that meant two major representatives of the people were against it. "Not so," said Jack, not waiting for the MD, "Six CABs out of almost 400 nationally replied which firstly indicates that the vast majority couldn't care less and of the six, only one was against publishing both sides addresses, the other five were happy for the Applicant's to be hidden but not the Respondents." She looked at him and the A4 pad in his hands from which he had obviously read the data.

"What else do you know," she asked. Jack looked at the MD who nodded and Jack said, "Well, Minister, out of the 165 responses received by that Department…" she interrupted again, "How do you know that?"

"Because I went down to their library where they are stored and went through them." She looked astounded. "Only three, including the CAB one I have quoted, said the address of neither parties should be published, 96 said that the Applicant's should be hidden but not the Respondent's which makes up 99 and the rest expressed no opinion but did comment on the other points raised in the Green Paper."

At that he turned to the last page of the A4 folder on which he had handwritten the relevant quotes from their replies, some 45 pages in all, and the final figures analysed as he had just described. He then said, "The figures analysis published by that Department is completely at odds with the facts, how do you explain that?" At that she stood up and as she walked out, she said, "I can't but I will!" They never did hear from her and the law was changed to hide the details of both parties and that remained until the Tories won the next election and changed it to publishing the Respondent's addresses. So much for the honesty of politicians!

Chapter 49

The Company was growing at an enormous rate and had hoovered up almost all the potential Applicants in the shape of especially, potential Advisers. Most of the existing ones were mature Personnel professionals, many redundant from struggling companies and delighted to be employed in their 50s and 60s when they could have expected to be sent to the scrap heap! Jack was called to a meeting where it was announced that they had taken over a company in Leicestershire which was in the same field as themselves but much smaller.

It also had the advantage that it was within the same catchment area as their main competitor who was known to be struggling financially and whose staff might be looking to jump ship to safer waters, so they hoped this would be a rich source of recruitment. The deal having been done Jack and Tony drove down to see what they had.

The offices were in the middle of the town but everything after that was downhill. A few minutes conversation with the Advisers revealed that their knowledge was not up to the standards needed and attained by the Delta people. So, Jack had to run two courses, one for the existing Advisers and one for the eight they recruited two weeks later. One of the most detailed lessons was that relating to Disability. Jack had attended the Sky Studios in West London to talk about it and the implications to employers of the new law.

He started with an explanation that the old system, introduced just after the Second World War, was designed to force employers to employ disabled people, not just ex-service people, but civilians injured by war as well, who were being left on the shelf. The original requirement was that every employer should have at least 3% of their work force as disabled people—even with certain jobs only to be carried out by disabled people, such as Lift Operators or Car Park Attendants. The problem was that as time had gone by the disabled by war people had retired or died off and the numbers left represented far less than 3% of the working population, indeed Jack had never been able to recruit anywhere near that percentage even though he wanted to.

The definition of someone as disabled was also to change. Originally an individual would be assessed at a special clinic run by and assessed by Doctors—this was expensive, time consuming and they were short of Applicants as the war population grew older and either retired or died off! The Government came up with a new definition of disability and estimated that some 5% of the population would qualify! The definition was that someone was disabled if:

They suffered from a mental or physical impairment (this was wrong for a start because it should have been 'and/or' since people, which included Jack, could suffer from physical and mental impairments at the same time!) which substantially, adversely, affected daily life long term.'

The biggest faux-pas was that although they gave guidance on what substantial meant, they also defined long term as being a year or more. Both of these definitions were substantially altered by 'interpretations' by Tribunals and the EAT but worst of all was that whether a problem was to be defined as a disability was to be decided by Tribunals and not Doctors!

Having described why the law had arrived at where it currently was and what each of the sections meant, Jack would then start with a list of medical problems and get the class to analyse whether the problem fitted the definition and was therefore a disability. He started at the head and worked down with:

Ill mental health such as Depression lasting more than a year.

Hearing impairment, permanent requiring hearing aids.

Skin cancer, both Squamous Cell Carcinoma and Actinic Keratosis.

Nasal drip at the back of the throat causing severe, crippling coughing.

Hiatus Hernia.

Obstructive Sleep Apnoea.

Atrial Fibrillation (heart beats too fast and stops erratically).

Pacemaker.

Arthritis of the ankles, hips, facet joints of the spine and shoulder.

Hay fever (severe).

Enlarged prostate with severe side effects.

Diabetes Type 1.

Type 2.

Gout.

(The original list did not include the type of skin cancer, the sleep apnoea or pacemaker, but I have added them as they were diagnosed for Jack a short while later!)

Any questions they asked regarding the substantial adverse effect to daily life Jack answered making sure that each time it pointed towards it being a disability. He would then ask them if someone applied to them for a job and had one, no say all of those disabilities described on their application form, would they employ them—and he wouldn't tell authority if they said no! Time after time all the attendees would say they would make an excuse and not employ such a person, even if they had only one of them.

That's a pity Jack would say because it means none of you would offer me a job—with the exception of Type 1 diabetes I have all of those disabilities. I arrive at work at about 7.30am and I leave after 6pm, longer hours than anyone bar the Director of Consultancy. As an Advocate driving a thousand miles a week outside of 9-5 and often on Saturdays coming home and Sundays leaving for somewhere far afield, was quite normal. So, the point he forcefully made was not to look at what someone could not do but to look at what they could! A lesson he preached frequently and loudly.

Chapter 50

His final role was one which Jack enjoyed although it had its unpleasant moments. He was still involved in training Advocates and Advisers but his role training and organising the training of Sales personnel changed slightly with his becoming the Compliance Manager as well as his other duties. This role besides training was also a monitoring and correcting/chastising one. Sales people were always willing to bend the rules for a sale—even to break them if necessary.

The problem with that was breaking the law attracted heavy penalties and it was Jack's job to ensure they didn't do it. He wasn't on too many Christmas card lists as a result. He even had one new start call him a liar. The guy was due to meet Jack at 9am but turned up at 10.30 breezing in with casual 'sorry, fog.' Jack was not happy. So, he said, "Why are you late?"

Looking more than annoyed, the Rep said, "I've already told you, fog."

"That's not a reason, that's an excuse. The fog was forecast last night—you should have left to be here on time."

The guy decided to fight rather than apologise and said, "That's rubbish. Everyone is late this morning."

"I wasn't, I was here at 7.30am as usual because I left half an hour earlier knowing that there would be slow moving traffic. In fact, I have never, ever, been late in the 48 years I have been working. Your Telesales will have worked hard to get you an appointment to sell Delta to a senior decision taker, you breezing in with a 'sorry fog' having kept him waiting an hour and a half creates an awful impression; even if he will see you that late, and it is highly unlikely to lead to a sale. I suggest you sort yourself out and quickly."

The guy looked at Jack for several moments and then said, "I don't believe you."

"About what?"

"Never being late." Remembering the power of silence Jack gave him the stare for several minutes while he brought his temper under control and then said,

"I haven't, you were, get out and take these notes with you. Fail to learn them at your peril." And threw him out! That day, a Friday, was the last of two weeks of his induction at Head Office.

The following Wednesday he received a call from his Area Manager who asked for Jack's opinion of him. Jack described his meeting and finished with, by the way I haven't signed him off as competent to sell insurance so he will have to come back here for that and apologise profusely as well! The Area Manager laughed and said, "He won't be coming back, he was late Monday, Tuesday and this morning meeting me and I was just about to ask you if you agreed with my giving him the bullet?"

"Do I really need to answer that?" asked Jack? The phone went dead and so did the bloke's career with Delta.

Jack continued to be the spokesperson for Delta and employment law. He was asked to speak at a conference of Travel Agents in Limerick, South Western Ireland. It meant flying into Dublin to meet the Rep who had arranged for Jack to speak and then driving with him almost right across the country—it would have been easier to fly to somewhere nearer Limerick but the Rep wanted to brief Jack, so drive it was. In those days, other than a short distance of motorway near Dublin, Ireland was all poor main roads and it took so long they were late arriving for the pre-conference drinks!

Not that Jack minded as he was dead tired and when he saw the state of the attendees the following morning, he was quite glad they had. He had made a point of going into the main conference room where he would be speaking, to check it out—the old motto, time spent in reconnaissance is rarely wasted, was again proved to be true as he was able to hand his memory stick to the Technicians for them to set his presentation up ready for him. The Rep had set-out that he would do the first half of the 30 minutes to sell Delta and then Jack could deliver the details to show their competence. In fact the Rep chickened out—the room, with more than 500 seats set out, was enormous and the thought of being in front of all those eyes scared the hell out of him.

Jack was positioned at the end of the front row, with a woman speaker next to him who was to speak immediately before him. She was scribbling on paper all morning and he realised that she was preparing there and then for her delivery. She was introduced to the audience and it became clear that she was, in fact, an ex-Minister of the Irish Government who had just lost her seat in a recent election and had been given a role in Government even though not elected.

She was dreadful, rambling, contradicting herself and highly, offensively political. She clearly had no sympathy with business and said a lot that was contentious to the audience who were all business people. But worse, she over ran by more than 20 minutes and since Jack was the last speaker before lunch, he knew he could not over run in turn. He was also a bit pissed off that the Chairman didn't stop her but he didn't so Jack had to think how to curtail his delivery while at the same time doing a proper job.

He walked up onto the stage as he was introduced and quietly said 'good morning, ladies and gentlemen.' As he expected he only received a few muttered replies so he repeated himself, 'GOOD MORNING, LADIES AND GENTLEMEN.' And he got a much livelier response. *Got 'em'*, he thought; *it always paid to make them respond to grab their attention,* He followed with, 'I checked all this technical doodadery, pointing at the screens and stuff but I thought for one minute that these, pointing to his hearing aids, had gone on the blink. Now I understand that I should start with a joke or funny story, and he then gave his delivery about I haven't got one but I can tell you about a problem that we are dealing with at the moment relating to the new disability legislation.

'Your Government has not yet published how you intend to introduce the new EU stuff so it might turn out different for you but the problem we have is this. A lady went to her Doctor to complain that her husband was no longer carrying out his husbandly duties and she wanted to complain and get a solution. 'Well, the solution is easy' said the Doctor 'but I don't know about the complaint. The solution would appear to be that I prescribe some Viagra tablets for him'. She immediately said that that wouldn't be any good because he wouldn't't/couldn't take tablets. The doctor thought for a moment and came back with, 'we could always make it an Irish Viagra by grinding the tablets up in his coffee'.

At that the woman's eyes lit up and, forgetting about the complaint, off she went. A few days later the Doctor happened to be walking along the high street and who should be coming the other way but the lady in question. Greeting her he asked how things were and she said in reply, 'good and bad, and I want to complain'. Whatever is the problem he asked her and she said, 'well, I ground up three tablets, just to be sure, and put them in his coffee like you said. After about 10 minutes his eyes started to sparkle and after another 10, he suddenly jumped up and tore off all his clothes, then mine and proceeded to do his duty three times'.

The Doctor looked at her for a while and came back with, 'but surely that's what you wanted, where's the complaint?' The woman looked at him and said, 'I want to complain that I can never show my face in Starbuck's again'. The room erupted much to Jack's satisfaction and relief he wasn't sure how the reference to Irish Viagra would be received! He carried on with a shortened delivery about the real problems they were facing and how they were resolving them and finished with his pitch selling Delta. He received much the loudest and prolonged applause of the morning.

Even so the room emptied pretty quickly but not before the Rep ran out of cards and had to ask those interested in a visit by him for their cards for him to contact them. As Jack walked past the female who had pinched half his time, she hissed at him, "Remind me not to share a platform with you again, you made me look like a right amateur prat."

Jack looked at her for a moment, a bit stunned by what she had said and then he replied, "Yes, I did," and walked away.

They did not have time to stay for lunch as Jack had to get to Dublin for the last flight. They only made it with 20 minutes to spare—its's a long way from Limerick to Dublin. The flight back was uneventful until they came over the North Wales coast and the fireworks and rockets started coming up at them. The Pilot came onto the microphone and commented that the fireworks, it being the 5th November, were nothing to worry about! At first, they were way below them but as they came down for Manchester Airport they were bursting above the plane and Jack was quite glad of the two Nuns sitting in front of him praying like they didn't really want to go to Heaven just yet! And they didn't!

He had been appearing in the press and media quite a lot but he did not expect the next two events. His phone rang one day and Reception announced in a reverential voice, "Jack, it's the CABINET OFFICE on the line for you."

"No, it isn't," he said, "It'll be a Rep playing a trick I bet, but put him on anyway." The phone clicked and Jack said, "Hello, Jack Hughes speaking, how can I help you?"

The chap introduced himself and then said, "I'm speaking from the Cabinet Office and we have set-up a Small Firms Committee to look into the problems caused by legislation for small companies and it is clear from your appearances on the television and in the press that you have a considerable understanding and familiarity with the problems such firms face and I would like you to address the committee for say an hour and then answer questions for an hour—would you be willing to do that?"

"Yes." So, they arranged a date and Jack duly appeared at the time and place appointed. He initially thought that the Cabinet Office might be in No 10 and he fancied trying to arrange a photo of him going in but it turned out that the Cabinet Office was round the corner and that had not the same attraction! He was taken into a room that was set up with a horseshoe shaped table around which the Committee sat and a smaller table across the open mouth of the horseshoe at which Jack sat.

After the introductions and Jack was asked to deliver his presentation, He reached into his wheeled briefcase and started extracting book after book. The first one he pulled out had a green cover and he introduced it as a Butterworth's Employment Law which he started using twenty years or so ago. It was quite a slim volume no more than 3/4inch thick. He then pulled out another one which was over 2 1/2inches thick. He told them that was it now and that was how much just employment law had expanded and that in just the last 10 years there had been more than 270 pieces of legislation regarding employment law by the present Government. He was challenged on this by the Chairman who tried to say that it wasn't more than three or four at the most and all of them justified.

Tony, Jack's boss had kept a running total of the legislation since Delta had been set-up in the 80s, and Jack had collected a copy from him. He handed a wad of them to the Clerk to hand them out. Once he saw that the Chairman had read it, he said, "As I was saying, if you look back up the list you will see just how many there have been and since 1960 and the Redundancy Payments Act there have been hundreds and hundreds of laws passed affecting employment which employers have to cope with. That is just employment law. I want you to imagine you are the chap I am representing in Tribunal next week. He owns four lorries; he drives one himself and employs three drivers to drive the other ones. His wife runs the office. His real work is running the business but he has to know all that lot," pointing at the Butterworth's, "and he also has to know," and he pulled out of his briefcase two Tomes on accounting, one on Health and Safety, Transport Regulations and a few other massive books he had pulled off the shelves in Accounts and all the other departments at Delta.

He stacked them on top of one another but had to hold the stack to prevent it falling over and then he let it go so that the collapse made an even bigger impression than the pile itself. "You have whole departments to advise you on all those things, he doesn't so what he does is, he ignores them and hopes he doesn't get caught out breaking some of them. If you really want to help such people you have a number of options, exempt small companies entirely, reduce and simplify the law enormously or provide help and advice, such as Delta does, either free or for a minimal fee."

He answered questions for an hour and then left. He didn't expect to receive a Christmas card from the Chairman and he didn't but he was disappointed when the deliberations of the Committee were published and they ignored every single thing Jack had pointed out, went out and bought themselves a big shiny, yellow digger and proceeded to dig an even bigger hole for small companies!

The second event was not a phone call but a letter. It was from the Royal Society of Arts and started:

"Dear Mr Hughes, Election to the Fellowship of the Royal Society for the encouragement of Arts, Manufactures & Commerce is only open to those whose achievements set them apart. The Trustee Board has noted your success and has asked me to invite you to stand for election…"

Jack read the rest of the literature included with the letter which listed former Fellows such as Charles Dickens, Nelson Mandela and Cherie Blair—*well two out of three isn't bad thought Jack*. He was only too happy to stand and was duly elected. He was thus entitled to place the letters FRSA after his name along with MIPD—he had been offered the opportunity of a Fellowship with the IPD but had turned it down.

One issue, not to occur until after he retired, of which he was also very proud, was when he sued the MOD and won. Jack had been to see his GP who immediately referred him to a cancer Specialist at the hospital in Canterbury, Jack then living in Ashford. He was referred for a rash but the Specialist took one look at a spot on his forehead and said, "That needs to come off and now. I can either put you on the list and you will be seen in about 12 weeks, much too long in my view, or I can do it now; what do you say?"

"Now." And just over half an hour later it was gone and Jack had a huge dressing on his forehead and a wife driving him home rather than to lunch in Canterbury as had originally been planned! The Specialist had told him that he had a Squamous Cell Carcinoma, the end result of the rash being untreated; the rash being Actinic Keratosis and normally caused by prolonged exposure to the sun.

She asked him if he had and he had explained that he had served two years in Aden as a young soldier and she had said, "That'll do it every time. I'll give you a form to claim from the Army for that," and she did. And he did. And when he did so he added the hearing damage he had received from the unprotected shooting he had done in the Cadets and the Army and also for the arthritis in his ankles, hips, spine and shoulder caused by his service. The MOD rejected his claim for hearing loss and the arthritis but offered a measly £1,000 for the potentially fatal tumour removed from his forehead.

As it happened, he saw an advert for Poppy Day wherein the RBL (Royal British Legion) were advertising their services for ex-Army personnel so Jack approached them. He had a meeting with one of their Legal Department people who, having listened to what Jack had to say, adopted a negative, you don't stand a chance attitude but nevertheless offered to represent him if he so wished. He didn't—and he was glad he didn't.

He arranged to sit in and listen to an appeal against a MOD decision in London and who should be representing the Appellant than the woman from the RBL In the conversation he had had with her she had laid great stress on the fact that she had six years' experience to back her judgement. Jack thought I have 35 years' experience and watching her performance he was appalled at how little she had learned in six years.

The Tribunal, a variation being a Medical one, still functioned in the same way as all Tribunals but obviously with a knowledge of medical matters. So, Jack spent a lot of time on line researching the three claims. It was clear that the hearing one was rigged in the MOD's favour. The calculation of loss and damage was based on low frequency sound and thus useless because the exposure to loud bangs caused high frequency hearing loss. He obtained a report from the Specialist who had identified his loss stating categorically that the loss was due to the exposure to loud bangs but the Tribunal ignored it, which Jack expected they would, but he had introduced it to make them feel guilty about the fixed calculation.

He quoted an American Veterans Association report showing that the percentage of ex-soldiers with arthritis problems was 20% higher than in the normal population but the Tribunal ignored that too on the basis Jack couldn't quote the research they had carried out, but they were stuck when it came to the tumour. Jack had British Government figures showing, for two years previously—the latest available—that nearly 900 people in the UK had died from

Squamous Cell Carcinoma and that therefore the offer of £1,000 was entirely inadequate especially as the Army knew the dangers of exposure to prolonged sunlight which was why he had been issued with a wide brimmed floppy hat for protection.

When he reached that point, he reached into his pocket and took one out of it and placed it on his head. He then said, "Having been issued with these protective hats the RSM forbad us from wearing them as they were not smart and soldier like. As a direct result of that order, I developed a potentially fatal skin tumour and all that lot" pointing at the MOD representative, "can offer me is a pathetic £1,000!"

They reserved their decision, rejected his first two claims and increased the cancer award to over £6,000! He then wrote to the RBL complaining about the advice he had been given and was invited to a meeting. There were some six senior personnel present who listened intently to his description of events. At the conclusion one of them, who described himself as the Head of the Legal Department, said, "I do not have an Advocate who could do what you did." Jack responded with, "Well, let me carry out a training session with them so that they can—ex-servicemen deserve that at least."

They did not take him up on his offer, even though he said he would not charge! He wrote to them a few weeks later reminding them of his offer. He received a telephone call from a Secretary to say that they already had a training contract with a consultancy and intended to stay with them. "What the ones that are not as good as me…" He paused, thought, *fuck 'em*, and simply said, "Thank you for telling me." What a pity, servicemen don't deserve better than that!

Chapter 51

One final problem presented itself to Jack via the MD. He was called to his office and asked to produce a 'contract' for a Solicitor who was about to start with them. The MD explained that he was to be shared with the Betting Shops Company for whom he had been carrying out work for a number of years, mainly licence applications for the shops, but he was also an expert in health and safety law and would be representing Delta clients in the event they should be facing prosecution or problems with authority. He was told that the partnership in which he worked was being terminated on the retirement of the other partner and he was due to start the following day having accepted the offer of employment made by the Chairman and MD. Jack had to ask a number of questions about job title, salary, holidays, sick pay, pensions etc and wasn't best pleased to discover that he was to write a Contract of Employment Statement for a Solicitor who was about to be paid twice the salary Jack was getting!

He went back to his office and thought about it for a while. He didn't know why but something was not quite right and it wasn't the fact he was having to write the contract for someone on twice his salary—why couldn't the bugger write it himself, he was after all a Solicitor? No, it was something else at the back of his mind. He thought about it some more, but couldn't pin it down, so he decided to go onto the Law Society website, one he had used often before and which he had found to be very helpful. Scanning through he came to a paragraph that he had to read twice before exclaiming 'Oh, shit!' The wording he was reading was quite specific, it said, in effect, 'No Solicitor employed by a company may work for a client company of that employer.'

He did not want to but had to, to tell the MD. He ran off a copy of the relevant section and took it with him. The news did not go down well. He had to sit there whilst the MD got the Chairman on the phone and then said, "I'll let Jack tell you what he has discovered," and handed the phone to Jack! *Thanks very much, thought Jack,* as he took the phone and told him.

There was silence for what seemed like eternity until the Chairman said, "Bring it to me, now," and rang off. So, Jack found himself driving to the Head Office of the Betting Shops on the other side of Manchester somewhat quickly. On arrival he was shown straight in to the Chairman's office who simply held his hand out for the download. He took it, read it and said, "Thank you" and it was clear Jack was thereby dismissed. As it was pretty well going home time and he had to traverse the whole of Manchester again he went home!

At three o'clock in the morning Jack had another of his Eureka moments. He suddenly realised how the situation could be resolved; he was tempted to ring the MD then but thought better of it and was waiting at his office when he arrived. He explained his thoughts and the MD immediately picked up the phone to the Chairman and said that Jack had come up with an idea as to how to solve the situation, "Send him over," said the Chairman. So, Jack went all the way across Manchester, and as he did so he thought *I should have come straight here anyway*!

"Well?" said the Chairman once Jack had been sent in.

"He could remain an independent Solicitor as he still has his Practicing Certificates. We could provide him with an office and admin support for a Peppercorn Rent and he could put up a plate outside. He could submit invoices monthly or whenever, and he would be free to take on any work he wanted to should someone walk in off the street, although he is likely to be fully occupied with work from us but it is important that he would be free to reject it or not as he saw fit. I suppose we might need to provide two offices, one at each site, but as I understand it most of the betting shop work could be done from an office in Delta anyway as it is mainly correspondence with authorities and sometimes visits to courts or sites." Jack waited.

"Do it."

So, Jack did. He produced an outline contract for the Chairman and MD to consider and it eventually arrived back with a few amendments for him to add. One of them was the amount to be invoiced each month. Two things immediately occurred to Jack that should not be stated because the figure should vary with the amount of work done and secondly the figure was wrong! He did not know why—it was just one of those moments that had occurred infrequently before when he had spotted something no-one else had noticed.

It was obvious that someone had taken the annual salary and divided it by 12; but that was wrong. The Solicitor would be entitled to annual leave, four weeks as per the original salary offer letter, so therefore he would only work 11 months and therefore the original salary should be divided by 11 not 12 to arrive at a monthly figure. Guess what? He told the MD who phoned the Chairman who said, 'Come.' So, Jack did. Jack could have found his way across Manchester blindfolded by that time!

The Chairman looked at his figures and picked up the phone to someone who arrived moments later. The Chairman said, "He," pointing at Jack, "Says your figures are wrong, what do you say to that?" He handed the paper Jack had written, by hand—no records of this to be dug out of a word processor in the future! The Finance Director, for that was who it was, read it and then in a very faint voice said, "He's right."

"Thank you," said the Chairman dismissing him so Jack left. He also dismissed the FD—he had been warned about a number of failures and this one was one too far!

Chapter 52

The stress of the job—he had to get every decision right all the time—with his disabled daughter and all the health problems he was experiencing meant that he was finding it difficult to cope so he went to Tony again and asked to reduce his hours which was agreed that he would now work a three day week but extend that if a particular problem arose.

For six months or so, this worked well but Jack's health continued to deteriorate, especially because of the Atrial Fibrillation when he started to have more bad days than good caused by his heart stopping for short periods of time quite frequently on the bad days.. The Specialist said that when they increased in length to over three seconds at a time, he would insert a pacemaker. On asking how long his heart was stopping for at the moment, he was told 2.95 seconds!

He could not see much difference between 2.95 and 3.00 but the Specialist would not be moved nor would he authorise a seven day monitoring of Jack's heart, only a 24 hour one and Jack kept pointing out that the last two had been carried out on good days and were almost certainly not representative of the situation. Eventually, at the age of 63, Jack handed in his notice to retire in six months' time. Tony tried to persuade him to reduce his hours even more rather than leave but Jack did not feel well enough to cope even with fewer hours, so he refused.

Jack told his boss and Secretary that he did not want a fuss when he retired, he did not want a presentation and would like to go quietly. He was asked by his Secretary, Nicola, what he would like as a gift and said that he would much prefer nothing. However, she persisted and, as he had had a hankering to build a model railway, he suggested that maybe vouchers from a model shop would do very well. On his final day he had a lot to clear and had been working solidly trying to do so when just after lunch, Tony buzzed him to pop through.

Jack was astonished, the area was jam-packed with people. Although appearing in front of hundreds of people did not faze him at all when it was necessary to speak etc he normally avoided crowds as he felt more than somewhat uncomfortable. As he walked through the throng to smiles and claps on the back, he could see the MD and Tony waiting for him and wished he could just turn around and walk away because it was obvious there was to be a presentation which he had specifically asked should not happen.

Tony spoke glowingly of just how unique Jack was, how he had a set of skills that no-one else in the Company had, and would be sorely missed. The MD said much the same and then Jack was presented with a number of items. He did not want to deliver a speech; indeed, he had not prepared anything because he had asked that there would be not presentation but the cries rang out and Jack delivered a short address. The breaking up of the crowd took a long time as they all wished to speak to him, wish him the best, shake hands or in the case of many of the women, give him a hearty kiss—*perhaps this isn't so bad he thought*! In fact, they had given him a number of items which he didn't really appreciate until he more closely examined them at home the next day.

There was, of course, a huge card signed by so many people that they had run out of space and signed on the back, but that was all it contained, just signatures, no comments. The comments came in a book in which at least a 150 people had written. Reading them Jack was astonished. He had not made friends with anyone he had worked with for many years as the roles he had held had meant that he might have to discipline or even fire them so he had been friendly but not friends with people. What surprised him most was the affection that was evident towards him and the very high esteem in which he was held. He had not realised how highly he was regarded and in just what awe he was held. Tony, in his speech, had referred to how irreplaceable he was, there was no-one who had the skill set that Jack possessed and indeed they were going to have to replace him with three people.

One of the Advisers Jack had recruited had even gone so far as to write and insert into the book a poem which follows. The other comments, some of them, are included in an Appendix at the back of this book should you be so interested as to read them. Jack did, from time to time, and took great comfort from them.

An Ode to the 'Hughesmister'
When a man has done what he set out to do
Then comes a time to reflect
How a man did what he set out

With the values he sets and reflects
His story has shown that right from the start
Jack's been a man of great integrity and passion
And with fire in his belly and warmth in his heart
At Delta an advisory service did fashion
An ever prospering career and advice family that grew
A leader and mentor was needed
To the challenge he rose demonstrating significant repose
Letting nothing and no one impede it
With a family that size, problems arose
That caused occasional distress and dismay
But with a patient approach and presence of mind
His good counsel saved the day
His legend is huge
His phrases unique
His training in a class of its own
But we'll never forget
The experience we've had
And the man that we've known
Now when a man has done what he set out to do
And he's had the time to reflect
He should keep fire in his belly and warmth in his heart
And set out what he does next
This chapter starts soon
It's sad you must go
We wish that you'd give us more time
We know that you can't
We will miss you so much
And hope that retirement's sublime
It merely remains for us to say
We wish you the happiness and the pleasures you seek
Live life to the full
Remember that work is dull
And your holidays are every day of the week.

By Sharon O'Shaughnessy

Jack was humbled every time he read it that he should have been so highly regarded—he had not realised it at all.

When he retired, they were living in Swinton, West Manchester in a small cul-de-sac of five houses built on a brown field site previously a telephone exchange. Initially the neighbours had been great but three of the properties were rented out and over the three years Jack had lived there the renters had changed and not for the better. Jack and Janet saw a property in Warrington and so keen were the builders to sell that they purchased Jack and Janet's house in Swinton and paid all the fees other than the actual removal costs themselves. So keen to sell were they that they even offered a guarantee that, if in two years' time, or longer, they sold the property at a price less than they had paid the builder would make up the difference!

They moved to Warrington only six weeks after Jack retired. This was at the completion of the third stage of the development with the fourth stage about to begin of a similar mix of properties to the first three. In fact, the start of that forth stage was continually put off until the bombshell that the builders had sold the land to the Council and it was to be built on with blocks of social housing flats exploded around them.

At the same time the management of the estate was transferred from the property management company originally appointed by the builders to maintain the grass and grounds, the playground, blocks of garages etc for the residents, to a company to be run by the residents. The property management company had doubled the charges every six months from an initial £20 to £160 when Jack got cross. He wrote to the MD of the company asking for a breakdown to justify the increases. His first two letters were ignored and the third one received a curt 'costs have gone up' reply. Jack wrote back asking for a breakdown and was ignored so he wrote again saying that when the management of the estate was handed over to the residents, he would stand for election to the new company board and as a Director his first act would be to terminate the contract of that management company.

And yeah, it did come to pass, that the management was handed over, Jack became a Director, along with his two next door neighbours and another property owner. He took great pleasure in writing to the MD pointing out that he had written to say he would sack them, if he was appointed, that he had been, and, as the contract required, he was giving one month's notice. They also terminated the contracts of all the companies appointed by that management company and recruited new ones such that they were able to reduce the monthly fee from £160 to £30. The rest of the Board asked Jack to become the Chairman and he did for just over a year.

Again unfortunately, Jack's health continued to decline and matters were made worse by the people who were installed in the new blocks of flats built by the council. There must have been some decent people amongst them but they were not evident; who was evident, late at night, roistering and generally noisy and anti-social, were the ones who Jack discovered had been dumped there having been evicted from other properties owned by the council. Protests to the council were ignored and Jack, for the first time ever, called it a day and gave up the fight. He put the house on the market, notified the builders that he was exercising the guarantee claim since he had been there for more than two years, in fact three, and since the property was now worth £69,000 less than he paid for it, due solely to their actions in selling the fourth stage development to the council and the very considerable drop in desirability of the estate as a result.

He expected a problem but they paid up promptly although they did refuse to honour it for a near neighbour who had neglected to get the guarantee in writing as had Jack. Because of the continuing deterioration in his health, they decided that the best move would be to move south to be near his son who now lived in Deal.

The two ladies in Jack's life, his wife and his daughter, wanted to live in the 'big city' so they explored Canterbury. It was phenomenally expensive and the best Jack could afford was a garden shed, and a dilapidated one at that! One of the Estate Agents with which they had registered sent them details of two properties in Ashford by mistake. Jack wanted to throw them straight in the bin as he had done a number of Tribunals there starting in 1992 and hated the place. He had been booked into a pub/hotel on the High Street and the noise and discomfort had been unacceptable; so much so that he had threatened to resign if booked there again. But the properties looked promising and more importantly, affordable! And as they hadn't seen anything else he and Janet went to look. He was amazed at the change in the town.

A by-pass had been built and the High Street had become almost a pedestrian precinct transforming the town into a very pleasant place. They visited three times in all, the original properties they saw being unsuitable for some reason or other. They eventually found a property a short walk from the town centre with all the facilities, Doctor, Dentist, papers in a garage, all no more than 10 minutes' walk away. So, they bought it and moved making eight houses in all that they had owned with another six properties they had lived in before buying their first one in Nottingham in 1972 when they left N Ireland. The house in Ashford turned out to be the best they had ever owned for insulation and keeping the heat in and thus proved to be the cheapest to run they had ever owned.

Initially Jack used to walk to the Library but after three years or so it started to be a bit too far, but he was an avid reader so by car it was. Opposite the Library was the Citizens' Advice Bureau and Jack started to think about the number of times he had been up against one of their people in Tribunal. He could remember clearly a half dozen cases, although he was sure that there had been more, especially the first case with the CAB representing in Scotland where the chap was hearing and sight impaired and the room had had to be reordered to accommodate him. That was the case where he had involved the Manager of the Job Centre and had the case thrown out as being out of time. He had also acted in a number of cases for an insurance company involving self-employed agents claiming to be employees when their contracts were terminated.

Of the three cases, two had been conducted by CAB personnel and all of them were poor, both in preparation and presentation. Two, at least, he felt he should not have won but he had because the representation was so bad. He thought about it for a long time and then went in, one day, having decided to offer his services as a Volunteer, perhaps on the telephone a couple of afternoons per week, to advise on employment law issues. Having explained why he was there he was handed an Application Form and asked to return it completed whenever he liked.

That, was a week later when he returned to the Library. Having dropped it off he received a phone call that afternoon asking him to come in for an interview the following day! When he arrived, he was greeted by the Senior Manager a woman of mature years with an unmistakeable aura of power. After offering him a coffee or tea and the normal social introductions she immediately explained that they were in the process of seeking to recruit two Trustee Directors and looking at his CV he would appear to be ideally suited to the role, would he be interested?

Really, he wasn't, but he asked to be told more about what the role involved. She explained that it would take a commitment to attend at least four Board meetings a year plus the AGM. As Trustees and Directors, they had an oversight role to ensure compliance with the law and to provide guidance as to policy. He asked a few questions and agreed that he would like to be considered. He was asked to return the same afternoon to meet the Chairman and his Deputy and by the end of the day was a Trustee Director!

He joined the CAB at a time of great change. The CAB was structured as more than 350 separate limited companies with a major set-up in London, to which they all subscribed, which provided guidance and assistance as required, Jack discovered that the centre had been reviewing its role and the role of the individual companies and seemed to be on a route to assume command, direct command of the individual companies. He was handed a very considerable document and asked to comment on it. It turned out to be the proposal for changes to the existing relationship as a way forward. Jack had expressed concern when given it that he knew nothing of the existing one and so could not compare the original and proposed one in any meaningful manner but the GM said that didn't matter she wanted his view on what the relationship would be if the proposals were accepted.

So, Jack read it. By that time Jack was 75 years old and had dealt with, worked with and for, literally hundreds of companies, possibly thousands and he could honestly say that the document he had been handed was the worst, most disgraceful proposal he had ever seen, bar none. The grammar was awful; the structure abysmal with arbitrary changes between bullet points, abc, 123, no paragraph numbers or letters whatsoever and changes to the font every so often as though written by different people on different word processors at different times with no coordination between them.

Jack was deeply ashamed to think their 'head office' should not only have produced such rubbish but should have sent it to over 350 companies nationally as the suggested way forward. When he came to the content the purpose of the update was clear—it was a power grab pure and simple; and not a good one at that. The standards they were seeking to introduce were just wrong. There was to be an annual, in-depth appraisal of the staff and business with severe penalties if the highest standards were not met and, judgement to be by 'HO' and any appeals against any marking to be made to an appeal panel appointed by the same 'HO'!

Not only that, there were to be formal appraisals of all staff every three months with informal appraisals to be carried out monthly. Copies of all appraisals were to be sent to 'HO'. Jack did some quick maths, 350 companies by, say, 35 staff each by 1 annual, 4 three monthly appraisals, and 7 informals, assuming monthly was not in addition to annual and three monthly meant some 343,000 appraisals arriving at HO every year or 28,583.3 arriving every month.

Clearly no-one would read that number, or if they did the staffing required would be absolutely absurd—it was just a bureaucratic nonsense—and Jack didn't believe in appraisals anyway, they were a great idea like Socialism, but like Socialism, they just didn't work in practice and Jack had visited or worked with literally hundreds of companies and never found one that worked as advertised. As for those 365-degree ones, where not only did the boss appraise subordinates but subordinates appraised their bosses, he had found that there was, in practice, tacit consent that if you give me a good one, I will give you a good one, making a complete nonsense of the practice.

He then came to one which he felt certain would be a deal breaker. The vast majority of their funding came in the form of a grant from the local authority and the wording and conditions were quite specific; it was to be solely for funding help to citizens living in the local authority area only. They regularly turned away people from Folkestone, where the CAB was only open for a couple of days a week and where they told their people to go to Ashford if the problem was urgent.

They had to be turned away and yet the 'HO' was proposing to set-up a national telephone service where it would be possible that someone living in Inverness or Penzance ringing the central number would in fact be put through to Ashford. As so many issues related to Landlords, rent or property repairs—about 60% of their total—it needed a local knowledge as to areas, particular Landlords etc to be able to give advice and that could not be done for someone from outside the Borough as well as being against their funding requirements.

Also, there were contradictions, repeats, omissions and generally a very poor document but which, if accepted, meant the end of their independence as an operating company and probably against their Articles of Association. Somewhat reluctantly, because it would be obvious that they would face severe problems, Jack recommended that it should be rejected as it stood and added a long list of amendments which would be needed before he, as a Trustee Director, could sanction it. He was not sure how it would be received by the GM, who clearly ran the business, and was delighted when she exclaimed that she knew her faith in him was upheld.

The Chairman and Deputy were also delighted with the analysis and as a result it was put to the full Board and passed! The outcome was a long letter to

'HO' and then a series of increasingly acrimonious letters between them. When it became clear that none of their points, even the ones about the poor grammar, structure and layout had been accepted, the Board voted unanimously to send a formal notice of intent to cease to be a member of the 'HO' organisation in three months' time as required by the rules. That really did light a bomb under them. So much so that they wrote saying they believed they might have a solution to the issues bothering Ashford and could they come and visit to discuss them?

The GM, in the meantime, had been contacting a number of other companies to sound out their views to find that the suggestions in the new document were roundly condemned and hated. But only a few of them were prepared to do anything about it. Jack had been introduced to a Barrister who provided pro-bono advice to Ashford and had done so for many years. He attended a meeting, along with Jack, the Chairman, deputy and GM to discuss their meeting with the 'HO' lot. Prior to the meeting the Barrister produced a paper arguing the points they wished to make and Jack thought it one of the best he had ever read; it really was that impressive but when the Barrister outlined how he intended to start and deliver it Jack felt very uncomfortable.

He didn't say anything but listened to the reactions of the others present to what they thought of it. All were in agreement and then the Chairman pointedly said to Jack, "Jack, you haven't said anything, what do you think?"

"Well, I think the analysis is brilliant, I don't think I've ever seen anything better presented, but I think the proposal as to how we start is wrong." They all looked stunned.

"Why do you say that?"

"In a negotiating situation which this really is I would want to keep my cards close to my chest and see what the other side ante up first. For example, if someone is asking what are you prepared to offer me to go away if you say £100, they might snatch your hand off because they were prepared to go away for £50. In which case you've paid much more than you needed to. My response in such a situation would be, rather than answering, would be to ask, 'what are you looking for?' If they say, £75 0r even £100 you know that they would probably accept much less so I would offer, say £30-£35, and see what they come back with.

"The principal being, make them answer first. In this case they have written saying they have some ideas as to how the problems we have with their document might be solved. I think we should open with, you as the Chairman, welcoming them, sorting out the coffee/tea etc and then sayings, 'we are very pleased to have this opportunity to meet you and listen to the ideas you have, would you like to set them out?' and then we listen! Who knows they may agree to all that we want or at least have solutions we can live with and everyone is happy. If what they come up with is rubbish and unacceptable then we hit them with that analysis and they leave here knowing they have a real fight on their hands."

Silence. The Deputy Chairman then said, "I think he's right." The Chairman then asked Jack to repeat the words he had suggested to start them off and wrote them down. And that's what they did. And it worked. 'HO' came up with all sorts of concessions covering all their points bar two. It became clear that they were determined to go ahead with a national telephone line and although they were prepared to reduce the number of appraisals by a small amount they would not concede regarding an independent appeals procedure.

The Chairman concluded the meeting with a 'thank you for coming—we need to consider all this and will be in touch soon' and the meeting ended. They could not accept those two issues so it became a voting matter for the next Board meeting, six weeks later, and the Board unanimously decided the proposals were unacceptable and a letter followed confirming their decision to withdraw. At the end of that Board meeting the Chairman asked Jack to remain behind.

Once everyone else bar him, Jack and the Deputy, had gone the Chairman said to Jack, "Jack, both I and the Deputy, are intending to retire, both because of age and health, and we have been so impressed with your performance, especially how you advised on the negotiations with 'HO,' that we would like you to take over as Chairman. It would be subject to a confirmatory vote at the next Board meeting, of course, but we feel you are the man. None of the other Board Members have your knowledge, skill and ability. Will you accept?"

Jack paused. He recognised the honour that was being done him but he wasn't sure he wanted it—not because of any inbuilt reluctance but he wasn't sure if he wanted the amount of work and would be able to cope with the stress that would come along with it. He refused an answer then and asked for time to consider it but the allure was too strong and he accepted a few days later. He served for the next two years. Much he enjoyed but some of the problems less so.

Almost immediately he had a problem with the Deputy General Manager, another woman, and a falling out between her and the GM which became stressful in the extreme. He also had a problem with the 'HO' and their attempts to bring them to heel. 'HO' tried offering their services directly to the Council at a reduced cost to that of Ashford but it was easy to see that this was just a short term offer and would still lead to having to provide services to people resident outside the Borough, a very considerable no-no for the Council. Jack was having to go in almost every day and it gradually became too much for him with his health continuing to be a problem and his age creeping towards 80! So, he resigned and retired again.

This time he was talking to Janet one day and something she said reminded him of their time together in Aden and so he raised the issue and she said, "You know, with all these stories you tell, you should write a book." So, he did, three in total and this is the last one. Thank you for reading them!

Epilogue

This book, the last in the Trilogy, covers a much longer period than the first two. Nevertheless, on the whole, the stories are true, how true is for me to know and you to guess, and are a result of an author to create his own characters, events and timelines, so if you think you can identify yourself, good for you, but you can't, you are not in it, but my characters are!

I referred earlier in the text of the comments made in a book presented to my hero when he retired and presented for your information a poem written by Sharon which much affected me. Some of the other comments are as meaningful and a delight for me to read but are, generally, so much shorter. Read on if you wish—I hope you enjoy them.

Mike, We have worked together for nearly 17 years!

Remember the interview in my 'Advocacy Manager's' office on 19th August 1992 when you came for a job as an Advocate—so impressed was I that I was able to put a job offer in writing to you later the same day!

You started as an Advocate on the 7th September 1992 and excelled in that role. You were then my first choice for the role of Advice Manager following (name deleted) exit to join the (name deleted) taking up position on 11th September 1995.

It was then early in 1999 you asked to take on a different role and I was very pleased to be able to arrange that and appoint you to the position you have held since of Senior Employment Law Development Manager plus Compliance Manager as a side line! Over the years however you have acquired or inherited many responsibilities that neither of us envisaged back in 1999!!

Well, have a great retirement—you—will be a hard act to follow—well, impossible—which is why we have to split up your duties to a range of different people.

All the best, Tony.

(Very sadly, a few years after this was written Tony went to bed one night and did not wake up in the morning. He was 10 years younger than me and I miss him.)

Mike, All the very best for a long and happy retirement.

It has been a pleasure working with you over the years whilst not without its ups and downs. You have always been ready in with a joke or two each day.

Your painstaking proofing of the Bottom Line will be missed and if you are really good, I'll send you a copy for old time's sake.

Once again all the very best.

Cheers, Mike

Dear Mike, What can I say apart from you have always been there for me. You gave me the confidence I needed and was always there for me when I needed you, no matter how busy you were. You will always be the best spokesperson with the Media. And who else am I going to send to Sky News at such short notice?

Have a long, healthy and enjoyable retirement and thank you for everything you have done for me.

Take care, Sammy x

Mike, Thank you for all your help and wise counsel over the last six years. Hope you have a long and happy retirement.

Above all however, thanks for the jokes.

Terry.

Dear Mike, Wishing you all the very best on your retirement…
What are we going to do now for the jokes at the conferences??
All the best anyway, enjoy the rest and take it easy…
With love from

Debra

Mike, I cannot believe this day has arrived. Where have those 16 years gone? I was only a 'young' 23 year old when you started at Stamford House.

That's frightening!

I will certainly miss our 'little chats' and I'm sure (not) that you will miss my Salfordian 'morning' greeting! Our little office won't be quite the same.

At least you can put your feet up and get on with building your model railway and getting out more on your motorcycle.

Only another 26 years to go for me!

I wish you all the very best Mike—you take it easy and enjoy it, as I'm sure you will.

Fondest memories, Vicki

Mike, One of the leading authorities in the UK on TUPE transfers…!

Will have to change my pitch now!

All the best in your retirement, Simon,

Mike, Not too long a time working together but I wish you the best and enjoy your retirement. Great Boss!!!

Love, Rosa

Dear Mike, I wish you the most contented, long and fulfilling retirement…

You will, of course, be missed by all of us in Advice, but no doubt your legend will live on.

Do keep in touch and maybe one of these day I'll have you a race,

Lots of love, Lisa

Dear Mike, I wish you and yours a happy, restful new chapter in your life…

I will always remember my interview with you when I wanted to tell you all about what I could bring to the party and you just asked me when a year's service was a year!

That was nine years ago now!

You have helped me to operate the Advice Service and have always been willing to advise, interview and train the staff and I thank you for that.

Be happy and write that book! (I did—this is it!)
Kindest regards, Ann

Hi Mike,

Your advice and support has been invaluable since I joined the company 9 years ago.

You'll be sadly missed by all of us, of that there is no doubt. You're a legend!

My very best wishes for your future retirement and good health.

Kindest regards and affection, Elaine

Mike, You recruited me into the company 11 years ago, so you owe me (sorry, I owe you one!)

Seriously, as my first Manager here I really appreciated your help and support in what to me was a totally new environment.

That support has been available ever since, and your knowledge and experience invaluable.

Many thanks!

(Also for your fund of jokes—always of course in the best of taste)

Have a great retirement Mike—we will all miss the legend.

David

Dear Mike, Hi Super Star—what a man. Star of stage, screen and TV!!!

I trust all your Personnel data is compliant!

We shall miss you—you are a fountain of knowledge and always helpful—have a great retirement—you deserve it.

Best wishes, Ray

Mike, Thank you very much for all your assistance with setting up (name of insurance company) and helping to get it off the ground.

Where do I go now for correct punctuation!!!

Best wishes to you for a super retirement.

Best regards, Des
Mike

We almost met in 1966, you had just left and I took over your job at Middle East Command, Aden.

Nearly 40 years later you interviewed me and gave me a job.

Have you held this grudge all these years?

Have a long and happy retirement and I am sure Janet will love you being at home all day!

The pleasure has been mine.

All the best, Ray

Mike, Like lots of others I remember my first interview with you and your comment some years later (after my proudest career appointment as a Director for Health and Safety of the company) that you advised my now fellow directors how I was right for the Board.

Thank you!!

Your professionalism is something I have always admired and even now, only days away from retiring you are still maintaining that standard.

Please enjoy a long, happy and healthy retirement, give me your number so I can steal a few jokes for the golf club.

All the very best, Noel

Mike, Your contribution to the company in many and varied roles over the last 16 years has been greatly valued.

I would like to express my personal appreciation of your commitment and loyalty throughout your employment with us and wish you a long, happy and well deserved retirement.

All the best, Keith
(Financial Director)

Dear Mike, Just a note to say thank you for the big contribution you have made to the success of the company from Advocacy to Advice Service Manager, and recently working through the minefield of FSA Compliance.

You have always done a fantastic job.

I hope you have a long and happy retirement and don't forget to come back and see us.

All the best, Peter
(MD)

(There are/were another 82 which made reference to their interview, the training, support and advice/help received, or some combination of which, for which I am very, very grateful but to include them all would simply be too much—so thank you for your kind comments; they are much appreciated, no less so than those quoted—but there simply isn't room for them all. The balance of the 150 simply expressed good wishes, etc.)